Praise for mad Dash

"A fun, light, well-written novel, and likely to resonate."
—*Tampa Tribune*

"Gaffney keeps both Andrew and Dash likable. She's found the sweet spot in relationship humor: funny but not malicious. The result is a true-to-life portrait of a marriage at the crossroads." —*Free Lance-Star*

"A book just long and sweet enough to get you through the night."
—*Good Housekeeping*

"[A] good-humored story of a marriage in trouble . . . So much fun."
—*Boston Globe*

"Vividly set, and we actually come to care about these two diametrically opposed veterans of twenty years together . . . Gaffney has a blunt and convincing insight into her characters, particularly the women. . . . There isn't a phony bone in Dash's body, and we definitely want to hang around to see how the pieces finally end up on the matrimonial chessboard." —*Washington Post*

"Read this one for the pure charm of Gaffney's writing."
—*Library Journal* (starred review)

"The writing is lively. . . . The denouement is just rosy. It's a lot of fun."
—*Publishers Weekly*

"With humor and compassion, Patricia Gaffney tells the story of a marriage, and the flawed and fascinating people inside it. Both touching

mad dash

a novel

Patricia Gaffney

THREE RIVERS PRESS

NEW YORK

Copyright © 2007 by Patricia Gaffney

Reader's Group Guide copyright © 2008 by Three Rivers Press, an imprint of the Crown Publishing Group, a division of Random House, Inc.

All rights reserved.
Published in the United States by Three Rivers Press, an imprint of the Crown Publishing Group, a division of Random House, Inc., New York.
www.crownpublishing.com

Three Rivers Press and the Tugboat design are registered trademarks of Random House, Inc.

Novel Thoughts colophon is a trademark of Random House, Inc.

Originally published in hardcover in slightly different form in the United States by Shaye Areheart Books, an imprint of the Crown Publishing Group, a division of Random House, Inc., New York, in 2007.

Library of Congress Cataloging-in-Publication Data
Gaffney, Patricia.
Mad dash : a novel / Patricia Gaffney.
p. cm.
1. Midlife crisis—Fiction. 2. Married women—Fiction. 3. Middle-aged women—Fiction. 4. Domestic fiction. I. Title.

PS3557.A296M34 2007
813'.54—dc22 / 2006039295

ISBN 978-0-307-38212-2

Printed in the United States of America

Design by Lauren Dong

10 9 8 7 6 5 4 3 2

First Paperback Edition

For James Holmes Gaffney,

1909—2006

dash

one

The puppy and I trip over each other coming through the door, just as the phone stops ringing. I go down hard, but Andrew's voice on the machine loosens something that was tight inside me, a dry sponge in water.

"Hi, babe," I say, full of relief, as if he can hear me. Sprawled on the plank floor, craning away from the puppy's exuberant tongue kisses, I rub my sore knee and listen to my husband say, "Dash? Hello, are you there?"

I start to get up, but his tone changes. "I know you're there." He's annoyed, so I stay where I am. Andrew is mad at *me*? I have really whacked my knee, and now I'm seeing it as his fault.

"Dash, answer the phone, please." He sighs. What a martyr. Oh, what he has to put up with.

"We said we'd talk this evening," he reminds me. I can hear classical music in the background; I picture him in his big chair in the living room, feet up on the ottoman, enjoying his record collection without interruptions. He must be having a ball without me. "Dash, would you please pick up the phone?"

Again I start to get up, but he heaves another piteous sigh and I change my mind. "Very well," he says. Who says "very well"? No one but Andrew. He says "indeed," too, and "quite right," and "em" instead of "um." You'd think he was English.

"Very well, call me back, that is if you can find the time." His sarcasm is usually subtler. "But I might go to bed early," he warns. "I didn't sleep at all well last night."

I wait through a small pause, wondering if he misses me. Probably, but he won't say it. Oh, I ought to get off the floor and pick up the phone, talk, resolve things. But I stay where I am, holding the puppy's warm, panting sides. Sometimes prolonging even bad things, painful things, is better than getting them all nice and neat and settled. That's what Andrew would like, for us to get this silliness behind us, tidy it up like a messy room. Put everything back exactly where it was before.

"Also," he goes on, "I've got a raging headache, so maybe you shouldn't call. It came on all at once, I didn't take a pill in time." Now I can hear it, that pinch in his tone that means he's squinting, holding himself stiffly to ward off his migraine. If he even has one. Andrew is a hypochondriac, but I suppose an imagined headache is just as painful as a real one. A *raging* headache—how dramatic, like a nineteenth-century heroine. If I were there with him I'd be sympathetic, though. I'd rub his neck, make him a cup of tea. Funny how bitchiness comes a lot easier when you're seventy-five miles away.

"Mrs. Melman called," he says. "I don't know what you want me to tell her. Tell anybody, so I didn't say anything. Just that you weren't here."

I don't know what to tell anybody either, even Mrs. Melman, who lives next door. Maureen knows, but no one else. If this is a separation, it isn't real yet. I don't know what it is, and I ought to. I started it.

"I'm not going to keep talking to this damn machine. I'm hanging up." Andrew's dignity means everything to him. "They're calling for snow here, so who knows what it'll do down there. So . . . you be careful," he says gruffly, and hangs up.

Now I'm bereft. There's no pleasing me; I could have eight husbands, or none, and I'd still have this edgy, empty feeling. It's not even depression, which I imagine is at least relaxing. This is more like an illness, one that's not serious enough to warrant any sympathy. Just a long, long stretch of feeling lousy.

It started to snow down here about an hour ago. I'm surprised Andrew didn't know that, since the Weather Channel is one of the three he watches; the other two are PBS and the History Channel—naturally; he's a history professor. The snow is what made us fall over each other in the doorway, the puppy and me. My hiking boots left wet blotches on the kitchen floor, melting snow seeping into the cracks between the old pine boards. First snow of the season. What if I were snowed in for Christmas, the unspoken date by which Andrew and I are supposed to reconcile? Snowed in at our cabin all by myself; alone at Christmas for the first time in twenty years. The thought makes me shiver. Not with dread. An illicit thrill, like shoplifting must be, or committing a victimless crime.

The dog waddles over to her bowl, toenails clicking, pudgy belly bulging from side to side. I sigh and pick myself up, go outside to retrieve the armload of wood I dropped in my haste to answer the phone. Mr. Bender, the man who does odd jobs and out-of-season maintenance on our cabin, has taken to stacking the wood he brings all the way out by the shed. He's such a surly old coot, I think he does it on purpose, so I'll have to walk farther.

We bought the cabin three years ago, but it might as well be three days as far as Mr. Bender is concerned. Or thirty years—we'd still be "the new people," rich Washingtonians spoiling the pristine Virginia countryside with our traffic and pollution, our estate developments eating up the beautiful old farms. Never mind that Andrew and I are anything but rich—in fact, we're poor now that Chloe's in college—never mind our cabin's been here since the forties and we have personally saved it from rotting into the mossy ground with a lot of improvements we couldn't afford. We're still "the new people" to Mr. Bender, and still not welcome.

I've become an expert at keeping the fire in the woodstove going, formerly Andrew's job. The stove is tiny, but so is the kitchen; if I close the door to the living room it's warm as a kiln in here. I sprawl in my mother's old padded rocker with her shawl around my shoulders and my feet on one of the couch pillows I use for a footstool. I love the quiet, just the hiss of the stove and the tick and slide of snow against the window. The dog, asleep beside me on the rug. Not chewing it for a change.

I wonder if I would be lonely without her. I never used to come down to the cabin without Andrew; I thought I'd be scared by myself. But I'm not, and she's certainly no watchdog. I was thinking of naming her Sock, because she has one white paw. Dogs are supposed to be especially sensitive to the *K* sound, I've heard. Is that funny, "Sock" instead of "Socks"? I like funny names for pets. Andrew would come up with something funny. When Chloe was little, he'd make her laugh by christening her dolls and stuffed animals Uriah or Orville, Saffron, Primavera.

But, of course, consulting Andrew is not a possibility in this case. The way we got the puppy, or rather what happened afterward, pretty much squashes that option.

We were coming home from the history department trimester break party. Exams had ended the day before, vacation was starting, so everybody was in a good mood and drank too much. Everyone but me, anyway; I probably drank too much, but I was in a bad mood.

But I've been in a bad mood since last summer, when my mother died. Then Chloe went off to college and, I don't know, I can't seem to find my footing, my old self. I go around like a ghost, no bones, no blood; I feel like I barely cast a shadow. The doctor thinks I might be hitting menopause early. Trauma can do that, she said.

Something was wrong with me that night—I mean, obviously; I walked out on my husband, apparently over a *dog*. The only warning I had, and only in retrospect, was that every time I looked at Andrew— who stood almost the whole night in Richard Weldon's dim foyer with his back to the wall, as far from the thick of things as he could possibly get without going outside—it was as if his outline had blurred or faded and I were seeing him in duplicate, two Andrews slightly overlapping. It wasn't the rum punch, either, because everything else was in perfect focus. It was Andrew.

He had on his uniform: khaki trousers, blue Oxford shirt, tweed jacket. And, touchingly, the paisley tie I gave him years ago, back when I had hopes of varying the uniform. Naive me, I used to buy clothes for him. He'd get a pained expression while he'd praise my selections— sweaters, slacks, shirts in colors besides blue—and then he'd never wear them. I wonder what his students make of the uniform, I wonder if he's the butt of jokes—he'd hate that. Probably not, though. His students always love him.

He stood in the foyer with his hands in his pockets, head back, looking down his long nose at Tim Meese, his best friend, his fellow escape artist. The two oldest men in the department, not counting ancient Dr. Cleveland, and neither one a full professor. Not that there's anything wrong with that.

I always add that, like making a cross against vampires. So I don't sound so much like an ambitious, political, calculating faculty wife.

"Oh, hello, Dash," I heard from behind me. "What an amusing cape. Where's Andrew?"

Elizabeth O'Neal, I knew without turning around. She has a low, staccato, order-giving voice that pauses in unpredictable places; if you close your eyes, you'd swear she was Captain Kirk. She slouches; she always wears black; she's not pretty in the least, not to me, but her students are fascinated by her. If the college rumor mill is right, and so often it isn't, she's having an affair with Richard Weldon. Poor Allison, his indecently young wife, who used to be one of his students. I guess you reap what you sow.

"Elizabeth, nice to see you," I said. "Andrew? He's over there."

"Oh, mmm," she said in a different voice, not Captain Kirk's at all, and I looked more closely at my husband to see what she was seeing. He's handsome, certainly to me, but he's got the kind of face that doesn't exactly bowl you over with admiration, not at first when you might be distracted by his thick glasses, or put off by his everyday expression of worried melancholy. And he's tall, but you don't notice right off because of his sort of hollow-chested, self-deprecating stoop. I can see him growing old like Mr. Chips, thin and tweedy and dignified, and never losing his hair.

Before slouching off toward the foyer, Elizabeth made dutiful chitchat about her plans for the break—Jamaica with some guy—and asked me about mine and Andrew's. "Oh, we're staying home," I said carelessly, "keeping it quiet this year. Chloe's school is on a different semester system, so . . ." I'd only just found out, so the wound was fresh: Chloe wasn't coming home for the Christmas holidays. She was going skiing in Vermont with one roommate, then visiting the other in Connecticut over New Year's, even though it's her freshman year and we haven't seen her since Thanksgiving. She doesn't even ski.

I think that's when it started. My unwinding. Elizabeth, I presume unwittingly, put her bony finger on the most recent sore spot in my heart. But there was an older, tenderer one right under it, and by picking at the top one she pierced the tissue-thin scab over the other. Fresh blood.

The sandwich generation: I'm so tired of that expression. In the last nine months, both halves of my sandwich have been pried off and eaten. I'm the soft, squishy center, exposed, unprotected. *Unsafe,* that's the word. All I have now is Andrew to protect me.

"Didn't you see me?" I asked him on the way home, holding my hands closer to the heater for warmth. "I gave you the signal." Everything about him annoyed me. That should have set off another warning bell, but I only remember clenching my jaw over the obsessively careful way he drove, the highbrow music station he always has to have on the radio, his utter obliviousness to my mood. The hypochondriacal loop he kept going around in about tonight's spiced shrimp's probable effect on his gastrointestinal system, the migraine he wouldn't be at all surprised to wake up with tomorrow from all those flash pictures Richard's wife wouldn't stop taking—

"But didn't you see me? You looked right at me, you couldn't have missed it." I'm not as practiced at giving the "Let's go" signal as Andrew, for the simple reason that he always wants to go home before I do. Still, it's not brain surgery: You raise your eyebrows and rub your left wrist, careful not to touch or look at your watch, which would give it away.

"I thought you were having a good time," he said. There was no traffic, but he put the turn signal on to change lanes. That annoyed me, too. "You were dancing with Richard."

"No, I wasn't, Richard was dancing with me. Oh, *God.*" I slumped, overcome with exhaustion. Everything was the same, the Weldons' holiday party, Mason-Dixon College, the ancient flirtations, the politics, the *people.* Nothing changed except how old we were all getting. How many more faculty parties would I have to go to in my lifetime—fifty? A hundred? I didn't even have my friend Maureen to commiserate with anymore, not since she split up with her husband. She says that's the only good thing about her divorce—she never has to go with Phil to another damn faculty party.

"Did you hear Richard's giving up the chairmanship?" Andrew asked me, and I said of course I knew, it was the hot subtext all evening. You couldn't be there and *not* know (I didn't say) unless you stayed in the foyer all night and only talked to one or two of your closest friends.

"You never even moved," I complained. "It was like your shoulder was glued to the wall. Couldn't you just . . . can't you ever . . ."

I didn't finish, just sighed again and stared out the window, and I think that's a point for me. At least I don't nag. I used to consider Andrew's complete indifference to office politics admirable, a mark of his honesty and integrity, but I don't anymore. When you think about it, it's kind of selfish. His academic career is . . . how best to put it . . . languishing, but he would rather teach class in a kilt than do anything so undignified as network, so who has to do it? Me. I have to dance with drunken department heads and pretend to like it. Our daughter isn't putting herself through her expensive college.

"Let's go to the cabin for the weekend."

He finally looked over at me. "The cabin?"

That's all, two words, but as soon as he uttered them I knew we weren't going. And even though the idea had just occurred to me, I was suddenly convinced of the rightness of it, the urgency. It was the answer.

"Oh, Andrew, let's go. Just us. It'll be romantic." I squeezed his arm, but he felt brittle to me, untouchable. My fault; I've been so rotten and moody lately. "We could drive down late, come back whenever we feel like it." What I really wanted to do was go *now,* turn the car around, get on the Beltway and drive and drive and drive.

"Hm," he said with feigned thoughtfulness. "I've got exams to grade. Plus all the journals." He made everybody in his Colonial America class keep diaries, as if they were living during the Revolutionary War or something.

"You could do them down there. Peace and quiet."

"There's no wood," he pointed out, turning onto our street from Columbia Road. "We said we weren't going back before spring."

"We could buy some fake logs on the way down."

"You can't burn them in a woodstove. Chemicals."

"We'll get Mr. Bender to bring us a load of wood. Or you could chop some. *I* could chop some."

"Don't we have something, a party on Saturday—"

"Just Amy and Dan's, and it's an open house, they'd never miss us."

He made his *long* humming sound, "Hmmm," which he thinks I think means he's taking the subject under advisement but really means it will never come up again unless I raise it, and then raise it again, then again, till we're both so tired of it it's a relief to forget the whole thing.

"Oh, never mind." I flopped back against the seat. "I'll just go down by myself."

He chuckled, not taking that seriously. He was right, I wasn't serious. Then.

We usually come and go through the front door, not the back, because we park on the street—no garage—and the back door doesn't lead to anything except the alley behind our block of town houses. That night was trash night, though, plus we were running late for the Weldons', so we'd hurried out the kitchen door with a plastic bag of garbage each, dumped them in our spot in the alley, and walked around the corner to the car.

Which is all to say—what if we'd done that again for some reason, parked and then gone into the house from the back? What if we had? We'd have tripped over a dead dog on the front porch the next morning, that's what.

Andrew had the door key, so he saw it first. "What—" he said, and started back, scaring me. I saw something black, the size and shape of a soccer ball, wedged between the storm door and the door. We'd forgotten to leave the porch light on; we only had the streetlight to see—an animal, a sweater, someone's purse . . .

"It's a dog," Andrew exclaimed, bending close. He took off his gloves and touched it. "A little dog. I don't think it's alive." He handed me the key, scooped his hands gingerly under the lifeless black mound, and lifted it. I felt frozen; I squinted instead of looking at it directly, the way I do at scary movies.

I think of that, how squeamish Andrew took it up in his bare hands, dead for all we knew, while I, the great animal lover, shrank back in fear and distress. All I could do was unlock the door.

I turned on a lamp while Andrew set the dog on the rug in the living room. It lay perfectly still—but then it moved, shivered or twitched or something, and after that I could act. Silly, but once I knew it wasn't dead, I was all right.

Its eyes were open but not fixed on anything. "Is he hurt? Is he just cold? Andrew, who could *do* such a thing, put a dog in somebody's door on a night like this and leave it there? I think he's freezing. Should we take him to the vet? He's not even shivering. No, there, he just shivered. Are you calling?"

"They won't be open, we'll just get the answering service."

I sat on the floor and pulled the puppy into my lap. "Call and leave a message, then." It could hardly raise its head. The blue-black eyes finally focused on mine, but only for a second before the dog dropped its heavy little head, *thump,* on my thigh.

We had a dog when I was young, a stray we named Tramp. My mother let me keep him even though Daddy had just died and she was working two jobs and I was only nine and not that responsible. What a softy she was. Sitting there on the floor, I had a wave of longing for my mother that was so intense, I had to squeeze my eyes shut to keep from crying.

Andrew was talking on the phone in the kitchen. Huddled over the puppy, trying to warm it with my body, I didn't notice Hobbes till I felt his wet nose on my cheek. "Hey, Hobbes," I said loudly, so he could hear me. He's deaf. "Hey, boy. Look here, we've got a—"

Hobbes finally noticed the puppy and jumped back—much as Andrew had on the front porch. Hobbes, Andrew's father's fourteen-year-old cocker spaniel, is the only furred creature I've ever known Andrew not to be allergic to. Which is interesting since, in so many ways, Andrew is allergic to his father.

"I left a message at the vet's," he told me from the doorway. "They're supposed to call back. In the meantime—"

The phone rang.

"Wow. Fast," I said, and Andrew went away again.

Under my coat and my amusing red cape, I had on velvet pants and a fancy silk shirt that buttoned down the front. I unbuttoned the shirt and put the puppy next to my skin, noticing in the process that it was a female. I pulled my clothes around her, coat and all, making a cocoon, and after a little while she wasn't a deadweight anymore. Her soft, solid body twitched, her little toenails grazing my skin, the breath from her cold nose tickling me. I got up from the floor and carried her into the kitchen.

"I don't know," Andrew was saying, "lethargic, yes. I think so. Did it shiver?" he asked me.

"She's shivering right now."

He reported that to the vet, a man we've gotten to know well because of Hobbes's arthritis. "That's a good sign? A good sign," Andrew relayed. "It means only mild hypothermia."

"But what should we *do*?"

He held up his hand. "Yes. Right, right. Four teaspoons in a pint. But first—okay. Yes."

Finally he hung up. "That's the first thing he said to do, put it next to your skin."

"Really?" I hugged the puppy closer, feeling relieved and gratified and smart. This was going to have a happy ending.

Fill bottles with warm, not hot, water, the vet advised, and lay them next to the puppy's body, especially her chest and armpits. Don't overheat, and definitely don't use a hair dryer. Try to feed her a little sugar water.

We did all that. She went through a phase of violent shivering—an excellent sign, Andrew reported; shivering increased metabolism and generated heat. Gradually that subsided and she began to relax, sprawled out on a towel in my lap, her silky belly rising and falling with natural breaths. She had short, woolly soft black fur all over, except for that one white foot.

I was asking Andrew if he thought it would be a good idea to let her sleep between us tonight so she could get nice and warm, and running names by him like Lazzy, short for Lazarus, or what about Feeney for Phoenix—when he sneezed.

"Of course we can't *keep* it," he said between honks into his handkerchief, as if I'd suggested adopting a wild boar, a baby python. He was getting out the little enamel pan he heats a cup of milk in every night just before bed. *I'm married to a man who drinks warm milk.* The horror of that closed in on me, like being sealed in an envelope, like being buried alive. *Mama!* I thought—I did, I had that very conscious thought. I wanted my mother back, and Tramp, and my youth, my freedom, I felt like running away so fast and so far that nothing looked familiar.

I should've left right then. The die was cast, and it would've been easy—I still had my coat on. I'm not sure why, it seems a bit mad to me now, but I was beyond angry. I had skipped that step and gone directly to finished.

So I should've left, but instead I stayed to say hurtful things about Andrew's father's dog, already snoring again in his smelly bed beside the refrigerator, and how convenient, no, how *bogus* Andrew's allergies were. Which naturally led to his hypochondria, and somehow that led to a rant about the colossal stupidity of a world order that would let a horrible old man like Edward Bateman draw *one more breath* after my sweet, loving, tenderhearted mother was gone.

Andrew thinks I'm a drama queen, he was sure this was just another pointless emotional flare-up that would die out sooner if ignored, so he didn't fight back, even when I gave him a dog-or-me ultimatum.

"Dash, sweetheart," he said, "you're upset. We'll let the dog sleep here with Hobbes tonight, and tomorrow we'll find it a good home. A really good home. Now come to bed." Then he leered at me. Andrew Bateman, who is not a leerer, leered at me, I can only assume because my white cotton brassiere under the blouse I'd never rebuttoned had inflamed him.

"Maybe when pigs fly!"

The rest is a blur. I said some more regrettable things, then left. That felt great—I loved the whole flouncing-out part, finding my purse, wrapping the puppy in a chenille throw, hauling open the front door and slamming it behind me.

Andrew immediately opened it and called out from the porch, "Have you completely lost your mind?"

If I had, it's still missing. None of the rationalizations I've come up with to explain what I did that night really work. It seemed like a good idea at the time. (But so did proclaiming myself "Dash" at age thirteen, because I despised "Dot," short for Dorothy.) The puppy—I think if I went to a shrink he might say, or she might say, taking the puppy out from under my shirt to save its life was like a ritual birth. In the last six months I've lost my mother, and I've virtually lost my daughter. Andrew was trying to rip away my last chance to have something belong to *me*.

That's all I could come up with as I sped down I-66 at midnight, caught between competing urges to keep driving forever and turn around and go home, where I supposedly belong. It beat Andrew's explanation, at least, made me sound more thoughtful and complicated than irresponsible and idiotic.

But it's just as likely his diagnosis is correct and I've simply lost my mind—that's still better than perimenopause. Although I don't suppose they're mutually exclusive.

two

My cell phone rings as I'm merging into traffic on I-66. Overnight the snow turned to rain, which is good, but traffic's still crazy and it's not even rush hour anymore.

"Dash?" an unfamiliar male voice says. "This is Mike Warner." I don't know anyone named Mike Warner. No, wait—it comes to me just as he says, "Barbara's husband?"

"Oh, hi, Mike. How's—oh, no, is everything—"

"We just had a baby."

"Oh my God!"

Mike, whom I've never met, has a raw, breaky voice, as if he's been yelling. "Yep, a boy."

"Oh my God! Congratulations!"

"Thanks. Thanks. Um, so Barb asked me to call and tell you she can't"—Mike starts laughing—"she can't come in today for the shoot."

"I guess not!" I join him; we both have a good laugh, although his is more sincere than mine. My mind is skipping ahead—who am I going to get to help me at this late hour? My phone book's in the office and I've only got a few numbers on this cell.

"She went into labor yesterday about four in the afternoon and she told me to call you last night, but I forgot. So it's my fault this is such short notice." He's trying to sound repentant, but he's too tired and too excited to pull it off.

"No problem, don't worry about it. This is so great! Give Barb a big hug and a kiss for me. And the baby! What are you naming him?"

"Clive Otis."

"Oh!" That's all I can think of to say to that.

As soon as Mike hangs up, I call my best photographer friend in Washington, who thank God is in her studio, I don't get her answering machine. "Elaine! My regular assistant just gave birth, and I've got a studio shoot at one o'clock this afternoon!" Elaine shrieks in sympathy, and we go down the list. Neither of us has a full-time assistant, but we often use the same freelancers. She gives me two numbers and wishes me luck. "If you strike out with them, I know of one more," she says, "but I can't say how good she'd be—"

"Can she hold a light meter?"

"Well, she's had a year of photography school, so she must know *something*."

"You'd think. What's her number?"

Sock does her business three times on the two-block walk from where I finally find a parking place to the studio. "Good *girl*," I lavish on her all three times. I think it's working; she's only gone in the house once in two days. I really think she's getting it.

My studio is over a jewelry store on Ontario Road. The sign on the side of the building says Bateman Photography, and has for about fifteen years. If Andrew and I really split up, should I change it to Mc-Gugin, my maiden name, or would that just confuse people? The red brick facade and faded awnings don't promise much, but I like to think the interior is a happy surprise. Somebody once told me people actually prefer seedy-looking photo studios, and the iffier the neighborhood the better. Whatever you charge, they think it's a deal, plus you seem more like a fine artist than a commercial one. I wave to Mr. Federman, the jeweler, through his shop window, and unlock all the locks on the door to the stairs. That always takes a while, and by the time I finish, Sock's got her leash wound around my legs twice. She's scared of the steep steps; I have to pick her up and carry her.

I turn lights on in the lounge, the echoey studio, my little office. The answering machine is blinking like mad, which is good, means business, but it's probably just clients making sure their prints will be ready before Christmas. After the holidays, things will slow down a bit and not get hectic again till Valentine's Day.

I make a few calls, tidy up the lounge and the bathroom, start getting the studio ready for the shoot. I keep checking my watch. One of Elaine's freelancers didn't answer and the other one said he was busy and couldn't make it, but the third one, the one Elaine had reservations about, naturally she was free and promised she'd be here by a quarter to twelve. Greta Cantwell is her name. She sounded very young, and like I woke her up, but also eager and grateful and enthusiastic—which are the things you want in an assistant anyway, I'm telling myself, more than a look at her portfolio or her degree. With Barb out of commission indefinitely, it's *better* if this Greta person is unformed; that way I can mold her in my own image, so to speak. All photographers operate differently, and I want an assistant who operates like *me*.

Greta shows up at twelve-thirty.

"I'm sorry, I'm so sorry," she keeps saying as she strips off her wet coat. "My car's in the shop and I missed the bus and then I just missed the subway, and then I had to walk from Dupont Circle because there weren't any cabs because of the rain. I'm really, really sorry."

"Never mind, that's fine. Can you bring your coat over here? I like to leave the lounge area clear for customers' stuff," I say, leading her through the studio to the office.

"Oh!" She spots Sock on her pillow in a corner of my office. "Oh, a puppy!" She drops down on her knees, and Sock licks her nose. "What a *beautiful* dog. How old is he?"

"She. I'm not sure, a couple of months, I think. Okay, so are we ready?"

Greta jumps up, coloring a little, as if she's suddenly remembering she's a professional. She's got on a short, tight skirt, no stockings, and platform boots. She's blonde, I can tell by the roots, but she's dyed her hair a dazzling, comically vivid carrot orange, done up in cornrows tied off with beads. She crosses her bare arms in front at the wrists. I can see gooseflesh; I think, *Honey, why didn't you wear a sweater?*

We go out to the studio. I start to explain the layout I've got in mind. "It's twins," I tell her, "six-year-old boys, and it might get a little dicey because of the grandmother."

"Oh," Greta says, "the mother's dead? My mother died when I was six, too."

"I'm sorry. But—no, the mother's not dead, but it's the grandmother who's commissioned the portrait, so she's the one bringing the kids.

And I don't think there's—well, we'll see what happens, but when I did the preshoot consult, I didn't notice a lot of affection between the boys and their grandmother. But we'll see."

"So you met the kids already?"

"Yeah, I always do that."

"Wow." She has squinty blue eyes, pale-lashed and pink-rimmed; they look intelligent but myopic. I hope she's wearing contacts. "I love what you do," she says. "I think it's the coolest job."

"Why?" I ask, amused.

"Well, working with kids and all, plus you're an *artist.*"

"Ha. Sometimes. But there's a lot to it that's not all that artistic." It's good to hear she wants to be an *artist,* though. A lot of the young ones these days are only in it for a quick buck, and because they think it's easy. God, I sound old.

Very quickly I show her where the basics are: the hair light, the fill, the key lights, what props I expect to use. "The bathroom's over there, the kitchen's there, that's a little dressing room. I can do most of this by myself, and I usually do, but since it's twins . . ."

"Oh, sure. Double the trouble."

"Right, plus the whole grandmother deal. This isn't a Christmas shot, by the way. It's for the kids' birthday, January fifteenth, so that's why we won't be using Christmas props."

"Gotcha."

"What else? Mrs. Thorpe, the grandmother—when I asked her what the boys were into, she said chess. So I got a chess set and we can put it on this table, these chairs—but you know, I just doubt it, they didn't seem like chess guys to me. But, again, we'll see."

The doorbell buzzes.

"Damn, they're early. Okay, Greta. Are we okay?"

She takes a deep breath; her skinny shoulders go back, little breasts stick out. "I'm ready."

"Good. Oh—no, never mind."

"What?"

"Nothing." I started to give her the most important instruction, which is, basically, keep quiet and in the background so everybody focuses on me. Makes things much simpler. But in Greta's case, I don't think it's necessary. Unless I'm mistaken, this is her first pro shoot. Her problem's more likely to be taking initiative, not taking charge.

Mrs. Thorpe is a ghastly woman on almost any level I can think of. Why Mrs. Thorpe the *mother* didn't come today with her children and protect them from her I can't imagine, unless she's as scared of the old lady as they are. She should've come anyway: These children need her. Grandmother Thorpe looks particularly humorless and formidable, like a Cold War Russian soldier in a full-length sable coat she won't take off—my studio's too cold, she says—matching hat, and knee-high leather boots. It's not going to be easy keeping her out of my way.

The twins, Kevin and Eugene, are identical, but I can tell them apart by Kevin's slightly darker crew cut and Eugene's glasses. They're six, going on seven. When I greet them, they give no sign of having met me before, but they're cowed little guys; they don't meet anybody's eyes, and even though their sullenness is a cover for fear right now, any minute it could morph into really bad behavior. Already I don't like how this is going.

I have to roll the backgrounds down myself because Greta has never seen a motorized lift before. What are they teaching in photo school these days? We set up the chess scene with a background that looks like wood paneling; Mrs. Thorpe is going for that two-gentlemen-in-a-library look, I presume. Greta takes flash meter readings like a pro, thank God. We get something preliminarily okay for the lighting, but it doesn't work. Kevin and Eugene, especially Eugene, can't relax, they look like mannequins, like firing-squad victims.

"This isn't what I wanted *at all*," Mrs. Thorpe tells me in a loud aside. "This is just not right. I'd heard good things, but frankly . . ." Her blonde pageboy doesn't move when she shakes her head. "I must tell you, Dash," she says, and my name sounds sillier than usual in her society-lady voice, "this was by way of a test. If these pictures were good, I planned to have you photograph my very *favorite* grandchild for her birthday in April. But. Frankly."

The twins pretend not to hear, but they do, they must. I happen to catch sight of Greta hovering behind the soft box. She's wincing, her teeth bared in sympathy for these poor children. Right, then. We're a team.

We try again with the chessboard. I act goofy, say something to make the twins giggle. "Don't grin!" Mrs. Thorpe orders. "Kevin! We discussed this!"

I must not have heard right. "Did you say, 'Don't grin'?"

She looks at me coldly. "They've just lost their front teeth, both of them. Of course they mustn't grin. Toothlessness is not cute. Smile, yes, with lips closed, but I don't want bare gums in these photographs."

That's when I banish her. It's never easy, but sometimes it's necessary, and with Mrs. Thorpe it's essential. Her son is a congressman—she told me that early on to impress me, intimidate me, who knows. It's true, I want more clients like her—who wouldn't? I'm a low-volume high-dollar photographer, and they can afford my premium fees—but I can't let her stay. I use fake confidentiality, trying to disarm her. "They're high-strung," I say, guiding her casually into the lounge, holding onto her furry arm. "Such bright boys, so intelligent, and this is, really, let's face it, an artificial environment. Forgive me, but when you're here, their *anchor,* their *compass,* they can't—naturally!—focus on anything else. I never do this, I hardly ever do this, because it's necessary only in the most special circumstances, really extraordinary children and their families—but Mrs. Thorpe, I really must insist, and I know you understand—you must go."

She does! It's amazing! She doesn't just take a seat in the lounge, either—she *leaves,* exactly what I was hoping for but not expecting. "I'll be back in one hour." She points a finger at me, as if this is her idea. Up close, her face is puffy around the eyes; she looks more frazzled than formidable. She's glad to get out of here, I realize; small children make her crazy—they probably always have—and her only defense is becoming a shrew. "See you later," we say to each other with mutual relief.

"Okay!" I shout, clapping my hands. I'll turn cartwheels to change the mood in this place. "Let's have some fun!" I don't have long to get the twins out of the funk they're in and up onto the Happy Plateau, and they'll only last about thirty minutes, max, once they're up there. Time's a-wastin'.

The only thing that's piqued either one's interest so far is the camera, my brand-new Canon. They want to play with it; I've had to shoo them away from it twice already. It gives me an idea.

"You know what, I'm tired of taking pictures of you guys. I don't suppose you'd like to take some *for* me for a change?"

They look at me with suspicion. Eugene glances at Kevin, who's the leader. "You mean like Polaroid or thomething?" Kevin asks.

"Yeah, like Polaroid." Good idea.

"We've done that before." Eugene squirms in the three-piece suit Grandma dressed him in. "Our dad leths uth blow on the picture."

"Tho it'll come out fathter," Kevin explains. They have identical snub noses and stick-out ears. Fabulous-looking kids. They have identical toothless gums, too, and by God, I'm going to photograph them.

"Oh, wow. Well, hey, if you can do that, you can *take* pictures, too."

I don't use Polaroid as much as I used to when formatting shots, not since digital, but I've still got unrefrigerated film somewhere and a very old Nikon with an NPC Proback. The twins hover around me when I crouch down and explain how it works. It's lovely to see the nerves and wariness leak out of them as they become their own age again, turn back into children. They're so small and slight, their bones like sticks through the tough little-boy skin. Their bowed heads smell like hair tonic. I can never have enough of children. I want to gather these two up in my arms like a bunch of flowers.

They take turns shooting pictures of each other. I give them my watch and explain about the second hand, and just let them go. After a while I start messing with the lighting, taking shots of them taking shots, and that gives me another idea.

"Hey, guys, let's really do this right, whaddaya say? How about if . . ." I explain what I'd like, a formal picture of Kevin taking a formal picture of Eugene, and then vice versa.

They don't get it.

"Okay, look. Tripod," I tell Greta, pointing, and she brings me the one leaning in a corner. "And a nice formal background . . . like . . . this?" I roll up the wood paneling and roll down a dark blue cloth. "Or—no, I know! A scene! Check this out." Up with the blue, down with an extremely nifty hand-painted mural I've never used. I paid much too much for it, but I couldn't resist. It's an outdoor scene, a split-rail fence in the foreground, funky old farmhouse in back, leafy green tree limbs at the top throwing great shadows. It's corny, but I love it.

"Ith like the Wetht," Eugene observes. "Like cowboyth?"

"Old-fashioned," I say, suddenly not sure. Maybe they like space better, or dinosaurs.

Kevin, whose word is law, goes up close and touches the screen—which is forbidden, but I keep quiet; I'll worry about oily little fingerprints later. He sweeps the scene with his whole hand, in fact, petting it, as if he'd like to get inside it. "Ith pretty," he pronounces. And we're off.

Now that they know how Polaroid works, they want to shoot fast, and the trick is slowing them down. I pose them in profile, facing each other before the screen. I make Eugene sit bolt upright in a chair with his hands on his thighs, serious-faced—that's another challenge—with Kevin bent over the tripod, staring into the Nikon's viewfinder. We do that for a while, then switch, which involves Kevin rolling down his shirtsleeves, buttoning up his vest, and putting his tie and jacket back on, Eugene reversing the process. I'm seeing the whole thing in soft sepia, but who knows. It's a joke setup, sort of Norman Rockwellian, but the boys' wonderful faces, earnest on the surface, bubbling with merriment just underneath, rescue it from cuteness.

"What do you think?" I ask Greta, who is doing a pretty good, low-key job so far, except during pauses she can never remember to turn off the molding lights or check the flash heads for heat; I have to remind her every time. "How does it look to you?"

"It's great! It's so sweet, and so, I don't know, simple, I mean it's like just two things, but it works."

Precisely. It's these great kids in an adorable pose, at the same time they're being exactly who they are. So I have enough of that, but I want a backup, something completely different. And I can't help it, I want to knock old lady Thorpe's socks off. With what, though?

Greta thinks of it first. So obvious. So perfect. "Why don't you let them play with the puppy?"

Fabulous idea, although not without a million built-in difficulties. Like getting Sock used to being mauled by two excited six-year-olds, and after that, getting all three to stay *roughly* on a new set and within range of cameras and lights. Refocus, refocus, refocus. "We'll just let it go," I say to console Greta, who's looking harried by all the changes and adjustments that keep coming and coming. "We'll get something, don't worry about it. That's the fun part—not knowing what's going to happen. Relax, Greta, have fun."

The twins are having fun, that's the main thing. Clicking cameras and flashing lights are old hat to them now, they don't even notice. I told them to take off their ties but keep their jackets on, and I love how rumpled and wrinkled they look. Grandmother may or may not agree, but she's got to like their red cheeks and their laughing, relaxed faces, gums and all. I step around with the camera in my hands, using the motor drive. I get even better shots using the tripod and remote, because then the puppy comes to me and I can get the boys alone, and sometimes they're posed *perfectly,* sitting on their heels and grinning right into my lens. I've heard photographers say they don't know if they've got anything good till the shoot's over and they're checking the proofs, but I always know. And today even the timing's right: Everybody, including Sock, starts getting cranky at the very moment Mrs. Thorpe returns.

Fun's over. End of shoot.

Greta is exhausted. Me, too, but I love it, even the letdown, all that energy spent, the tension and uncertainty, the near disasters, the mini coups. I feel like a flat balloon. It's like I've come down from a drug, but there's no hangover because I brought the high with me—it's in that little stack of memory cards on my desk.

I send Greta out with money and directions, and she comes back from World's Best Deli on Columbia with hot pastrami sandwiches and all the fixings, including truly the world's best pickles. We eat in the cramped office while I download some of today's cards and check out a few proofs. I just like to check, make sure nothing nightmarish has happened—not that it really can anymore with digital, but still, I like to check—but I don't pore over proofs the day of a shoot, and I *never* show them to clients. They're too tired, it would just get them all revved up again. Better to wait and build up all-new anticipation.

"God, this is good," Greta says over a mouthful of salty french fries. "I was famished."

"Me, too. Nothing since breakfast." I'm half surprised she's not a vegan or something. At the very least she looks like a picky eater with her freckled, sugar-white, cheekbony face and her long white arms. She's a bit clumsy, I found out today; she makes wide, scary gestures with those long arms, sometimes when she's standing near tripods and light stands. I thought of a Labrador retriever beside a low coffee table, its thick tail sweeping the drinks over.

"Show me your book," I invite—there was no time this morning to look at it—and she spreads out her portfolio on my desk.

"I was an art major in college. I guess you can sort of tell."

"How do you mean?" I wipe my greasy fingers before turning the photos over carefully. They look like photo-school pictures: not bad, not great. Competent. Luckily a beginner can be a mediocre photographer and a terrific assistant. Attitude is everything.

She sneaks the puppy a bite of her sandwich. "My stuff is very young and self-conscious, it's not really me yet."

"No, it's good. Lots of promise."

"I probably should've stayed in school, but it didn't seem like I was learning anything new after the first year or so."

"Well, I've got nothing against photography schools in general. You can certainly get a good grounding in the basics, if nothing else. And, of course, some schools are a lot better than others." Greta's is one that some are a lot better than, so I don't pursue that. "But to really learn the business, I don't think there's anything like assisting."

"Absolutely. I learned so much just *today*, watching how you kept changing things to make it work. And really fast on your feet, and always right inside their heads, the kids' heads, like practically *being* them. And then the pictures, God, they're so great, the lady won't even be able to *pick*."

"Well, let's hope she likes one or two," I say, thinking, *Now, that's the kind of attitude I like.* "With children, though, you're always improvising. Today was pretty much par for the course. If you go into a shoot with a fixed idea about how things are going to go, you're just asking for it. Kids will *always* find a way to surprise you."

"I bet."

"Are you interested in children's portraiture in particular?" Her portfolio only has one or two kid pics.

"I'm not sure. Maybe. Before now, all I've done is product photography, to tell you the truth. Like fruits and vegetables, and one time just close-ups of nails."

"Nails?"

"For a hardware store catalog."

"My God."

"But this—I love kids, and this was so much fun. And having your own studio, that must really be amazing—but then again, I also like playing with computers, you know, designing things, graphic art. But then—sometimes I feel like what I really want to do is study to be a photojournalist so I can travel, you know, see more of the world before I settle down. I see myself as"—she snickers, self-conscious—"like, Christiane Amanpour." Next comes a giddy, full-throated laugh. "But then *again*—I have no money!"

"I think you should *definitely* see the world before you settle down," I say, laughing, too. "Before you get old and gray like me. This is the best time of your life, so don't waste it! Whatever you do, don't let all that energy go for nothing, that's my advice." Which I am never shy about giving—ask Andrew—but I look at this girl's odd face, the eccentric clothes, her strange but marvelous hair, and even though there is absolutely *no* resemblance, I see myself twentysome years ago. In her spirit and her impracticality. Her talent and her cluelessness. Her big, vague ambitions, with no plans to achieve them.

Why can't you just give people money when you can see they need it? I could give Greta . . . a thousand dollars, say, and she could take a photojournalism course at Maryland or American U. while she saves up for the next course. Or she could just *go*—she could go to Africa or Asia or anywhere and start taking pictures. That's how to see the world, just *go*, and she's the kind of person who'd have the guts to do it.

She starts throwing napkins and wrappers in the garbage. "Sorry about the modeling lights," she says. "What a dolt."

"Forget it. Once I plugged the flash meter cord into the wall socket instead of the power supply."

She gasps. "What happened?"

"Blew out everything. Luckily it wasn't my studio. Or unluckily— I got fired." Unfairly, I always thought. I was young and dumb, the photographer should've been paying more attention.

"Did you go to photo school?"

"Not me. Self-taught in the beginning, although I've picked up some degrees since then. But that was a long time ago. If I were coming up now, I'd do what you're doing. And the *desire* to learn is half the battle, more than half. No, you were great today, Greta, very intuitive. You're the one who thought of using Sock. That was totally inspired."

She beams. Then—it's as though my praise is too much for her—she picks Sock up and hides her face in the dog's furry neck. "Thanks," she says, muffled. "Thank you very much."

I offer to drive her home.

"Oh, no, I'll just get the subway."

"No, it's late, I'll drop you off."

"Oh, no, really, I couldn't. Thanks, but it's too much."

"Don't you live in Arlington? That's not out of my way. Much."

"It's not?"

Then I realize: She thinks I live practically around the corner. So then I have to explain that I'm staying down in Virginia these days, a fact I wouldn't have bothered mentioning otherwise. Her squinty eyes open wide, but she doesn't ask me any questions.

I hate winter. I hate five-thirty in the evenings, everybody's lights on, glare in your eyes, the day's over and all you've done is work. Why don't they keep daylight saving time year-round? Winter is when we *need* it.

In the car I ask Greta about her family, her life. She's from the Philadelphia suburbs; her father and stepmother are schoolteachers. Her boyfriend's name is Joel.

"Actually," she confides with a short laugh, "we're fighting." Her bare legs look bluish in the flicker of streetlamps; I keep turning the heater up. "He thinks we should move in together."

"You don't want to?"

"Well, I sort of do. We've been going together for five months."

"That's not so long."

"I know, that's what I tell him. I want to slow things down a little, but he says if, you know, we're *serious,* we should be living together." She heaves a deep, soulful sigh. "He's older than I am."

"How old?"

"Thirty-one. He's divorced. Has a little boy. Joint custody. What he'd really like to do," she says, looking out the side window, "is get married."

I bet. "What does he do?"

"He's a systems analyst."

"Uh-huh."

Another heavy sigh. "So anyway. I don't know what to do."

Andrew would be proud of me. I know exactly what she should do, but I say nothing, not even the two words that would throw Greta's dilemma into spectacular, blinding relief: Christiane Amanpour.

She lives on the first floor of a low, sterile apartment building in the kind of featureless, aging, redbrick complex Arlington's full of. I stop in front of the curb. She points her place out to me. "The one with the lights on. That's good, that means Cindy's home. My roommate. Good, I didn't much feel like being by myself tonight. Frankly," she adds, half laughing, trying to make that sound less pitiful.

I think again of me at twenty-three, twenty-four. Out of college but not on any of the career tracks I thought I might be on by then. Hanging out with iffy guys, drinking too much in bars, taking too many dead-end jobs to pay the rent on my overpriced efficiency apartment. Confused. Thrilled with my independence, just *delighting* in being on my own, the whole world open and available if I could ever choose, ever commit—and then I fell in love with Andrew.

And that was the end, if you look at it like that, if you take that perspective. The end of all my choices. After that, everything, like it or not, fell into place. Dash's life, settled.

"Greta."

She smiles at me, hand on the door. "Dash. Thank you so—"

"I could use some help. I'm not in the office as often as I should be these days because of, you know, circumstances, so I'm thinking I could use a good, reliable assistant. It would be part-time, and mostly what you'd do is answer the phone and sound intelligent, but you'd also help me out on shoots like today, when it can get complicated. I think you did really well today—"

"Oh *wow*."

"—especially considering the limited amount of experience you've had in portraiture—"

"Oh, this would be so *great*."

"Now, you wouldn't get rich, and we should probably try this out on a trial basis before either one of us commits—"

"Oh, golly, the answer's yes. Trial basis, that's fine, whatever you think. I'm up for it, I'm ready." Her whole face beams in the yellow light of the streetlamp. "Even if it's not that much, a steady income right now would be perfect for me. Oh, I'm excited!"

"Me, too. When do you think you could start?"

She throws her head back and laughs that crowing laugh, orange hair flying, beads clacking. "Tomorrow?"

She's so funny. I have absolutely no reservations about this, even though it's a spur-of-the-moment decision. "How about Monday? It's a light day for work but heavy for phone calls, people calling for appointments because they made up their minds over the weekend. I'll come in Monday and we'll go over everything, how's that?"

"Monday, perfect. I can't wait to tell Joel." She hugs herself. "I am the *luckiest* person." Suddenly she collapses, shoulders hunched, head bowed. "God, I'm being so unprofessional. Thank you, Dash, I accept your job offer." She dissolves in giggles.

This is going to be so much fun. It's like I've hired myself.

three

Driving back to the cabin at night doesn't scare me, although if something happened, no one would know. No one's worrying about me. I guess I miss that. It was a comfort, a pillow between me and danger, that someone (Andrew) was worried about me. Then I didn't have to worry about myself.

I put music on to break the silence. I make a cup of tea. There's a message on the machine from Andrew saying that he's going to bed early, he's got another headache, but we need to talk.

The puppy smiles at me as she sits on her little haunches on the hooked rug by the woodstove. She has the biggest brown eyes. "Hi, sleepy," I say in a cooing voice. "You were so *good* today. Weren't you? Yes, you w—— Hey!" She might be smiling, but she's not sitting on her haunches. She's peeing.

We go outside.

I still can't get over how quiet it is. No cars, airplanes, sirens, radios, children, televisions. Another light, wet snow is starting to fall, just like last night. It's unusual, everybody says, snow down here this early; it's not even officially winter yet. I lift my face to the pearl-bright sky and let snowflakes tickle my eyelids. When I take a deep breath, it smells like innocence.

When I was a little girl, my mother taught me how to make snow cream: Fill a pot with clean, fresh-fallen snow, add milk, a lot of sugar, some vanilla, stir it up. Give half to your mother and eat the rest right out of the pot. Makes your head throb and your teeth ache.

Just thinking about it makes me crave some snow cream now. I've been thinking, part of the reason I could do such an unspeakable thing as walk out on Andrew, actually *leave my home,* is because I'm an orphan. My mother and I carried home between us, even though we didn't live together for the last twenty-five years. She tied me to my past—she was the history of me. My mother was my home. Storming out of that other place, the brick town house in Adams Morgan that Andrew and I bought as soon as we could afford it, the house we loved and fought and built our lives and raised our daughter in—leaving that house seems almost like a technicality. Like checking out of an especially comfortable bed-and-breakfast.

That's not true, what am I saying? But still—where you grow up, for better or worse, that's home. When I dream, Mama's old clapboard house in Greensboro is always the setting for *home,* even when I people it with anachronisms like Andrew and Chloe or my dentist. All the domestic dramas in my sleeping dreams unfold in that kitchen with the faux redbrick tile, the dog's big wicker bed forever blocking the broom closet. Or in the beige-carpeted living room with the baby grand piano nobody could play—Daddy won it in a contest. Or in the deep window alcove at the top of the stairs where I kept my hamster cage and read movie-star magazines. Home.

The puppy can't walk far; snow gets stuck between her toes and makes her limp. I pick her up. We'll go to the end of the driveway, watch the cars go by. This is not much of a snow; the flakes are already growing fat and feathery. It'll stop soon, but I wish it would last all night, snow and snow, keep snowing till the whole white world came to a halt. A nonviolent, temporary interruption of my life.

I have another snow memory, a sweet one that's warmed my heart for two decades. If I get amnesia, if I get Alzheimer's, if any physical misfortune befalls me except blindness, I won't forget this one. It's engraved inside my wedding band: RUBBISH.

Andrew and I had a traumatic courtship, defining courtship as the interval between meeting and sleeping together. He was twenty-eight, had just passed the D.C. bar exam, and was fighting with his father over what to do next: teach while he got his Ph.D. in history or join the family law firm. I had a degree in sociology (I asked Chloe if that's still what you major in when you have no idea what you want to be; she said no, it's communications now) and lots of dreams and ambitions, but except for dog walking and house-sitting, I was pretty much unemployed. At twenty-four, I was just beginning to worry about that.

I wasn't free when we met. I was going out with, in a raggedy, undeclared way, one of the musicians in a garage band I was singing with. Practicing with, rather; we hadn't had any gigs yet, never been hired to play anywhere for actual money. (I remember Andrew's face when I told him the name of the band was Goon Squad—he'd imagined I sang in a chamber chorale or something, I realized later.) My boyfriend called himself Hood, but his real name was Larry Heigle. He had peroxide hair and a silver spike in his bottom lip, and this was *years* before body piercing went mainstream.

In the morning after the first time we made love, Andrew sat on the edge of my bed to pull his socks on and told me it was all a mistake.

"It's not you, it's me," he said. And "I hope we can still be friends."

I'd just woken up. I lay amid the tangled covers in dawning shock, still dazed from the most thrilling, most *complicated* lovemaking of my young life. "What? Say that again?" He did, and it felt as if I were being wrenched out of a good dream by a punch in the nose.

"I don't think it's going to work out," he said sorrowfully. He was dressed in an early incarnation of the uniform, the winter version, khakis and a charcoal-gray crewneck over the blue Oxford shirt. One of the reasons I'd fallen for him was because he wasn't like anyone I knew, not in those days. Compared to my friends, he was the exotic one, an earnest oak in a crowd of gaudy palm trees.

"What's wrong? What's going on?" When I grabbed for the sheet, I grabbed back all the inhibitions—not that I had so many, hardly any compared to Andrew—that I'd joyfully sloughed off during the long, amazing night. "Are you leaving? This is over?"

He stood up to buckle his belt. He poked around and finally found his wire rims amid the clutter on my bedside table. Then he faced me in military at-ease posture, hands behind his back, legs apart. Defenseless—taking it on the chin. Behind his glasses his eyes were the clear, bewildered blue that still melts me and, I really think, makes me a better person. Because I don't want to be anything but kind to him.

"It's just that we have nothing in common." He puckered his serious brow. Just like now, only not as deeply, it furrowed in three places when he frowned. "You're terrific, but I can't see this going anywhere. So I think it's better to break it off now instead of later."

"But we've *always* known we have nothing in common. We *joked* about it." In a flirty, indirect way, during the period when we were still pretending I was being faithful to Hood. Everything was bittersweet and forbidden then—how could we not fall in love? Twelve hours earlier we'd quit playing that game, though, or so I thought, and now Andrew was telling me it was over? I threw a pillow at him—I'd have thrown a bomb if I'd had one. *"What is wrong with you?"*

He put his hands out in the baffled, hunch-shouldered gesture of earnestness that always gets me. "Dash," he said gently. "Look." The fact that he didn't want to *hurt my feelings* made me so angry, and so horribly alive to what I was losing, I burst into tears. "Oh, please," he mumbled, but out of distress, not impatience. "Please don't do that."

"Last night you liked everything about me," I threw at him, wiping my face on the sheet. "About us. What a jerk you are. Go if you're going, just go." I couldn't look at him, the way his bony wrists hung there, helpless-looking, under the cuffs of his shirt, the unfamiliar body I'd just seen and made terribly familiar, a feast covered up with a cloth before vanishing. Oh, he was so wrong, but I didn't have the words to *explain* it to him.

"We're different people, that's all. No one's to blame, we're simply—"

"Are you *trying* to sound like the woman?"

"What?"

"Go away!"

He started to, his relief obvious.

"But don't think you didn't break my heart!"

That stopped him. "I'm so sorry. That's the last thing I wanted."

"What *do* you want? I don't understand you. Just tell me."

"I'll send your records back."

"You'll *send* them?" I'd lent him some CDs, hoping to turn him on to punk rock. The pain and politeness and the badly disguised anguish in his face while he listened to them had wrenched me even deeper into helpless love. "You'll *send* them?"

"I've thought about it all night," he said—a patent lie; I'd heard him snoring. "Relationships are hard enough anyway and, em, I just believe two people need to have as much in common as possible before they . . . before they even start."

"My parents had nothing in common." I couldn't believe I was *ar-*

guing with him—how low could I go? But I thought of my mother and father, how different they were and how ecstatically happy together. I wanted that, but until then I'd never realized it, I think because my mother and I were everything to each other after Daddy died. Andrew—not that he was like my father, but he was the only man I'd ever met whom I could imagine *being* a father. Or a husband. He seemed ready-made.

And here he was turning me down. "You and I," he said, "we're like . . ." He squinted in thought; he's always been horrible at analogies. "We're like Nixon and James Brown. I just don't think we're right for each other."

"What about opposites attract?"

"Attract, yes. Yes," he agreed. "But then they repel."

Repel. The sting of that was scalding. "Didn't you like fucking me?" I said on purpose. He *hates* it when I swear, so I don't anymore, or hardly ever. But I did then, like a sailor, and I wanted to see him blanch.

"There, that's—exactly it," he said. "Don't you see?" I saw, but then he rubbed it in: He made a gesture that took in everything I suddenly realized he hated about my room, the messiness, the—oh well, the chaos. It's hard to keep a one-room efficiency apartment neat and tidy. I'd noticed his veiled incredulity the night before, and I'd imagined he was comparing my place with the spare, barrackslike apartment on Twenty-fifth Street *he* called home. I knew a symbol of incompatibility when I saw one, but I resented having it thrown in my face by *him*.

"Okay, leave!" I shouted. "Leave right this instant!"

He slunk out.

All day, while I moped, it snowed. Late in the afternoon, Hood and the rest of the guys picked me up in the band's ancient van, a noisy, foul-smelling, smoke-spewing rust heap they kept registered in Maryland because the inspection laws were looser. We were going out to College Park to practice with another band, maybe hook up with them and start playing country rock, since our punk careers weren't going anywhere.

I'd spent the day watching snow swirl past the window, comforted a little by its erasing power, able occasionally to imagine not feeling wretched but cleansed and free, the way I used to feel. Like, *yesterday.*

I was young, and I was also young for my age, but the hurt was real and I knew what I'd lost. Numb as a widow, I stayed all day at the window and watched the snow, trying to make sense of this massive personal catastrophe, this violation of my deepest instincts. I loved Andrew. I did, and it wasn't infatuation or lust, although it certainly was those, too. I'd met my match, my man, and I knew it, and he'd said, "We don't suit," and walked away. The *injustice.*

I took my seat in the back of the stinky van, wedged between an amplifier and Hood, who kept trying to cheer me up—last night had meant absolutely nothing to him, which somehow made it even more distressing to me. "Hey, whatever," he said while he patted my knee, "it's not like this big, like, *love* affair, right? Right? Guy's an asshole, you'll—" I looked away, out the window, and there was Andrew waving to me from the snowy sidewalk.

Just then Eddie, the drummer, started the van and it roared into rattling, hacking life, belching plumes of foul blue smoke. Andrew started shouting and windmilling his arms. Hood turned to see what I was staring at. "What the fuck?" he said. Eddie said the same thing, "What the fuck?" but he was talking about the van. It wouldn't move, even when he tromped on the accelerator.

"Who's that guy?" wondered Greg, the guitarist, before his attention joined Eddie's on the mystery of the motionless van. I sat still, imagining hopeful things one second, hopeless ones—Andrew had decided to *bring* my CDs back rather than send them—the next. His mouth kept forming the same phrase, but I couldn't make it out over the engine roar. He flapped his hands; he grabbed his neck, made a slashing gesture across his throat. He wanted to kill himself? The last snowplow had left a high, filthy bank of snow between us and the curb; Andrew couldn't get closer to the van without going around to the other side, but rush-hour cars and the slick street made that a potentially suicidal idea.

"Are we stuck on the ice?" Greg said.

"What's he doing?" Hood asked, looking out the window at Andrew.

Hatless in a camel chesterfield coat, he seemed to be walking around in circles on the steep slope in front of my apartment building. Not walking, more like shuffling, pushing snow aside with his loafers, and every few seconds he'd take a giant step to the side and start shuffling again.

"It's the clutch," Eddie said. "It finally burned out."

"He's writing something," Hood said. "What is that, R-U . . ."

I craned closer, crushing Hood against the window. "R-U-B . . ."

"Rubbish." Hood looked at me blankly. "He wrote out 'RUBBISH.' "

Andrew's trousers were white to the knees. His hair hung wet and blackish over his pale forehead. His glasses were fogged. His mouth moved again, and over the noise of the engine I finally figured out what he was saying. "That was all rubbish."

Well, it certainly was. As miserable as I'd been, I'd never believed for a second all that nonsense about people needing to have as much in common as they possibly could, relationships being tricky enough to begin with, blah-blah. Absolute rubbish.

I climbed over Hood, practically fell out of the van. Andrew did fall, scrambling down the bank to the sidewalk, and we cannoned into each other in an ecstatic, terribly romantic embrace, kissing and laughing, Andrew murmuring in my ear the loveliest things about what an idiot he'd been. I was in heaven, pure bliss—but I'd have been even more jubilant if I'd known then how rare a gesture my dignified husband-to-be, whose personal idol is Thomas Jefferson, had just made, all for my sake. A once-in-a-lifetime gesture.

That's a dear memory, immortalized inside my wedding ring all these years, twenty years this coming May. It's taken me almost that long, twenty years, but I suppose I finally got it straight that night we found the puppy on the doorstep. Turns out Andrew's dithery, womanish misgivings about us weren't idiotic at all. They were prophetic.

I call the machine at my studio for messages, but there aren't any. Good. I lock up, turn out the lights, a long process since most of the switches in this cabin are nowhere near the lights. It's early, but I'm tired. Going to bed.

The puppy's snoring in her box, dead asleep. I reach down to stroke the soft line between her eyes, and she doesn't even twitch.

Every night since I've been here, I make a conscious decision not to miss Andrew. In bed, I mean. I crawl under the covers by myself and make a point of thinking, *Yes, he's not here, but he's safe, and you're safe except for the mice in the kitchen, and you can live without sex. You can fall asleep without him because, luckily, you were never the kind of people who have to cuddle and spoon and sprawl on each other in order to get a good night's sleep.*

I wonder if I left him for the same reason I married him, only in reverse. When I was twenty-five I wanted the Mommy-Daddy-little-girl ideal I'd had when I was a child, the sort of thoughtless, complacent security you take for granted when you're fortunate enough to have it. I had it only until I was nine, and that's too bad, but afterward I got another model, another ideal—the mother-daughter one—and in its sadder, more intense way it was just as sweet. Us against the world, that's how Mama and I saw ourselves, survivors, an inseparable unit always compensating, compensating, usually successfully, because we were two, not three.

I'm so lucky. A terrible loss split my childhood in half, and yet on either side of it I was happy. The people who loved me made sure of that, or maybe I'm just predisposed to happiness, or maybe there's a happiness "set point"—you read about that in magazines—and I always return to mine, eventually.

But I don't know. If Andrew's driving me crazy and I don't want his husbandly, fatherly *security* anymore, if I don't need the safety and the thoughtless contentment of *three*—how do I imagine I can return to the bittersweet closeness of *two* when my mother and my child are both gone? I don't understand myself. Maybe *three* and *two* are equally irrelevant (how sad; if I think about that for long, I'll cry). Maybe all that's left is to find inside myself a coherent and reasonably well-functioning *one*.

I should call Andrew. But he's probably asleep. He makes a head sandwich with his two pillows so he can have absolute quiet, and he sleeps that way all night. Never on his back anymore; he read somewhere that causes postnasal drip.

My hip hurts when I lie on my right side. Arthritis? I'm getting so old. People who say forty-five is young are always old, but objectively they're right. I could live to ninety—forty-five more years. I could take up a whole new career, people do it all the time. The only reason I got into portrait photography was to help Andrew pay for graduate school after his father wouldn't. Our first Christmas together, I got a job taking pictures of kids on Santa's lap at the mall. How *ridiculous,* I've been thinking lately, that my entire professional life was determined by something so haphazard.

I used to have grand ambitions. Confused but grand. Everything looked right and attainable to me, an endless horizon of choices like stars on a clear night. Veterinarian—that was one of the big ones. Foreign war correspondent, a journalist for *Audubon* or *National Geographic.* A blues singer or a talk-show host or a TV news anchor, something big and show-offy. But also, the person who sits all alone in the fire tower, scanning the vast green forest for smoke.

Children's photographer—when you come down to it, what kind of a job is that? Today was fun, but, frankly, I get tired of other people's children. I wanted three or four, but after Chloe we couldn't have any more. Andrew denied it, but the truth is, he didn't mind. That infuriated me. *It's not your womb that's barren,* I shouted at him—I got quite biblical in my grief. I spent half of Chloe's first year of life in a dreary blue funk.

That's what it feels like now. Yes, suddenly it's clear to me: I'm living the middle-aged version of postpartum depression. *Post* is "after"; partum . . . what is that, birth? I look it up in the dictionary in the bedside table drawer. *Partum,* from *parere,* "to beget."

Well, there you are. God knows my begetting days are over. My mother's gone, and Chloe, light of my life, she's almost as lost to me as the other children I couldn't have. It's just me and my barren womb now. Andrew—Andrew's a rumor. I'm by myself on a wide, flat plain, no one else in sight, just boneless me who can't even cast a shadow. And Andrew wanted me to *take this puppy to the pound.*

To hell with his imaginary headache. I punch the number, the phone rings twice, and he answers, his voice clogged with sleep.

"I'm taking my name back."

"Dash? Is everything—"

"Tirva, not McGugin—why should I take my father's name? That's as silly as taking yours. Tirva." My mother was Lithuanian. "Although," it occurs to me, "that was just *her* father's name, so what's the difference? Even if I took her *mother's,* it would just be her *grand*father's. You guys really stacked the deck, didn't you?"

"I was asleep," Andrew mumbles accusingly. "Hold on, hold on." I can hear him poking around, looking for his glasses, like that'll make him hear better.

"I'm just telling you, Andrew, this is not for a few days. I don't know how long, but it's not going to be just a few days." As soon as that's out, I feel better. Whatever else is the matter with me, I'm not a wishy-washy person. Making decisions peps me up.

"Wait now, hold on, this is why we said we'd talk."

"I know, but I don't care, Christmas isn't the deadline anymore. Without Chloe it's just another day anyway, so let's let it go."

"Let it go?"

"It's just another day, and frankly—frankly, I don't want to do it anyway, the house, the tree, lights, all the *cooking,* the presents, my *God.* So let's skip it."

"Fine. Very well, no Christmas."

"Oh, yes, *that* should please you. You *never* want Christmas. Oh, this'll be right up your alley! I should've married a Jew."

"God." He's rubbing his face, I hear his whiskers, and probably making that pained expression. "You're not making sense. We'll talk it all out tomorrow."

"I'm not making sense? I'm the most sensible, the most *boring* person I ever met. You even know where I am. I'm right here in our cabin, all nice and safe—"

"Dash—"

"I'm not driving across the country, am I, I'm not taking interesting side jobs, not having an affair with Brad Pitt."

"What are you talking about?"

He's touched a goddamn nerve. "I let myself get too old. I'm not one of those women in books who just—walk off the beach one day—I'm not Susan Sarandon or what's-her-name, my time has passed. Men start a whole new life—you can go to ninety, a hundred, but it's all over when we turn fifty. I heard that all my life and never believed it, I thought it was feminist bullshit, but you know what, Andrew? It's the goddamn truth."

"Now, listen—"

"It's the goddamn truth, and this is my last chance."

"Last chance to do *what*?"

"Don't ask me questions, I don't have to answer any of your questions. Okay—find myself. Are you happy? I said, 'Find myself.' I am now a walking, talking cliché."

I hate his exasperated silences. I start to say good-bye, but then he says, "Come home, Dash," in a voice that slips past my defenses. It enters my whole body through my ear. "Whatever you want, Christmas or not, it doesn't matter. Just come home."

"No, no, no, no, no." I have to drown him out to stay clearheaded. "I'm not. Andrew, I'm not. You'll see, this will be good for us."

"How can it possibly be good for us? Good for *us*?" *Good,* I think, now *he's* mad. "How can being alone at Christmas possibly do either one of us any *good*? For God's sake—I don't even know where my shoes are."

"Your *shoes*?"

"That's not the point, of course—"

"Your *shoes*? They're at the shoe repair."

"Which one, the one on Columbia or the one on Eighteenth?"

"You just want your maid back, that's all this is."

"No, that's not all this is."

"Eighteenth Street, the Korean guy. Now I have to go to bed, I've got a long day tomorrow. Hang up," I say, so he'll know I'm not hanging up on him. A long time ago we promised each other we would never, ever do that.

"Look," he says, "I'll be in the office all day tomorrow. Call me. We can have dinner. Here, not out—I'll make beef Stroganoff."

It's all he knows how to make. "What did you have for dinner tonight?" I picture him pouring spoiled milk over a bowl of Cheerios. Can he even make a salad?

"I went out. I had dinner out."

"By yourself?" No, I don't want to know. "We can have dinner," I say, "but I don't know when. Not tomorrow. I don't know when. Tomorrow's going to be another long day for me. We'll set something up. Maybe Christmas Eve."

"*Christmas Eve?*"

"I don't know. Yes, maybe. Okay, signing off. Good night, Andrew. Hang up," I say, and hang up.

Well, that accomplished nothing. There are good, sound, solid reasons for what I've done, I just don't know what they are. That is, I don't know how to *express* them. It's like when I try to argue politics with him. I always lose because he knows more and he argues better, not because he's right and I'm wrong. I wish I could organize my grievances, all the *second*-to-last straws—the dog was the last straw—and make Andrew shut up through a long, eloquent, uninterrupted presentation. And be convinced at the end, say, "Oh, I see. Yes, obviously, you're absolutely right."

That won't happen, so my next-best course is to stay out of his way. Dinner—I don't think so, not yet. I don't want to normalize things, pour oil on the hinges so they don't squeak anymore. There's something the matter with the whole *door*.

How humbling. I see Andrew is not the only one who's horrible at analogies.

andrew

four

*I*t was Wolfie, the boy from the next block, who pointed out to Andrew that his shoes didn't match. "Yo," Wolfie greeted him on a frosty Thursday morning as Andrew was unlocking his car, preparing to drive to school. "Whassup with your shoes, man. Where your ol' lady at? She let you go out like that?"

The incident unnerved him, especially since it was the kind of thing much more likely to happen to his old lady than to him. He went back in the house and changed his shoes—one dark-brown brogan in place of one black one; not that alarming; could happen to anyone—and went on to work.

Then he forgot about a history department meeting. Tim Meese stuck his head in the door to his office. "Where were you?" Andrew all but slapped his forehead. "I forgot!" Tim was as amazed as he was. Faculty meetings were skull-crushingly boring and frustrating wastes of time, but Andrew never missed them, at least not by accident.

A little later, Mrs. Melman, his next-door neighbor, called to say that the key wasn't in the mailbox, so she couldn't get in the house to let Hobbes out, a favor she'd been doing for him since Dash left on the days when he had a late class. The key, the key . . . it took him too long to remember: It must be in the pocket of his sweatpants, where he must've slipped it instead of in the mailbox after his morning jog. More absentmindedness, but still, nothing to worry about. Just because his father was going senile didn't mean he was.

Then, proving things could happen in fours in one day as easily as threes, his car sputtered out of gas at a red light on Sixteenth Street. Evening rush hour; honking horns; the humiliating push from good Samaritans; a ten-block walk, round-trip, for gas in a freezing wind. *What the hell?* The last time he ran out of gas he was sixteen years old.

Unbelievably, Wolfie was loitering in front of the house when he got home. He was bouncing the same basketball he'd been bouncing this morning, but he couldn't have been there all day; he had on different clothes, a hooded sweatshirt instead of a Windbreaker and stocking cap.

"Aren't you freezing?" Andrew asked.

"No." His full name was Wolfgang Coleman. He was eight years old and small for his age, almost frail; when he grinned, his permanent teeth looked too big for his face. "So, man, where your ol' lady at?"

He'd dodged the question this morning. Wolfie was Dash's little pal more than he was Andrew's; small children made him uncomfortable. "She went on a trip," he said, turning his back on a shock of cold wind whipping up the sidewalk.

"A *trip*."

"Yes, a trip."

"She be back?"

"Oh, yes."

Wolfie's large eyes gleamed with skepticism. "My ol' man went on a trip." He waited, palming the huge-looking basketball in his wiry palm until Andrew said, "Really?" "Yeah. Only he *never* come back."

He didn't care for the implication. They stared at each other. "Do you want to come in?" Andrew asked finally, more out of exasperation than hospitality.

"Don't got time. You need your walk shoveled?"

"Now?" He glanced at the stretch of clear, windswept walkway to his front porch. "No, thank you."

"Tomorrow?"

"If it snows, if it sticks—very well, tomorrow."

Wolfie raised his free hand. It took Andrew that telltale, old-white-guy second to realize it was for a high five, and by the time he did, Wolfie had spun around and started for the corner. His basketball made tinny, echoey thuds on the sidewalk in the icy quiet.

I'm falling apart. Andrew studied his face in the black window of the microwave while his Hungry-Man Steakhouse frozen dinner circled inside. He looked gaunt, beaky, a raptor in glasses. Were the whites of his eyes jaundiced? He squinted, going closer, closer—then jerked back. Now they claimed electromagnetic emanations from microwaves were harmless, but not long ago they were saying just the opposite.

The problem was, he wasn't thinking about what he was doing while he was doing it. He wasn't *awake*. Right now, eating his dinner on a stool at the kitchen counter, he couldn't remember what he'd had for breakfast this morning, or lunch for that matter, or precisely how he'd passed the time between classes this afternoon. Yesterday was mostly a blur, too, except for the fifteen minutes he'd spent talking on the phone to Chloe. How to account for these lapses? Dash was the day-dreamer, not him. It had something to do with time, which was passing in a peculiar, unfamiliar way, going by in a rush and yet taking forever; no wonder he couldn't keep track of it.

And no wonder he'd missed the department meeting this morning—it just occurred to him: He'd forgotten to make his list last night. What would Dash say about that? She thought his list making was obsessive-compulsive behavior, a "fetish," she once called it. Nothing of the kind, merely a tool for time management. He liked making his at night in bed, last thing before going to sleep. Last night he'd forgotten, and look what happened.

What Dash failed to appreciate was what a leap of faith list making was, touching, really, and how many positive things it suggested about a man's certainty in the future. Things, frankly, Andrew wasn't alto-gether sure he believed in, given his family health history. And yet—the lists didn't lie. If he could jot down "$$ to Chloe" or "drugsto.," think how sanguine his expectations must be of indefinite check writing and Pepto-Bismol dosing. He would tell Dash that the next time she called him a pessimist. "How could I be," he'd say. "I make lists."

He put his empty plate in the trash and washed his fork. Start to fin-ish, dinner had taken nine minutes, including cooking it. For the first few days after she left, he'd sat in his usual place at the dining-room table, enjoying his hot dog or bowl of soup with a cloth napkin, some-times a small glass of wine. But over time that got to be too much trou-ble, or else more noticeably pathetic, and now he ate in the kitchen, frequently standing up.

Not that she was a slob, not precisely, but one unexpected side effect of Dash's absence was a new cleanliness, he might even say radiance, around the house. He liked to stand in the kitchen door and survey the shiny, uncluttered surfaces of counter and stove, the crumbless kitchen table and footprintless floor, Hobbes's clean, sweet-smelling blanket jumble beside the refrigerator. Everything remained just as he left it, the dish towel folded lengthwise in thirds over the swing-out holder by the sink, dishes not languishing in the drainer but put away, the sink empty and bright. Each evening he would perfect the space a little more, clean a new cabinet, rearrange the spice rack, but he'd finally run out of improvements. Tonight everything was just right.

He made a cup of tea, disposed of the bag, added a teaspoon of sugar, wiped the stove with a clean sponge, and carried his mug out to the living room.

Here the differences were subtler but even more satisfying. At last, all of Dash's photographs on the walls were at precise angles to one another, and they stayed that way because as soon as one went out of alignment he righted it. He could sit in his easy chair and look around at perfect symmetry: no small pleasure. He knew where the newspaper was, and he knew it was all there, his wife hadn't taken the Style section upstairs or into the bathroom and abandoned it. The oak doors to the "entertainment center" stayed closed unless he was actually watching television, a rare occurrence, and the CDs were no longer scattered all over the credenza but neatly stacked in the holder and back in alphabetical order by music genre. He even knew where the remote was.

Hobbes, who'd followed him in from the kitchen, wobbled blindly in the middle of the room, waiting for him to settle. When he did, the dog collapsed at his feet with a tragic sigh and fell back to sleep.

Andrew rested his mug of tea on the scarred arm of the leather chair that had once belonged to his grandfather, Edward Bateman Sr. Andrew had inherited it via his father, Edward Jr., who, instead of keeping it for himself, had given it to twenty-year-old Andrew as a bribe. As if putting his backside in the wide, creaky, redolent chair would make the profession of law seep into him osmotically, would make the desire to be anything but an attorney in the Bateman family firm miraculously, physiologically disappear. It hadn't worked out that way, and yet, over the years, Andrew had never associated the chair with winning, never taken any gloating pleasure in the fact that he hadn't had to pay for it in the way his father had wanted. Just the opposite, actually. As comfortable as it was, the chair always seemed to exude faint reproach. *Failure*, the cushions sighed in a disappointed, paternal whisper. His uneasy chair.

He looked up from a student essay he was grading on the Second Continental Congress, recognizing the piece he'd unthinkingly put on the stereo. Mozart, the D-minor piano concerto. He dropped his head back, enjoying the sinister opening. Dash could listen peacefully to the whole first movement, not even wagging her head in time, and during the romanza she stayed relatively subdued. But the moment she heard the first five-note trill of the rondo, she would leap to her feet and start conducting. Move aside, Igor Markevitch. She turned the piece into a ballet with her wide, theatrical arm sweeps, putting her whole body into it, her fingers mimicking the piano notes, and her face—what tragic drama in the tightly shut eyes, the painfully furrowed brow, what *sympathy*. It was a bit like watching a silent film star conducting an orchestra, every emotion exaggerated, telegraphed.

He used to enjoy the concerto in a modest way, a bit of a guilty pleasure, because compared to, say, the C minor, it was more facile (as Dash would say, "It's catchier"). But now he couldn't listen to it without seeing her conducting it. In a way, she'd ruined it for him, turned it into dance instead of music, an opéra bouffe. But in another way, he liked the D-minor concerto much better than he used to. It happened all the time: Dash took over one of his simple, straightforward pleasures and made it at once more enjoyable and less what it was in the beginning. Less his.

The next day, he put on shoes that matched, made certain Mrs. Melman's key was in the mailbox, drove to work without mishap, and arrived at a curriculum meeting with time to spare. It was all in the list.

The last item on today's list was "Write Chloe." He had a few minutes before class—he'd send her a quick e-mail.

As usual, his computer mailbox contained a post from Dash, one of her mass mailings to every person in her address book. This one was about breast cancer awareness, but it could've been saving gorillas, voting for the feminist candidate, sending money to this or that charity or cause; or worse, some feel-good joke complete with music and graphics that took eons to download. None of her friends complained, though. It was so Dash, they said, exuberant, generous, activist. Exasperating.

Dear Chloe: Trust check arrived and you are not spending it all in one place, ha-ha. You're right, a credit card would probably be handier for you, simpler for me. Still see no need to rush into it, however. Would only note, you turn 19 in two months. Tangible proof of our faith in your fiduciary trustworthiness may then be forthcoming.

He suspected Chloe found his notes ponderous and hard to wade through, eminently skimmable, probably because of sentences like that. He meant them humorously, but to be sure she took them that way he would have to add more "ha-has" or even smiley faces. Unthinkable.

Glad to hear you're enjoying your independent study break and putting it to good use. You should do even better this term than last, if only because everything's not brand new anymore. And that's not pressure! Your mother and I simply could not be prouder of you. You're handling college the way you've handled every other challenge, with confidence, enthusiasm, and good sense. If we've set high standards, it's only because we know you always rise to them.

Nothing much new here. They're calling for snow again. Wish you were here, we could go sledding in the park.

Rushing—more later. Love always, Dad.

His finger hesitated a second before he hit Send. Leaving out the most important thing, that he and Dash weren't living together, made him uneasy, as if he were telling Chloe a lie. But Dash thought it would be better to keep it between themselves for now, and deep down, he wasn't sorry. As long as no one knew, it stayed in the realm of the temporary. The not-worth-mentioning.

Dash thought she had a monopoly on missing Chloe. As if that were her exclusive domain, as if maternalism trumped paternalism by definition. He didn't bother to dispute it; he sensed it gave her a perverse comfort to believe it. But she was mistaken. When he thought of his daughter, he felt a sharp pang of sadness perfectly mixed with delight, the strangest combination; like biting into a delicious piece of fruit with a sour spot, a sudden bitter taste. He missed the sound of Chloe's voice, he missed her bizarre music playing in her room. The way she slouched in front of her computer, intense as a hawk. Mostly, he missed his last chance to be her father, at least in the old way, the father of a girl. His time was up.

He wished he had a blood pressure monitor here in the office. There was one at home, but why not have two? He put his fourth finger on the inside of his left wrist and counted the beats of his heart to the second hand of his watch. Twenty seconds, twenty-three times three— sixty-nine. Good, but he was sitting calmly in his office in Douglas Hall with nothing scheduled, no meetings or student conferences, nothing remotely stressful in the offing except his Early Republic class, and he looked forward to that.

Besides, it wasn't his heart rate that concerned him, it was the irregularity of the rhythm. His doctor had spotted it at his last checkup, and now that Andrew knew it was there he could easily discern it: His heart sped up when he breathed in, slowed down when he breathed out. "Perfectly harmless," Dr. Bukowsky had said; "nothing to worry about. Very common, in fact." Maybe; maybe not. If Edward hadn't ignored breathlessness and fatigue for so long, who could say what condition his heart would be in today? One of the hundred or so ways in which Andrew tried not to be like his father was in the ignoring of symptoms.

"What's that smell?"

Richard Weldon came in without knocking and threw himself down in the chair across Andrew's desk. Andrew glanced at his watch: fourteen minutes until class, and Richard was a gasbag. "What smell?"

"Like a—Jesus, did you bring that dog again?"

Andrew rolled his chair back and looked down at the scruffy heap of Hobbes sleeping at his feet. Hobbes had lost his shape in his old age; he'd gone flat, like a damp bathroom rug. "He smells?"

"You can't smell that? Jesus. It's like an old well. An old abandoned mine." Richard jumped up and began to prowl around the room, pulling out books on the shelves and pushing them back in. He was

short and slight, not quite forty but almost bald, always pacing, cracking his knuckles, bouncing on his toes. He chaired department meetings in constant motion, circling the conference table in uneven jerks,
never lighting.

"You're looking well, Richard," Andrew said pleasantly. "Like a man
about to drop a great burden."

"It's not a great burden." The corners of his mouth sagged in disapproval. "Not in the least. I've enjoyed the job. Hate to give it up. I
wouldn't, but it's time to share."

Share? Richard could hardly wait to relieve himself of the chairmanship. "I'm tired of it," he'd told Andrew only a month ago, in a weak
moment. "Sick of all the endless goddamn den-mothering."

"How come you never have any pictures of Dash?" Richard asked,
picking up one framed photograph after another from Andrew's careful grouping, putting them back in the wrong places.

"Because she's the photographer."

"No, here's one." Richard reached up and pulled their wedding
photo down from a top shelf. "Who took this one?"

"Dash's mother." They'd gotten married in Arlene's house, spent
their wedding night in her bedroom while she'd slept downstairs on
the couch. Andrew's father and stepmother had sent an expensive gift.

"Jesus, she looks about eighteen." Richard smiled fondly. He liked
Dash. A lot.

"She was twenty-five." Andrew wished he would put the photo back.
Richard didn't know about the separation, and it made him uncomfortable to discuss Dash with him. Another lie he was almost telling. "Did
you want something in particular, Richard? I've got a class in—"

"Right, I won't hold you up, just wanted to put a bug in your ear." He
gave his nervous, throat-clearing laugh, put the photo back, and came
over to the desk. "Here's the deal." His hands clamped the edge; he
leaned in close, so close Andrew had an urge to pull on the goatee
Richard had started growing over Thanksgiving. "I won't beat around
the bush." He tugged on the Orioles cap someone had put on Andrew's
plaster bust of Thomas Jefferson. "Okay, here's the thing. We've talked
about it, and you're it. You're the one we want, but we're not comfortable giving the job to an associate professor, it doesn't look right. So
you know what that means."

"What job?"

Richard straightened. "The chair! So you'll have to bite the bullet and write something good, something impressive. It's the only way. Which you can easily do, and I've got an idea along those lines, too."

Richard Weldon was offering him his job. Andrew couldn't have been more astonished if he'd offered him his wife.

"*I* don't want it." He rolled backward on the wheels of his chair. He held up his hands, like a trampoline spotter. "Don't give it to *me*."

"Damn it, I knew you'd say that! Okay, okay, listen." Richard grimaced, struggling to make his face patient again. "You don't have to decide right away, this is just a feeler. But think about it. We want you, Andrew, you're the man."

"Who's 'we'?"

"Everybody I can get to agree on it."

"Ah. Two people?" He relaxed; all was well. "I haven't got time to write papers right now, Richard," he said with feigned regret. "Gilded Age is going well, but it's a lot tougher than I anticipated. It's the first new class I've taught in a couple of years, and I didn't take into account the learning curve."

"Well, you wanted to teach it. I thought it was too much, but you insisted. So, in a way, you owe me."

He ignored that. "Give it to Dominic. He *wants* the job."

Richard's face went red. "Brodsky would be a disaster, don't even think about it."

"He's hard to get along with, yes, but—"

"Forget it. No, you're the man."

"Look, Richard. Apart from everything else, if I took on the chairmanship I'd have to give up two of my classes. Teaching is the part I *like*."

"Yes, but think what you could do for the department." Richard jolted up on the balls of his feet, making himself taller. "You've been saying for years we need to rejuvenate the history club, get the students more involved, get 'em active again. Here's your chance! You stand for the students, that's your strength, more than scholarship. *Even* more than scholarship," he corrected hastily. "The pendulum swings back and forth, but only when somebody's got his hand on it. I'll admit, we've probably gone too far in the direction of research and publishing under my watch—so here's a chance for you to move us back toward the center. And the young faculty—everybody knows how you feel about mentoring the assistants. You and Peter Flynn couldn't be farther apart there."

"No," Andrew agreed. "Or on most other things." But why had Richard brought up Flynn?

"Speaking of Peter," the chairman said casually. "I've talked to him, and he'll get on board for you, too."

"I don't think that's likely."

"No, you're wrong. In fact, he says he'll let you write a chapter for the book he's editing. To help you get that leg up."

"Peter Flynn will let me write a chapter for his book." Andrew stood, began shoving notes and books into his briefcase. "How extraordinarily generous. Look, Richard, I've got to go." *Brilliant,* just what he needed, Peter Flynn to the rescue.

"It is generous," Richard insisted. "More important, it's exactly what you need. It'll get you over the hump, don't you see? Put your prejudices aside, write this chapter, and you'll get the full you need, I can almost guarantee it. You're so *close.*"

"I don't need a full professorship to chair the history department— *if* I wanted to chair it, which I don't. Hobbes!" he shouted, to wake up the dog.

"I don't get you. Here I am handing you two gifts on two separate platters, and you're saying no. It's not laziness—what is it? I've known a lot of TAPs, but you're much brighter than that, always have been."

"TAPs . . . ?" Teaching assistants? Andrew looked at him quizzically.

"TAP—terminal associate professor." Richard laughed. Then he turned red. "Don't tell me you've never heard that term."

The bell rang.

"This is just a beginning," Richard said, giving him a chummy slap on the shoulder, letting him go through the door first. "It's not a formal offer, just a feeler. We'll talk again, keep the dialogue going. Let's get a drink one night this week. We'll talk again, Andrew. *Think* about it, that's all!"

"Yes, all right," he mumbled over his shoulder as he tugged on Hobbes's leash, trying to make him go faster. TAP. The word kept him company all the way to his first-floor class; he set it to the rhythm of his footsteps. Smiling falsely at people he passed in the hall, it occurred to him why he'd never heard it before. Nobody used the word *terminal* around a dying person, either. Simple decency.

The worst was that there was no one to whom he could repeat this conversation. Not Dash, certainly; never, ever. And not even Tim Meese, his best friend in the department. Tim was as big a TAP as he was.

He could think of one person who would really enjoy hearing about it. His father would throw his head back and open his mouth in silent laughter, flaunting eighty years of fillings, bridges, and graying crowns. He'd slap his hands on his knees and grin up at him from his motorized wheelchair. "What'd I tell you?" he'd rasp. "Yes, sir, that's my boy. I raised a TAP!"

"Hobbes!" cried Heather Kuhn, Andrew's shiest student, when he brought the dog into the classroom and led him over to a sunny spot under the window. She even rose from her desk at the very back of the room to help get Hobbes settled. Heather was like a nursing-home resident who only comes to life on therapy pet day. "How is he?" she asked. "You haven't brought him in lately, Dr. Bateman, so I was afraid . . ." She trailed off delicately. "Is he still lonely?"

The question puzzled him until he remembered: That was the excuse he'd used for bringing Hobbes to class last time, that he was lonely in the house by himself all day. It had seemed kinder to the old boy than "He pees on the rug if somebody doesn't walk him every three hours."

"Yes," Andrew said solemnly, "still lonesome."

"Maybe you could get him a playmate. Another dog for company."

"Yeah, or a cat," said Marshall Denny, reaching down from his desk to pet Hobbes's graying haunch. "We had a dog who was thirteen when we got a kitten, and she perked him up, he lived three more years."

"Good idea," Andrew said, "except that I'm allergic to dogs. Hobbes is an anomaly." What if Dash's puppy had been an anomaly, too? Would she have stayed then, or would she have stumbled on another excuse to leave him—he drove too slowly, he left whiskers in the sink?

"Thomas Jefferson wasn't much of a dog man," he said in his professor's voice, rising from a crouch beside Hobbes to some good-natured groaning at the obviousness of the segue. "He greatly admired the sheepdog, though. In fact, in 1809, his good friend Lafayette sent him two sheepdogs from France, and Jefferson immediately put them to work at Monticello. 'Their sagacity is almost human,' he wrote, 'and qualifies them to be taught anything you please.' Think about that, class. 'Their sagacity is almost human'—do you see how relevant Jefferson still is? He could've been speaking of anyone in this *room*."

Laughter, more groans. It was an excellent class. All history majors, although most of them would go on to careers in law, journalism, government. But a few would become teachers, and some of them would regard that as a comedown. Andrew never had. Teaching had always been his first choice, and it was always history. Nothing else had tempted him.

Today they were comparing Jefferson's draft of the Declaration of Independence to Congress's final version. "There's a revolutionary sentiment in the second sentence," he began, leaning against the blackboard. "Who knows what it is? Something brand new in the history of governmental doctrine." The usual hands went up. He called on Heather, who never raised her hand but always knew the answer.

"The pursuit of happiness?" she guessed almost inaudibly.

"Correct. And why was it new? What was the old trifecta in political doctrine? Life, liberty, and . . . what?"

Even more softly: "Property?"

"Yes. Brilliant," he declared, and Heather's pale cheeks pinkened from pleasure and embarrassment.

"Life, liberty, and the pursuit of happiness," piped up Derek Berenson from a front-row desk. "Unless you happened to be a *slave*."

First Richard Weldon and Peter Flynn, now Berenson. Andrew brushed chalk off his hands and strolled over to the lectern. Defending Thomas Jefferson was a job he relished less and less because of the position it put him in: apologizing for a presumed racist. "Interesting point, Derek. We could spend the rest of the day discussing that, but let's stay on topic for now."

"But Jefferson owned slaves," Berenson, a smart, good-looking, smooth-talking third-year student, persisted. "You could pursue happiness, but only if you were a white guy, right?"

"Well, it's complicated. We'll talk about it, because it's important, but for now, let's agree it would be an easy mistake to evaluate a historical figure using modern criteria. Judge an eighteenth-century man by twenty-first-century values, in other words." The party line; it seldom failed. "At the moment, we're discussing the drafting of a document that, however many flaws we might anachronistically find in it *now*, changed the course of history *then*."

Evading difficult issues wasn't his style, but he didn't have the heart today for a debate over Jefferson's racial ethics. Besides, it wouldn't change anything. The winds were shifting. Not that he'd ever had much clout in the department—not that he'd wanted it—but seeing what little he did have slip away, like the painful passing of knots in a tug-of-war rope when you're losing . . . it was demoralizing. If he was the old guard, Peter Flynn and his bunch were the new, and Andrew could feel their hot breath on the back of his neck, their loafer-shod toes on his heels, hounding him into obsolescence.

"Hey, don't be in such a hurry to say no. Think about it," Tim Meese said around a mouthful of Boston cream pie, Friday's dessert special in the Student Center cafeteria. "If you were the chairman, you could get me out of teaching Western Civ forever. I'd want a summer session this year, too, I need the money. And no eight o'clocks, ever again."

"No problem." Andrew finished his coffee and reached automatically for the roll of antacids in his pocket. "How about a raise while I'm at it?"

"That's a given." Tim smiled, watching him bite down on a couple of Tums. "Don't let it get to you. Flynn's an ass. It's a con, this deal with his precious book."

"You know what he's calling it? *The Great Cover-up*."

"He knows you won't do it, that's his trick. And when you refuse, it makes you look, you know . . ."

"Ungrateful. Misguided."

"Well . . ."

"Inert."

"Inert, no, no—that's *me*." Tim's laugh rumbled up from his barrel chest; his fleshy Irish features reddened. "I'm the deadwood around here, not you."

"You're not deadwood."

When he shrugged his beefy shoulders, the tops of Tim's plaid suspenders briefly disappeared. He was letting himself go; no wife to take care of him anymore. "Anyway, I'm telling you, Sink-or-Swim's an idiot. Have you ever heard him lecture? He just reads the notes from whatever article he happens to be writing. It's a joke."

"Sink-or-Swim" Flynn—they called Peter that because of his indifference to the junior faculty or anyone else struggling with advancement. The concept of mentoring was unknown to him; he never helped anyone but himself.

The cafeteria was stifling, as usual, and the noise level, always high, was deafening on Fridays, everyone revving up for the weekend. "Why don't *you* take the job?" Andrew had to lean across the table to ask.

"*Me*." Tim pushed back on his chair's hind legs and burped leisurely, drumming his hands on the soft mound of his belly. "No, thanks. I fly low, low, low under the radar. I like things just the way they are."

So did Andrew. Was he as sedentary and complacent as Tim, though, who never published, never presented a paper or went to a conference? At least Andrew still felt alive in the classroom—Tim didn't even have that anymore. At fifty-six, he was just counting the years until retirement.

"Besides," he went on, wiping a chocolate smear from the corner of his mustache. "They didn't offer me the job."

"Maybe they will. The only criterion seems to be a pulse." Andrew laughed quickly, to show that was a joke. "I mean, if they asked *me*—"

"No, the criterion is somebody who doesn't threaten anybody. A uniter instead of a divider. You're not on anybody's team, never have been. Nobody hates you—that's your big advantage."

Andrew patted his heart with his fist. "I'm . . . touched."

"The more I think about it, the more I can see where Richard's coming from. People trust you. You're not going to walk over 'em, stab 'em in the back, you're not so ambitious that they're afraid of you. You don't intimidate anybody."

"Oh, I wouldn't say that," said a low female voice from behind Andrew's shoulder. He knew better, but Tim started to get up before he caught himself. "At ease," Elizabeth O'Neal said with a twist of her villainess lips, sliding into the chair next to Andrew's. Elizabeth never hid her disdain for the quaint, old-fashioned courtesies men of Andrew and Tim's generation hadn't had beaten out of them. "What are you talking about?" She opened her paper napkin with a violent flap, slammed her straw on the table to pop the wrapping.

"Nothing interesting," Andrew said before Tim could answer. Moving his tray out of her way, angling his chair toward her, he wondered if Elizabeth was one of the colleagues Richard had talked to about who should be the new chair, and if so, if she'd supported Andrew. She was an up-and-comer, one of the young, hungry ones, so—probably not. But he couldn't be sure. About anything where Elizabeth was concerned.

"*This . . .* is inedible." She speared a hefty triangle of gravy-covered meat on her fork and devoured it in one bite. "Who can eat this crap?" She finished off the meat and started on a gluey pool of mashed potatoes. "What do the vegetarians do? If we have any. Probably not, this place is forty years behind the times. Nutrition being the least of it."

No one dared to challenge Elizabeth when she got on one of her Mason-Dixon bashings, not even Richard, the college's peppiest champion. She was too intimidating and contemptuous. She taught Middle Eastern history, the currently hot specialty, and that gave her some leverage in the department. But her preferred method of getting her way was by scaring people.

She scared Tim, who took the first opportunity to excuse himself. "'Bye, kids, gotta run. Places to go, people to see." He scooped up his tray, snagged his jacket from the back of his chair. The buttons of his shirt strained across his middle, his tie stopped shy of his belt. The last time they'd played one-on-one in the gym, Andrew had barely worked up a sweat before Tim had his hands on his knees, shaking his shaggy head, panting, "Man, man, I gotta get in shape." Behind Elizabeth's back, he made a face of comical terror before shambling off.

"*So . . .* Andrew."

"*So . . .* Elizabeth." He shook himself. Mimicking her choppy speech patterns was a habit he'd caught from Dash.

She ate like a man, fast, businesslike. "I heard something about you," she said, scooping up yellowish pudding in her spoon.

So she *had* talked to Richard. He waited, curious about her reaction. Politically, Elizabeth was a bit of a dark horse. If Andrew didn't scare people because they trusted him, Elizabeth scared people because they didn't trust her. She spooked them. Something predatory about her expressionless face, the way her eyes never seemed to blink . . .

Last term, over the bowed heads of 130 students taking the Western Civilization final, she'd trained that stare on Andrew. Or maybe she hadn't. They were helping Tim proctor the exam, Elizabeth in front of the lecture hall, Andrew in back. She'd sat on the edge of the table by the lectern, slouching, both hands gripping the table edge, while she swung one crossed leg back and forth, back and forth. Surely he couldn't hear it from that distance, but it seemed real, the soft *shush* of nylon on nylon. He'd heard rumors about her, that she'd slept with Richard Weldon, she slept with students, she was a lesbian, but he always dismissed school gossip; nothing was more unreliable. Still, an aura of sexual catastrophe seemed to hang over her, and Andrew surprised himself by being as attracted to it as he was repelled. She'd lifted her head from the open book on her lap and looked at him. He didn't turn and glance behind him, but only because he was in the last row, there *was* no one behind him. *Is she looking at me?* Her heavy-lidded eyes were like eyes in a painting, omnidirectional; perhaps everyone in the room imagined she was looking at him. Or her. Andrew stared back, captured, only looking away from her eyes to look at the slow, swinging leg, the slight muscular flare of calf rubbing its twin in that agonizingly suggestive rhythm. *Are you looking at me?*

He never knew. After that he watched her surreptitiously, searching for a hint of interest, flirtation, awareness. But if anything she was sharper with him than before the lecture-hall incident. She'd sniff her breath out or raise one fatal eyebrow at any mild suggestion of his in a faculty meeting. She'd slump lower in her chair and cross her hands over her stomach, as if he disgusted her.

Now she pushed her tray away. "Yes, I heard something quite interesting. I heard you're on your own these days."

He hid his surprise by blotting a drop of spilled milk with his napkin. "Oh? Who told you that?" No one knew but Tim. No—Dash must've told her friend Maureen by now, and Maureen's ex-husband taught in the English department. So everyone knew.

"Is it true?" Elizabeth folded her arms and looked directly into his eyes.

He hated exposure, his private life on display. "It's temporary. Just a . . ." He coughed. "Blip."

"Want to go to a wedding this weekend? My ex-stepfather's marrying a teenager."

He stared.

"Or close enough." Her red lips curled cynically. "The flower girl's their love child."

"Your ex-stepfather? So—your mother . . ."

"She won't be there. She's in Seattle with her new husband. Number three. *Numero tres,* I should say—his name's Carlos. So? Do you want to go?"

"Em, well, it sounds . . ." He assumed she was serious. Her waiting smile turned sardonic when he hesitated, but he couldn't picture it, his mind went gray imagining himself at a family wedding with Elizabeth O'Neal. "But, em, sorry, I don't think I can make it this weekend. Sounds interesting, though. Perhaps if you'd asked me a bit sooner—"

"I didn't know you were available sooner." She looked him straight in the eye again. It made him reevaluate the things she said, search for double entendres. He began to apologize again, but she cut him off. "Relax, Andrew." Her voice dipped low with disdain. "You didn't break my heart." Behind the dismissal and the contempt, though, he thought he could see a much younger woman. Maybe one who'd learned how to hide hurt or neglect behind a sneer.

"Call me sometime," she said in a kinder voice. "A sympathetic ear." She had long, dark, wavy hair she always wore down, a style incongruous with the sober, black-wearing rest of her; too feminine, too obviously provocative. She smiled, showing the small, sexy gap between her front teeth. She pushed a long tendril of hair behind her ear. To show him how sympathetic it was.

He watched her go. She had a distinctive gliding walk, as if she didn't care to straighten her knees all the way. She was someone he thought about often, and after today he would think about her even more. He felt a need to sit her down and interrogate her, solve all her mysteries. Where were you born? How many siblings? How many sex partners? What's your favorite food?

What did she want from him? Did they have things in common, perhaps because of their shared experiences with difficult stepparents, that he couldn't see but she had somehow intuited? He was used to that dynamic, God knew, living with Dash. Which was like living with a psychic. Like being autistic and living with a psychic. It was hard to imagine how strange, fascinating Elizabeth could have much on Dash in the intuition department.

dash

five

The cabin isn't much to look at, even with the new coat of white paint we put over the peeling clapboard, or the red shutters that match the tin roof. Technically it's two stories tall, although Andrew has to slouch in the two upstairs rooms or his head brushes the ceiling, with a chimney in the middle and another one on the left. The comfortable but sort of slatternly porch sits low to the ground, only a half step up from the yard. The cabin's not ugly, just unprepossessing, nothing out of the ordinary—which was a blessing for us, because otherwise we couldn't have afforded it. The pond is what makes it special.

It's behind the cabin at the bottom of a long, low slope: half an acre of fresh springwater in a bowl so pleasingly shoe-shaped we were sure it was man-made. But the fellow who dug out the runoff channel for us the first year, eliminating the scum problem, said no, it's natural and has probably been here as long as the mountain. (*Mountain* is an exaggeration, but it's what people around here call this Blue Ridge foothill two miles west of the town of Dolley, population 649.) The water drains into a creek that gradually widens as it trickles downhill, till at the bottom you have to cross it over a wooden bridge. I love the sound of my car tires on the bridge, that low, rickety rumble. It means I'm almost home.

When we first bought the property, I'd walk around pointing at trees and saying, "That's mine, that one's mine, that maple is mine, that's my oak tree, I own that little sassafras." I had no idea I was so *possessive.* Or what a difference private property ownership makes. Rock Creek Park is wonderful, I used to go there all the time, especially when Chloe was little, and then later to jog or walk or just bask in nature. But it's nothing like having your very own 5.2 acres of mountain to roam around on whenever you like, *naked* if you like, confident you won't be observed by another soul.

The first thing we did, even before painting, was hire Mr. Bender to build a pier across two points of land that jut out at the "shoelace" part of the pond. It's only eight feet long, no handrails, nothing fancy, but all summer it's my main vantage point, my throne. Andrew prefers the deck off the living room, but I sit on the little wooden dock, sometimes on a pillow if my rear end's sore from a long spell of gazing, and observe the many wonders and changes of pond life.

It's December, so there's not much pond life going on, not to my amateur eye. The bullfrogs have stopped galumphing at night, which I miss, and the gray, shadowy fish are swimming so deeply now, they look like ghosts. Our wood duck couple flew away in October. But the water won't freeze till February, and in the meantime I can watch cloud reflections or trace the direction of the wind from the way it pleats and ripples the surface. The tans and grays and russets of winter are only drab until you give up expecting more. Then they're gorgeous, infinitely varied, just across a smaller color spectrum.

I'm coming back from a misty early morning stroll, carrying my empty coffee cup and thinking about Mr. Bender—as I always do when I pass the soft, squishy part in the path around the pond caused by the tunneling of muskrats; Mr. Bender wants to exterminate them (he considers them rats, I consider them proud cousins of the beaver)—when I see a flash of dented red metal through the nude tree branches between the pond and the driveway. Mr. Bender's pickup truck. Did I conjure him?

"Hi!" I call out, hurrying up the hill. He touches the bill of the green cap I've never known him to take off, but doesn't call back. A man of few words is Mr. Bender. Sock runs ahead, tail spinning, thrilled we have a visitor. She loves everybody. I told Andrew she's a great watchdog so he wouldn't worry about me being here on my own. That was a fib.

"Morning, Mr. Bender, how are you today? Think it's going to rain? Or snow again, I wouldn't be surprised. That's unusual around here, isn't it, snow this early?" His taciturnity always makes me chatty.

He mutters something vague about the weather, rubbing a work-rough hand across the denim chest of his overalls, then gets down to business. "Can't change that kitchen faucet for you like I said. Got some business at home needs tending. Take at least a week."

"Oh, well, that's okay."

"Won't be able to get to any o' those other chores either, the stuck door and whatnot. I'm outta commission."

"You are? I hope it's nothing serious."

"Not me. Wife." He scratches his whiskery chin, a nervous habit. He's a small, intense man, narrow-shouldered, slightly bowlegged, with black, piercing eyes. "She's just outta the hospital."

"Oh, I see." I've never met Mrs. Bender, but I've seen her in her yard, a tall, rangy woman hanging laundry or bending over the plants in her amazing garden. Once, driving by, I saw the two of them in the window of the Velvet Cafe in Dolley, having lunch together. He still had his hat on.

"You got enough wood to last till next week?"

"I think so. And if not—"

"If not, I can get somebody, prob'ly get my son-in-law, drop off a load."

"That'll be fine. Don't worry about me," I say, although he doesn't look worried. "I hope it's nothing too serious with your wife."

"Heart. Be laid up a while."

"Oh my. Mr. Bender, if there's anything I can do, please just let me know."

"Church ladies got it covered."

He starts around to the driver's side of the truck, but then he stops. "Thank you for offering," he says with formal politeness. For a second, before he tips his cap again and climbs in the pickup, I think I see something in his eyes, a shadow of fear or helplessness. As if he's holding back an emotion that would be too much for him if he let it go.

The look haunts me; I think of him off and on all morning while I strip sixty years of paint from another kitchen cabinet door. One a day, that's my goal. It's too chilly to work outside, though, and here in the kitchen the paint-remover fumes are making my head ache.

That's my excuse to stop in the middle of the job and stare into my doorless cabinets, mulling what I could make the Benders out of the limited ingredients I have on hand . . . something the church ladies won't have covered. I've got soba noodles, got anchovies . . . here's coconut, I make a very good Indian tomato soup with coconut. Nothing seems right. If Mr. Bender isn't a meat-and-potatoes man, I'll eat this jar of kimchi. There are chicken breasts in the freezer. I could thaw them in the microwave and make some kind of casserole.

The phone rings while I'm sautéing onions in olive oil. The real phone, not my cell, so I know it's not a client; also, the first thing the voice on the other end says is "I just had sex with Viagra."

"Maureen, hi. You took Viagra?"

"No, I didn't, *Charles* did."

Charles, Charles . . . Mo's boyfriends are starting to overwhelm my memory bank. "The real-estate appraiser? That *young* guy?"

"He's forty," she says with a tiny bit of frost. "Not that young."

"I didn't mean young for *you,* I meant young for Viagra." I'm not sure what I meant. Maureen is forty-eight. "So? How was it?"

"Weird at first. You know, the waiting. We listened to music, drank some wine. Necked. Then . . . well, then it was just normal. Only longer."

"Huh. That's good. I guess." Depending on how *much* longer.

"I still don't know why he needs it. He never said, so I didn't ask. But he wasn't embarrassed at all, he was very matter-of-fact."

"He made no bones about it?"

Mo cackles. "I don't think I'm going to go out with him again, though."

"Welll . . . I guess it isn't very romantic."

"Oh, I don't care about that. I don't care about *romantic.* Charles is all right, but I'm not ready to give up the process."

"What process?" I hold the phone with my shoulder while I slide the chicken breasts into the pan. Maureen of all people has become a serial dater. I would never have predicted it, she was such a homebody before, a mother hen perfectly happy making the nest cozy for her rooster and chick.

"It's completely different, Dash, the whole dating scene, when you're not looking for Mr. Right. There's no pressure, everything's just for fun. A man isn't going to save me, I've evolved enough to realize that, so now I can just enjoy myself."

"The way men do."

"Precisely."

I'm not sure I buy this, it's so antithetical to the Mo I used to know. The predivorce Mo, who wasn't bitter, who couldn't have *imagined* sleeping with a man one time and then casually deciding not to see him again.

"Men are right about monogamy," she says, "it's not natural. Romance is a female construct, and it's very seductive, but it's a conspiracy. We foist it on them to keep them at home, and they pretend it's working to keep the peace."

"God, Maureen, you are so depressing."

"That's because you're a romantic. Phil's got a new girlfriend, by the way."

Aha. No wonder; that explains this uncharacteristic cynicism, which doesn't sit well on my sweet-natured friend. "Of course he does," I say. "I hope she's older than the last one."

"Oh, who cares, I'm just thankful she's not a student."

Every professor's wife's nightmare. "Are you at work?" I ask.

"I'm parked outside a three-bedroom colonial on Twenty-eighth Street, waiting for a guy who wants to see it." Maureen had to go back to work after the divorce; for the last year, she's been selling residential real estate. "What are you doing?"

"Making chicken divan with green beans instead of broccoli." I tell her about Mr. Bender's visit, his wife's heart trouble. "He just . . . I don't know. He seemed kind of lost."

"So he reminded you of Andrew."

"Ha! No, believe me, Mr. Bender is nothing like Andrew."

"So you never worry that Andrew's lost?"

"You know—I can't think about that right now. Just not right now."

"Absolutely, you have to worry about yourself. You're doing exactly what you should do, Dash, taking some time off."

"I hope so."

"Are you doing okay? Don't you get bored down there?"

"Never. Hardly ever."

"You're really not lonely?"

"No! Well, the time between dinner and bedtime, that can get . . . but the trick is to have a schedule and stick to it, not eat breakfast at noon, or eat popcorn for dinner at midnight just because I can."

"Does Chloe know?"

"Not yet."

"She'll be all right." Maureen sounds confident. "She's very grown up."

"Well, she's a lot more mature than I was at eighteen." Or forty-five. Sometimes I wonder where Chloe came from. She's so *calm*. I'm not calm, and Andrew only pretends to be.

"Gotta go—here's my guy, I think. Oh, excellent, he's driving a Lexus."

"A live one. Mo, thank you for calling. Thanks for everything."

"Is it too much? I don't want to harass you."

"It's not too much."

"But you took care of me when Phil and I . . ."

"Yeah."

"So now it's my turn. Hey, this guy is cute. Don't you love salt-and-pepper hair on a man when he's not old? This one's tall, too. I think I'm turning into a thigh person."

"I hope Phil knows he's created a monster."

Maureen and I met fifteen years ago, sitting next to each other at one of the awful spouses-of luncheons they used to have at the college. After we bonded over our mutual sense of irrelevance and superfluousness, not to mention boredom, we stopped going to the luncheons and started having lunch with each other. We've been friends ever since.

She's always been a very serene person, very soothing and maternal. She does yoga and meditation, she eats a completely organic diet, she's lost fourteen pounds since the divorce. Even though she's New Agey, I always considered her my most sensible friend, not counting Andrew. I don't like to hear "monogamy is unnatural" coming out of her mouth. I wouldn't chide her for it, she's got plenty of grounds for bitterness, but even if it's true, we don't have to *live* like that.

A romantic, she calls me. I guess it's easier to be a romantic when you're married, even if not 100 percent happily, than when you're recently divorced. Every time Maureen tells me a story about one of her dates or her sexual adventures, naturally I put myself in her place, try that role on for size, see how it suits me. She's gone out with passionate men, impotent men, charmers, drinkers, fathers of small children, older men, married men—so I have a wide variety of imaginary partners. But it's not the specifics of the individual men that preoccupies me, it's imagining the kind of woman I would be if I had the freedom, like Mo, to choose almost anyone I liked.

Not that that's a brand-new fantasy. Heavens. I entertain it almost every time Andrew and I have a serious fight. It's always been *just* a fantasy, though, so it must be because Maureen has so *many* boyfriends that it seems to come to me more and more often lately.

Actually, I have a full-blown single-gal fantasy. Or more of a reverie, slow-moving pictures I can fall into if I need a little soothing. The day-dream equivalent of a child's blankie. I have good legs, so in this day-dream I'm wearing high heels: slingbacks, very chic. And a smart suit, short-skirted, but the jacket is tunic-length and I wear it with no blouse, just simple gold jewelry.

Maybe this isn't so much a fantasy as a clothes fetish.

I'm riding in an elevator with those light-bronze reflective walls and that flattering light they give, in a tall, modern office building. I'm wearing my hair in a simple chignon. My expression is pleasant but se-rious. I'm a professional, consummately so. Professional what? I don't know, it doesn't matter. People on the elevator, women as well as men, admire me—I see them watching me in the mirrored walls—but that's not really the point of the fantasy.

The doors open and I stride out through an airy brass-and-glass lobby, through the revolving front door and out onto the wide white sidewalk, which is busy but not congested. It's dusk. The streetlights are on, but the sky is still a soft, hazy indigo. Nothing glares, everything is muted; the city at its gentlest. I'm heading somewhere, perhaps a stylish bistro where I'm to meet an interesting man, perhaps just to the corner to flag a taxi and go home, but I'm very purposeful, swinging briskly along in my high but perfectly comfortable slingback heels.

That's it.

Why is this little vignette so comforting and seductive? I think it's be-cause I'm alone, and I'm confident. Two things, and one's no good with-out the other. Solitude is nothing if you're frightened or lonesome or bored to tears or without a purpose. And confidence is easy for couples, relatively speaking; much more complicated and difficult for singles.

So the point of the fantasy is that I am both, the perfect Dash caught in a snapshot moment, and everything is possible. Instead of all the mundane knowns of my real life, I'm a walking (literally) manifesta-tion of opportunity. Nothing ties me down. Freedom. Total freedom, and I'm not scared of it—I *thrive* on it. I stride out, chin up, heels click-ing, toward my unknown but significant destination.

The Benders' house is on Tolliver Pike, the road to Dolley. *Right* on the road, one of those old farmhouses it must've seemed like a good idea, eighty or ninety years ago, to build twenty-five feet from the sleepy lane the milk truck trundled down every day to pick up your product. Not that Tolliver Pike is much more than a sleepy little lane *now,* but at least it's got two lanes instead of one, which means they widened it since the olden days, which means the Benders' front porch is fifteen feet from the road and completely out of proportion, house to yard. The place isn't even a dairy farm anymore. Various Bender fore-bears sold pieces off over the years, and now there's just the old gray frame house set so close to the road you could almost reach out and skim your hand along the daylilies as you drive by.

I've always admired it, though, even before I knew our handyman lived there. It's got the classic box shape with a steep gable front, very popular around these parts. Two aged, peeling sycamores shade the long porch on either side, and I just think that's a miracle, that nothing has happened to at least one of those old beauties in all this time. There's a spectacular flower garden in the backyard—too bad it's not in the front, but the sycamores make too much shade. Plus there's no room.

I park in the driveway, pick my way around winter-naked shrubbery to the front. I don't recognize the man who answers the door. Then I do. Mr. Bender—without his hat! Why, he's bald, there's only a smoky fringe of hair in back from ear to ear. He looks younger—no, older. I can't decide. I'm discombobulated.

"Hi, hello, I hope I'm not disturbing you—I wanted to ask after your wife, and give you this." I hold out my foil-topped glass casserole. "You probably don't need it, but I thought you could freeze it, and don't worry about the container, I can get that any old time—"

"Who is it, Shevlin?" a woman's voice calls from inside.

His black beetle brows come down. He looks as welcoming as an old, irritable rottweiler. He stands still, moves nothing but his head to call back: "Miz Bateman."

"Who?"

He turns back, vindicated. "Wife's not up to—"

"Oh, Bateman, from up the mountain? Well, let her in, don't leave her standing out there on the stoop."

I say, "That's okay, really, I just wanted to—"

"Come on in," Mr. Bender—*Shevlin*—says in a resigned but commanding tone, and opens the door wide.

"I won't stay *two minutes*," I promise, and step inside.

A grandfather clock in the hall takes that moment to chime the hour. I have a hasty impression of country decor and comfortable clutter before an upright, elderly woman in jeans bustles toward me from the low-ceilinged living room, pulling a white cardigan tighter around her and smiling with her whole face. "Mrs. Bateman," she says, almost as if she's been expecting me. We shake hands; her grip is calloused and firm. "How nice to meet you, I've heard all about you."

What has she heard? "Dash," I say, "call me Dash. I'm sorry—I thought—Mr. Bender said . . ." But now I don't want to say what he said; if he was fibbing to get out of doing chores for me, how embarrassing for everybody. I stutter some more. Mrs. Bender looks puzzled.

Then her face, which is long and creased with laugh lines, and also pink as if from exertion, clears. She turns to her husband, who's shifting protectively from foot to foot beside her. "Oh, did you tell her I'm an invalid? Shevlin, I swear." She puts her hand on the back of his leathery neck and gives it a soft squeeze, the gentlest admonition, and Mr. Bender's face undergoes a profound change. The black eyes unfocus; a foolish half grin uncovers straight, tobacco-stained teeth. He ducks his bald head and mumbles.

"I had a valve replaced, is all." Mrs. Bender pats her chest lightly. "I'm not only good as new, I'm *better*."

"And you're already up and around," I marvel. "Wow, that's amazing."

"They cut her open like a rabbit," Mr. Bender says. "Had to stop her heart and then start it up again. She was in the intensive care for fifty-three hours."

"All right, now."

"She got this ball contraption in her chest, which they sawed right down the middle. Cracked 'er ribs—"

"Shevlin, she doesn't want to hear that."

Well, I do and I don't.

"Why, look here, did you make us a casserole?" She gestures toward the bowl in her husband's hands. "That was awfully nice, you surely didn't have to do that."

I begin again on how they can freeze it, they must have a refrigerator full of meals by now. Mr. Bender interrupts me.

"She can't eat salt."

"Oh. Uh-oh—"

"Oh, I can eat *some*. Let's go in the kitchen, I bet you'd like a cup of coffee, Mrs. Bateman. Did you say *Dash* is your name? That's unusual. Mine's Cottie, my grandmother's name. It's not short for anything, it's just Cottie." With a hand on my back, she ushers me through an unused-looking formal dining room into the sunny kitchen. "Or would you rather have tea? Take a seat, sit right there—"

"She can't drink coffee, either." Mr. Bender has followed us in.

"Tea's fine—anything," I say, sitting down on a padded chair at a wooden spool table. It's crowded with flower arrangements in baskets and jars and vases, some with the cards still in them.

"From the hospital," Mrs. Bender explains, plopping down next to me. She's taking deep breaths; the short walk winded her. "Silly, I should've left 'em there, but I can never resist flowers."

"She had twice that many. Some died, some she left for other people. And cards like you wouldn't believe."

"Put the kettle on for us, would you, hon? And get down some of those cookies Gladys Lejeune brought."

She wears her gray hair in a braid down her back. Her face is thick-skinned, not delicate, with heavy brows and a large nose and pale lips not yet thinning with age. She has a high voice, almost childish, but she tells me that's because of the tube they put down her throat in the hospital. I guess her age at around seventy, but I still can't decide about Mr. Bender, who never stops hovering while Cottie and I—she insists I call her that—talk about flowers and the pleasures of gardening, country life versus city life, and the fact that we both have one child, a daughter.

"Our Danielle's in Richmond and she's doing real well, working for a cosmetics company."

Mr. Bender makes a sound like "Hmpf."

"She's got a little boy, Matthew, who we don't see nearly enough. Seven years old, and so funny and smart—here's his picture." Framed, half-hidden among the flower arrangements on the table; a freckle-faced redhead in a shirt and tie, grinning for his school photo. "We're old even for grandparents, because we had Danielle so late, me forty-one, Shevlin forty-six. We'd given up thinking we could have any, and then along comes Danielle."

"I always wanted lots of children," I say, drawn in by her candor, even though Mr. Bender is glaring as he sets cups of tea in front of us, put out by all this personal woman talk on such short acquaintance. "But after Chloe, we couldn't have any more."

"But you photograph children—maybe that's a comfort." She pats my wrist once with gentle diffidence; there's a Band-Aid over the top of her hand, half covering a large purple bruise.

"Oh," I say, "sometimes."

"And your husband, Shevlin tells me he's a teacher at a university. My, my."

"History professor at Mason-Dixon College."

"Isn't that something. My goodness." She shakes her head and smiles, so pleased with me and mine. Some of the locals in Dolley are suspicious of us Batemans because we're outsiders; I can tell by the narrow way they eye us in the hardware store or at the gas station. Mr. Bender was the most suspicious of the lot, and now here is his kind-faced wife beaming at me, impressed with my life, my husband's career. I feel accepted and embraced—it's almost as if I've been forgiven for something. All of a sudden, I'm flooded with an intense longing for my mother.

"Does he just get down on weekends, or sometimes during the week, too? Depending on his schedule, I guess."

"Andrew? No—he—we—" She was only making conversation, but she's caught me flatfooted. I'm thinking too slowly to say something vague and change the subject; I stutter some more until, inevitably, understanding unclouds her face.

"Sweetheart, would you go get my pills for me?"

Mr. Bender squints at a cuckoo clock on the wall. "It's not time yet, not for—"

"I know, but would you go get them anyway?"

I can tell by the look he gives her that he's recognized a tone inaudible to me. He leaves the room without another word.

"I'm sorry—" she begins.

"No, no."

"—and I just wanted to tell you that by *myself,* so as not to make it even worse."

"It's absolutely nothing."

"But I would never have asked anything personal if I had my wits about me. I'm not all here yet, the doctor said I wouldn't be for a while. Why, this morning I tried to put Shevlin's teeth in instead of mine." We look at each other with straight faces for a long second. Then, thank God, a light glints in Cottie's eyes, and we let out whoops at the same time. Her shoulders shake; she throws her head back, mouth open— I could swear she's got her own teeth in there, not false ones.

"Wooh, that felt good for a change." She puts her hand flat on her chest. "In the hospital, I had to keep telling Shevlin, *'Don't make me laugh.'* "

I have trouble imagining that. Mr. Bender, the cutup.

"Anyway. I'm sorry for butting into your business."

"You didn't, and it's not a secret, it's just—new. Andrew and I are taking a little time off, that's all. So he's up there and I'm down here. I'm sure it's temporary." I'm not sure of that, but I feel like reassuring her, fitting myself into what I imagine is this woman's stable, sensible, old-fashioned world. I wonder how old-fashioned it is, though. She's a surprise, not the Mrs. Bender I was expecting. She has clear hazel eyes that look directly at me with a wry knowing.

"How long have you been married?" she asks.

"Almost twenty years."

"Oh, yes. Well, that's when it starts to get pretty serious, isn't it?"

"How about you and Mr. Bender?"

"Forty years this January. You're lucky to have a place to go to while you sort things out. Once Shevlin and I didn't talk for three weeks. I don't remember what started it. Something to do with Danielle, probably, since that's mostly what we've fought about in our lives."

"You didn't talk for *three weeks*?"

"I kept holding out for a change in him. But I expect we wouldn't be speaking to this day if I'd kept on that way. One thing I know, staying together doesn't depend on feeling the same way about everything."

"What does it depend on?"

She scrapes her fingernails over her chin, thinking. "Depends on letting a lot go. Not being so proud and sure of yourself."

"But then, aren't you the one who always compromises?"

"Well, somebody's got to." Her infectious laugh draws me in again. "If a woman marries a *difficult* man, she's got her work cut out for her, that's for sure. But if she knows it from the start, then she's probably got a stronger kind of love to help her get through it with him."

"Andrew's not . . . well, I guess he is a difficult man. In some ways." Let me count the ways. "But I'm no picnic at the beach," I add in fairness. "Matter of fact, I drive him a little bit nuts."

She flaps her hand, as if that's to be expected. Or as if she already knew it. "Back when you were courting, was he the pursuer?"

This conversation seems perfectly natural. "Well," I say, "yes and no."

"Shevlin was just *set,* he was *not* going to be denied. I felt like a dandelion in a hard wind. So I fall back on that in the bad times, because he's still the same man."

I hear his footsteps, heavy and measured, coming through the dining room. Cottie does, too; she leans back, assuming a bland expression I do my best to copy. Perhaps we're too bland: He looks at us with suspicion as he thunks a plastic pill bottle down on the table. *A dandelion in a hard wind.* I try to imagine Mr. Bender in passionate love with the Cottie of forty years ago, a pretty woman with long legs and laughing eyes. She's still tall, but spare and rugged now, as if the years have whittled away everything not absolutely necessary. He's shorter, scrawnier, a bantam rooster to her tough old hen.

He puts his chapped hands on her shoulders, standing behind her chair, and announces, "She could've gotten a pig valve if she wanted."

Cottie laughs.

"Pig valve, she could've had one o' them put in if she'd rather. This contraption lasts longer, though. Looks like a Ping-Pong ball in a cage."

She lays her cheek on one of his hands. "I swear, Shevlin wishes they'd given me the old valve in a little jar so we could set it in the kitchen window."

At last! Humor gleams for an instant in Mr. Bender's closed, narrow face. Cottie tips her head back to let it rest on his stomach, and he looks down with that soft, sappy expression I saw before. I think he would run his hands over her smooth, Quaker-gray hair if I weren't here. Or lean over and kiss her forehead. I have an ache in my jaw, a longing I don't know how to fill. And a great frustration, as if satisfaction or the answer or some kind of relief are just over *there,* but I'm blindfolded, my hands are tied, and I can't walk.

The other thing I feel, the last emotion I expected when I set out on my little mission of friendship an hour ago, is envy of the Benders.

He raises her gently but firmly out of her chair. "Time for your rest." I get up, too. She gives a helpless shrug and starts to thank me for coming—just then there's stamping at the back door, it opens, and a man in heavy boots and an old red barn coat tramps in on a blast of cold air. He smiles politely at the sight of me, pulling off his wool hat and hanging it over a hook by the door.

"Oh, Owen," Cottie says, "good, you can meet Mrs. Bateman. Dash, this is our son-in-law, Owen Roby. Or do you two already know each other?"

"You look familiar," I say, but I can't really place him, a fortyish, solid-looking man with fair hair thinning on top, his face ruddy from the cold. His hand swallows mine when we shake, and his fingers feel rough as bark. He smells like pine.

"You've prob'ly seen me around. You live on the mountain, the cabin with the pond," he says, which would be a creepy thing for a strange man to know about me in D.C., but not down here, where everybody knows where everybody lives.

Mr. Bender clears his throat. "Owen can change that kitchen faucet for you."

"Owen can do anything," Cottie says fondly, tilting her head at him. Her smile looks tired; she's holding on to the back of the chair. "There's no reason you can't do it, though," she says to her husband. Then to me: "Shevlin is *determined* to be my nurse, and I don't need one. I haven't felt so well in months."

"Come on, Mother," Mr. Bender says, face stern, moving her toward the door.

"Dash, come back and see me. Don't bring anything, just come and talk. If you have time. Or if you ever get lonesome up there—" Her husband is rustling her out of the room like a sheepdog. "Thanks for the casserole. Do you like piccalilli? Owen, go down and get her a couple of jars of piccalilli, will you?" She waves from the dining room. "Give it to somebody else if you don't care for it!"

"Piccalilli," I say to Owen. That's a word I haven't said in a long time.

"It's like a relish—"

"I know, my mother used to make it."

I'm probably imagining that he looks surprised. "I think I know where she keeps it," he says, opening the door to what I thought was a cabinet, but instead I see it's a wide, shelf-lined pantry on two sides, and straight ahead are steps to the dark basement.

While he's gone, I wash the cups and saucers Cottie and I used and put them in the dish drainer. There's a sun catcher in the window, rainbow-hued; pots of greenery in various stages of germination line the sill. Outside, snow dusts the ridges and furrows of what you'd never guess is a fabulous garden, alight with masses of color and bloom from spring until fall. I've always wanted to grow flowers like that, planning ahead so as each amazing display starts to fade, a new one takes its place, week after week, all season long. I study the diagrams of perfect beds and borders in the plant catalogs and think, *Oh, I could do that,* but then I never order the right flowers in time, or when I go to the nursery I forget my list. Apparently a gorgeous, summer-long perennial garden is one of those things, like black hair and blue eyes, or my own horse, that I'm never going to have.

Owen stumps back up the steps. He's not especially tall, he's certainly not fat, but he's one of those men who just take up a lot of room. Or maybe it's the coat and boots—whatever, the kitchen gets smaller as soon as he comes in. "Here you go." He sets a couple of mason jars on the table. "Shev told me about your kitchen faucet. Says you've got a door that sticks?"

"The front door, but it's nothing that can't wait. I mean, unless you've got absolutely nothing else to do."

"I'm a farmer, there's always plenty to do. But this is the slow time of year, and I like to help the Benders out when I can."

"Oh, you don't live here?" He came in like he lived here.

"I'm a couple miles south, out along the river."

But if he's the son-in-law, isn't he married to Danielle? Who's in Richmond, a two-hour drive from here? Andrew jokes that I can find out everything about anybody I meet in five minutes, but Owen Roby's going to take a little longer. He's perfectly friendly, but also formal with me in a courtly, old-fashioned way. Any minute now I expect him to call me ma'am.

He walks outside with me, talking about hot and cold fixtures and spigot sizes. He parked his tan pickup next to my car; there's a rifle in a rack in the back window. I'm used to that around here, but I still shake my head when I pass a truckful of bundled-up men in orange, firearms on display. Owen has a bumper sticker championing his right to bear that rifle, I see, and a couple of others supporting our troops. I feel comparatively insubstantial; my only car sticker says WE ♥ THE NATIONAL ZOO.

"Mrs. Bender seems so well," I say, looking out across her snow-covered garden. "It's hard to believe she just had major surgery."

"Yeah." He puts his hands on his hips inside his open coat and stares down at the ground, shaking his head. "She was bad all fall. Before that, too, but we didn't know—she didn't say. She had rheumatic fever when she was little, that's what caused the heart failure. If she's as good as new . . ." He looks up, his eyes frank with hope and gratitude. "If she's okay now, it'll be a pure miracle."

"It will be."

We saunter over to my car.

"How're you fixed for firewood, Miz Bateman? I can drop off a load for you when I come up."

"I'm probably okay for a while—would you please call me Dash? I don't use that much wood since I'm not here every day. I drive to D.C. a couple of times a week. I have a photography studio, but I don't have to be there every day." He's a little more talkative, but he's still almost as good as his father-in-law at making me chatter. "So I probably have enough for a while."

"You up there by yourself?"

I nod, feeling no apprehension admitting that to him. Odd, since I don't know him from Adam. I wonder what he thinks of me. I bet he and the Benders will talk about me later on.

A crow flaps over our heads, moving from one sycamore to the other. "What's a good day for you to come up?" I ask, opening the car door.

"What's good for you?"

"Well, not tomorrow, I have to go into town. The day after?"

We settle on Friday. I get in and start my car; we say it was nice meeting each other and all that.

"Might want to take a look at that left front tire sometime," he says before I close the door.

"Uh-oh. Is it bald?" Imagine him noticing.

"Just wearing down in the middle. You'll want to check your pressure."

"Okay. Thanks."

"See you Friday." He has very definite lips, slightly jutting and aggressive, but his smile is small and reserved. But genuine. I like him. I like all the Benders, even *Shevlin,* whom I picture right now wafting a homemade quilt over Cottie in their bed, so she'll be warm for her nap.

There's no room to turn around, so I back out of the driveway. Carefully, hoping to stay on the gravel in case Owen is watching. When I bump up onto the road and level out, though, I see he's already gone back in the house. Too bad, because I did it perfectly.

six

*W*hy am I so nervous? It's like a first date.

I'm jiggling my foot at a corner table in a restaurant called Isabel's, sipping a glass of the house white too fast and wondering why this place is so crowded on Christmas Eve. Who goes out to eat on Christmas Eve? People on dates, people who don't want to be alone tonight—that's what I'd have thought, but right across from me is a family, mother and father and three kids, including one in a high chair. What kind of Christmas tradition is that to set for your children? Thanksgiving I can see, especially if you hate to cook, but Christmas is different. *Go home,* I channel to the family, leveling an intense, disapproving stare. I guess they could be Jewish. Or traveling. Visiting the nation's capital for the holidays, and they picked Isabel's because it's close to their modest Silver Spring family motel. Oh, all right, then. Merry Christmas to all.

The reason I picked Isabel's, aside from it being close to the college, is because Andrew and I have eaten here before, so it won't be a fun new dining experience, incompatible with the serious business at hand; but not very often, and not on any special occasions, so it's not loaded down with a lot of emotional nostalgia. Bad enough it's Christmas Eve, the least we can do is eat our dinner in neutral territory. Hence, Isabel's, the Switzerland of restaurants.

Why is Andrew late? I'm the one who's never on time, so says the comfortable old myth in our family. But we get our reputations early on, and then nothing can dislodge them. Dash is always late (except for work), Dash is unorganized and impulsive (except at work). Andrew's the sensible one, steady and sober, you can always depend on Andrew. Personally, I don't think he's that sensible. He's getting more quirks all the time, he's heading toward eccentricity. The nutty professor.

As for me being impulsive, that's another figment of the family imagination. Even Chloe's in on it. "You always jump in with your clothes on, Mom," she said to me once, I forget in what context. "You don't *think* first."

Chloe always thinks first. When she was seven, she asked Andrew (not me; interesting), "Does every single other person in the whole world think they're as important as I think I am?" Pretty astute for seven. I myself was much, much older before I recognized I wasn't the center of the universe. And even now . . .

Andrew, needless to say, agrees with Chloe: That Dash, she's so impulsive. It's a flaw now, but I remember when he thought it was one of my most bewitching charms.

Either way, they're both wrong, I do think first, but too fast for them to register. Then I jump in with my clothes on. Because if someone's drowning—keeping on with Chloe's analogy—he could die while you're still shucking off your underwear. The only advantage to thinking before jumping is that it might turn out the person *isn't* drowning, he's playing, or just seeing how long he can hold his breath under water. So then all you accomplished by taking the time to strip was trade one kind of embarrassment—*Oops, didn't mean to drag you out of the pool*—for another—*I'm naked!* It's not worth it.

I signal the waiter for another glass of wine.

I keep thinking about the Benders. I wonder if they still sleep together. I bet they do. Even though she's been ill, I bet they share the same bed they've had all their married lives. A double bed, not queen- or king-size. And he tries to be careful now, worried he might throw out a leg or an arm in his sleep and accidentally hurt her. I keep remembering his scuffed old hand on her shoulder, the goofy smile on his face when she teased him. I'm sure he's the one who wrapped the elastic support bandages around her ankles and calves. I picture him kneeling in front of her as she sits on the edge of the bed, or maybe the toilet seat, with her foot on his thigh while he gently winds the elastic cloth round and round her leg, thick with edema. I bet he's doing all the cooking this week, even though there's no reason she couldn't heat up the church ladies' casseroles in the oven as easily as he.

Andrew took care of me last year when I had the worst flu of my life. I thought I was dying. "This can't be right," I whimpered, gagging into the toilet for the dozenth time, nothing but spit left to throw up.

He rubbed my back, he rubbed my feet. He kept quiet and didn't try to cheer me up. When I could finally keep liquids down, he went out and bought a bag of oranges and hand-squeezed glass after glass, keeping me hydrated. They tasted delicious, cool and sweet and tart, just the perfect thing. "You saved me," I told him. "You saved my life."

There he is. Looking very cold and pink-cheeked, his hair tousled from the wind. A sight for sore eyes. Is he nervous, too? I can't tell. He's giving the hostess his name while he looks over her head for me, but he doesn't have his glasses on, so that's hopeless. Now he's shaking his head, no, he'll keep his overcoat, thanks—I could've told her that. This way he'll save two bucks. It's not that he's cheap, *exactly,* it's more that he sees no sense in coat checking. And 15 percent, that's his absolute tip limit. Me, I love to tip. Why not, if you've got the money? Even if you don't, you've almost always got more than the person you're tipping. I like to have long lunches with girlfriends, over the course of which we get to know the waitress so well that by the end she's practically one of us, and then I like to leave her a tip so big her eyes bulge. "But, Dash," Andrew says, "that makes no *sense.*"

He sees me and smiles carefully. I'm glad to see him, but I don't want him to know how much, don't want to send a false message. He hasn't said it, but I know he thinks I'm going home with him tonight.

That's why I'm so tense: I want him to understand how serious I am about this separation, but I dread the moment when he does, when he gets it. That gulp moment. The look on his face. I want to get it over with—I want to put it off indefinitely.

"Hi." He leans down to kiss me, and there's an awkward, fumbly second when neither of us can decide where, cheek or lips, so the kiss ends up half and half. He takes the seat next to me instead of across the table. "Sorry I'm late. I had to drop something at the office, and Richard Weldon caught me just as I was leaving. Have you been here long?"

"I was on time." We raise our eyebrows together at the wonder of that. "You look a bit bleary," I notice. "You've been reading journals." Two-thirds of the grade in one of his classes is these journals the students have to keep for two semesters. They pretend they're living in 1789 or whatever, and they have to choose characters or personas to portray, like silversmith, slave, politician, tavern wench. He doesn't set a limit on the length, and some of the kids really get into it, pages and pages of details about their made-up lives.

"I finished the last batch this afternoon." He rubs his eyes, which are bloodshot. He needs a shave, too. Did he forget to shave this morning? Impossible. He's the most fastidious person I know. "That's what I was taking in to school," he says, "when Richard caught me. You know how he goes on once he gets started."

"Have they picked his replacement yet?"

Andrew scans the wine list. I already did, so I know what he'll order: a glass of red, probably the cabernet, not the cheapest and not the most expensive. Moderation in all things, that's my man.

"Not as far as I know," he says without looking up.

Well, that's no surprise, that he doesn't know. Andrew's not a company man, not a member of any of the factions or sects or splinter groups always scheming and sniping over their petty differences in the history department. He doesn't even keep up with the gossip. He teaches his students, who adore him and vice versa, and he goes home.

"Whoever they get," he says, putting the wine list down, "I hope it's someone more student oriented than Richard. Although almost anybody would be an improvement in that department." He's starting on one of his pet peeves, and I catch myself rereading the menu instead of listening. I used to care about the politics; I knew who was who and what they wanted, who was going to get in their way and why. I took a lot more interest in all of it than Andrew did, in fact, and once I realized that I stopped paying attention. All that knowing wasn't going to change anything, because Andrew was above the fray. Another way of saying out of the loop.

We order salads. While we wait, he takes a piece of paper out of his pocket, scans it, puts it back, and asks if I got my flu shot yet. It's nice to know I'm still on his lists.

"Speaking of job changes," I tell him between bites of lettuce, "I hired a new assistant. She's young, but I think she'll be good." I tell him about Greta, the photo shoot with the twins, Joel the boyfriend. "What? What's that face mean?"

"No, no." He waves his hand, erasing the face. "It's just good to know you're still saving people."

"I'm not *saving* people."

"The lovelorn, the needy, the misunderstood."

"Oh—poohy." I'd like to say worse, but it's Christmas Eve. Another family myth is that I'm naive about people or something. A few sets of steak knives—for *gifts*—from a really nice door-to-door salesman, a cleaning lady from Guatemala who didn't quite work out—that's it, that's all they have on me, but now I've got this completely undeserved lifetime reputation as a soft touch.

Andrew's smiling at me over his wineglass, his eyes warm in the candlelight, and I love that look. The acceptance, the pleasure he takes in me. I could fall right in and forget about climbing out.

"Did you get a Christmas tree?" I ask at random. "Or a wreath or anything?"

"No."

"Nothing? I wasn't going to either, but then yesterday I went out in the woods and chopped down a little tree. About this high." I show him with my hand. "I decorated it with popcorn. God, that was tedious. It still needs something." This is a sad conversation. "Owen came over and fixed the faucet."

"Who?"

"Mr. Bender's son-in-law—I told you about him, I told you about Mrs. Bender and her heart—"

"I remember," he says, defensive; I always tell him he doesn't listen and he always denies it. "Owen, Owen something or other, the son-in-law who can fix anything."

"Owen Roby. He says he can plow me out—he's got a plow thing on his truck, he can clear the driveway for me if it snows."

"Handy."

"Oh—he had the best idea. Instead of refinishing the kitchen cabinet doors and staining and varnishing them and all that, Owen says he could cut the centers out with his saber saw, put grooves around the edges with his router, and then set *glass* in the grooves. So we'd have beautiful glass cabinet doors inside about a two-inch square of stained oak all around—is that incredible? And it would cost almost nothing, just the glass and Owen's labor, and he doesn't charge any more than Mr. Bender did."

"I thought you liked doing the cabinets yourself. That was your winter project. You said you were into it."

"Yeah, but there are a million other things I can be doing. I've been trying to figure out a way to brighten up the kitchen and still have stained wood cabinets, and this is it. On the *cheap*."

The waiter comes for our order.

Andrew's feeling okay, he says when I ask. Except for a pain, more of an ache actually, just above his solar plexus—he opens his jacket to show me exactly where. He's had it for two days. An ulcer? I suggest. I always play along with these fantasy ailments. No, probably not, he admits; stress, more likely. Or indigestion. Besides, an ulcer would be lower down.

"Oh," he remembers, "I brought you some mail."

"God, not more Christmas cards." He sent a huge batch down to the cabin a couple of days ago. Dozens of unrequited lovers, it felt like. "This is the first time in our *lives* we haven't sent any. People will think we *died*."

He smiles in a whose-fault-is-that way as he pulls a sheaf of envelopes out of the pocket of his overcoat.

"Oh, I don't want to look at them now."

"Just read the one on top. That will interest you."

It's from the Caplans, I see by the return address. We used to double-date, that's how long we've known them. But then, years ago, they moved to New Mexico, and we never see them anymore. "What?" I say, pulling the card out. "Oh, Andrew, don't tell me somebody died."

"Nobody died."

But it's almost as bad. "Not such a merry Xmas this year," Nancy has scribbled on the back. "Ed and I have gone our separate ways, as the saying goes. It's even pretty amicable (for a divorce). He sends his love to you guys. Me, too. Will fill you in on gory details soon—promise. Happy New Year, N."

"I can't believe it." I read the note again. "I can't believe it."

"Why not?"

"Ed and Nancy. They got married before *we* did." The irony in Andrew's expression registers on me. "I just didn't expect it, I thought they were, you know . . ."

"Devoted?"

"Yes. Or at least *together,* I thought they had a good relationship. Didn't you? It looked like it worked, didn't you think? Wow. Ed and Nancy. Ed and *Nancy,*" I say again to distract him, but it doesn't work.

"I thought we worked." He pitches his voice lower, so no one can overhear. "I thought *we* had a good relationship."

"We did."

"We did? Then what happened?"

I sip water. "I don't know." I didn't want to go here yet, not this early in the evening. We haven't even eaten.

"You don't *know*?"

"No, I don't know. Stop saying what I say. And I'm allowed not to know."

He folds his hands at the edge of the table. He's trying to be reasonable, but he'd like to reach over and shake me.

"Let's call Chloe," I say, and not only to change the subject. I miss her.

"Call her here? Now?" He disapproves of cell phones in public places. Well, who doesn't, but right now I don't care. "Actually," he says, "I've already spoken to her. I called this afternoon."

"So did I—but Andrew, it's Christmas *Eve.*"

"All right. What are we going to tell her?" About us, he means. So far it's been easy: We simply don't bring up the tiny detail that we're not living together. Naturally Chloe doesn't ask—it's the furthest thing from her mind. So we're lying, I know we're lying, but only indirectly. And we hate it, him more than me; Andrew's an honesty absolutist, whereas I'm more of a . . . pragmatist.

"Nothing. We won't tell her anything," I say, dialing. "Or whatever; we'll just see how it goes. Play it by ear. Okay?" I pause before pressing the last number. Playing it by ear isn't Andrew's strong suit. He hunches his shoulders and shakes his head in disapproval. "Okay," I say, since he won't answer.

Chloe answers on the second ring. "Merry Christmas!" she sings out, and I laugh, glad she's so happy, sad she obviously isn't missing us one bit. "Merry Christmas, yourself."

"*Mom.*" There's a definite note of surprise that she's hearing from me again in a matter of hours. No irritation, though—that's good. Chloe is the *sweetest* child. If college ruins her, I'll die.

"I know, you can't get away from us. Your father and I just wanted to say Merry Christmas again—together. Honestly, we're not stalking you."

She laughs her full-throated *uh-huh-huh,* the perfect echo of my mother's laugh, and I see her, clear as an etching, the flyaway hair and baby skin, her slender wand of a body, her serious face. I've taken a million photographs of Chloe over the years, the history of my daughter in pictures. Always and forever, she's my favorite subject. "No, it's great," she says, "Emily's talking on her cell right now to *her* dad, so it's like a 'rents moment."

"Oh, good." Emily's parents split up in the fall, and Chloe and the other roommate, Valerie, were her faithful support group all semester. Now the three of them are inseparable. "So this party you're going to," I say casually, "does everybody know everybody, or nobody knows anybody, or what." I am so curious about Chloe's social life. I try to be cool, but I fail; I'm wild to know everything.

"I don't know anyone but Em and Val," she says in a patient voice, "and Em doesn't know anyone but Val and me, but Val knows lots of people, in fact most of them she went to high school with."

"Well, that'll be nice, lots of new people. Interesting men."

She doesn't respond to that, or not audibly. I'm glad she's not the kind of girl to roll her eyes. At least I don't think she is. She didn't used to be.

"What are you wearing?" I ask.

Here we're on firm ground. We discuss what shoes go best with the outfit she's chosen, we segue to jewelry, specifically the little crystal drop earrings or the long, dangly red bead ones, and I catch Andrew watching me with that soft-faced, mellow look again. I smile at him. "Here," I say to Chloe when we've run through all her accessories, "your father wants to say hi."

I miss her, oh, I miss her, I want her back. I was thinking of all the things we would do before I found out she wasn't coming home, all the fun things we like to do together, and not just shopping—art galleries and ice skating, movies we've been dying to see. Staying up late watching TV with microwave popcorn and Coke floats and brownies made from a mix at one in the morning, snuggled under a blanket on the couch like a couple of cats. I miss the clean, rainy smell of her hair, the way her contacts make her wide blue eyes blink, the way she says "Mo-om" for a joke, mimicking the cadence of a different kind of teenager whose mother's being a pain. When she's really aggravated with me, Chloe gets quite dignified and calls me "Mother." I miss that, too.

"He's about the same," Andrew is telling her—she must have asked about her grandfather. "Not much change lately. I think he's . . . yes, settling in. Finally." He chuckles. "Well, not since that time. No, nothing since then, to speak of."

Nothing since Edward threw a vaseful of zinnias at the night nurse at his assisted-living place. Andrew can smile now, but it wasn't funny then; we thought they were going to kick him out. His heart disease is bad enough, but now he's going dotty, too.

"Em, really? Well . . . No, well . . ." He looks at me with worried eyes.

"What?" I mouth.

"Well, yes, actually, we are. Yes, em, a restaurant, we just thought it . . . Isabel's. In Takoma Park. Yes." He laughs falsely. "Well, I guess your mother—I guess she didn't feel like cooking just for the—just, em—she didn't feel like cooking," he finishes. *Just for the two of us* would be a lie, and Andrew doesn't lie. Simultaneously, he says, "Well, here's your mother" and I mutter, "Oh, give me that," and he hands the phone back.

"Hi," I say brightly, sending him a look. *Hopeless.*

"What's wrong with Dad? He sounds funny."

"Well, he's had a glass of wine."

"Oh." Chloe laughs politely. "So you guys are having dinner *out*?"

"Sure, why not? Why cook a big meal when we can get people to wait on us?"

"I guess." I can imagine her adding this to the mental list of changes going away to college has brought to her life, her loved ones. I do it, too. No one thing is a big deal, you just make a small adjustment in your outlook; it's when you add them all up that you notice the sea change. *Nothing* is the same anymore.

Which must be why I say next, "Don't you miss us at *all*?" At least I say it in a humorous wail, and take care to laugh at the end. "Aren't you *ever* coming home again?"

"Mo-om, I was just there in November. One month ago, four mere weeks. And I do miss you, but I'll be home again for the long weekend in February. And then don't forget Easter."

I want to wheedle and nag, but we've already done that. She'll bring her roommates here, finally, over spring break, but for now she's spending Christmas and New Year's in Vermont and Connecticut, because that's where Val and Emily live. And all that's left for a mother to do is pretend she's thrilled for her.

She has to go, they're calling her, they'll be late if they don't leave right now. "Have a *wonderful* Christmas, sweetie." "Okay, Mom; you, too." "We love you." "I love you, too. Merry Christmas!" "Merry Christmas, and be safe. Have fun, but be careful, whoever's driving, tell them to be careful, and be *happy.*" "Okay, Mom. Love you." "I love you, Chloe."

I could go on indefinitely like that but, wisely, Chloe hangs up. I take a deep drink of wine to keep from bursting into tears.

Andrew's a little misty-eyed himself. "She sounded fine," he says consolingly. "Very happy, I thought."

"I know."

"She aced her history independent study paper, did she tell you?"

"God, how did she get so smart? She's smarter than *you.*" She's following in his footsteps, too, majoring in history, which she's always loved. She wants to teach it.

"We sabotaged ourselves," Andrew says. "Our daughter's a tribute to our parental brilliance because she doesn't need us anymore." He makes a mock sad face, but personally I don't see the joke.

"It's *true,*" I say. "Sometimes I think, what if she had a problem, she was a drug addict or she had fetal alcohol syndrome"—Andrew looks shocked—"no, I know, but then at least she'd *need* us. But she's growing up in the most normal, easy way, and we're just obsolete. Really, we're just irrelevant. The Pattersons, at least—"

"Oh, come on, Dash."

"I know, but at least they've got him for life, poor Teddy." The Pattersons' son has schizophrenia and can't live on his own. "I'm just saying you're right, we sabotaged ourselves, and now look, she's *gone.*"

"She's not *gone.*"

"She has her own private thoughts. She has a secret life, her own life. Yes, of course, it's healthy and right and a good thing, but that doesn't mean it's not *painful.*"

The food comes, thank God; otherwise I might get emotional and ruin the evening. That's not supposed to happen till the end.

As usual, I like the look of Andrew's dinner better than mine. Ordinarily I would suggest sharing, but tonight I stick to my own plate, for the same reason I chose Isabel's: to keep us from falling into those undermining little intimacies. And I make small talk, I amaze myself by how deftly I dance around the big coiled snake on the table. I can't keep it up indefinitely, though, and by the time coffee comes I'm worn out. Andrew doesn't waste any more time getting to the point.

"Okay, Dash. What are we doing?"

Deep sigh. "I can't answer for me in one word, or one sentence. One paragraph, it's too—"

"Write a short story, then. An encyclopedia. I don't care, but you have to explain to me what's going on." He pats his fingertips on the tablecloth very gently but intently. He's so controlled. I know what he'd rather do is bang his fists.

I bow my head. "Okay. I'm just . . . I'm not myself. I want a lot of things to change. I want *change*"—that's it—"and you . . ." He's watching me with a patient, baffled expression that makes me feel hopeless before I start. It's as if we speak two different languages; I'm fluent in his, or at least I get the *words,* but mine is completely incomprehensible to him.

"We have nothing in common," I start over. "Last year, remember we were trying to decide on the ideal vacation, and I said Machu Picchu and you said riding our bikes around Colonial Williamsburg. There. I mean—"

"We've *never* had anything in common. What's new?"

"That's not it anyway, that's just not helping right now. It's more me than you," I say, to be nice. "I hate getting old. I feel like the best is behind me."

"You're not old." He smiles patronizingly. "Wait'll you're fifty."

"I'm going to die, and for the first time in my life that's not just a rumor. I believe it."

"Because of your mother."

"I suppose. I mean, yes, obviously. Without her there's no . . . no guardrail between me and dying. She was the buffer."

"I can understand that."

"But that's not *it.* It's not death. I'm never going to be famous for anything, I'm never going to get better looking, my sex life has peaked, Chloe doesn't need me anymore. All the best things are over."

"But what's that got to do with us? That's depression, you're having a classic mid——"

"If you say *midlife crisis,* Andrew, I swear I will throw this glass of water in your face."

He puts up his hands. He knows I'll do it. "Far be it from me to minimize your experience. I want to validate your experience."

Snort.

"I do. I'm not joking, I'm taking this very seriously. I think you could use some help. What about your friend Amy's therapist, or a referral from him, somebody you could talk to about these things that are depressing you."

"I'm not depressed."

"Dash." He leans forward. "Clearly—"

"I'm not. I'm not depressed, Andrew, and I'm not going to some shrink who'll put me on Prozac and make me *talk* for the next five years."

The waiter comes over to ask if we'd like anything else. No, I say, just the check.

Andrew is shocked. "You want to leave? But we've just *started.*"

"I know, but I hate this place. Claustrophobia. Come on, let's just go."

It's better outside, even though it's freezing. We parked our cars adjacent to each other in the lot; we stand next to mine, facing the busy street, cars whizzing by in both directions like it's any night, not Christmas Eve. "Where the hell is everybody going?" I grouse, pulling on my gloves. "Why aren't they at home?"

"Why aren't we?" Andrew ducks his head and shoves his hands in his pockets. The frosty exhale of his breath is like a cartoon balloon of frustration.

"Look," I say, "I know this is lousy. It probably seems selfish to you, but I can't help it. If I could help it, I wouldn't be doing it."

"That's it? You're finished telling me why you left? Because if you are—are you?" He's shivering from the cold, but it's his own fault, he doesn't zip the lining into his overcoat until January 1. Why? Who knows. His little eccentricities, the hypochondria, the list making, the wacky but unalterable life rules—usually they irritate me, in fact more all the time, but now I feel a perilous tenderness.

I slip my hand under his arm. "Sorry," I say softly. "I hate this, too. Oh, I wish we—"

"No." He backs up. "No, I just want to know. Is that it, are you through? Because if you are—"

"Because if I am, what? It doesn't make *sense?*"

He gives a humorless laugh. "You could say that."

"The worst *possible sin* in your book."

"It's ridiculous, is what it is."

"Oh, but you didn't want to—disparage my true feelings, you wanted to *validate* them. Thank you so much!"

His eyebrows meet in the middle; his ascetic face looks anguished, Christ on the cross. "Dash, I don't *get* it. How can I deal with it if I don't get it? If you could, for two minutes, be reasonable. Is that possible? Two minutes."

I open my handbag, fumble for the car key. "I'm not talking anymore."

"Great." He kicks the tire.

"Except to say—" I sag against the door. "Oh, I don't want to fight, not tonight."

"I don't want to fight, either."

"It's just, I want things to change, and . . ."

"You already said that."

"And you don't. You never do, you love the status quo."

He holds out his hands. "Why is that *bad?*"

"You like the past better than the present. I'm now, you're . . . then. I was thinking of going back to school. Something completely new and different. I could train Greta to take over the studio."

He takes a step back.

"Not right away, I'll have to wait till Chloe's through college, I know that. But I'm thinking about it."

"Back to school? To study what?"

I feel a bubble of giddiness in my throat, almost like hysteria, but I manage to say "Veterinary medicine" with a serious face.

He stares for a second, and then—then he laughs. *Laughs.* I want to punch him, I want to kick him in the shins! He sees my face, says, "Oh, wait—" But it's too late, it's way too late.

"Yes, it's very funny, it's a riot! It was so funny when I put you through graduate school, too, I just laughed the whole time."

"You didn't put me—"

"Almost! And I could've been anything, anything at all, I was young and smart, I had potential!"

He presses his fingertips to his temples, a familiar gesture; it means I'm driving him crazy. "But you *love* what you do, you'd never give it up."

"How do you know? How do you know anything? You don't know anything about me."

"Veterinary medicine? You're right, I don't know anything about you."

We glare, him stiff and foursquare, me practically on tiptoes, until Andrew realizes people coming out of Isabel's are listening to us—something I knew all along; who cares?—and turns away. "This is futile," he says with dignity. "And it's not getting us anywhere. Dash, come home with me now. Just come home."

"I can't. I'm sorry. I don't like the way things are. And—it's not just you, you know."

"No, I didn't know."

"It's not. It's all kinds of things. It's *me.* I have to do something to fix myself, and I have to be by myself to figure out what."

This time I don't blame him for looking skeptical. I'm not a loner; I usually find myself, on the rare occasions when I've been lost, by gathering the people I love *closer,* not pushing them away. But this, whatever "this" is, is different. I have to hibernate. It's essential.

He stares down at the ground and doesn't say anything for a long time. "Couples counseling," he mutters at last. It's barely audible. "Therapy. Christ Almighty."

I nod grimly. "Kill me now."

"Do you know anyone?"

"Maureen does. I can ask her."

He makes a sound of distress or disgust. It's just now sinking in for him, the truth of what's happened to us. *Dash and Andrew are separated.* Maureen recommending a therapist will make it real.

"One of us has to tell Chloe," I say. "Do you want to?"

"No. I don't."

"Okay, I will. I'll call her tomorrow. No, it's Christmas—I'll call her the day after."

"Shall I start sending your mail to you?" he asks coldly.

"To the studio, I guess. If you would."

"I'll keep paying the bills, same as always."

"Yes. And I'll keep depositing my checks in the joint account. I don't think anything has to change, moneywise. I guess there will be more bills since we'll—we'll have two different households, but it shouldn't be much, just the electric down there, and Mr. Bender for chores. . . ." I trail off because he's not looking at me, he's gazing away, not appearing to listen. This is the moment I've been dreading. I can see it now, it's clearing like a photo in a tray of developer. How much I've hurt him.

All right, I think, *let's forget the whole thing,* and for a second I let myself imagine going home with him. We'll light a fire in the fireplace, because it's Christmas Eve, and we'll hold hands on the sofa while we listen to something predictable like *The Messiah.* Then we'll take glasses of brandy upstairs, for a treat, and make love. "Merry Christmas," we'll tell each other afterward. "I love you."

The temptation makes my head reel; I'm actually dizzy. What am I playing at, anyway? This is self-indulgent. It's not like he *beats* me. And I'm not the *kind* of woman who leaves her husband, I'm a loyal person, I'm *slow* to anger, I don't fly off the handle at the least little—

Andrew says, "You know, this is the third time."

I flinch. He couldn't have been reading my mind, though, because I was softening, I was going over to his side. Now I'm back on my toes, defensive. "Those weren't anything like this. Don't say that, it's not fair."

"Really? What's the difference, exactly?"

"You're just being snotty. I thought you said you didn't want to fight."

"I don't."

"The difference is—those were emotional times for me. And one was hormones," I rush on, because I can't stand the incredulity in his face. "Hormones, Andrew, it's not that damn uncommon. And the other was cold feet. It's not like we haven't discussed this."

"I'm only trying to comprehend the difference."

"I told you, those were emotional, this is—that's the whole *point,* this is not emotional because I'm not myself, I can't *find* myself, I don't know if I'm *two* or *three.*"

"What?"

"Or one! I just have to do this, okay? Quit talking to me, I mean, pretty soon it gets to be abusive, you know?"

His face turns black.

"No, wait!" He starts away, but I catch him from behind. "Don't go like this. I'm sorry, I'm sorry."

"Dash, for the love of Christ."

"I know. And it's his birthday." Feeble joke.

"You want too much. You want to leave me, and you want me to tell you it's fine, go, here's my blessing."

"No, I just want . . ." We're sort of holding on to each other's arms. My hands grab higher; I want to hug him and hold him, front to front. I want him to kiss me and then let go of me.

"You're right." I step back. "I was being selfish. This is bad, any way you look at it, and I was trying to soften it or something, have it both ways. But the more I talk, the worse it gets, so can we just say good night? Please?"

"Yes, I think that's best." He's offended, and there's nothing I can do. It's true, I want too much, including his blessing as I drive off down the road.

"Good night," I say, not touching him. "I still love you."

"That's something." He holds the door while I get in my car. "Be careful. Try not to tailgate. I hate this drive at night for you."

"I never tailgate." This is an old argument.

"You do it unconsciously. It's infuriating—someone unstable could fly into road rage. Try to drive defensively." He goes on advising caution, reminding me he's programmed 911 into my cell phone, all I have to do is hit 01, or 02 for AAA; don't speed, pull over if I feel sleepy— it's endearing when he goes through this litany for Chloe, not so much for me.

"Merry Christmas, Andrew," I interrupt. "Will you call me tomorrow?"

He feigns surprise. "If I *may.*"

"You may."

We can't quite smile at each other. I want to, so we can end this frustrating evening on a friendly note, and to send the message that underneath all the trouble and pain there's still hope, still plenty of sweetness between us.

But that's just me wanting too much again. I start the car, and he slams the door.

It feels strange, driving away from him. I don't suppose anybody gets used to this, but I can't get over how peculiar it feels to go off in opposite directions. However, just because it's unnatural doesn't mean it isn't right.

I wipe sudden tears out of my eyes. In a wave, everything I love about Andrew swamps me, everything I don't recedes. What in the world am I doing? And why can't I decide on one course and stick to it? Either one I picked, I would be so much *happier*. I, who can't stand being alone, am driving straight into total, absolute aloneness on purpose, and on Christmas Eve. What madness.

I don't remember until I'm merging onto the Beltway that I forgot to give him his Christmas present. He didn't give me one, either. Did he forget, like me, or did he mean not to give me one? His is still in a shopping bag in the backseat. A joke gift, not suitable at all for our current circumstances: *The New Encyclopedia of Men's Health*. It weighs a ton.

andrew

seven

Half an inch of wet snow fell on Saturday night in the middle of January. At eight o'clock the next morning, Wolfie rang Andrew's doorbell. He and his snow shovel were the same height. He cleared the walk in five minutes and charged ten dollars. "You got any cocoa?" he asked, blowing on his mittens, chattering his teeth. Andrew said he didn't think so. "Yes, you do, man. On that shelf with the cookies."

In the kitchen, Wolfie banged his heels against the chair legs and looked around the room as if he'd never been in it before. "How come it look different in here?" He wouldn't take off the sweatshirt over his jacket, wouldn't even put the hood down. Gnomelike, he hunched over his mug of hot chocolate, peering around critically. "Look like nobody live here."

Andrew cast around for a good conversational topic. Sports didn't work; he followed college teams, Wolfie liked the Redskins and the Wizards. Wolfie had two sisters and a brother, all older. He looked shocked when Andrew told him he had no siblings, no relatives at all except a father. "Do you like him? Do he like you?"

"It's . . . we have a . . . it's not . . . yes, we like each other."

Wolfie studied him with searching eyes, running his tongue around the inside of his mug. When he went home, leaving footprints on the kitchen floor and chocolate circles on the counter, the house fell absolutely still, as if he'd sucked all the sound out with him.

Rattle around. That's what they said about men who lived on their own, but not women. *He just rattles around in that house all by himself.* A cliché.

All morning, Andrew wandered from window to window, staring out at the dull view of the street or the dull view of the alley. He wanted to call Dash, but somehow they'd gotten into a routine of talking to each other every other day, and this was an off day. He thought of going for a run, but the temperature was hovering around freezing and he hated running in the cold. A dull pain under his ribs on the right side came and went. His mother's cousin had died of cirrhosis of the liver. This pain was lower, though, nearer his large intestine. He did a load of laundry, a small one, just his underwear and socks. The phone rang. He raced to it, said, "Hello?" eagerly, but whoever was on the other end waited a second, then hung up.

He called his father. Edward had a new telephone with a dial on the receiver to turn up the volume, but he didn't like it: "All it does is make everything louder." The conversation took a familiar absurd turn when he couldn't understand the word *church*. Andrew said it over and over, even spelled it. "Church, Dad, did you go to *church* today?" "Hurt? I hurt every day." "No, *worship*." "Warship!" his father exclaimed, disgusted, sarcastic. "Did they take you to the *chapel* today? In the *main building*?" He was shouting; Edward was growing furious. "Never mind, Dad, it doesn't matter." "What?" "I'll call you tomorrow!" They hung up with mutual antagonism.

A few minutes later, Chloe called.

"Hi, Dad! Happy Sunday. How's it going?"

His pleasure in hearing her voice was diluted by something almost like shame: In the last few weeks he'd turned into the sort of person his daughter felt she needed to call often and cheer up.

"I went to the coolest concert last night," she began, and launched into a spirited description of it: the venue, the kids she'd gone with, what they'd done afterward. If she'd stayed in the dorm and played computer games last night, he suspected she would regale him with that story in the same lively, energetic way. It had been like this since Dash had told her about the separation. Chloe's solicitousness made him feel pathetic—the exact opposite of her intent.

"You know Becca, that girl in my English class? Remember, the one who wants to be a playwright? Her psych teacher flipped out. He's gone, they're saying a 'leave of absence.' Did I tell you about him? The day they're doing personality disorders he dresses up for class like a hermaphrodite. Seriously, he had on, like, half a wig, one high heel and one sneaker, one earring—for a *teaching* aid. Can you imagine?"

"Too well."

"I know—everybody's talking about it like it's so bizarre, so unusual, but I told them it happens all the time. Professors going bonkers."

"Perhaps not *all* the time."

"No, but it's not that unusual, right? Even at Mason-Dixon, which is tiny, it happens what, once a year? To somebody?"

"That sounds about right."

"So how are you doing?"

"My, what an artful segue." He laughed, genuinely amused, and after a second or two Chloe joined in.

"No, but, you know, I was just asking."

"I'm fine, sweetheart, I'm just fine. Haven't even been *tempted* to wear my tricorne to class."

"Oh, Dad."

"Or shoot the place up with my musket. How are you?"

"I'm fine, too. Did you get my last move?"

"Indeed. Very bold." They'd started playing chess via e-mail. Chloe's idea; another kind, transparent attempt to buoy his spirits. He felt like a social studies project.

"How's Mom?"

"Haven't you spoken to her?"

"Yeah. I was just wondering if you had."

"Not today."

"Emily said . . ."

He stifled a sigh. Lately, more and more of Chloe's sentences started with "Emily said."

"Emily said her parents probably wouldn't have split up if she hadn't gone away to college. Because then they had time. You know, no distractions, they could just concentrate on all the things that were wrong, whereas before, when she was there, she was like the focus, so they didn't have anything to argue about." She left a pause, thoughtfully allowing time for him to speculate on whether that was what had happened to him and her mother.

Was it? Had Chloe's leave-taking merely cleared away the obstruction between them and their incompatibilities? No, Andrew decided. Not for him, anyway. For Dash—who could say?

"Sweetheart," he shook off some strange, creeping inertia to say, "this is just temporary, you know. Your mother and I are going to be fine."

"I know."

"Emily's parents, whatever they're going through, it's got nothing to do with us. And as for us—*that's* got nothing to do with you. Understand?"

"Yes."

"You do know that, don't you?"

"Right, I do."

"Good. Okay."

"But Dad?"

"Yes?"

"I could come home. I could go to Maryland or Georgetown, George Washington—I could even go to Mason-Dixon."

He wavered between laughter and—he didn't know what. She was kidding, wasn't she? An embarrassing lump in his throat made it hard to speak for a moment, and after that it took awhile to josh Chloe out of her sweet, crazy offer—which he feared was only half a joke. Even when she said, "Well, think about it, Dad. For you, I could join a gang and flunk all my courses, I could get deeply into drugs, have a baby—then Mom wouldn't have *time* to go to the cabin."

"You'd do that for me?"

"Only for you."

She hung up laughing, but as soon as the line went dead Andrew's grimacing smile faded to nothing. He stood with his arms limp at his sides, hands heavy as dumbbells. *I'm not well,* he thought. *My daughter feels sorry for me.* He pressed his fingers to the side of his throat, monitoring his pulse. *I'm not doing well.*

Dully, he watched the red light on the answering machine flash on and off, on and off. He'd been erasing every new message but that one for the last two weeks, which was foolish, not like him. Time to get rid of it.

He pressed Play.

"Happy New Year! Hi, it's me—I guess you're out. We're here, just Sock and me. We went for a walk and now we're sleepy, we're going to bed. Not even going to watch the ball drop. Couple of old poops."

Pause.

"Well, I hope you're out somewhere having fun. But not *too* much fun—ha-ha. Okay, I guess that's it. Love you. Miss you. Happy New Year."

He'd called her as soon as he got back—from walking Hobbes, not partying—but the conversation had been perfunctory, superfluous, not nearly as satisfying as the message.

He erased it.

Dash was the only adult he knew who genuinely liked New Year's Eve. He hated it, the mandatory socializing, the antic fun required, the undiscriminating hilarity. The only thing good about it as far as he was concerned was that it marked an anniversary for them. They'd met on New Year's Eve.

At a horrible party one floor up from his two-room apartment in Foggy Bottom. He'd climbed the stairs at eleven o'clock in the evening, aware of the joke he was about to make of himself, the studious, uncool jerk come to complain about the noise. But he was in a bad way, preparing for the D.C. bar exam while trying to convince himself that a single cell in his body gave a damn about the practice of law. It was one of the worst times of his life; he'd felt as if his head were a test site or a proving ground, the locus of explosions and collisions years in the making.

Dash opened the door. She'd been thinking of leaving, she told him later, because her musician boyfriend had abandoned her to get drunk in one of the bedrooms with his band mates. She had stiff, spiky short hair the color of fake mahogany and a great deal of blue makeup on her eyes. Strange clothes, boots that came up over her knees, a sort of crocheted skullcap on her head. The first thing she did was look him up and down and laugh, as if he were the one in the eccentric costume. A sweet, sunny, surprised kind of laugh, but he was about to take offense anyway when she took him by the wrist, pulled him inside, and kissed him. "Happy New Year. Friend of the bride or friend of the groom?"

"Em . . ."

It turned out the party givers were celebrating not only New Year's Eve but also moving in together, but he didn't know that, and Dash's question was only the first of many mysteries that would puzzle him that night. The second was why this odd, laughing girl wanted to be with him. But she did, and as soon as he understood that, he forgot his gloomy mission and gave himself up to fate. Or rather, the unique allure of sex and chumminess Dash radiated, at least for him. Then and now.

Awful, thumping music made it impossible to talk even in the kitchen, where she led him to get plastic glasses of someone else's wine out of the refrigerator. The run-down apartment building had only two virtues, low rents and spacious fire-escape landings overlooking a bit of the distant Potomac River. "Get some air?" Andrew shouted. Dash looked confused until he led her through the packed, stifling living room, out an open window, and onto the fire escape.

"Wow, this is great!" she said, turning in a circle, arms out as if she were blessing the city. "How did you know? Isn't this *fabulous*?" His first experience of being made to feel as if he'd saved her. She charmed everyone that way, he knew now, an all-inclusive generosity of spirit, but that night he'd thought it was just for him.

On the icy iron stairs under a pinkish sky, they got to know each other. "A *lawyer*?" she repeated, like "A *cannibal*?" when he told her his prospective profession. Her patent horror thrilled him. He laughed for the first time in days. Well, she said, at least he'd find a job right away, since the town was lousy with lawyers. He was aware of casting a pall over the conversation by answering, "Well, as a matter of fact. My father wants me to come into his firm. He's expecting it."

One step above him, she put her chin on her fists and leaned close, eyes alight with sympathy. "Don't you want to?"

"Actually, I don't want to practice law at all." She was the first person he'd said that to straight out, no ambivalence.

"What do you want to do?"

"Study history. Teach it at the university level."

"Then that's what you should do."

"Think so?"

"Yes, of course. It's your life. What do you care what your father thinks?"

He might have dismissed that as naive, except that he'd been arrested from the first moment by a way she had of looking at him as if she already knew him. As if she were waiting for him to catch up, and in the meantime, being with him was exciting and sweetly amusing to her.

"Have we met before?" he almost asked. And yet mixed with that was the contrary sense that she was slightly on edge with him, perhaps even on her best behavior because, in fact, she'd never met anyone like him.

"This isn't really me," she said at one point, making an artless, looping gesture.

"Who is really you?" he asked.

She grimaced thoughtfully, tapping her front teeth together, and then laughed. "That is an excellent question."

She told him what she was doing with her life, which dazzled him in its directionlessness, and he told her what he hoped to do with his. "It sounds like I'm having more fun," she deadpanned, but sympathetically. As much as he was drawn to her, his practical side, the one that could always be relied on to prophesy failure, insisted they would never work, they were too different. Temperaments, interests, outlooks—they had nothing in common, so why begin? Why raise false hopes?

"Look, I've got goose bumps," she said, showing him a bare thigh under her short skirt. "It's freezing! Oh, but let's not go in." Of course he gave her his sweater, a cardigan he ripped off like Walter Raleigh's cape and put over her lap. No, now *he'd* be cold, they must share, she insisted. So they squeezed together on the same step and put opposite arms through the sleeves of his sweater, stretching it tight across their fronts. She was flirting, yes, but also, she really didn't want him to be cold. His first experience of the way she could comfort and excite, be his friend and his lover at the same time.

Then Hood came.

Andrew had seen men who looked like Hood around the campus, the city, but had never met or spoken to one in person—no common ground on which to strike an acquaintance, obviously. His head was clean-shaven and shiny-bright, as if he polished it, and he had more piercings in one ear than Andrew had orifices in his whole body. He had black-painted fingernails and a wristband covered with spikes, a cigarette, or maybe a joint, dangling from his lips. He stuck one scrawny leg out the window and straddled the ledge. Holey jeans, a tank shirt, and steel-toed boots completed the outfit—and still he didn't look tough. He had sleepy eyes, a benign, crooked-toothed smile, and when he spoke—"Hey, honey, it's two minutes to midnight!"—he sounded more like the boy next door than a storm trooper.

For a moment—how long? a second, two seconds, yet uncommonly momentous to Andrew—Dash didn't move. She sat still, the left side of her body warming the right side of his, while he wondered what she would do. A tiny sigh—and then the awkward untangling, the clang of cold metal when they stood up, the clambering back through the window. Someone turned off the music. Andrew got shuffled aside as people gathered around a TV set in the living room to see what was happening in Times Square. They slung their arms around one another and swayed, counting down "Ten! Nine! Eight!" Trapped in the drunken crush, he saw shiny-headed Hood wrap his tattooed arms around Dash and give her a long, ardent kiss on the mouth. Her arms stuck out straight behind his head, her hands limp; when she closed her eyes, the blue makeup glittered with silver specks in the light from the television.

He told himself he should stay, learn the situation, intrude, pretend it didn't matter—but as soon as he could, he fought a path through the hot crowd and got out the door.

In his own apartment, weirdly quiet except for the muffled racket overhead, he thought, *Lucky escape,* for a while, then *What did you expect?* He wasn't used to losing women, who usually liked him, but he was used to not getting what he wanted. Or possibly (Dash's theory, years later) what he was used to was being prepared not to get what he wanted—a defense mechanism, a way to save face. Either way, blighted expectations were no strangers to him, and his usual coping method was weary resignation. *What else? What did you expect?* He was trying and failing to console himself with that sort of shoulder-shrugging fatalism when a quick knock came at the door. Dash.

And Hood, a few steps behind, carefully cupping a lighter to his cigarette. Or joint.

"Hi," Dash said.

"Hi," Andrew said.

She had on a feathery, spangly half poncho for a coat, and long red gloves. And she had that look again, as if she knew him unnervingly well and were only waiting, with tender amusement, for him to catch up.

"I wanted to use the fire escape," she said softly. So Hood couldn't hear? Not that he was paying any attention. One knee gave out and he lurched sideways, had to start over with his cigarette. He was drunk, but Dash wasn't.

"It's so high up, though," she said. "I got scared."

"The stairs are much safer," Andrew agreed.

"Yes. We were wondering. Do you like black-eyed peas?"

He just smiled. He wanted to see her in daylight. Was she beautiful? Already he didn't care.

"I'm—we're having a party tomorrow. I make this thing of my mother's called hoppin' John. It's a southern tradition. For every black-eyed pea you eat on New Year's Day, that's how many dollars you'll make that year. Actually it's more of a superstition."

"Do I look that hard up?" He meant that as a *joke*; he was so *stupid*. "I'd like to come," he said quickly. "Where do you live?"

So it began, their confusing, undercover, thankfully short period of courtship. Hood proved to be a congenial rival, and before long Andrew and Dash were a couple. Happily ever after. She made hoppin' John every New Year's Day, and he pretended to like it. This was the first time in twenty-one years he hadn't had gas all New Year's night.

Sunday morning dragged on. Now that it was too late, he felt guilty for not going to church. It wasn't that he had nothing to do; he just couldn't stand the thought of doing it.

He wandered into the downstairs office he and Dash shared, then forgot what he'd come in for. It used to be a pantry off the kitchen. With no window, it was a dark, gloomy room, and so, about ten years ago, Dash squeezed up against the house behind the shrubbery and shot a wide-angle photograph of the backyard. She blew it up and hung it on the office wall inside a window-shaped frame she made, complete with curtains. It fooled people for a few seconds—they thought it was a real window. But only in summer; in wintertime, the sunny greens and pastels gave it away. They were depressing, too, unless you were in a hopeful frame of mind and the thought of springs past and to come cheered you up. Andrew wasn't in a hopeful frame of mind.

He'd liked Dash's faux period, though. She would take close-ups of light switches around the house, enlarge them to their exact dimensions, mount them on thick cardboard, and glue them on the walls in unexpected places. Same with the thermostat and the heat registers, the doorbell. People halted at the sight of them for a minute, then laughed. But after a while, she'd tired of her domestic reproductions and taken them all down. All but the window.

Nostalgia washed over him. He felt heavy, homesick. If he could find them, would it be even *more* depressing to hang up a few fake light switches now, or would it make him smile? He knew where they were, in a drawer in the oak file cabinet. She kept some of her early work there, pre-Chloe, back when she'd done all her own developing and printing in a tiny darkroom in the bathroom of her apartment.

She kept other photos in that file cabinet, too. They were in a brown envelope at the back of the bottom drawer, the made-up name "Municipal Boro Council" scrawled on top in her spiky printing—"in case Chloe ever looks in here." He went to the cabinet and pulled out the envelope, carried it to the desk, turned on the lamp. They used to look at these pictures together, but not in a long while. He couldn't remember the last time.

The good ones were in the middle, between batches of dull cityscapes and parking lot scenes for camouflage. They were in black and white— she'd have had to send color film to a lab. In the first few, they were kissing. "We never get to *see* ourselves when we kiss," she'd said. "Don't you want to see how we look?"

They looked like lovers. In this one she was perched on his lap, in the kitchen at his place, he in his boxer shorts, Dash in nothing. He'd felt self-conscious; she hadn't. She looked like a sleek, smooth fish, her skin glowing pearl white. In another photo she had her tongue in his ear for a joke, but the joke was the expression on his face, mirth battling consternation. Even then, his dignity was not to be trifled with.

The next ones were in her apartment, in the old iron bed she'd found somewhere and painted red. Horrible bed; the springs squeaked, the mattress had a trough in the middle that forced them to sleep jammed against each other because of gravity as much as desire. The first pose was artily tasteful, Andrew on his back, Dash pressed against him with her bent knee covering his groin, her elbow coyly hiding the tip of her breast. They had their eyes closed, pretending to sleep, but their secret smiles gave them away.

They got bolder in the next shot: full frontal nudity flat on the bed, holding hands and grinning into the camera. Dash's blinding smile took up her whole face, squeezing her eyes to slits. Her pale nipples, her innocent knees, the shadows of her rib cage, the triangle of hair between her legs . . . His chest felt clogged. He stood up and sat down again.

Their intimacy had been so thrilling to him, and at the same time so natural. Dash never felt any shame, but she was never immodest or coarse. Just free. And so kind to him. Before he knew her, he could never have thought of himself as the sort of man he looked like in these photographs, sleepy-eyed from sex, shaggy-haired, lax, his body stretching and languorous. A sensualist. She'd taught him to be who she wanted him to be, and that was what he'd been hoping for, one of the reasons he'd fallen in love with her—so she could make him feel truer to himself. Not such a stranger.

He picked up the phone and dialed her number at the cabin.

The machine came on. Disappointment made his mouth taste sour. He didn't leave a message.

God, her apartment. He remembered that lamp on the bedside table: seashells filled the clear glass base, and the shade revolved when you switched on the bulb, illuminating a beach scene with rocking waves. She'd throw a gauzy scarf over the lamp when they made love, and they'd lie on their backs afterward, talking, talking, following the colored lights around the ceiling until they hypnotized themselves to sleep.

I don't belong here, he would think at times, staring at the crumbling plaster walls or smashing a roach in the bathroom or trying to endure the music on her cheap stereo. But the very things that made him recoil also drew him in, as if his neat, scrupulously planned life needed the relative squalor of Dash's for balance. It wasn't that he'd felt superior— merely out of place, a Young Republican at the Socialists' convention. A small-town private whose first leave is in Paris.

The last photograph made him hiss in his breath. She'd destroyed all their "porn" shots eventually, the ones in which they were actually having sex, but she'd kept this one. At his request. It still aroused him, dirty-movie pose and all. There was nothing in it of him except his hairy legs and his testicles. Dash sat with her back to the camera, spine arched back like a wand, her streaky hair splashing her shoulders. Her heart-shaped bottom was so beautiful, so . . . beautiful. He grabbed the phone and called her again.

"I'm coming down," he blurted into the machine. He took a long, deep breath. "Emmm . . . nice day, think I'll take a drive down your way, see how things are. I've been meaning to." It wasn't a nice day at all. He paused. He had things to say, but they were too jumbled and raw; he needed to organize his thoughts first. "Are you out for a walk? How are you? Em, well, then, see you in a bit." He waited a beat before hanging up, hoping that would make the farewell *click* sound more careless.

eight

Nothing looked familiar to him here in winter, the fields and trees bare and stark, dreary brown instead of vivid green and overgrown. They didn't have a mailbox; he almost missed the turn, which was unmarked except for the corner of the rotting fence of the Speichers, their nearest neighbors, behind which a few cows grazed in summer. The ruts were deeper than the last time he'd driven up the long dirt lane, which would be treacherous in snow or ice. Why did Dash like it here so much? A place in the country was her dream, not his. Rock Creek Park had all the nature he needed, and then some.

But the sight of their red-roofed, clapboard-sided cabin emerging from the last thicket of laurel and pine gave him an undeniable stab of pleasure. And there was Dash's little white car, so dearly familiar, a piece of home in this wintry no-man's-land. He pulled in slowly, parked beside it gently.

The crunch of gravel under his tires made a racket, though—she must've heard, was probably looking out the window now to see who it was. He climbed out of his car with smooth movements, slammed the door athletically. He surveyed the murky tangle of trees surrounding the front of the cabin, featureless to him, beautiful to her, with an interested, approving expression, hands on his hips. Then he turned and walked up to the cabin with confident, unhurried strides.

Blue canvas covers draped the porch furniture, pushed to the side farthest from the weather. Nothing but dirt and dead stalks filled the dozen or so flowerpots she'd planted last year. She'd made a winter wreath for the door, he saw, tangled vines twisted in a circle and studded with dried flowers and purplish berries. It took up the whole top half of the door; he had to knock at belt height. He straightened his shoulders, made his face casual. She was going to like this. Spur of the moment. One of her complaints about him was that he wasn't spontaneous enough—a completely bum rap. This would show her.

He knocked again after a minute, louder. He put his face in the middle of the wreath and tried to look in through the window. A twig poked him in the eye, under his glasses; he jerked back, blinking, watery-eyed. He tried the doorknob. Locked. Odd; she loved to brag that she never locked the door.

Out in the yard, he looked up at the chimney but could see no smoke, only gray, unmoving sky above the red roofline. The flat stones they'd set two summers ago in a mossy, curving path to the back of the cabin were slippery even when it wasn't raining; he almost fell before he got to the steps up to the deck. His footsteps rang out on the wooden stairs. He tramped to the glass sliding doors, also locked, and peered into the living room, making a visor with his hands to block the glare.

The empty room looked cold, as if the woodstove had gone out a long time ago. He could make out sections of the Sunday paper strewn over the floor and the coffee table. That was his job, driving into the little town of Dolley for the *Post* on Sunday mornings; he couldn't help hoping she found it inconvenient, having to go get it herself. An empty plate and glass sat on the hearth beside the ratty old shawl her mother had made her. He could see her glasses on top of an open book. He put his hands on the cold glass and stared in until his breath fogged the view.

She was probably down at the pond. Her favorite place. She would sit on the pier and stare out at the water until she lost track of time. He'd have to go get her, tell her it was time for lunch, time to go home. She'd turn to him with a glazed, erased look, her eyes the color of the water.

But she wasn't in her spot, or anywhere else along the meandering pond bank. He called out; his voice echoed back from the other side. He thought of the time, two summers ago, when she'd talked him into going for a swim, and afterward he'd fallen fast asleep, facedown on the dock. When he woke up, she was paddling innocently at the far end, and his whole backside was covered with seaweed. Not seaweed, the green stuff growing at the bottom of the pond, algae or whatever. He looked like a science-fiction-movie freak. He put his arms out and stalked around the bank toward her, making monster noises while she squealed in pretend fear. They ended up making love in the cold water.

He went around to the front again. Since her car was here, she must've gone for a walk. He made a megaphone with his hands and yelled, "Dash!" in three different directions. Why didn't they have a key hidden outside someplace? They'd talked about it, never gotten around to doing it.

He turned in a frustrated circle, surveying blankness. Had she never gotten his message? He'd left it over two hours ago. She was always going on tramps in the woods, but he seldom accompanied her—he preferred sitting on the deck with a book, or better, sitting inside with a book—so he didn't know her trail system, where to even start to look for her.

Calling the police would probably be overreacting. She'd think so, anyway. He could hear her: "Oh, Andrew, you *didn't.* My God, you are so neurotic." Half an hour, that's how long he'd give her. At four o'clock, he was calling the cops, and he didn't care if she mocked him.

He needed something to occupy his mind in the meantime, keep it off horrible scenarios. Dash's foot caught in a hole or a bear trap, Dash abducted by mountain men. Dash dying or freezing to death because of a heart attack. Her health was excellent, but she could have a sudden stroke, an embolus, an aneurysm as easily as anyone else. They'd have to send dogs out to find her, and it was going to be pitch-dark in two hours. He had to do something.

He'd chop wood.

Her pile was running low. She complained about old Bender's habit of including wood in his drop-offs that was too big for the woodstove. She could chop up the smaller pieces herself, but the logs were too much for her; she had to leave them on the ground where Bender dumped them. Here was a chance for Andrew to do something helpful and admirable. Knightly. Something she would be grateful to him for.

He found the ax in the woodshed and gripped the handle experimentally, trying to recall if he'd ever held one before. Perhaps in Boy Scouts. Shouldn't there be a platform to put the log on, a base of some sort, so it was at a more convenient height? He'd never thrown his back out before, but if this wasn't a golden opportunity for it, he didn't know what was.

He took a few practice swings, wishing he'd brought gloves. He set a bulky log on end. It wobbled, but it was only about twelve inches across; if he put his foot on it to steady it—good-bye foot. He spread his legs, dug his heels into the ground for traction, like a baseball player. Lifting the ax high overhead, he brought it down with all his might.

Not bad. His whole body vibrated, but he'd driven the ax into the log a good three inches.

Now if he could only get it out. He jerked and yanked, he hoisted it, log and all, and tried to smash it against another log, against the ground, against the side of the woodshed. It never budged. He was sweating, swearing—

A man's voice. Coming from the side of the house, and now a laugh. Dash's laugh. He froze.

His wife and a man he'd never seen before strolled around the corner of the cabin. Dash was in the act of elbowing the man in the ribs, a bit of shtick she reverted to when the joke or pun she'd just made was especially lame or obvious. The man, a burly fellow in a plaid jacket and a hunting cap, chuckled in appreciation. They looked up and saw Andrew at the same time.

She faltered, almost stopped. She was too far away for him to read her face precisely; the widened eyes and the *O* her mouth made might mean gladness, might mean shock. Otherwise, she looked relaxed and fit, light-footed. She had on clothes he couldn't remember seeing before. Her cheeks were bright as cherries. She had on earmuffs.

"Andrew!" she called, waving a mittened hand. She said something inaudible to her fair-haired, thick-necked companion, who had to be Bender's son-in-law, and they came forward together. A small black dog bounded out of the woods and ran past them, skidding at Andrew's feet, turning in circles, giddy with welcome. Sock, he presumed. The watchdog.

"Wow," Dash said, stopping just shy of him, "what a surprise." She looked healthy. She looked beautiful. She swung her arms in a restless, girlish way, as if—he hoped—she'd have embraced him if they'd been alone. "Did you call? I've been out walking. With Owen. Have you two met? No, of course not. Owen, this is Andrew—Owen Roby."

They shook hands; Roby's was thick and meaty, like a baseball glove.

"We've been tracking muskrats along the creek," Dash went on; she chattered when she was nervous. "Owen's so smart, he knows what all

the tracks are, possum, raccoon, squirrel—he can tell the difference between a gray squirrel's footprints and a red squirrel's footprints. Can
you imagine?"

"Truthfully, no."

"Oh, and we saw a wild turkey. As close as that tree, and then it
flew away. Very clumsily. When did you get here? Have you been waiting long?"

"No, no. A couple of minutes."

"I wish I'd known you were coming. Why didn't you go inside?"

"The door's locked."

"No, it's not."

"Yes, it is."

"No, it's stuck. Owen's going to fix it, he has a plane. Oh, Andrew—
are you chopping wood?"

"No. Yes." He tried to swing the log by the ax behind his leg, but it
hit his ankle. Without wincing, he said, "Well, just getting started."

"Oh, gosh, you don't have to do that. Owen's been doing it for me."

Two minutes he'd known Owen, and he was sick of him.

"Where's your wedge?" Roby said, or something that sounded like
that, and started looking around on the ground. Andrew wrinkled his
eyebrows, as if trying to remember where he'd left his wedge. What
was a wedge?

A heavy, rusting, metal thing, wedge-shaped. Roby found it in the
woodshed. "Here it is." He tossed it in the air a few times, catching it in
his paw. Before he could toss it to *him,* Andrew dropped the log on the
ground, ax and all. Excalibur in the stone.

The logo on Roby's hunting cap said WORMER'S ORGANIC FEEDS. His
fine, pale-yellow hair and the pink streaks on his windburned cheeks
gave him a naked, unprotected look that didn't match the rest of him,
which was rugged and planted-looking, quietly self-assured. He didn't
look at Dash or Andrew, didn't smirk, didn't flex his halfback's shoulder muscles—which only made it worse when he took hold of the ax in
one hand and slammed the log off it with a single hard chop to the
ground.

Andrew heard himself say, "I loosened it." His cheeks burned.

Dash wore a gentle, amused, wistful smile he couldn't look at.

Next Roby tapped the wedge into the white gash the ax had made. With the same gallingly unassuming efficiency, he slapped the flat end of the ax against the wedge, and the log's two halves fell neatly away.

"Ah, yes. Much easier that way." Andrew gave a good-natured laugh, as if nothing pleased him more than a lesson in manly wood chopping in front of his estranged wife.

Dash's echoing laugh was the one she used when she was trying to save someone's feelings. "Oh, let's not chop any more wood now, guys. It's getting cold; let's go inside and get warm."

Let's? Guys?

Roby pulled off his cap, ran his wrist over his thinning hair, and tugged it back on. "I guess I'll be heading on back now."

"Okay," Andrew said.

Dash had a lot more to say, though, about the sticking front door, the kitchen cabinets, the stacked washer-dryer unit Roby was going to buy with his contractor's discount and install in the bathroom. "Although I'll kind of miss the Laundromat," she added in a jokey voice, and Roby grinned and said, "No, I told you, the Velvet Cafe's even better."

"But only at the counter."

"Right, not a table."

"And especially on Mondays."

"Because all the good stuff happened on the weekend."

They laughed together, fond and easy.

"Gossip," Dash explained eventually, noticing Andrew's look. "Town gossip, at the Laundromat or at the café—"

"I got it."

Roby finally left, walked off down the hill. It didn't occur to Andrew to ask where he was going until he was almost out of sight; he was too happy to see him go.

"He left his truck down at the Speichers'," Dash said, moving toward the house. "He's putting in their new hot-water heater."

"I thought he was a farmer."

"He's everything, it's amazing. He raises beef cattle, he does construction, he delivers mail over Christmas, he works for a logging company sometimes, sometimes for the county extension service. Plus he hunts and fishes and grows a big garden every summer . . ." She stopped talking to open the front door, which involved turning and pulling up on the knob while hip-butting the bottom panel and pushing in. "See? It wasn't locked, I never lock it."

The cold cabin smelled like ashes. Dash went around turning on lamps, picking up plates and carrying them into the kitchen. "I'll make some tea," she called to Andrew. "Do you think you could make a fire?"

Was she being sarcastic? He watched her punch the blinking light on the answering machine in the kitchen; she had her back to him, so he couldn't see her face while his message played back. Did he sound desperate? No, he decided; just unusually alert.

"Shall I make one in here, too?" he asked when he'd finished building a fire in the woodstove. They had a potbellied stove in the kitchen, but seldom used it. Dash said no, that was fine, while she took cups down from the cabinet and got milk out of the refrigerator.

He drifted back to the living room to hold his hands over the clanking, slowly warming stove. "Yes, very cute," he told the dog, who had pulled a piece of kindling from the wood hoop and was trying to lure him into a game by repeatedly dropping it at his feet. Wasn't it cats who were supposed to zero in on people who didn't like them? His nose was itching already; he got his handkerchief out just in time to sneeze into it twice.

The cabin's decorating theme was still Shrine to My Mother, he saw. Arlene's old armchair sat in the corner; her dusty oil paintings from a long-ago hobby had replaced Dash's photos on the walls; her fake Oriental runner bordered the brick hearth in front of the woodstove. Her knickknacks lined the small bookcase alongside her book club copies of *The Thorn Birds, Hawaii, Ship of Fools, The Forsyte Saga.* He didn't really mind the gradual eradication in the room of almost everything connected with himself—there hadn't been that much to begin with, although he did miss his foot-high stack of unread *New Yorkers*—and if it gave Dash comfort to be surrounded by her mother's things, how could he resent it? Everything looked so settled, though, so cozy and self-contained, and that he resented. It looked as if one woman lived here by herself. Contentedly.

He turned over the library book on the hearth to see the cover.

Religions of the World. Dash? Impossible. On second thought, maybe: The subtitle was *An Illustrated Overview.*

He started guiltily when she came in with a tray, catching him stirring through the mail on the coffee table. She set the tray down with a small, admonishing clatter. "I sent away for that."

"What? This?" He held it up innocently: a course catalog from the University of Pennsylvania.

"I know you think I'm not serious about vet school, but I am."

He looked again at the catalog. "This is in Philadelphia."

"It's the closest one there is. Except for Virginia Tech."

"But . . ."

"What?" She set her hands on her hips.

"Nothing." He put the catalog back and sat down. The idea of Dash giving up her career, her successful business, the work she was born to do in order to take up the study of *veterinary medicine* was so ludicrous to him, so unbelievably wrongheaded—if he said one word, it would start a fight.

He didn't want to fight, he wanted to take her to bed. He'd figured that out halfway down Route 29, and spent the other half imagining it.

She sat at the opposite end of the sofa from him, drawing up her feet in their woolly socks. She worried too much about getting old. She stared in the bathroom mirror at night and complained about her crow's feet, her jawline, the barely perceptible wrinkle between her eyebrows. Everything was the beginning of the end. She never took his consoling remarks to heart, but he meant it when he told her she still looked beautiful to him. She was just right. She had been twenty years ago, and nothing had changed. She was simply his type, medium-tall, fair-skinned, fine-featured. Softhearted. His own Dash, who had turned on him for reasons she didn't understand herself. Part of her quarrel with him was that he didn't take her leaving him seriously, but how could he? It made no sense.

"I spoke to Chloe this morning," he mentioned as they sipped tea. Chloe was always a safe topic. "We've started playing chess, sending each other moves in e-mails."

"She told me." They smiled at each other across the expanse of couch. "I wish I had something like that with her," Dash said, worrying a torn thread in the knee of her jeans. "Something to keep us close."

He put his hand on her foot, the only part of her he could reach. "You? You two will always be close."

She sighed. "She's more like you than me."

That was true, so he said nothing. He thought of sliding his hand up the leg of her jeans and holding her bare calf. In the past, if Chloe hadn't come down with them, they used to make love on this couch, Saturday or Sunday mornings after breakfast, usually, the newspapers strewn everywhere, crackling underneath them. He hated sleeping alone. Did she? Her hair was coming down in sexy tangles from a barrette on top of her head. She was talking about the two geese she'd seen on the pond yesterday, and he loved her expansive gestures, the way she looked behind him and to the left when she concentrated on what she was saying, then back into his eyes. He loved her intensity and her vitality. She woke him up. She was right, she wasn't depressed. If this was premenopause, it had just made her more ... it had just made her *more.* On the other hand, Dash times two was a mixed blessing. One of her had always been as much as he could handle.

He missed what she said next, but came to when he heard, "Did you know you can *eat* muskrats? Yeah, they're very clean animals. I asked him what they taste like and he said chicken—he didn't even laugh! He gave me a suet feeder he built himself—I'll show you, it's outside. He says we get woodpeckers all winter, and they really need suet for energy. And cardinals, chickadees ..."

Suet. Wedge. Crossword puzzle words he'd heard all his life, and yet he had to admit he didn't know precisely what they meant. It wasn't like him to resent the acquisition of knowledge.

"You're seeing a lot of Roby, are you?" he said, leaning over to brush a spot of mud off his pants cuff. Was he jealous of Roby? Yes, but not for any good reason. Of that he was sure.

"Well, I guess. He's doing everything Shevlin used to do."

"Who?"

"Mr. Bender. That's his name, Shevlin—I know, all these years and we never knew. Cottie and I are starting to be friends. I'm not sure why she likes me, but I like her, too, right from the beginning we just hit it off. I've been going over there in the afternoons sometimes for coffee. We talk about gardening, things like that." She shrugged, smiling at the unlikeliness of a friendship that didn't surprise him at all. Mrs. Bender, who sounded like a nice woman, must be about Arlene's age.

"I'm glad you have someone to talk to," he said, stroking his finger over the toes of her foot.

"I'm trying to get Greta up to speed to take over the office for a whole week, so I can stay down here. Things are still slow, I could move some appointments around and get an *entire week* with no shoots." She closed her eyes. "Think of it. I could really get somewhere if I had one long, uninterrupted week."

"Get somewhere?"

"With myself." She opened her eyes. "I know it's a drag, but you have to be patient with me. It's an important time. I've been meditating. I go for long walks in the woods with Sock, and just think. I'm learning lore."

"Lore?"

"Don't you dare laugh. I've been reading nature books and learning to identify birds and trees and things." She pointed to a jumble of dried leaves and poddish-looking objects on the table; he had thought it was one of her winter flower arrangements. He couldn't help it—it made him smile. "Andrew, I'm warning you."

"No, I think it's great. Really. But . . . aren't you ever lonely?"

"Nope. Not lonely." She ran her thumbnail over the place on the cup where her lips had been. "Or if I am, it's a good kind. Scary, but educational. I'm having a genuine learning experience."

"You could take an adult education course at Mason-Dixon. I think they've got one on wildflowers."

She narrowed her eyes, not sure if he was making fun or not. He didn't know himself. If she wasn't lonely, then she didn't miss him. But he was expected to be completely supportive while she played at Thoreau or Thomas Merton or whatever the hell this was.

The dog, who had been dozing in front of the stove, roused itself to jump up on his knees and deposit a moist stub of rawhide in his lap.

"Pet her," Dash said, her face breaking into a smile. "Oh, look, she likes you."

"How big is it going to get?" He patted the dog's head with three fingers.

"She. Medium, the vet thinks. Knee-high, the perfect size for a dog." The puppy nosed its chew toy into his crotch. His eyes began to water. "She's very smart. She knows 'sit,' and she comes when I call her. We're working on 'stay.' Show Andrew how you can shake hands. Watch this—Sock, shake hands. She has to be sitting, put her feet on the floor. Sock, *sit.* Good girl! Now, shake hands. Put your hand out, Andrew. Sock, shake. Shake hands. Usually she can do this. Get closer. *Sock.* Shake hands, honey. *Shake.*"

When Andrew had time to control them, his sneezes were discreet, choked-off affairs in his hand or his handkerchief. When they came without warning, like this one, they were startling, ear-piercing explosions that made people jump, then made them angry.

"Achh!"

The dog leaped high in the air, squealed, and flew out of the room.

"Oh, *honestly.*" Dash got up and went after it. Andrew tried a laugh, but she called back, "It's not funny!" and kept going.

Usually it would be funny. Nothing was working today, though. Look where impulsiveness had got him. If he'd stayed home, he'd still have some dignity left. Nothing gained, but nothing risked.

Then he remembered—he had something of a trump card. A dubious ace in the hole.

"Guess what."

In the kitchen, Dash was holding the perfectly fine puppy in her arms. She kissed the top of its head and set it on the floor. "It's getting late. You know how you hate to drive after dark." She turned her back on him, opened the refrigerator, and took out a plastic container.

"Guess what."

Her shoulders rose and fell. "What."

"Richard Weldon offered me his job."

She turned around in slow motion, huge-eyed. "As chairman? Of the department?" He nodded. "Oh, *Andrew.*" She put the container down and clapped her hands. "Oh, I'm not surprised at all!"

He laughed—clearly that wasn't true.

She laughed with him. "Oh, this is outstanding. *Good* for you."

Too late, he began to see that his trump card was a two of diamonds. "Hang on," he said lightly, "there's a catch. Nobody's comfortable with me taking the job as an associate professor—not that it *couldn't* happen, but now, you see, the push is on to get me a full."

"But that's *good*. And about damn time."

"Richard says the quickest way is if I'd agree to write a chapter in a book Peter Flynn's editing."

"But you hate Peter Flynn, you—" She stopped. Her head came forward on the long stem of her neck; her voice rose higher on every word. "So you're not going to do it?"

"You don't understand. It's called *The Great Cover-up*—Flynn's book—*The Great Cover-up: A Reexamination of Race and Gender Issues in the Framing of the Constitution.*" His lips curled. "I'm amazed he didn't get 'deconstruction' in there somewhere."

"Oh no. Andrew, for God's sake." She wilted against the counter. "I can't believe this."

"Don't you see, it's going to be a hatchet job. Flynn's not a historian, he's a number cruncher. Regression, quantitative analysis—that's his field, it's not history, it's *math,* and all in the service of *proving*"—he made derisive quotation marks in the air—"that Thomas Jefferson had little black children, Washington was a slaveholding hypocrite—"

"Oh, save it. Why didn't you say so? No wonder—this is about Jefferson, your *hero*. Which means the end, case closed."

"There's no point in trying to explain this to you," he said coldly.

"You don't have to explain it."

"I don't want the job anyway."

"Why not?"

"Because I'd rather teach. That's what I do; I'm a teacher."

"You can do both!" She came after him when he went back into the living room. "Damn it, you deserve this job, and you'd be great at it. It's more money, isn't it?"

"That's the whole point for you, isn't it?"

She gasped. "How can you say that? About *me*?"

"Why not about you?"

"I care about getting Chloe through college, if that's what you mean!"

"Right. So I should take the job so you can give up yours and go to *vet school*." He grabbed his coat.

"You are so unreasonable! This is why we need counseling," she threw at him, following him out on the porch. "I made the appointment, by the way—it's this Thursday night at seven. Put it on your *list*."

"I will."

They stood under the porch light without looking at each other. Dash wrapped her arms around herself, frowning, dissatisfied. "Well, go on, then. Be careful driving."

It was hard to see how he could've made a bigger hash of this visit, especially in light of his hopes at the outset. "Go inside," he said, "you're freezing."

"Okay. Be careful driving," she repeated, not moving.

He took a chance and put his arms around her. Strangeness and familiarity warred, but only for a second; then everything was fine. "Sweetheart," he murmured. Holding her was like slipping into a favorite shirt still warm from the dryer. "You're too skinny." He didn't even realize until afterward what a perfect line that was.

"Oh, I am not. I have lost a couple of pounds, though." She went looser in his arms.

"From not eating right." He hadn't kissed her in five weeks. "I'm not, either. I'm living on ice cream and frozen potpies."

"Poor baby."

"God knows what my cholesterol is. It was one-ninety-seven at my last checkup, which is borderline, but that was four months ago." He nuzzled her neck. "They sell kits, home monitors, I was thinking we should get one. My father's LDL—"

He was surprised when she bussed him on the cheek, pushed him in the chest, and backed out of his arms. "Good night, Andrew." She went inside and closed the door. The porch light went out before he could get to his car.

dash

nine

"*Y*ou fell asleep during meditation," Mo accuses me.

"I did not."

"Did, too."

"I did not. I was deeply, deeply into the present moment. Look, those guys look like they're leaving, let's get their seats."

"She was asleep, right?" Mo turns to Greta for support. "You heard that little snort?"

Greta, my loyal employee, merely casts down her eyes and smiles. Mo made us come to her yoga class this morning, and Greta didn't fix her hair afterward. I see now why she always wears it in braids or dreadlocks or some other bound fashion: otherwise it explodes like Easter basket filling, like orange tinsel glued to her head in piles and left to wander. I like it this way, myself. Free.

We're waiting for a table at a restaurant I've either never been to before or they've remodeled out of recognition. That happens a lot in my neighborhood, which is nice, lots of variety and everything, except as soon as you get attached to some little Milanese bistro, you come back and they've turned it into a cigar bar. This place features high round tables with uncomfortable stools, a long, lively bar, and a shiny black counter along the front window, behind which you can sit, eat, and watch the world go by. My first choice every time—and lo, the three businessmen I've been watching all stand up at the same time. While they're still putting their coats on, we swoop down and take their seats at the counter.

"Isn't this nice?"

"I love people watching."

"I could do it all day."

The waiter comes. We're examining our menus when Mo says, "What an incredibly good-looking man."

Greta, sitting between us, murmurs, "Mmm."

"He was," I say, not looking up, thinking of our yoga instructor.

Greta giggles. "Not him. *Him*."

"Oh. *Him*." Out on the sidewalk, a tall man with his hands stuffed in the pockets of a soft brown leather coat, his shoulders hunched, back to the wind, is talking to another man, older, not as attractive. They shake hands, say final words, and the older man walks off. And then, as if our collective, barely conscious wish has been granted by the god of oglers, the Leather-Coated Man makes a quarter turn and strolls into our restaurant.

He takes a seat behind us at the bar, invisible unless we turn completely and gracelessly around, as if looking for the waiter or at the clock. How many times can you do that? Twice, I decide, and return to my menu, but Mo is much bolder. "Doesn't he look familiar?" she muses, openly staring, resting a finger on her cheek. "Like someone we know?"

"No."

"I wish," Greta says.

"I'm sure I've seen him before."

"Go ask him," Greta says, giggling again. She really does not know who she's dealing with. I wouldn't be surprised if Mo asked the hunky yoga instructor for a date. But maybe that's not fair, because she was really into it today, incredibly focused and precise. She says she goes three times a week now, and it shows. She looks fabulous. She's cut her hair and stopped coloring it since I saw her last; now it's a cap of streaky gray, and she's an aging Joan of Arc. There's a new sharpness in her face, too, as if living a Phil-less life has scraped away all the soft curves and made her pointy and avid. But attractively so. I think.

"I've met somebody," she says, closing her menu with a snap. "Christ, there's not one healthy thing to eat here."

"Who?"

"His name is Anwar, but he's British. He's something in the consulate—I found him a condo. Get this: He only has one ball."

"Like Hitler," Greta and I say in unison.

"Yes. How do you know about Hitler?"

"Everybody knows about Hitler."

"It doesn't affect anything; I mean, he's still potent and all."

Oh good, this is going to be easy. I wasn't sure how Mo and Greta would like each other, and now I see it was silly of me to worry. We are getting *right down to it,* heavy-duty woman talk before the water comes.

"So?" I say. "Do you like him?"

"Yes, except he smokes. Tonight I'm going out with a guy from the office, and he smokes, too. I don't get it. Don't these people—"

"Whoa, wait—what about Anwar?"

"Oh, Dash. If God wanted us to be monogamous, he wouldn't have made us multiorgasmic."

Ha-ha, we laugh. That's funny in a sort of *Sex and the City* way, and here we are, girlfriends at lunch dishing on men, nothing missing but the Cosmos. It doesn't feel quite real to me, though. I feel like the oldest one here, and I'm not. I feel as if I'm *impersonating* a frank, breezy girlfriend. I'm in a funny mood.

"Seriously," Mo says, moving her head oddly, peering at what I take for bare tree branches outside until I realize she's found a way to see Leather-Coated Man in the window's reflection. "Monogamy doesn't work, obviously, because it shuts out so much of *life.*"

Here we go. "Maureen is recently divorced," I inform Greta—not very kindly, I suppose, but she deserves a warning.

"Two people can't be everything to each other forever, it's just not possible. We're not built that way. Or if you *must* institutionalize monogamy, then everyone gets three husbands. For ten years each, and in between you can have as many lovers as you want. I've given this a lot of thought."

Greta and I mull that over, searching for flaws. It does have an appealing sort of symmetry.

"Maybe you have to keep falling in love with the same person? Over and over again?" Greta ventures. "And sometimes you just have to wait?"

"Yeah, but too bad you keep falling *out* of love over and over, too." Maureen signals the waiter, asks for the fruit salad with yogurt dressing and a side of asparagus, no butter, no salt. "So then your only hope is that your remarriages ultimately outnumber your divorces."

Greta and I order the zucchini omelet with *pommes frites.* "Why are you eating like a bird?" I ask Maureen. "You're getting way too thin. It's not healthy." We've even discussed this: It's what people who wish they weighed less say to their slim friends. A snarky defense mechanism. Deliberately tarnishing your idol.

"Those fries are what will kill you," Mo says in a superior tone. "Before yoga, I only eat fresh fruit. The rest of the time, vegetables, fruits, and whole grains, mostly. Very little alcohol."

"You're a *vegetarian?*" News to me. Although not that surprising, on second thought.

"Practically. Virtually. Anyway," she resumes, "monogamy is unnatural, that's the point. Because all it comes down to, after all the pain and heartbreak, all your hopes and dreams, the struggling—all it comes down to is money."

I sigh. Greta's shoulders sag.

"Well," I rouse myself to say, "nobody's saying there should be monogamy—or *marriage,* that's what we're really talking about— without love. That would be slavery. That would be lack of imagination to the point of lobotomy. Apathy to the point of coma."

"Love," Mo says, thinning her lips. "Good luck. All you can trust, bottom line, is lust. Outside of eating, sex is the most natural thing we do, but we suppress, suppress—women, not men—and then we wonder why married women have the worst mental health and married men have the best."

"Is that true?"

"It's absolutely true." She's turning around again, craning her neck to see Leather Coat. He's taken it off; underneath, he's wearing that sort of thick beige cable-knit sweater men never buy for themselves— it's always a gift from the wife or the girlfriend. He looks very *taken* to me.

"Lust is great," I say, "but it's not what holds two people together for a lifetime."

"What does?" Greta asks. She and Joel are still an item, but she doesn't talk about him as much as she used to. Good: I don't like the sound of him, and I was afraid his hold on her was lethal.

"What does," I say ruminatively, cronelike. "The details. A million little details, like threads in a tapestry. Weaving our lives together."

Maureen coughs behind her napkin.

"No, but lust is great," I backtrack, "you gotta have that. Absolutely, it's a prerequisite."

"So do you and Andrew . . ." Shy, Greta lets that trail off.

"Have lust? Well . . . yes. You know. Peaks and valleys. Good times and bad, mostly good."

Both women look skeptical.

"No, we *do*. Really." I've put it too mildly—they think I'm equivocating. "We definitely do. We had sex in Andrew's office not that long ago, last fall sometime. On the *desk*." Now I've got their attention. "And it wasn't because we wanted to get caught, nothing kinky like that, I mean, we locked the door and everything."

"Then . . ."

"Well, we just wanted to. So we did."

I don't know who's looking at me with more subtle amazement, Greta or Mo: Greta, because she finds it incredible that two old fossils like Andrew and me can still get it on at all; Mo, because she's wondering why I've left him if my husband is still so virile and desirable. (Phil was a dud in their bedroom for a year or two before the divorce. But not, it turned out, in other women's bedrooms.)

"Wow," says Greta. "That's . . ."

"A fucking miracle," Mo finishes.

"Is it?" I watch a couple of teenagers out on the sidewalk, moving fast arm in arm, their breath visible as they laugh at something one has said. They look so healthy and vigorous with their jutting knees and swinging arms. Like nothing can stop them. "I guess I take it for granted."

Andrew used to tell me it was *my* doing, the fact that we're good at lovemaking. I was happy to take credit, but the truth is, there's never been a time with him when I haven't felt safe. In every conceivable sense of the word, and you have to have that, you absolutely have to have that firm, friendly ground under you, like your native land, before you can . . . take off and go flying around in the wild blue yonder, so to speak. And by the same token, maybe he needs me to yell at him from high up in the thin air, "Come on, let's go for a ride!" So we're a team. Of acrobats, the flashy woman on top, laughing, going "No hands!" the strong, silent man on the bottom, steady as a rock.

It's true—I've had that for so long, I take it for granted.

Mo shakes her head, as if clearing it, and stops staring at me. "Lust is a fever," she pronounces, "and marriage is the powerful antibiotic that cures it."

"Oh *God.*" I make imploring gestures toward heaven. "Would you stop? Poor Greta, she's going to think you're a misogynist."

"A misogamist, you mean. Which I am. Okay, okay—I'm tired of *myself,*" she says, laughing, sprinkling a dash of forbidden salt on her asparagus—and this is why I love her. Just when she starts to get really tiresome, she always pulls up short and boomerangs back into my funny, normal friend. "Greta," she says, stabbing at a piece of dry lettuce, "tell me about yourself. All I know from Dash is that you're perfect."

"She is! She's smart, she's creative—look, she's beautiful." She's blushing. I put my arm around her. "And she's going places, the sky's the limit. Oh yes, I can see it," I say, squeezing poor Greta's shoulders while she wobbles and grins, looking down. She likes it, though. And she needs it. I was lucky, my mother spoiled me with it almost, if you *can* spoil someone with encouragement.

Mo asks Greta if she has a boyfriend, and she glances at me, says yes, and sums up Joel in about two sentences. I trust she's not skipping over him so quickly on *my* account. True, I have very little use for Joel, but I've kept that to myself. I'm sure I have.

"And you like your job, Dash isn't too tough on you? Not too bossy and demanding?"

That's a joke, but Greta's a bit of a literalist. "Oh *no.* She's terrific, I'm learning so much. Today—well," she defers, "you tell her."

"No, you."

"Well . . . this afternoon we're doing a studio shoot, and I'm going to sort of, um . . ."

"Be in charge!" I crow.

"Yeah." She stares out the window with a half smile, rubbing her bare white arms in what I'm sure is nervous anticipation. She's excited, but she's trying to hide it.

"Well, now," Mo marvels, looking at me. "That *is* something."

It is, and she's right to be impressed. Mo knows I'm not one to relinquish control, not in the studio, where my undemocratic reign is supreme. This is a special occasion—but I have confidence in Greta, whose only weakness is lighting. Which, okay, is the whole ball of wax, but I lent her the money to take a lighting seminar to get her up to speed, and in the meantime what she needs most is hands-on *experience*.

"Who are you photographing?" Mo asks.

"A thirteen-year-old girl," Greta says.

"Oh my God, what a horrible age."

"Isn't it?" Greta agrees. "The worst."

"There should be a moratorium on photographing children between the ages of twelve and seventeen," Mo says. "For girls. For boys, eleven to eighteen."

"Thanks, just put me *out* of business."

"Well, really. Go back and look at pictures of yourself when you were a teenager."

"I know," says Greta. "It's a wonder we survived."

"Oh, please, you guys are talking about yearbook pictures. Don't insult me, I'm an artist. And so are *you!* Greta—this girl has no idea how lucky she is. For the rest of her life she's going to look back at the work we do today—*you* do today—and think, 'God, I was cute.' Or '*God,* I wish I'd known how pretty I was, I'd've been so much *happier.*' "

"Really?"

"Really. We're going to take her in hand. That's our job, it's what they pay us for. We're *magicians.*"

"Magicians of light."

"Precisely!" Bright girl.

After lunch, we sip coffee with our elbows on the counter, staring out at passersby, cars, sparrows pecking at the ground under a stalky, municipal maple. At least that's what I'm watching; if he's still there, Mo is probably watching Leather Coat's reflection. I wonder why I'm not more interested in good-looking men, more *personally* interested, not just as fantasies borrowed from Mo's storied love life. For some reason that makes me think of Owen Roby. "You know what I'd love?" I say to my friends. "What I'm really longing for?"

"What?"

"A week off. One whole week away from everything. I want to hole up in the cabin with nobody but the dog and do nothing. Except whatever I want to do."

"Don't you do that already?"

I return Mo's humorously snide look in kind. "No, honey, I'm always interrupting that to come *here*."

"So you need a vacation," Greta prescribes.

"It's more than that. I need aloneness."

"Yes." Mo nods understanding. "I used to have to have that."

"God, not me," says Greta. "I hate aloneness. My roommate's moving in with her boyfriend, she keeps saying. If she ever does, I don't know what I'll do."

"Because you get lonely?"

"Yeah. I mean, it's scary and creepy, it's boring. It's, like, a total waste of time."

"You're single," Mo says kindly. "You have to be married to understand the allure of aloneness."

"That's true," I say. "But then it's practically universal."

"Men, too, or just women?" Greta asks—humoring us.

"Just women."

"Men *hate* being alone," Mo says.

"But we love it. My friend Amy, her husband takes the train to New York on Mondays and comes back Fridays. It's *perfect*."

"Perfect," Mo agrees. "Although it only works if you're married, because then you know they're coming back. It's not that you don't love them *necessarily*—"

"No, no," I say, "it's not that."

"It's just that it's so *great* when they're gone."

"Why?" Greta looks mystified. "If you love them and you have a good marriage, why is it so great when they're gone?"

I'm not sure. I turn to Mo.

"Because you can finally hear yourself think. Gather yourself back together. You've been in a lot of little pieces because you're always dealing with him, listening to him, checking on him, trying to find out what he thinks instead of what you think. Do that long enough, you can lose yourself. Just disappear."

"Yes." Well put.

Mo and Greta get up and go to the ladies' room.

Outside, a woman walks by wearing a long red wool coat exactly like the one my mother used to wear. She wore it for years, all through my childhood. "Red goes with everything," she said, which is true, even if that was the sort of bright, sunny screen she'd use to hide our chronic money worries behind. I myself have owned one red coat or another all my adult life. I make a point of it.

Yearbook pictures. Talking about them reminded me of eighth grade, the day we got our new yearbooks and I raced home to show mine to my mother. I was excited because I was in so *many* pictures, not just the standard class shot but all my various clubs and organizations, even some gratuitous extras like me at my locker, me in the cafeteria, me smacking a volleyball over a net. I was *everywhere,* and just thrilled about it, bursting with pride. I was thirteen, but to this day I haven't outgrown the need to share moments like that with my mother. My biggest fan.

She never disappointed me. That day she was busy in her office— a section of the dining-room table where she did bookkeeping for a paint supply company. She shoved all her work aside, and I remember hanging over her, hugging her neck while she leafed through the pages of my yearbook. "Okay, now go to page 126," I'd say, and she'd look at the next picture of me and rave, "Oh, you look so *cute,* your hair is *darling,*" while I beamed, warm and satisfied, letting that mother-inspired complacency seep through me. That's how it was with us, that's how I remember my childhood: Mama telling me how wonderful I was and me believing her.

"What are you looking at?" Greta bumps me as she sits down, jarring me out of my memories. Sometimes she makes me smile just to look at her. She was the youngest person in yoga class, but not the most graceful. Ah, no. Her golden retriever ungainliness was on full display, her long white arms flailing around more like a children's music conductor's than a yogi's. She wasn't clumsy, though—that's what we old folks are. Clumsy young people are coltish.

"Are you excited?" I ask her.

And sometimes she can look blank as a bison. "About what?"

"The *shoot.*"

"Oh! Yeah. Really excited."

"Don't be nervous, you'll be terrific." I consider going over the lighting design again, but no, that would be information overload at this point. "Where's Mo?"

Greta makes an eloquent gesture with her forehead.

I turn around. "Oh."

Maureen's right, Leather-Coated Man does look familiar, like someone on a book jacket. He's gotten off his stool to speak to her. They look smart and sleek against the bar, one in beige and one in gray, like gracefully aging protagonists in one of those world-weary Woody Allen movies from the nineties. Maureen cocks her head up, coquettish and serious at the same time, listening carefully to everything Mr. Leather Coat says.

"He has an art gallery around the corner, the Unicorn—I knew I'd seen him," she tells me on the street as we're about to part. Greta's said good-bye already and gone on to the studio. "His name is Liam— he invited me to an opening tonight. Ceramics, some woman. Want to come?"

I laugh.

"What? I didn't pick him *up*, you know."

"No, I know."

"No, you're shocked."

"I'm *not*."

"I can see you are." She slips an arm through mine and draws me close as we cross Columbia Road with the light. "But you know, I haven't always been like this. You work up to it, it takes time. If you and Andrew, you know, if it doesn't work out in couples counseling, God *forbid*, you'll get a whole new perspective on men, too. You will."

"Will I?"

"Being single changes everything, it's like waking up from a long sleep. Everything's possible, because nothing's forbidden. Life *throbs* again, Dash—your eyes are *wide open*." She opens her dark eyes wide, for a demonstration. I see alertness and nerves; I see no peacefulness. We hug, and Maureen moves away from me with long, muscular strides, her head up, pocketbook swinging.

I'm aware of setting off with much less confidence, practically tentatively in comparison. Owen Roby crosses my mind again, but only fleetingly, just his shadow. Am I sleepwalking? Without Andrew, would I have a rebirth? Do I *want* a rebirth? Well, of course. I suppose. In the crosswalk, I have a vision of a door opening; it's the front door of a house, soft gold light falling through the crack and shimmering on the ground. What the hell does *that* mean? Nothing, is my hunch. And I can't call it back to look more closely—I'm no better at visions than meditation.

Nothing to do, then, but huddle tighter into my coat and hurry. Don't want to be late for my young protégé's first solo shoot.

ten

Neither of us has ever been in therapy before. Which isn't to say we exist in perfect mental health, ha-ha, far from it, especially Andrew. The truth is—and nobody knows this, not even our closest friends, because for one thing it sounds arrogant, and for another it might hurt their feelings—secretly we think therapy is silly. The quickest way to stop a quarrel between us is for one to say to the other, "What I hear you saying is . . ."

Nevertheless, long ago we made a solemn vow that if, laughably far-fetched as it seemed, anything ever seriously threatened our marriage, we would bite the bullet and go for couples counseling. We wouldn't go down without a fight.

How the mighty have fallen. But this is worse than either of us could ever have imagined. Dr. Fogelman, our new therapist, has just told Andrew it might behoove him to try to cultivate an attitude of gratitude. Andrew's face—I couldn't look at it, but then he pretended he'd misheard the doctor, and said, "A platitude of gratitude?" so then I *could* laugh. Dr. Fogelman even joined in.

"Don't make any snap judgments," Maureen instructed when she gave us his number. "See him at least twice before you decide." "Why, what's wrong with him?" "Nothing! Just don't make up your minds about him right away." We said we wouldn't, but we're both hoping he does better for us than he did for Maureen and Phil. They saw him for six whole months, then split up.

I think Dr. Fogelman is older than he looks, but it's hard to tell. He has thin, whitish hair with a pink tint where his scalp shows through, and a round, boyish, almost whiskerless face. Bifocals. His slacks look like cashmere; his sweater definitely is. When we shook hands, his felt just-washed and unused, and precious to him somehow, like a surgeon's hand. He's a Ph.D., it says on a license over his desk. William B. Fogelman, Ph.D., Marriage and Family Therapy.

He doesn't sit at the desk, though; he sits in one of three large black leather recliners, and Andrew and I take the other two. Dr. Fogelman uses the gearshift thing on the side to make his recliner go back and shoot out the footrest, but Andrew and I just sit in ours. You have to know someone a lot better than we know Dr. Fogelman to recline with him in matching La-Z-Boys.

"Let me tell you a little about myself," he says, which is not the way I would begin a counseling session, but I'm not the one with a doctorate in marriage and family therapy. While he speaks he's careful to look at each of us for the exact same length of time, not a second over, lest we think he's already got a favorite. "I'm one of the half fulls, I'm the kind of guy who tries to make lemonade with the lemons," he says between equal-opportunity glances, crossing his loafers, crossing his hands over his belt. "So far I haven't met a couple I couldn't help, and it's not because I'm so great"—he holds his hands out in mock grandiosity; I assume it's mock—"but because there's never been a couple who couldn't be helped. I believe that, and I hope you do as well, because attitude is everything. Attitude. And the foundation for what I try to give people who come to me, the basis I base my counsel on, is a concept I call— now, don't laugh—the House of Love.

"The House of Love. We'll use all kinds of things in here as we go along, we'll do active listening, role-playing, clarification and communication exercises." From the corner of my eye I see Andrew put his forehead in his hand. "But I always like to start off with some *orientation,* if you will, some locating of where we're going to be spending most of the time during our time together, what *room* in the House of Love we're going to be dealing with most. Or rooms, often it's more than one, or sometimes each party has a different room, or rooms.

"Now, what do I mean by the House of Love? The House of Love has many rooms, and some of them are self-explanatory. The bedroom is self-explanatory—it's where you express your physical affection for each other, it's the physical intimacy place, so that one's easy. The kitchen is the center of your domestic life—it's where your day-to-day life occurs . . ."

And so on through all the rooms of the House of Love, including the attic, which is our past, and the basement, which is the past, too, I think, but also our subconscious minds or something. I know he's going to wind the house tour up by asking us which room we're having the most trouble in.

When he does, Andrew and I just look at each other.

But only for a second, because I am *this* close to cracking up. Andrew knows it, and he also knows that sometimes when I get started, I can't stop. He clears his throat, but luckily I pull myself together and get out before he can speak—because who knows what he might say to baby-faced, optimistic Dr. Fogelman—"I don't think it's any particular room, really. No one room more than any other, anyway. Well . . . it's not the bedroom, I think I can—Andrew, wouldn't you agree? It's not the bedroom?" If he says yes, it is, then all that stuff I told Mo and Greta was a hallucination.

He's not going to answer. He's thinking this question is insupportable on so many levels but primarily inanity, that he's not going to respond.

"And not really the kitchen either," I blather on. "Possibly the attic . . . But no . . ." I peter out. Even to save the doctor's feelings, I have no more to say on the rooms in the House of Love.

Andrew raises one finger. I wait in suspense, thinking of our promise to Maureen. And promise or not, you should give your new therapist longer than twenty minutes before you walk out into the Corridor of Dismay and press the button for the Elevator of Pent-up Snickering. Dr. Fogelman's expression remains pleasant as the silence lengthens; no doubt he's used to waiting his patients out. But if he says, "It's your fifty minutes," there's no telling what Andrew might do.

"I think it might be useful," Andrew says at last, "if perhaps Dash talked for a bit about her mother."

Dr. Fogelman's nose twitches. He lifts his eyebrows at me for permission to be enthusiastic about this suggestion. "Your mother?"

"Really? I should talk about my mother?" Imagine Andrew taking the therapeutic initiative. He nods to me encouragingly. Maybe he's just trying to postpone getting called on himself. Or maybe this is a subtle way to communicate to the doctor that the whole breakup was my fault and he's an innocent bystander.

Or maybe he's right and this is the logical place to start.

"All right, well. My mother . . . died last summer." Incredible that it's still hard to say that word. "It was sudden. And I have ... grief, of course, but it's mixed with so much guilt that it's taking me longer than I think it should to get on with things."

"There's no timetable on grief."

"No, I know, but—"

"Guilt?" Andrew interrupts. "You feel guilt?"

"She was sixty-seven years old and she was still working. She was a bookkeeper, she lived in North Carolina," I tell Fogelman. "We were saving for Chloe's college—that's my excuse. I wanted her to retire, but I never did anything about it. She started working when I was nine because my father died, and she never stopped." I yank a Kleenex out of the box between Andrew's recliner and mine.

"She was my best friend. And she just ... loved me. So much. She thought I was a riot—I could make her laugh till she cried, she'd put her hand on her side and go 'Wooo!' and beg me to stop." I laugh through my tears. "She was so pretty. Wasn't she, Andrew? She could've married again, but I was selfish, I kept her to myself. She could've started a whole new life after my father died, but I wouldn't let her. She thought her main job was to take care of me, make sure I was happy all the time, and I ... I just let her. And then I went off to college and never came back. I abandoned her."

"You went back," Andrew says.

"For visits. It's not the same. I was *her* best friend, too. We should've brought her up here—*I* should've brought her up here. You said you wouldn't mind if she lived with us."

"I wouldn't have."

"I'm sure I haven't thanked you enough for that," I say, blowing my nose with another tissue. "You were always so nice to her. I just wish ..." I wipe my eyes for Dr. Fogelman's benefit, but he might as well know now, I'm a crier. "I wish I'd had more time. To thank her, to tell her I loved her. And everything."

"She *knew* that," Andrew says.

"She was planning to come up for our daughter's high school graduation last June, but then she called and said she was coming down with the flu. And two days later, she had a heart attack."

The men are quiet while I finish my cry.

Dr. Fogelman pats his palms together softly. "I suppose if we were to locate that experience in any particular room, we might say it occurred in the nursery. Because no matter what age we are, in many ways we're always children in relation to our parents. Dash, I hear you saying you weren't prepared to lose your mother, and in a very real sense you're still dealing with her loss. But every ending is a new beginning. You've commandeered a room, and you're not leaving, but can you imagine how that makes everyone else in the house feel?"

Andrew leans over with his hands up, palms out, making a barrier between us and Dr. Fogelman. "I didn't know you felt guilty. It never even occurred to me. Because you were as close to the perfect daughter as anybody could be."

"No, I could've done so much better."

"How? You were the light of her life. Don't you know that?"

"I'm having trouble hearing you," Dr. Fogelman complains.

"Andrew thinks I was a good daughter," I relay.

"And have you forgotten, you *did* invite her to move up here, and she said no."

"I should've insisted."

"She didn't want to leave her friends and come north."

"No, she didn't want to be a burden."

"Dash."

"I should've called her more often."

"You called her all the time. You sent photos, wrote letters, you e-mailed. No daughter could've been more devoted."

This feels like balm on my sore heart. I want Andrew to keep talking, I could listen all night, but Dr. Fogelman starts saying something about how guilt is subjective and the point is that I feel it, not that I necessarily deserve it. There are 1,440 minutes in a day, he says, and it's up to us how many of them we're going to fill with negative emotion. The opposite of "evil" is "live."

"Arlene was a wonderful mother, and you were lucky to have her," Andrew goes on in the same soothing, urgent undertone, "but she was lucky, too. She used to say it all the time, how blessed she was."

"Guilt, of course, is a great motivator. And often overlooked as a—"

"You're a good mother, too. As Chloe would gladly testify."

"Oh," I say, hanging my head in modesty. I want to sit on Andrew's lap.

"Probably because your mother was such a good role model."

"Well, if that's true, it makes the fact that you're one of the world's best fathers even more amazing," I say warmly. "Andrew's father was terrible, Dr. Fogelman. But he inherited *nothing* from him, thank God, not a single trait. Edward's mean, Andrew's kind; Edward's narrow, Andrew's generous and tolerant and open. Comparatively. Chloe adores him—everybody does. He's universally liked. He's been asked to be the chairman of his department."

Dr. Fogelman can't get any more out of us after that. What's left of our fifty minutes we spend lobbing softballs to each other in the House of Love's backyard. Our homework assignment is to write down three things that annoy us or we don't understand about the other, then be prepared to reverse roles and defend the irritating behavior.

We lean against each other in the elevator, smiling at our reflection in the closed doors. I take Andrew's wrist in both hands and squeeze the bones affectionately. "You know, Andrew, you can either be part of the problem or you can be part of the solution."

"Too true. It's nice to be important, but it's more important to be nice."

Out on the sidewalk, we look up and down K Street, happy to be out in the fresh air. We decide to have dinner, since neither of us has eaten. We're not far from Andrew's old law school. "Remember that corner?" he says, pointing across the street.

"Which one?" Washington Circle is a maze.

"You don't remember?" He takes my hand and we walk toward the lot where we left his car. (Why take two, he said, when we're leaving from the same place, practically? Why pay for parking twice?) "The most important turning point in my life, and you don't remember it?" He shakes his head in mock disappointment.

"*Which* corner?"

"The ultimate proof, if any more were needed, that you were the woman I should marry."

I crane my neck, looking behind us. Pennsylvania and Twenty-third? New Hampshire and Twenty-second?

"A hot summer night. We were hungry. And broke." Andrew sighs, as if the last clue pains him, it's so obvious. "You had some guy's guitar."

"Oh!" I laugh, remembering. "*That* was the turning point in your life?"

"Most certainly."

Hot and hungry, that I remember, and broke as usual, we were heading somewhere, me carrying the twelve-string guitar a guy in the band had been trying to teach me to play. We had about five dollars between us. "Let's see something," I said, and sent Andrew away to stand by the Walk/Don't Walk sign. I got out the guitar and began to play the only song I knew, "Mr. Tambourine Man," singing at the top of my lungs to be heard over the traffic. Lo, people hurrying by threw actual money in the open guitar case! That this was a significant moment for Andrew in our relationship surprises me, because I distinctly remember him pretending he didn't know me.

"How much did we make?"

"Twelve bucks and change," he answers promptly, "in just over fifteen minutes." I start to tease him about only wanting me for my money, but he goes on. "I'd never known anyone like you. I looked at you and thought, *She's irreplaceable.*"

"Irreplaceable." That's a funny word.

"You had on torn jeans and sandals, and silver earrings. And a red scarf around your head. Gypsy girl. You took my breath away."

I remember the scarf. I used to throw it over my bedside lamp to make the room look romantic.

Andrew puts his arm around me. "Let's have dinner at home," he suggests.

"Oh yes, let's."

Dinner is only a pretext, of course, a necessary detour on the way to the bedroom. We barely taste our scrambled eggs before we're hurrying up the stairs, Andrew behind me with his hand on the small of my back, not that I need any urging. I wasn't completely candid when I told Dr. Fogelman the problem wasn't in the bedroom. I didn't want to say it, though, in case Andrew didn't know. But he probably knows. Since my mother died, it's been hard for me to get in the mood. I never say no, but I'm not always there. And sometimes at the end, I pretend.

None of that is going on now, though. I can hardly wait. Everything is uncannily natural, I'm even laughing as we stand on opposite sides of the bed to take off our clothes. I do a little striptease at the end. It feels exactly as if I'm drunk.

Then we crawl toward each other across the bed, embrace, and fall over, and it's just right, no wrong moves. We're like acrobats slipping into a favorite routine we've done a thousand times—strong man on the bottom, gaudy woman on top. It's so lovely to kiss. What an intimacy; it's almost deeper than the lovemaking. I've thought of this since we separated, imagined how it would go; I was afraid we'd be self-conscious, too much in our heads, add all sorts of *meaning*. But no. I'm slippery and glad, Andrew is dear and familiar, and we're just our old selves. What made me think I didn't miss this?

Afterward we're languid and tender, making up for our one-track-mindedness before. We don't talk about what we just did. What is there to say? It was simple and it happened, no analysis necessary.

"Okay, now I'm starving," I tell Andrew, and we get up, put on bathrobes, and go downstairs. Hobbes, huddled in his bed by the refrigerator, struggles under all his blankets and finally pokes his head out. Crouching, I kiss him on the nose, sweet old boy. His breath is unbelievable. "Good thing Sock's not here," I tell him, "she'd never give you any peace. All she wants to do is play and play."

"Where is Sock?" Andrew asks.

"Greta took her for me. I'm supposed to pick her up on my way home." It's already ten o'clock. I open my mouth to say, "I should go," but what's the point? He'd talk me out of it so easily, why even start?

I call Greta instead, tell her I got "held up" and ask if I can pick the dog up at her house tomorrow, since neither of us is going in to the studio. She knows everything, I can tell, but she only says, "Sure, Dash, no problem. See you in the morning."

"I love that girl." I move Andrew away from the stove with my hip before he burns the eggs he's trying to reheat in the skillet. "Did I tell you how well she did with her first shoot? The teenager?" Andrew says I told him. "She's redesigning my whole website. 'Primitive,' she called it. Now it's got pop-ups. Andrew, why is there no food in the refrigerator except eggs, capers, and ice cream? What do you eat for breakfast?"

"Eggs with capers."

"Seriously, go to the store and buy some healthy food. You of all people. And why is it so cold in here?" And why am I being so bossy and territorial? Habit, I guess, but I should be wary of sending the wrong message. I'm not here for long.

"I keep the thermostat low if I'm at work all day. Want me to turn it up?"

"No, let's just go back to bed."

The house looks as if nobody lives here. I pause at the bottom of the stairs to survey the pristine living room, every throw pillow in place. "Wow" is all I can say. So this is how he's wanted it to look all these years.

We eat our eggs in bed, and for dessert Andrew pours us little glasses of cognac. He takes the words out of my mouth: "To Dr. Fogelman." Then he adds, "Failing to plan is planning to fail." I can't think of a good riposte. We snuggle against each other.

"Thank you. For the nice things you said about me and my mother."

"Same to you, for the nice things you said about me and my father."

"Do you think Fogelman knows what he's doing?"

"No."

"Maybe he does. What if he brings couples together by making them laugh at him? There's probably some German word for it."

"I suppose he could be an idiot savant."

We start to fool around. But we're so intent on taking our time this time, we fall asleep in the middle. "Old folks," I mumble, waking up enough to get untangled from Andrew and straighten out the bedclothes. "We're so far over the hill, we can't see it anymore."

"If you can't say something nice, don't say anything at all," he whispers against my neck, spooning me.

A few hours later I wake up and get a glass of water, but then I can't fall back to sleep. I'm thinking about my mother again. Andrew says I have nothing to feel guilty about, but he doesn't know. I never told him this.

What grade was I in, eighth again? Somewhere in there, thirteen, fourteen years old. One day I came home from school and Mama's boss, a man named Mr. Dreessen, was there, sitting beside her on the couch in the living room. That was strange—he never came to the house—but I figured he'd come to pick up some work or give her some work she had to do fast for the paint supply company. She only worked part-time, though; only while I was at school. I was never a latchkey kid.

I'd never thought a thing about Mr. Dreessen until that day. Or just that he was old (probably my age now), with reddish hair and wide-spaced eyes, and rather attractive acne scars on his cheeks. The most interesting thing to me was his voice, gruff and raspy from a freak childhood accident: His little brother shot him in the neck with a bow and arrow.

He looked at me in an unusually *aware* way that day, and tried to get me to talk to him—as if he'd never thought a thing about me until then, either. But I was short with him, almost rude. I certainly wasn't a rude child—I was as amazed by my behavior as Mama was, who frowned at me and told me to go in the kitchen and get a snack. I remember what I was doing—making a cottage cheese sandwich—when it hit me. What was wrong with this picture.

My mother had on perfume.

She was a beautiful woman, and not just to me. People were forever telling her she was, it was simply a fact, I grew up knowing it as surely as I knew she had heavy, wavy hair the color of rich coffee, and deep, heavy-lashed gray eyes that could look straight into yours and see all the things that were fine in you, nothing that was small or stingy. She favored flowing, unstructured clothes she made herself—she made all my clothes, too—and she had as little vanity as any woman I've ever known.

She never wore perfume.

She told me about Mr. Dreessen's marriage proposal while we made dinner together, our nightly ritual. I didn't say anything. I don't know what I was thinking, I can't bring my state of mind into clear focus now, but I know I didn't say anything. Nothing. And little by little, she stopped talking, too.

I couldn't leave her, though. I didn't want her out of my sight, or maybe it was me out of hers. After dinner, instead of starting homework or calling a friend or turning on the TV, I stayed with Mama. She always sewed in the evenings—her second job; she "took in sewing," an old-fashioned term even then. I helped pin a pattern for her that night, I pulled the basting out of curtain hems, I rearranged her thread box, neatened her stacks and rolls of material. Mostly I watched her, mesmerized by the deft, half-magical way her fingers flew, guiding a line of flawless stitches under the machine's presser foot. She liked to tell the story of her aunt Janna, who once sewed her own index finger, straight through the nail, to a pair of Grampa Josef's dungarees. I could never watch my mother sew without thinking of that story, and worrying about her. It's the reason I've never touched a sewing machine in my life.

I knew she was waiting for me to say something—marry Mr. Dreessen, don't marry him, are you in love with him, would he make you happy, *something*. But I didn't. As long as I kept quiet, didn't weigh in on either side of the issue, it didn't exist. Having an opinion—and I certainly had an opinion—would make it real, and then some kind of next step would have to be taken. I felt frightened—I felt powerful. I kept my mouth shut.

When I couldn't keep my eyes open another minute, I kissed Mama good night and went to bed.

And the subject never came up again. Soon afterward, she quit her job with Mr. Dreessen and went to work keeping the books for a husband-and-wife insurance company downtown. Mr. Dreessen faded out of my life and out of my mind, and my mother and I stayed at the center of each other's universe. Just the way I wanted it.

Windless mornings in Virginia are so quiet, sometimes the silence sounds like noise. Awakened by nothing, I'll lie in bed and listen as closely as if the stillness were some complicated symphony, alert for a sound coming from anything besides me, my breath, the slide of my skin on the sheet, my hair crackling on the pillowcase. In spring there will be birdsong around the cabin every morning, but now there's nothing. Nothing.

Unlike here.

Andrew singing in the shower isn't what woke me. It wasn't the dogs barking in the alley, or the sound of applause on the *Today* show coming through the wall from Mrs. Melman's bedroom. Two brick walls, some lath, some plaster, that's all that separates these old row houses. Relatively speaking, we paid nothing for ours twenty years ago—although it took everything we had and we're still paying—but prices have gone insane since then, and today it's far and away our biggest asset. If we sold it and moved to Dolley, Virginia, we'd be the Rockefellers.

What woke me up was the paperboy yelling to whoever he yells to every morning, his newspaper supplier, his kid brother, who the hell knows. I've called the *Washington Post* circulation department and complained, I've thrown open the window and shouted, "Quiet!" He's probably not even yelling, he's probably talking in a loud voice, but two unbroken rows of three-story brick town houses across one narrow strip of asphalt produce the acoustics of a rock canyon in Colorado. I'm a completely nonviolent person, and I've lain here dozens of mornings plotting revenge involving BB guns, deep trenches lined with upright bayonets, piano wire. It's not good for me.

I have to pee, but Andrew is still gargling, swishing, and spitting in the sink. The music of morning continues. I see I didn't miss it much.

I locate a clean blouse in the closet and put it on with yesterday's skirt. I don't like this blouse, that's why I left it here, but it'll put a smidgen of doubt in Greta's mind about where I spent the night. Not that it makes the least bit of difference.

Andrew appears in a cloud of steam, piney-smelling, wet hair slicked back. We exchange good-morning pecks in the bathroom doorway. Last night's urgency is over, and I wonder if he's thinking what I am, that maybe passion is simply uncertainty, not knowing if the other is a sure thing or not, and once you feel safe, it flies away. Then he's off down the stairs to take Hobbes out for his morning walk.

Chloe's room is depressingly neat and tidy. I miss the mess. What am I supposed to do with this room now? Make it a guest room, a gym, a sewing room, a present-wrapping room—the other abandoned mothers of my acquaintance have done all of those. It's so incredibly sad. It's pathetic. Why not a bomb-making room, or a chapel? *God.* We don't need another room; what we need is our *children* back.

On the bed are a couple of cardboard boxes holding all my mother's correspondence. I haven't had the heart to go through it yet. One box is nothing but my letters to her. She saved every one.

I have a little cry, but it's not too bad. Talking about her last night must have helped.

Hobbes is so slow, and he has to sniff every single blade of grass along their four-block route, so I'm washed, combed, and trying to figure out what's for breakfast before he and Andrew get back. They don't arrive alone; they picked up Wolfie somewhere en route, who bustles inside with them like he lives here. He greets me as if I've never been away—"Yo, you got any hot chocolate?"—and climbs into a chair at the kitchen table. He always keeps his coat on. We've been pals since the day he fell off his bike practically at my feet—I was planting petunias in the strip of grass by the sidewalk—and I took him inside and doctored him with Bactine and Band-Aids. Afterward I made him some cocoa, which is now the ritual refreshment, summer or winter, whenever he drops by.

"I've got some, but it'll have to be with water. Ditto the pancakes." There's food around here if you dig deep enough, including a box of frozen strawberries behind all the containers of ice cream. I could make strawberry pancakes.

"Where's your dog?" Wolfie asks. "You really name it Sock?"

"She's at a friend's house. Sock, yes. Don't you like it?" I'm not satisfied with the name myself, but it's too late now.

Wolfie shrugs. "What's that?" he asks next, and I turn to see Andrew wrapping the sleeve of his blood pressure monitor around his arm. He explains it to Wolfie, who must then have his blood pressure taken, too. "You sick?" he wonders, logically, when he sees Andrew's morning pile of pills. He has to know what each one is for, the multivitamin, the E, the baby aspirin, the saw palmetto, on and on.

Wolfie draws faces on his pancakes with syrup. "Hey, I missed you," I tell him. "What have you been up to? How's your mom?"

"She's okay."

"How's school?"

"Okay. Lookit this," he says to Andrew, sticking a syrupy finger on a photograph in the sports section. They start talking about basketball.

Andrew has the front page, as usual. He'll keep it until it's too late for me to read anything but the headlines.

"I want some more hot chocolate."

"Dash," I correct, "may I please have another cup of hot chocolate?"

His beautiful brown eyes twinkle. "I *said,* gimme some more o' this hot chocolate! Quick!" He and Andrew chuckle merrily, then look at me with identical complacent smirks.

"You guys are such a riot." I get up and boil more water.

Andrew takes out his leather pocketbook and his thin silver pen, begins making notations. "Hobbes is just about out of arthritis medicine," he says. "Could you stop by the vet's and get some?"

He takes my silence for assent and scribbles a line through an item on his list. He jots down a few more notes. When he's finished, he twists the pen, a gift from his father, closed and returns it with the notebook to the inner pocket of his tweed jacket. Why does he pat the pocket afterward? Always, one reassuring or fond or paranoid pat on the front of his coat whenever he puts his notebook and pen back in the pocket. And he folds the newspaper in half lengthwise, just so, as if he were sitting on a crowded bus instead of at the roomy kitchen table. He takes his pills one at a time, spacing them out so the last one goes down with his last sip of coffee.

I scoop up the sticky dishes and start to rinse them for the dishwasher, but stop myself. I dry my hands. I go out to the living room to retrieve my coat. They don't look up from their newspapers when I return; I have to say, "Guys?"

"Oh," Andrew says absently, "are you going in this early?"

"Just for a little while. Then I'll swing by Greta's for Sock on my way home." I don't say "home" on purpose, I'm not trying to communicate some mean message; it just comes out.

But Andrew's not sure what I meant. His high, handsome forehead creases; he blinks at me through his glasses.

"Buy some food that's good for you," I say, my hand on the back of his neck. "Better put Hobbes's medicine on your list. Last night was fantastic." I kiss him on the mouth. I want to tell him I'm not really leaving because of him—I didn't the first time, either. Not completely because of him, make that. In a way, Andrew's the scapegoat for everything that's gone wrong in my life for months. But I can't say any of that in front of Wolfie.

"And *you.*" Wolfie's shoulders feel bony when I squeeze them, even through the padding of his coat. "You don't be late for school." I lean over and kiss his dusky, syrupy cheek—he's too surprised to squirm away.

"You coming back, right?" he asks.

"Oh, sure." I pause in the doorway. "See you next Thursday," I tell Andrew, who's staring at me now like a fish. "Let's both pick Chloe up at the train station, shall we? And then go out for dinner someplace special. I'll call and cancel Fogelman for that night."

"She coming back, right?" I hear Wolfie ask again as I cross the dining room to the hall.

"Em . . ." I listen for the rest of the answer with the door open, but after a moment I have to go; cold air is blowing in the house.

chloe

eleven

They divide her perfectly evenly, two days with Dad, then two days with Mom, as if they're already divorced.

Chloe watches them tensely at dinner the first night—they take her to the Spanish restaurant she loves—but there's nothing to see. Are they acting? Her mother looks beautiful, candlelight softening her face, and she never stops smiling. She touches Chloe's hand, her arm, and stares at her with wide eyes, as if Chloe's been a hostage for months and the kidnappers just freed her. Her father is grave and funny, but he looks tired. They listen raptly to everything she says, regardless of how trivial. She can't get a fix on them—they're too intent on her.

Will they actually go off in different directions when the evening ends? She knows it's a possibility, but when it happens, it seems so foreign and wrong she can't quite believe it. She feels embarrassed for them. She can hardly say good night to her mother, and when her parents give each other peck-kisses on the cheek, she has to look away. "See you Saturday," her mother calls back cheerily as she walks toward her car. "Saturday," Chloe echoes, following her father toward his.

At home, her room is the same as always, neater but exactly the same, and yet it looks different to her. She remembers herself in it last summer, and that girl isn't her anymore. The difference is complicated, she only understands pieces of it. It makes her lonely and sad to think that her mother and father, for all their attentive watching and listening, don't understand any of it.

"Night, sweetheart." Dad pokes his head in the door, hesitant, always mindful of her privacy. He has on the tartan bathrobe she and Mom gave him two Christmases ago. "What are you studying?"

"*Antigone.*" She moves some notebooks aside and pats the bed, and he comes in and sits down at the end, crossing his long legs, keeping his hands in his pockets. In some ways, she misses the days when he would sprawl on the bed and "accidentally" disarrange whatever she had just arranged so carefully on it: paper dolls, stuffed animals, her homework. "Daddeee!" He'd pretend to be horrified and apologetic, putting everything back wrong, and she'd end up laughing, or tackling him and starting a wrestling match.

"*Antigone*," he says, impressed. "Lend it to me, I've never read it. Who do you play, again?"

"Eurydice, Antigone's boyfriend's mother. I commit suicide in the end."

"Why?"

"Because my son kills *him*self, and it's all Creon's fault—my husband." Her father smiles and shakes his head, looking pleased and perplexed. "You're really liking this drama course."

"I love it."

"I was surprised when that was your elective."

"You don't mind, do you?"

"Of course not. Mind?"

"You don't think I should've taken a writing course or public speaking? Something practical?"

"Not if you like this better. You can be practical when you graduate."

It's only since she got to college that Chloe appreciates how unusual her parents are in this respect. They never pressure her about grades, majors, careers, all the things her friends' parents are obsessed with. Her mother thinks she's brilliant; she jokes that Chloe is Andrew's *first* wife's daughter.

"What do you want to do tomorrow?" Dad asks. "I've got a pretty full day, a ten-thirty class and then a meeting at one, so—"

"Can I go with you? I could study in the library while you're in class. I've got plenty of work to do."

His face lights up. "Really? That would be great. You'll have to eat cafeteria food, though."

"I'm used to it." They grin at each other. She hasn't spent the day with him at school in a long time. It used to be one of their favorite things to do together.

"And then, how about a movie tomorrow night?" he suggests.

"Or a play. How about a play, Dad? Something incredibly obscure and avant-garde. With audience participation."

"Chloe, my God, it's uncanny. How did you know that's *exactly* what I wanted to do?"

"Dad?" she says seriously.

"Hm?" He takes off his glasses and leans over to polish them on the hem of his pajama bottoms. He thinks she's going to ask him about Mom.

That wasn't it, though. She was going to ask him what he would think if she decided not to major in history. But now she's afraid. What if it hurt his feelings? And he has so many other things on his mind. It might be better to go through Mom on this.

"I was just wondering how you're doing," she says instead. "You and Mom, it's so . . . weird, isn't it?"

Without his glasses, his eyes always look defenseless; tonight they look sad, too. "You know it's got nothing to do with you, right?"

"Right. I do."

"Good. Okay."

"So . . . what does it have to do with?"

He sighs. He rubs his forehead. His face looks craggier since the last time she saw him. He makes an empty-bowl gesture with his hands, then lets them flop back in his lap. "It's just a break. After twenty years, sometimes people need a break."

People. His discretion makes her want to cry. It makes her want to yell at her mother. Nobody has to tell Chloe this is all her doing.

She says, "Oh, okay," as if he's convinced her, and she agrees with him when he tells her not to worry, everything's going to be fine. They're seeing a counselor, and it's going very well. This is a *positive* thing, he assures her, something all old married folks should probably go through every twenty years or so, whether they need it or not.

She puts her arms out to hug him good night. He smells like toothpaste. He lets go before she wants to.

"Could you believe that guy?"

"What guy?" Chloe asks absently, slowing for a car trying to merge into their lane on the Roosevelt Bridge.

"Joel." Her mother gives Sock, who's sitting on her lap like a hood ornament, a kiss on top of the head. "Greta's boyfriend. What a *clinger*."

"I thought he was sort of cute."

"No, he's too old. Did you see how he held on to her? Like she was his birthday helium balloon. Greta could hardly *pivot*."

Chloe met Greta and Joel this morning at her mother's studio. He seemed fine to her, a typical young Washington professional—they're everywhere. And he wasn't old, he was about thirty. She can't understand her mother's hostility.

"Greta's great, though, isn't she? I just love her. So bright and creative. She reminds me of you."

Chloe laughs. She thinks it's more likely that bubbly, sweet, eccentric-looking Greta reminds Mom of herself.

"Mm, smell the spring. Can you smell it?"

"Mom, it's freezing. What spring, it's still February."

"Wimp." Her mother puts her window up. "The earth is warming up a little every day. I've had crocuses behind the cabin for a week."

"Is it weird being there by yourself?" Chloe asks casually.

"No! No, it's great, I'm having the best time, it's really . . ." She stops and backs up. "Well, no, I mean, but it's not . . . oh, you know, it's *fine*."

Chloe keeps silent. *Let her put her whole foot in her mouth,* she thinks. *I won't help out.*

Mom goes back to the subject of nature. "You could drop me down in an empty field and I'd know if I was in Maryland or Virginia just by the lay of the land." She throws an arm around the back of Chloe's seat. "And Maryland and North Carolina, they might as well be on two different sides of the planet. Mama used to say it's because of the color of the rocks—ours are brown and theirs are gray. They being northerners."

She talks about her mother a lot. Chloe thinks that's probably a good thing, therapeutic and all, but she wonders if her mother realizes that when she does it, she slips into a southern accent. It's unsettling.

"There's just something about the hills in Virginia, the way they get vaguer in the distance, the long views. It's . . . I don't know . . . tolerant or something. Forgiving. I just like the loose, slatternly look of things so much better than the neat, tidy, uptight North, don't you? There's an *attitude* here. 'Come on in,' it says—doesn't it?"

Chloe looks around at the shopping centers and apartment complexes on Route 29.

"Not yet," her mother clarifies; "when we get out in the country. The valleys and hills, the fence posts, the tumbledown barns. Whereas up North they say, 'Oh, hello. I wish you'd called first.' "

Mom's cackle sets Chloe off; they have a nice laugh. She sees that this is how the visit is going to go, her anger and exasperation with her mother constantly sidetracked by jokes and good times. The irresistible pull of her mother's charm.

Downtown Dolley looks dreary and even smaller in winter without the leaves of the maple trees practically meeting in the middle over Madison Street. It's only four blocks long, with a two-way blinking yellow light at the intersection of Madison and Monroe. Chloe doubts any cars have ever collided there, though; they probably put the light up just so no one could call Dolley a no-stoplight town.

Mom has a post office box, now that she lives here. She wants to get her mail, and she makes Chloe come in with her. "To show you off—you've never met the girls. They know all about *you.*"

Lori, Carla, and Margie, the entire staff of the Dolley post office, are there, and back in the car, Chloe can't disagree with her mother about how nice they are. "They'll call you up if they think you've got a package that's important," Mom brags. "If you're short on money, they say, 'Oh, pay me when you think of it.' They'll let you use their phone for a local call—I mean, try *that* at any post office in D.C."

It's true; you have to talk to the clerk through a scratchy Plexiglas shield at the one on Irving Street. Chloe thinks her mother's trying too hard, though. Why is she so gung ho Dolley and the Virginia countryside today? Is she planning to *move* here?

"You know who else is dying to meet you? Cottie Bender." Mom looks at her watch. "We could pop in for two seconds—but only if you want to. Really, we wouldn't stay."

"No, it's fine, whatever *you* want to do." They're being a little stiff with each other, still a little polite. Because of the circumstances. And because her mother, Chloe can tell, is terrified that she'll be bored. "Should we call first?"

Mom leans over the dog and digs her cell phone out of her purse.

Mrs. Bender isn't at all what Chloe was expecting. She's not glum and speechless like her husband, who scared Chloe when she first met him. Mrs. Bender comes to the door in jeans and a lavender turtleneck and says, "Well, hey! Come in, come on in, it's so good to meet you, Chloe. Let me look at you." She puts one hand on Chloe's shoulder and one hand on Mom's. "Both of you, you're so *beautiful*."

Chloe doesn't believe she's beautiful, but her mother is. She envies her carelessness, the way she never fusses with her makeup or clothes, and yet she always looks great. She's got so much life under her skin, she glows. She loves her mother's "postmodern pompadour"—Dad's term for her loose, floppy hairstyle. Next to her, Chloe always feels too well groomed. Buttoned down.

They sit in the kitchen, where Mrs. Bender says, "Eat, eat," like an Italian grandmother, pushing almond cookies, nut roll, peanut butter fudge, marble cake. "I see the church ladies are still at it," Mom says, then tells Chloe about Mrs. Bender's heart operation—she's forgotten that she already told her. The church ladies must not have heard of coronary artery disease, Chloe muses, sampling a brownie.

Mrs. Bender is good at drawing her out. She's usually reserved with strangers, but she finds herself telling Cottie—she insists on being called that—about her classes and professors, her roommate's parents' upcoming divorce, her role in *Antigone*. "She's majoring in history, though," Mom mentions, as if Chloe might've forgotten. "Like father, like daughter."

Cottie speaks of her own daughter, Danielle, who lives in Richmond. "She never went to college, just never had much interest in that direction. I wish we saw her more often, but she's got her life." Mom nods in sympathy. Chloe almost blurts out that she wants to live in New York City after graduation, but it doesn't seem like the right time.

They've stayed longer than they intended, but just as they're getting ready to go, old Mr. Bender comes in the back door with another man. They both have on filthy dungarees and stained jackets, and their hands are black with grease. They've been out back working on Mr. Bender's truck, Cottie explains, getting up to make introductions. "Shevlin, you know Chloe, Dash's daughter."

Chloe says, "Hi," and Mr. Bender actually grins, and tips his hat more pleasantly than he ever has before. Mom's doing: She's buddies with the Benders now, even grumpy old Shevlin.

"And Chloe, this is Owen Roby," Cottie goes on, "our son-in-law. Chloe's just home from college for the weekend."

She's heard about Owen from Mom, who hires him to do things around the cabin. He shrugs and makes a face at his dirty hands, as if he'd shake if he could. "Heard a lot about you," he says with a shy smile. He has gold-tipped eyelashes and pale-blue eyes, a thick, aggressive body just short of stocky. He's not that old, but he's going bald. He reminds her of Garth Brooks.

She says that later, in the car, when her mother asks what she thought of him.

"Garth Brooks!" Mom is indignant, practically insulted. "Oh, he does *not*. You're crazy."

"I thought he did. A little."

"He does not. Garth Brooks. Good God." She shakes her head and mutters wondering disparagements under her breath for the next mile or so.

Chloe perceives she's said the wrong thing.

"That was Emily." She closes her cell phone and resumes her seat in the easy chair by the potbellied stove. Mom's in the rocking chair beside her; they're sharing the footstool. Sock takes turns sitting in their laps. It's after midnight. The only heat in the cabin upstairs comes from the stove downstairs, so it's important to put off going to bed as long as possible. Which is easy to do when you're warm and comfortable and half asleep anyway from the long day and all the hot chocolate you've drunk.

"Everything okay?" Mom asks.

"Her parents filed for divorce. She just wanted to tell me."

"Poor thing. Is she very upset?"

Not as upset as I would be, Chloe thinks. "She's okay. Basically. She knew it was coming."

"You know, Mo . . . ," Mom says, then hesitates.

"What?" Chloe has known her mother's friend Maureen practically her whole life. She and Mom are always trying to get Chloe and Maureen's son Mark together. As if.

"Mo said her divorce was like living through a war. Like having her skin burned off and her limbs . . . amputated."

They look at each other gloomily.

Chloe cannot imagine her parents divorced. Apart from everything else, who would they be with if not each other? Worse, what if by some horrible miracle they each found someone exactly like them? It would be like inbreeding, like corrupting the gene pool.

Mom goes back to her laptop—she can clean out files and do simple photo work from here—and Chloe tries to go back to her play. *The message of a household woe smote on mine ear: I sank back, terror-stricken, into the arms of my handmaids, and my senses fled . . .*

"Mom?"

"Mm."

"Are we ever going to talk about you and Dad?"

Her fingers go still on the keys. "We can talk about anything you want. Always." She doesn't look up, though. But then, finally, she sighs, closes the laptop, and folds her hands on top. "Okay, first. I want to be sure you understand it has nothing to do with you, absolutely—"

"I know it has nothing to do with me. I get that, Mom, and I don't feel guilty or responsible or anything."

"Oh. Okay. Good."

"And you should understand that you don't have to tell me anything you don't want to."

"Honey—honestly, there's not that much to tell. We're taking a little break. That happens even in the best marriages."

God! It's like they rehearsed. "Do you still love each other?"

"Of course. Yes." Mom has black-rimmed gray eyes that can look positively ingenue-like when she's telling a gigantic whopper, Chloe's seen it a dozen times. She's not lying now, though.

Chloe feels less fear, more aggravation.

"But you still can't go home?"

Her mother shakes her head.

"But what if it becomes a habit? I mean, how can you be sure this is temporary? What if you give up, or you run out of energy? Shouldn't you at least be *trying* to get back together?"

"But we are, we talk all the time—we have a *therapist*." She laughs and shakes her hands, communicating that having a *therapist* is the ultimate sacrifice.

"Dad doesn't get it," Chloe says sullenly.

"Why? What did he say?"

"Nothing, no details, don't worry."

Twice Mom starts to say something, both times she stops.

Chloe plays with the dog's ears.

"It was nice of you to go with him to visit your grandfather yesterday," Mom says. "I'm sure Edward appreciated it."

"We took Hobbes. I think he's going a little mental."

"Hobbes or your grandfather?"

Chloe can't help laughing. This is how her mother dodges the issue, by changing the subject and making jokes. "Grampa. Although Hobbes isn't doing that great, either. I don't know which one is deafer."

They yawn at the same time.

"I'm going to go down to Greensboro in June," Mom says.

"You are?" She stops herself from asking if that won't conflict with the summer session in *veterinary medicine* her mother is thinking of taking. *Insanity.*

"Yeah. You'll be out of school by then—wanna come with me? Mama's anniversary. One year. I haven't visited the grave since . . ."

She pretends "since" is the end of the sentence, but Chloe knows she still can't say "died." "Hey, Mom, did you know . . ."

"Did I know what?"

"Did you know when you talk about Gran, you start talking in a southern accent?"

She snorts. "I do not."

"Yes, you do. Not all the time."

"I do not."

"Wanna come?" Chloe mimics. "Ah haven't visited the *gra*-ave . . ."

Her mother stares at her. "My God."

"It's probably normal," Chloe assures her quickly—Mom looks almost frightened. "You just miss her, so it comes out. I'm sure that's—"

"I gave it up in college," she interrupts, wide-eyed. "My accent—I got rid of it on purpose. I stamped it out. I didn't want to sound"—her voice breaks—"like a hick." To Choe's horror, she starts to cry. "Oh, Mama," she sobs into her hands.

Chloe stands up, but she doesn't know what to do. She hovers. After a while her mother lifts her head and sniffs the tears back on a long, deep inhale. "Sorry." She rubs her wrists over her eyes and gives a wet laugh. "Boy, that was stupid."

Chloe figures out what to do. She puts her arms around her.

Immediately everything is better. "I love you, baby," her mother says. "I love you intensely."

"Me, too, Mom."

Uh-oh, she's crying again. "I almost took my mother's last *name*," she says between little hiccups. "Dash Tirva. Dear God in heaven. But don't worry, everything's going to work out."

"I know."

"Your father and I are going to be *fine*."

"I know."

"We'll probably be *better* when this is all over."

"I wouldn't be surprised." Chloe's neck starts to ache from the bending-down position she's in. "Mom?"

"Yes, sweetheart?"

She squeezes her mother's shoulders. They're sort of bosom to bosom, cheek to damp cheek. "You've gone a little nuts, haven't you?"

"I have, baby," Mom says weakly, not even hesitating. She nods her head against Chloe's, tangling strands of their hair between their faces. "I've gone a little nuts."

dash

twelve

"*A*ndrew's coming, but he'll be a little late—he had a meeting that went longer than he expected."

"Ah."

"So I just came on. We thought it would be better if one of us was on time." *At the rate you're charging,* I don't say. It's on my mind because it's what Andrew, driving down Rhode Island Avenue, just said to me on his cell phone. After Chloe's visit, we had to skip two sessions in a row—first Andrew had something better to do, then I did—so it's a good thing Dr. Fogelman doesn't make you pay for missed appointments.

He smiles in a pleasant, professional way I don't quite know how to take yet. I wonder if psychiatry really works, or if we could do it almost as well by ourselves. On the other hand, I could see someone like, say, *me* being a very good therapist. I'd be nurturing and softhearted, totally sympathetic to almost everyone, because almost everyone deserves it. I'd give intelligent, healing advice people would be wise to take. So I don't know. Maybe it works.

"Would you like to hear a dream, Dr. Fogelman?" I feel like entertaining him while we wait. He's just sitting there, tapping his fingers together. He has on another cashmere sweater, yellow V-neck, with a button-down shirt and wrinkled slacks. He looks tired. Poor man. Long day, then Andrew and I show up at 7:00 p.m. and unload on him.

"Please, call me Bill."

"Bill." It sounds strange, but so does "Dr. Fogelman" out loud. This is the first time I've called him anything. "It's a recurrent dream," I say to entice him. "I've had it for years. It starts out, I'm on a highway or a road, and something's at the end that I want very badly, but I can't move toward it. It's a curvy road, not straight, so I can't see the end, either. Sometimes there's a brass band playing on both sides of the road: tuba, saxophone, drums. A triangle. And a conductor in a short-sleeved shirt with skinny white arms. I say, 'You can't keep me here,' or something like that, but he just keeps conducting. That's it.

"That's the dream," I say again when Fogelman just looks at me, his face blank but still pleasant. Maybe he's perfected a way to fall asleep with his eyes open. Or he's waiting for *me* to interpret the dream. In spite of the proverbs and the House of Love and all, I feel rather fond of Dr. Fogelman. I think of him as a required prelude to good times and excellent sex with Andrew. He's like homework you have to finish before you can go out and play.

He speaks. "Were you an only child?"

I'm nodding when there's a knock at the door. "Yes," he calls, and Andrew comes in, loose and jaunty in his school uniform, vigorous-looking, his hair a little mussed. The air is soft and sweet in Washington tonight, and it's cheering everyone up. "Sorry I'm late." We smile our public smiles, but underneath we're sharing a secret: *tonight*. We air-kiss self-consciously, brushing cheeks. His whiskery cheek smells fresh as spring.

Fogelman wants to get right to it: no pleasantries, straight to our homework.

"F-E-A-R," he begins. "False Evidence Appearing Real. That's what fear is, and it's what drives most of our misunderstandings with each other. And how do we defeat it? With forgiveness." He smiles, Buddha-like. He's really a nice man, but I thought shrinks mostly sat back and listened. This one gives sermons.

He quotes a Chinese maxim, he quotes Winston Churchill. He wants us to tell three things that we don't "understand" about each other—three things we hate, in other words—and then pretend we're the other and explain why we do what we do. "Remember, this is not an exercise in faultfinding," he says, leaning forward and making earnest gestures, "but in empathetic thinking, putting yourself in the other's place. Think of the African saying 'He who forgives ends the quarrel.' Let's get some of our disappointments and disagreements out in the open, and then we can start to shine the light of understanding on them. Dissolve the phantom of fear with forgiveness."

Okay. I'm in favor of forgiveness and understanding. But what a downer, like sleet on the cherry blossoms. Andrew and I look at each other—he's pulled the stick on his chair and is actually reclining along with Dr. Fogelman—with wry, helpless expressions. Fogelman asks who'll go first.

"I will," I say to be a good sport, but I've got no enthusiasm for this. I didn't prepare, either; I forgot the assignment as soon as he gave it to us.

And yet my first gripe slides out like cranberry sauce from a can. "Andrew's a hypochondriac."

I haven't said the actual word to him in a long time, not since his symptoms were just beginning. When they were still sort of cute. Before I knew I'd have to put up with them the rest of my life.

"I am not." He won't return my smile. I can't believe he's offended!

"Yes, you are. You are, Andrew. How could you not know that?"

"I'm careful about my health, as any reasonable fifty-year-old man with heart failure in the family would be."

"Your father's eighty—it doesn't count."

"Of course it counts. Why do you always speak of things you know nothing about with such authority?" He doesn't smile when he says that, either!

"Is that one of the things about Dash that bothers you, Andrew? Hold off on that for a moment if you would, I'd like to go in a different order."

"No, I just thought of it. It's not on my list."

I stare at him. "You made a *list*? Of course you made a list. Of course he made a list. That's Roman numeral I, Sub A on *my* list—his incessant list making."

"You can't have subnumbers. Three things, that's it. Believe it or not, the rules apply to you, too."

"Excuse me," Fogelman says, making a time-out sign with his hands. "Dash, I'm hearing from you that Andrew has issues about his health—and now it's your turn to role-play as Andrew, who's expressed some reservations about your opinion."

"Okay, all right." I can see how this could get very childish very quickly. "All right, I'm Andrew. This is what I have to say about my hypochondria." Andrew rears up. "What my wife *thinks* of as my hypochondria, excuse me. It started when we had Chloe. Before that I was normal—ha-ha, relatively speaking—but Dash had a hard time with the birth, in fact she almost died. So I *guess* that did something to me. I don't know how it works, why I'm now obsessed with *my* health instead of theirs, but that's the way it came out."

Andrew gazes at the ceiling, his martyred-saint look. "Do I need to point out that that's *not* what I would say?"

"Chloe fell out of a willow tree at my mother's house—sorry, my mother-in-law's house—when she was four and a half, and after that it got worse. He was a wreck, no help at all, my *rock,* and basically he went to pieces."

" 'I,' " Fogelman corrects. "Remember, you're Andrew."

"I, Andrew, me. Anyway—no, see, the problem is, Bill, I have no idea why Andrew is the way he is, so how can I explain it to you?"

Andrew's dramatic sigh is so heavy, I can see it filling the room with gray air.

"We're getting a little off track. It's important to stay in character when we role-play, really work on putting ourselves in the other's place. It's difficult but not impossible with a little practice and good faith. Before we go on, though, I'd like to sidetrack for a sec. Dash, you said something interesting—you said Andrew was your 'rock.' Could you elaborate on that?"

"Oh, you know, that he's steady and sensible, that I depend on him. My rock." I sit up. "But in the hospital, I was in a difficult labor with my first and only child, and he's yelling at the doctor, 'I knew it, I knew it! They're both going to die!' Such a comfort. Chloe got a concussion when she fell, and he *left* me. In the *emergency room.* I found him walking around in the parking lot smoking a cigarette—he'd bummed it from somebody, he doesn't even smoke! So that's the first thing on my list. It didn't used to bother me, but now it does. It's not terrible, and I know it's his problem, not mine, worse for him than me and all that. I guess I'm just tired of it. It feels like I'm living with a crazy man."

Something's happened to me in the last few minutes. I've lost my desire to soften what I say so it doesn't sound critical. I want to spit these things out like cherry pits, even if they hurt Andrew's feelings. It's Fogelman who's making it possible, and not in a good way, not like a kindly referee who'll keep us safe—more like a mob egging me on, urging me to let go of my discretion and inhibitions and my usually decent instincts. It's thrilling and perverse and irresistible.

"So, now what? Does he get a turn or should I keep going?"

"I think we'll give Andrew a turn," Bill says, as if he's breaking with his customary practice. Uh-oh. He wants to minimize the ganging-up factor in this game, but suddenly I don't want to hear Andrew's number one complaint against me. Why didn't Bill ask us to pick three things we *appreciate* about each other? Telling three things we're grateful for would bring us *together*, which you'd think would be the point of couples counseling. No wonder Maureen and Phil split up.

At least Andrew doesn't take out his notebook. Or is it worse that he has his list memorized? "My three are in no particular order," he begins, and immediately I resent it that he has a warm, clear, teacher's voice, carrying but not loud. It makes the words sound important even when they're not, like a British accent, obviously an unfair advantage to him and a disadvantage to me in the circumstances. "Number one is unpredictability. And I should say, in the same way my so-called hypochondria used to not bother Dash, her . . . I suppose *inconsistency* is another word, used to not bother me. But now it does."

"All right, very good. And if you were Dash, what would you have to say to that? *You're unpredictable.* What might be her response?"

" 'Yes, but it's part of my charm. What fun is consistency, the hobgoblin of little minds?' "

"I would never say that."

"Quite. Because you don't know Emerson. May I continue? As I said, this only became a problem within the last year or so. Before that—"

"A problem for who?"

"For whom. For me, but I should think also for you."

"Let's remember to—"

We wave Bill off.

"So it *was* part of my charm, back when you were the kind of man who could appreciate unpredictability or whatever you call it. *Spontaneity*—that's what you *used* to call it. And please don't correct my grammar in public."

"I don't mind unpredictability, actually. It's unreasonableness and irrationality I find hard to 'appreciate.' "

"Oh, now we're getting to it."

"Much less live with. My second item is 'constant upheaval,' and I see it's related—in fact, it's basically the same thing."

"Wait, you can't do your second thing first, it's my turn—finickiness. And if I were you, I'd say, 'It's not finickiness, it's neatness. I'm an orderly man, I have to have a place for everything and everything in its place. My wife's a slob. I alphabetize my record collection. You could eat off the floor now that she's left me. I wear the exact same outfit every day because—well, the hell if I know. No, I know—because it simplifies my life and I have more time to think deep thoughts. I don't bother communicating them to her, though, because they're mostly over her head. I have a Ph.D. and she barely got out of college. She probably had dyslexia or attention deficit disorder growing up, but it was a backward little southern town so nobody noticed.' "

Silence.

"Interesting. Some hostility, clearly, I think we can—"

"Emotionalism," Andrew cuts in. "Romanticism, sentimentality, illogic, exaggeration."

"That is so unfair! Tell him—he only gets one more. I could do that, too, if I wanted, but it wouldn't be fair. Like emotionally remote. And no sense of humor about himself."

"Emotionally remote—that's code for I won't join in when she tries to pick a fight."

"I'm not finished. Pride, too much pride—he gets it from his father. And it's his fault I'm a photographer, he forced me into it."

"Now, let's—"

"What?" Andrew grabs for the lever on his chair. He gets the ottoman part down, but not the seatback—he's stuck, he can't stand up.

I laugh.

He rocks back and shoots himself out of the recliner, stumbling from the momentum into the foot end of Bill's chair. My God, he's furious. He stalks to Bill's desk and stands behind it, as far from us, from *me,* as he can get in this small room. His face is streaky red. We look at him, Fogelman craning around backward, and wait for him to speak, but he can't, he's too angry.

It was nice of him to demonstrate my "no sense of humor about himself" claim so promptly. Bad form to thank him for it right now, I suppose. Anyway, I feel terrible; I'm not taking any pleasure from this at all. But it's *funny*. Why couldn't he laugh when he got stuck in his chair?

"What I meant was," I say calmly, "I was young and I had a lot of ideas about what I wanted to be. It's ancient history, yes, and it's a cliché, and I don't even blame Andrew for it—but it's true that after we got married I had no more professional choices."

"Professional choices."

Such sarcasm, such disbelief he says that with, I pitch the last dregs of my interest in saving his feelings. "Yes, Andrew, *professional choices.* I had a lot of promise."

"You walked other people's dogs."

"I had odd jobs while I was trying to find myself, but I had talent and it could've gone anywhere. But now we'll never know."

"We know it didn't go into Crowd Control."

"Goon Squad—that's a band I was in," I explain to Bill. "We had a very progressive musical sound, over Andrew's head."

"They had noise. Talentless decibels."

"That's right, only you had talent. *Your* career was important, mine was frivolous."

"I was getting a law degree; you were screeching into a microphone in your boyfriend's basement. You tell me which was frivolous."

I stand up, too.

"You talk of talent, promise, potential," Andrew keeps on. "The truth is, you had no direction at all. You should thank me, not hold it against me that you found your life's work trying to make some money for us when we were young and struggling. It's what anyone would've done—it's not heroic that you went to work while I went to graduate school."

It's not the words I hate so much as that infuriatingly reasonable tone, as if he's talking to a mental patient on a ledge. "You know," I say ominously, "I don't think you should talk to me about jobs."

"What does that mean?"

Fogelman's gone silent. He sits moonfaced, following us with his eyes through the tops of his bifocals. If this was his plan all along, to set us at each other's throat, it worked.

"It means you're stuck in a rut."

"Oh, this again." Andrew smiles thinly at Fogelman while he tosses a roll of Tums in the air and catches it. "My wife thinks I'm a failure, in case you hadn't picked up on that yet."

"I have never said that to you, never. I *would* never."

"You don't have to say it, you make it clear at every faculty event we've ever attended."

"I do *not*. And I *don't* think you're a failure, I just think you should admit it—you're jealous of Peter Flynn. What you're agonizing over is not a moral quandary, Andrew, it's not about Thomas Jefferson, it's about them hiring a younger man to teach the same subject you do. You were insulted and hurt, and you can't get over it. You'd rather stay stuck in your rut and not advance even though you deserve that job than give in and write one damn chapter in Peter's book. And you call *me* unreasonable."

"This isn't the first time she's left me, you know." Andrew circles the desk as he pops antacids in his mouth and crunches down violently. "It's just the first time she hasn't been able to run off to her mother."

"What does that have to do with anything?"

"Once before our wedding—"

"Cold feet!"

"And once before Chloe was born."

"Hormones!"

"Everyone thinks she's this Mother Earth figure: Dash is so generous, oh, Dash has such a big heart, she rescues people, she'd do anything for anybody—yes, when everything's going perfectly. When life is exactly the way she wants it, she couldn't be more obliging." He stops talking to Fogelman and rounds on me. "This may come as a shock, but you're not the first woman to lose her mother."

"Don't you *talk* about my mother."

"Or hit middle age, or have a child go off to college."

"You leave my mother out of this."

"Why?"

"Because I said so!"

"Here we go." He puts his hands in his hair. "The sprinkler system is on."

There's a fake fireplace in the corner of Fogelman's office. It has real gravel on the brick hearth, supposed to look like ashes. The knots and burls and burned ends of the logs look about as real as papier-mâché. A fat tear plops on the veneer mantel I'm holding onto with both hands. I want my woodstove. I want my mother's chair and the dog in my lap, silence all around, nobody talking.

Fogelman finally says something. "I'd like to change the focus, try something different. You've given some of your conflicts an airing, some ways in which there's not as much harmony as you want, and I think we've laid some groundwork for goals and directions we'll want to take and explore in the weeks ahead, months ahead. Let's keep going and talk about some positive changes you could begin to strive for in your relationship."

"Changes." I leap on the word. "I do want changes, that's what this whole thing is for—I never wanted us to separate for *nothing*. Andrew's the rock, and that's good, but rocks are sedentary. I'm trying to *do* things. I'm thinking about a whole new career. I'm reading about world religions, I'm making new friends, people as unlike me as I can imagine. I'm taking yoga."

Andrew's got his arms folded, unimpressed.

"What are *you* doing?" I challenge. "What do you want? You are so damned *passive*. Don't you want *anything*?"

"Yes. I want peace and quiet."

"Well, you've got 'em now, haven't you?" I say nastily.

"And I'm enjoying them more than I ever imagined possible."

"Good." Oh, that hurts. I thought he was lonely. He's still angry, but I can see he's telling the truth. I hate this game.

"What are you enjoying about it?" Fogelman asks.

"The calm. The lack of surprises. People have been very kind to me."

"Who?" I ask. "Who's being kind to you?"

He raises his eyebrows at me. He removes his glasses and takes out the special cloth he uses to polish them. "Mrs. Melman comes over to walk Hobbes every day. Women at work bring me food. Tim and I go out together in the evenings."

"Who brings you food?"

"Miriam."

Oh, Miriam. The department secretary.

"Elizabeth O'Neal."

"Elizabeth O'Neal! She can cook? What does she make you, black-bird pies?"

He ignores me, speaks to Fogelman. "What I like about it is the sanity. It's tranquil, there are no upsets, no drama. Before she left, I felt like I was shrinking. Dash got bigger, I got smaller." A sour laugh. "The incredible shrinking man."

The words are bad enough, they're like knives in the chest, but I can't believe he's saying them to *Fogelman,* a *stranger,* a man he's going to write a check to when this hour is up, if it ever is. I turn away, my hand on my throat. I keep swallowing; I won't give him the satisfaction of more tears. If you can't take the heat, get out of the kitchen—Fogelman hasn't used that one yet. I'm burned, seared, I've stayed in here way too long.

Andrew's not finished. "Since I've been on my own, it's as though I can breathe again, stretch out and be myself. I'm sorry Dash lost her mother, and I'm sorry that to her it's as if she's losing a daughter, but I can't do anything about it. I can't replace them. I wish I could, but I can't. And I'm exhausted trying. I need a rest. You ask what I want? I would love to be bored."

I rally for a second. "Bored? Is that what you said? That's a—that's a *terrible* goal. Obviously—I don't know who you are anymore. You want everything I don't—I assume vice versa. Do we even *like* each other?"

Andrew shakes his head, which I hope means "I don't know," not "no."

I'm learning how thin-skinned I am. I'm parchment, sheer as gauze. This has never happened to me before in a fight with Andrew. I was tough, flamboyant, I used to throw things. But he never said he was happier without me. I snatch up my coat, noticing too late that the sleeve has a split at the seam—my arm goes in the wrong track. My exit's ruined.

"I'm not coming back," I tell Fogelman as I struggle with the coat, struggle not to cry, not to look at Andrew. "I, too, am much, much better on my own, so there's no reason to keep pretending this is all going away soon, it's just a temporary glitch that's my fault, I'm the crazy one, mad Dash on another one of her drama-queen tears. I love it in Virginia. I love it, I could stay there seven days a week and be happy. *This* is unnatural, not that. And I'm so glad we've finally *admitted* these things to each other. Thank you, Bill—I didn't think it would work, but it did. So, this is great."

Nobody stops me when I head for the door. They look surprised, but neither one moves. "Andrew, I hope you have a nice, long, boring rest."

In the mirrored elevator doors, I look nothing like the me who rode down three weeks ago, smug and tickled, leaning against my husband's shoulder exchanging wisecracks. My eyes look like marbles; my mouth is a tight whitish line, tensed so it won't tremble. When the doors open, I squint in the too-bright lobby, wander out to the street. Start for my car, stop.

I have to see Andrew alone, not with Fogelman. I brace my back against a parking meter to wait.

May I be peaceful and at ease, may I be happy—the Buddhist metta prayer. "Try it," Mo said. "It works."

It's not cold, but I'm shaking. My blood feels sluggish, like water at the freezing point. Things have gone too far. If I could take back my life since last Christmas, would I? *May I be peaceful and at ease, may I be happy.*

Andrew pushes the glass door open with his shoulder, hands shoved deep in his pockets. Yes, I would take it back—I think—if I could have him right now, with his thin nose and his serious forehead, the wide strides he takes with his long legs. But he would still be himself and I would still be me, and after a time, wouldn't I just want him to go away again?

It's been a game until now. I was dancing on a thin edge, but part of me liked it because I knew I had a safety net. I could call the game off any time and skip back to safety—Andrew's infinitely tolerant arms would be wide open. Now he's taken himself away. "I feel more like myself," he said. So I was diluting him, my needs were camouflaging him; without me he's the pure, unretouched image. Well, if it's true, it's true. Neither of us was telling stories in Fogelman's office.

He stops short when he sees me. Pedestrians pass between us while we look at each other and don't talk. I push off from the parking meter and go closer; now people have to walk around us. "Did you mean what you said?"

"Yes." He paused before he said it, though. He leans forward, stork-like, trying to read my face. "Did you?"

I nod.

"Are you all right?"

"Peachy."

A little more staring, that's it. I have to squeeze my hands into fists and unsqueeze them, otherwise I don't feel real. I'm so stupid—I didn't know how precarious marriage was, mine, anybody's. I took it for granted, but it's a fragile envelope, delicate as human skin. People keep flowing past us. I keep my eyes focused on Andrew, the rock; I look at him so hard my eyes water.

He turns away first. We parked our cars in opposite directions, and we move toward them like shipwreck victims swimming for different shores.

andrew

thirteen

"Next item." Richard Weldon bounced from the window back to the conference table and checked his notes. "As you know, we still have no budget for next year, so we remain in the dark as to the summer schedule."

Groans; tsks.

"But not for long." Richard held up his hands with tired patience. "Next week, the dean assures me. Probably at our next meeting, I can let you know exactly how many courses we're going to have to cover."

"Assholes," Dominic Brodsky muttered, shoving his chair back and dropping his feet, *thud, thud,* on top of the table.

"It's like this every year," Peter Flynn said in his patronizing tenor, rearranging the tails of his tie over the front of his shirt just so. "They like to see us with our mouths wide open, cheeping like baby birds."

Every year. As if he'd know, Andrew thought; he'd been here all of three.

"But Christ, it's almost the end of March." Tim Meese scrubbed the ends of his mustache with both hands. "Why the hell can't they get their act together?" He sounded more worked up than he usually bothered to get at faculty meetings; in fact, the summer schedule was the only order of business so far that had roused a word out of him. But the meeting had been going on for over forty minutes, and after five o'clock Tim's focus had a way of about-facing, like an honor-guard soldier, from college business to a warm glass of stout.

From his perch on the tepid heat register, Andrew stared out at the network of illegal footpaths crisscrossing the winter-dead grass squares of Main Quad two floors below. The days were getting longer, but today it was almost dark out at—he pulled up his sleeve to see his watch—five-thirty. Late March: the time of year when students committed suicide most often, not at Christmas or during finals or senior comps.

Poor bastards; he could hardly see them down there in the gloom, bending into the raw wind or letting it hustle them from behind, using their books and book bags to shield their heads from an icy, spiking drizzle. The students, the sky, the wet stone faces of Mason Library and Burnham Hall, the whole blighted world today was the shade of gray of a rain-slicked cemetery. It was the first day of spring.

Richard bounced to the other side of the chilly seminar room and began to talk about a temporary vacancy in the fall term, when Dominic Brodsky was scheduled to go to some vowel-less Balkan country for a conference. Andrew couldn't concentrate on the topic, could hardly follow it. His mind stalled out these days, rushed forward to catch up and stalled again, like an old lawn mower. He ought to wake himself up by drinking more of the stale coffee Miriam had set out, but it gave him heartburn.

He caught Miriam's eye; she sent him a sympathetic look that brought him out of his stupor enough to sit up straight. He'd had his cheek and temple pressed so long to the windowpane, he had to rub them to get the circulation back. God. He'd be like old Dr. Cleveland soon, it was inevitable. There he was in his usual spot in back, snoring softly, fountain pen slack in his knotty fingers and leaking blue ink onto his notebook. He'd been emeritus for fifteen years, but he still came to school every day, to do God-knew-what in the closet of an office some sympathetic past chair had given him. He never missed a history department meeting, either, although he rarely said anything and he wasn't allowed to vote.

He came, of course, so he could feel as if he still belonged. And to get out of the house, empty since his wife died half a dozen years ago.

"We're almost done," Richard assured them for the fifth or sixth time. "Let's see . . . Elizabeth, did you have something on the women's studies department?"

Funereal in black boots, black stockings, black skirt, black sweater, Elizabeth O'Neal began to straighten from her languid slouch, a snake uncoiling—at the same moment Bonnie Tzach jumped up and started to put on her coat. "Sorry," she said in a stage whisper, "gotta sneak out."

"Wait, you'll want to hear this."

"Oh God, Elizabeth, I can't, I told Richard I might have to leave early if, you know, we ran over—"

"But this is about the interdisciplinary studies program."

"Right, well, I'm interested in that, but—"

"Yes, you said you were interested. Last term you told me you were. Otherwise I wouldn't have mentioned it to Professor Carillo. Now she's thinking you'll do something for them next year on women's roles in the Reformation. Along the lines of the lecture I did," Elizabeth couldn't resist adding, "in the colloquium series on contemporary women in the Middle East."

"Um, haa." Bonnie tugged her long, lank hair out of her coat collar. It used to be blonde and stylish. For that matter, her face used to be sunny and serene, not sallow and vague. "Well, you know," she said with a wan try at a laugh, "that was before I had twins."

Wincing, Andrew put his head back against the windowpane. Before he closed his eyes, he saw Peter Flynn's superior sneer, and in the brief pause before Elizabeth spoke again he could hear a subtle, communal downshift of expectation. Bonnie, for the love of God, he thought, why hand them the stick to beat you with?

If Richard would pay more than lip service to mentoring the junior faculty, this wouldn't be happening. Bonnie was a good, solid teacher—didn't that count for anything anymore? But she had three-month-old sons and a husband who couldn't help because he'd just opened a restaurant. She was falling behind, and when the time came, Richard or whoever replaced him would probably vote no on her tenure.

Elizabeth's face, normally inscrutable, seemed to shift between real sympathy for Bonnie and glee because, in the race to get ahead, she'd just pulled a couple of lengths ahead of her. "Right. No problem. I'll tell Dr. Carillo—maybe next spring?"

"Absolutely." Bonnie nodded vigorously, sidling toward the door. "Next spring, great, I'll start planning over the summer. Sounds like fun. Thanks, Elizabeth, I really appreciate it." She really did. Well, better to be naive than cynical and paranoid like everyone else. Hold on to it as long as you can, that was Andrew's advice.

"All right. Last on the agenda, this year's outstanding student. You were to give me your nominees, and I believe I've got everyone's but Bonnie's. Oh, and yours, Dominic. Would that be for the usual reason? No one worthy enough to warrant consideration?"

Brodsky grunted, not bothering to look up from the brutal manicure he was giving himself with a penknife. He and Richard didn't get along, but Brodsky's temperament with everybody was almost as bearish as his hairy, hulking body. But he was a brilliant scholar. Andrew rather liked him, even though their teaching philosophies were poles apart. At least you never had to wonder where you stood with Dominic, who was happy to call you an ass to your face if he thought you were being one.

"Let me guess," he said in his deep-chested rumble. "O'Neal's list is all women. Right?"

Elizabeth only blinked at him with slow disdain.

"Flynn's is the longest, because he thinks that'll give him a better chance to 'win.' " He made quote marks in the air. "Bateman's . . ." He shot Andrew a look of exaggerated contempt. "Bateman's is the most *sincere*."

Andrew clasped his hands together. "I do, I do hope so," he said sincerely.

"And Richard's." Dominic made a fake-earnest face and pitched his voice high and precise, like Richard's. "Richard's has a black, an Asian, and a female. Oh, if only there *were* a black Asian female. If only she were *gay*."

Peter Flynn laughed, flashing his white teeth. The sound wasn't quite real, though. The hollowness of it made Andrew glance at him, and he caught, quick as fingers snapping, a flash of hate in Flynn's face, before he bent his head and went back to sketching *X*s on a legal pad. Hate. No other word for it.

Andrew had to rub his eyes. He felt disoriented, practically dizzy. Peter and Dominic—weren't they allies? Prickly ones, perhaps, but didn't they vote together, eat together, mock their colleagues together? If not . . . Gradually a likelier possibility came into focus. It made sense, and it answered a question that had been at the back of Andrew's mind for weeks: Why would Peter, notoriously stingy, offer to help him over the "last hurdle" to the chairmanship, as Richard put it, by inviting him to write a chapter in his book?

One reason: to keep Dominic, the only other eligible candidate interested in the department chairmanship, from getting it.

Could it be? Was Flynn really so blinded by paranoia that he thought

Richard and the dean would agree on *Brodsky*—who'd be a *disaster* as chair, a human wrecking ball. He alienated everyone he came in contact with, plus Richard couldn't stand him.

Of course Flynn was that delusional, and absolutely he would try to sabotage his imaginary rival's imaginary chances. Minutes before this meeting, he'd buttonholed Andrew in the hall and made his chapter pitch again. "I could really use your voice," he'd said, jingling change in the pockets of his trousers. He favored turtleneck sweaters year-round, going for that author-photo look; all he needed was a dog and a fireplace.

"What voice is that?" Andrew had asked. Notwithstanding what anyone else (Dash) might think, his reasons for disliking Flynn were completely professional, not personal. He couldn't teach, he didn't have the decency or the common sense to try to hide the nakedness of his ambition, and, worst, he had no loyalty to the college.

"Oh, you know. Older—and wiser, of course." He'd laughed indulgently. "The conservative voice. Don't you think? Nothing wrong with a conservative voice."

"The foil, you mean."

"No, no. The foil?"

"The antagonist. Jefferson's racist defender, there to be set up and knocked down. No, thanks. Doesn't sound like much fun to me."

"No, hey, you've got it wrong. *Balance,* that's what you'd bring to the argument. No one's setting anyone up. Richard thinks this is all you'd need, Andrew, this little boost up to full professor. After that, the sky's the limit. Talking chairmanship, talking respect. For all your hard work. Everyone thinks you deserve it—I know I do. And if I can help, why, that makes it even better."

Andrew had almost bought it. He'd said no again, but more civilly than the first time, and for a moment he'd wondered if he might've misjudged Flynn.

And it turned out all he wanted to do was thwart Dominic, his so-called friend. It ought to be funny. The hypocrisy by itself might be funny. Or the petty treachery, or the cynicism. All three together, though, sucked the humor right out of Andrew.

"All right, we're done, I guess. If no one has anything else, thank—"

The rest of Richard's benediction was drowned out by the scraping of chairs.

"I've got a question." Dominic Brodsky folded his forearms on the table and hunched forward, wild eyebrows meeting above his globular nose. Andrew thought of Olive Oyl's bullying boyfriend—what was his name?

"Yes, Dominic?" Richard held up a hand to halt the exodus.

"Yeah, Richard. Some of us are wondering. How's the job search going?"

Bluto. That was Olive Oyl's boyfriend.

All movement stopped. The only sound was the faint scratch of Dominic's penknife under his thumbnail. His gall was impressive, considering everyone knew that he was the only interested party left, since Andrew had dropped out, in the search for Richard's replacement. And Richard loathed him.

"Ah, the job search." Richard yanked on his goatee, buying time. "Well, you know, that's a deliberate process. Can't be rushed. Naturally the dean wants just the right person, believes the department deserves the best. As do I." He looked down, patting his fingers on top of the table at random, as if playing a child's tune on a piano. He lifted his head, looked directly at Dominic. "As the time nears to step down, though, it's funny, I find myself feeling more reluctant than I thought I would. Matter of fact, I've been toying with the idea of staying on for another term or two."

Disbelieving faces locked gazes and glanced away. Dominic stopped cleaning his nails.

"Or we might seek an interim chair before we settle on just the right person." Enjoying himself now, Richard clasped his hands behind his head, ostentatiously stretching his shoulders. "Or"—he took a deep breath, held it, and said on the gusty exhale—"it's possible the dean may want to go outside the department for a new chair."

Brodsky looked ill. But he only had himself to blame. Politically, he was tone-deaf. You didn't broadcast your ambitions or go around lobbying other faculty for support; not visibly, anyway. You dropped a word in the chair's ear, or at most the dean's—but preferably vice versa—and let events take their course. Otherwise, look what happened. Public embarrassment, general awkwardness, unnecessary humiliation.

Obliquely, Andrew felt responsible. If he'd said yes to Richard's offer, repeated to him as recently as last week, none of this would be happening. But he had his reasons for declining, simple and complicated ones, obvious ones, ones he didn't quite understand himself.

One thing he was sure of, though: Spiting Dash couldn't possibly be among them.

He peered in the side-view mirror of Elizabeth O'Neal's speeding black Volvo, but a huge SUV, not Tim's little green compact, had run the light behind the Volvo at Georgia Avenue and Van Buren, and now who knew where Tim was.

"He'll catch up," Elizabeth said between puffs on a cigarette she kept in her mouth while she drove. She needed both hands, one to steer, one to shift and downshift the Volvo at noisy RPMs that threw Andrew forward and back in his leather seat but mysteriously didn't move her at all. She leaned over the wheel like a hawk, saying little as they turned west on Military Road and entered the gloomy, wind-whipped park. Going out for a drink after the meeting had been her idea, but she looked as if she regretted it.

"Mind if I tag along?" Tim had asked, overhearing the invitation in the faculty parking lot.

"Sure, no, of course not," Andrew had responded after a peculiar pause in which he'd feared Elizabeth might actually say yes, she minded.

"Great. Where to?" Tim had rubbed his hands together amiably. "Slidell's? The Cozy?" He named a couple of other Takoma Park bars. Students drank in Silver Spring; faculty drove a little farther to avoid them.

Elizabeth had made a face of disgust. "Follow me," she commanded, pressing a remote control to unlock the Volvo.

Andrew had hesitated. "Three cars?"

"No, *Tim,* follow me. He can drive you back."

Made sense; Tim lived a mile east, in Takoma Park.

Stopped at a light, Elizabeth tapped her fingertips on the steering wheel in a tight, impatient rhythm. Andrew noticed she bit her nails down to the quick. "Smells new," he mentioned for something to say. "The car."

She turned on the windshield wipers. Above the black boots, her black-stockinged thighs flashed dark and aggressive in the garish light of streetlamps. "Yeah, it's new." She flicked on the radio, and then there was no more conversation apart from her sneering asides or random curses at the woman reading the evening news.

They turned left on Connecticut, then right a few blocks later. She pointed across Andrew's lap. "That's where I live."

He saw an enormous three-story colonial, stone, with solid old trees flanking the walk. "By yourself?"

"Usually."

On Wisconsin, they turned into a small parking lot, full, beside a low brick building with a sign on the awning that said JERZY. Elizabeth drove around to the back. "They know me," she said as she backed into a tight spot beside a PRIVATE–NO PARKING sign.

"I think we've lost Tim."

"Have we?" She smiled.

"I'll call, tell him where—" But as he was reaching for his cell, Tim's car nosed around the corner and skidded to a stop just past Elizabeth's bumper. He took his hands off the wheel and lifted his shoulders; his face repeated the message: *"What the hell?"* Andrew sent back an innocent wave, trying to convey "Don't look at me." No place for Tim to park—insult to injury. Shaking his head, he drove out of the lot and into the crowded alley.

Tim had joked once, Andrew forgot in what context, about Elizabeth hanging out with vampires—so he was half expecting Jerzy to be a creepy, lightless bar full of pale, leather-garbed young people dancing maniacally or spouting angry poetry from a brick-backed stage. Happily, it was none of those, merely an upscale neighborhood restaurant-tavern decorated with a lot of mirrors and pale wood, a zinc-topped horseshoe bar, and taupe-colored upholstered furniture arranged in intimate, living room–style groupings. No television.

Happy hour was in full swing, but Elizabeth signaled with three fingers to a waiter with a shaved head, who smiled a greeting and led her and Andrew to a trio of low chairs and a table in a dim corner. "What can I bring you?" he asked Andrew but not Elizabeth, and a moment later he returned with a glass of wine and a gin martini.

"Well," Andrew said, lifting his wineglass. He tried to think of a toast.

"Cheers," Elizabeth said, and drank.

Tim showed up a few minutes later, wet, disgruntled, carrying the remains of his umbrella. "Look what the wind did. It's ruined." Definitely; the umbrella was inside out. Tim had difficulty fitting its carcass between his chair and the customer's at the next table. "What a lousy night." His lowering glance at Andrew and Elizabeth said he considered them part of it. "I practically had to park in Wheaton. Guinness," he told the waiter, then sat back and took a deep breath. "Well, anyway. Here we are."

Here they were. Andrew suspected Tim, no particular fan of Elizabeth's, had come along to protect him from her wiles. He watched them exchange stiff chitchat, Tim trying to fix his gaze on her gaze, not her chest; she'd unbuttoned her long black cardigan to reveal another sweater under it, also black but tight and plunging. She wore a single crystal on a silver chain, the crystal settling in the cleft between her breasts. It drew the eye like the only light in a dark room.

Tim's beer came. "Well, here's to another year of Richard Weldon." He wiped foam from his mustache. "How about *that*?"

"I know," Andrew said. "I thought Brodsky was going to take it."

"Me, too," said Tim.

"Never. Not while Richard is breathing." Elizabeth still had half a drink, but she stirred her finger in the air at the waiter, and presently another round appeared. "Richard would keep his job for the rest of his life before he'd give it up to Dom."

"He can't stand him," Tim agreed. "Never understood why, except for the obvious—Dominic's a son of a bitch."

Elizabeth extended her neck at him. "Are you serious? You don't know why Richard hates Dom?"

Tim shook his head. She looked at Andrew—he shook his head, too. Respectively, they were twenty and twenty-five years older than Elizabeth, and yet so often she made them feel like teenage boys with impure thoughts and no social skills.

"Because he fucked Allison."

"Who did?"

"Dom, who do you think."

Tim set his glass down. "Richard's wife? And Dominic? They had an *affair*?"

"Not technically. It was before Richard married her."

"God*damn*."

"Interesting," Andrew said, thinking this was a bit of gossip he might actually remember. Dash said he was worthless as a source of departmental intel, which was true, and that no one ever told him anything, which wasn't true. People confided in him all the time. It went in one ear and out the other. This was juicy stuff, though. Allison and Brodsky. What an unsavory image. And what a cesspool of vice and perfidy the history department was, too—because if what the gossips said was true, Elizabeth, who'd delivered the Brodsky-Allison news with such relish, was having an affair with Richard right now.

"You know what I figured out today?" Andrew reached for his drink and saw that he'd finished it. "I had a Eureka moment." Elizabeth and Tim leaned toward him expectantly, and he paused to heighten the suspense. "In actuality, Peter is no friend of Dominic." How gratifying to have an actual scoop.

"No?"

He told them his theory of Flynn's true motive for offering him a chapter in *The Great Cover-up*. Gossip wasn't always a bad thing, he realized; it brought people together. It created community.

"Huh," Tim said. "Well, it wouldn't surprise me. I wouldn't put anything past Sink-or-Swim. Yeah, no, now that you—"

Elizabeth cut him off. "So why don't you want to be the chair?"

"Me?"

"Yes, you. Isn't it just your kind of thing?"

"Em, how do you mean?"

"Responsible. A sacrifice. Idealistic." Her lips curled.

Tim said, "You think that's why Brodsky wants it?"

"Oh, please. For him it's a stepping-stone. He'd serve a few years, put it on his CV, and move on to better things. But you." She turned back to Andrew. "For you it would be a duty. A good deed. So. Why are you shirking your duty?"

If she'd asked him the question in a quiet place, his office, over the phone, in a car, he'd have had to answer. Here it was all right to sit back and look philosophical, move his cocktail napkin around, gaze over Tim's head at the backlit pyramid of liquor bottles behind the bar. The music was lively but low; he could hardly hear it above the chatter. There were no awkward pauses in a bar after the first or second drink, because there was no such thing as silence.

Elizabeth got tired of waiting. "Going for a smoke." She stood up and walked away.

Tim had his hands folded over his belly, a mellow look on his round Irish face. If his chair went back he'd have it on two legs, and if Jerzy were a little less upscale he'd have his big feet on the table. Andrew smiled at him, deep fondness coming over him like a blush. His friend, the hairy leprechaun. His boon companion. *We should go camping together,* he thought. *Or gambling. We should take a trip out West.*

"So why *don't* you take the job?"

Andrew's spreading smile reversed itself. He said the first thing that came into his head—"Dash wants me to"—but then he didn't know if it was the answer or a non sequitur. He excused himself to go to the men's room.

Washing his hands, he made faces at himself in the mirror, a sure sign of the edge his body had come to, the point at which his mind always said, Right then, that's it, and he put down the glass or shook his head at the bartender. A cheap drunk, Dash called him, but he didn't like to go past the feeling of weakness in his biceps or the urge to stare stupidly into space, the sensation that his cheek muscles had atrophied. Or else he talked too much, said things he hadn't thought out beforehand, and soon the intense conviction would overtake him that his ideas were not only profound and unique, but that he'd never had them before.

Back at the table, though, a fresh round of drinks had just arrived. He sipped from his without hesitating, and the thought process that led to the decision was as complicated as Oh, what the hell. A feeling of spectacular rightness lifted him, shone inside like a light. He was exactly where he wanted to be, with the very people he wanted to be with. He'd been so down, and now he was so happy. *Euphoria,* he thought. *I feel euphoric.*

Tim and Elizabeth were having an argument about art. No, about government. Or government control of art. Their intensity was a match, but she cared more and she was ruthless, so Tim didn't have a chance. Andrew listened, calm and judicial, the moderate one between two extremists. Tim said let the government fund the arts all it wanted, and if that meant fewer crucifixes in bottles of urine, fine with him. No, Elizabeth countered, that was state-sponsored censorship, the conservatives would finally strangle creativity altogether, only the most vapid, bourgeois, timid clones of art would be encouraged. How nice to see them engaging each other, even if it was in a fight. It made Andrew smile.

Elizabeth noticed. "Are you drunk?" she broke off the argument to ask.

Tim started laughing.

"What's so funny?" she demanded.

He laughed harder. "That." He pointed at his umbrella, the forked spokes and stretched nylon remains splayed across the floor like a huge black bird, dead in a horrible accident. The waiter had to step over it to deliver drinks.

"Why did you bring it in?"

"I don't know." Tim was convulsed. "I couldn't throw it away. It's new!" His loud, lusty guffaw always tickled Andrew; he began to chuckle in sympathy. Elizabeth caught it, too. It began in fits and starts, but soon all three were rocking with laughter. Tim's tears ran into his mustache; he held his sides and roared. Elizabeth put her arm on the table and her head on her arm, groaning while her shoulders shook. Tim's umbrella was the funniest thing they'd ever seen. It had a five-foot wingspan. Every time they looked at it they cracked up again.

Andrew felt weak, every muscle pleasantly used. Elizabeth sobered first, resumed her bored, lizard-eyed look, but the memory of her lax mouth and loose-limbed body and the helplessness of her silent laughter stayed with him.

"I should go home and grade essays," Tim said, signaling the waiter for another beer.

"Me, too."

"Me, too."

"You still assigning journals?" he asked Andrew, who nodded. "That's nuts. How many hours do you spend reading 'em?"

"They're a good learning tool. Easier than a formal essay. Students who have trouble writing, they're good for them."

"Do you set a page limit?" Elizabeth asked.

"No."

"No?"

"No, they're journals. The point is to animate the past," he said carefully; his tongue felt thick. "Instead of memorizing dates, they have to dig into primary research. They can't get away with dropping a few words like *chamber pot* or *candlestick* into a twenty-first-century narrative. And for some of them it's therapeutic."

"Then you're a voyeur," Elizabeth said.

"I'd be scared to find out that much about my students," Tim said.

"Sometimes I am a voyeur, in a way," Andrew admitted. "Yes. Sometimes it feels that way. What they write can be painfully honest. I don't take their confidences lightly."

"Do you have a . . ." She ran an olive on a pick around and around the rim of her glass. "What's your . . . you know, philosophy." She said it with a slight sneer. "Of teaching. I mean, do you have a *goal*?"

"Not me," Tim said. "I'm fresh outta goals."

Andrew thought. "To try to tell the truth. To get through the day without doing any harm." Did that sound pompous?

"Sometimes I feel like I'm dancing," Elizabeth said without looking up. "Juggling, dancing. I can't stop. If I do, they'll . . ."

"Not like you? But you don't need to wear a mask. They see through it eventually anyway. They always know."

"Yes, not like me, but also not learn. Do you know?"

"I think charisma can only take you so far. No one can inspire every day. The older I get, the more I think . . . the most important thing is to be kind. And competent, of course. But mostly kind."

"Do you digress a lot?"

"Sometimes."

"I don't. Should I?"

He laughed, but she was serious. "Well, for me, it seems they learn more, or just as much, on the byways, the scenic routes. Not the big highways I've taken so much time constructing ahead of time."

She scowled. She popped the olive in her mouth.

"It's all right to let yourself into the lecture. Let them see you as human—it helps them see history as human. I talk about music I like, about my daughter, a good mystery I've read. Places I've been. My thoughts. It seems to . . . wake them up. To possibilities. Sometimes you can practically see their minds turning corners."

She had her chin in her hand. "You really like them, don't you?"

"Yes. Don't you?"

Her eyes went out of focus while she thought, and he was filled with an apprehension, fear almost, that she might say no. "I haven't made up my mind." She rose abruptly. "'Scuse me," and she glided away.

"Ball breaker," Tim said, watching her. His tone was affectionate. "Can we get some peanuts or something? What the hell time is it?"

Andrew took a roll of antacids out of his pants pocket, and the foil-wrapped migraine pill he always carried in his coat pocket. He saw Tim lean back and smile. "What?"

"You got a headache?"

"I probably will have. You have to take one of these before it starts or they don't work."

"You got heartburn?"

"Yes. Not exactly heartburn. More a pain that comes and goes." He put his hand on the right side of his stomach.

"What's that, the appendix? Maybe you've got appendicitis."

"Or it could be my gallbladder." He expressed his darkest fear. "It could be my liver."

"Could be your head. Not saying it is."

Odd to swallow a headache pill with a glass of wine. "I'm not doing that well," he told Tim. "To tell you the truth."

"How so?"

"Insomnia. I get tinnitus."

"Ringing in the ears? What causes that?"

"Could be an infection." He looked at his hands. "Also, I think I have Raynaud's disease. My fingers turn white when they're cold."

"So do mine."

"No, this is a syndrome. The arteries suddenly contract, blood can't get to the digits. I put my hands in hot water—say, I've come back from walking Hobbes and I forgot my gloves—I put my white hands in hot water and they turn blue, then they turn red."

"That's it?"

"Yes, but it can lead to worse things down the road." He pulled his new gloves out of the pockets of his overcoat. "Look at these. Check this out." He wasn't going to tell anyone about his new gloves. For some reason they had vaguely embarrassed him, but now it was the embarrassment that seemed silly. He put the right glove on and blew into the little hole on top. "Then you snap the stopper back on." He recapped the glove, held it up. "Warmth!"

"Holy crap. Let me try." Tim put the other glove on, blew into the hole, snapped the cap back on. "Huh." They wriggled their fingers, high-fived each other. "Feels kind of wet."

"Moist air," Andrew said.

"I want some of these."

"I'll get you a pair."

They drank, smiling around the room vacantly.

"Did you call Dash?"

"Did I call Dash?" Andrew picked up the burning candle on the table, tilting it to let melted wax coat the red glass sides. If he held his fingers below the wax line, they didn't burn; above, they did. Over the flickering flame, he saw Elizabeth talking to a couple of men at the bar. She had her hands on her buttocks, as if in back pockets, her booted legs spread apart. She lifted her chin at one of the men, then at the other, accusing them of something, challenging them. They smiled back, hopeful but uncertain. Ball breaker, definitely. Why did he like her? She was certainly nothing like Dash. Except . . . chaos, he thought hazily. Chaos—they had that in common. He couldn't control either one of them. So he was drawn to chaotic women?

"Yes," Tim said heavily, enunciating. "Did you. Call Dash."

"We talk. I tell her how much I deducted from the joint account for the mortgage and the utilities. She tells me the cabin's porch roof is leaking."

"That's nuts. Call her up, go see her at the studio."

"Why would I do that? I'm not even thinking about her, deliberately. It's like an experiment. I banish her from my thoughts."

Tim wagged his finger. " 'The sleepless soul that perished in his pride.' "

"It's not pride. Nothing to do with pride. I simply don't wanna talk to her. Since the feeling's mutual, we're doing fine."

"Bullshit."

"I'm telling you. It was bad between us."

"So?"

"So now it's good."

"So how come you can't sleep, your hands turn blue—"

"One thing's got nothing to do with the other."

"Oh, yeah?"

Tim's pink, jowly face annoyed him; so did his elbows on the table and his burly shoulders hunched, like a cop interrogating a prisoner. "Yeah. And look who's talking. It's not as if you put up much of a fight to make Meg stay."

He regretted that instantly. Elizabeth came back just then, or he'd have apologized. It was the drink. He'd never said that to Tim about Meg before; he wished he could take it back, even though it was true. He loved Tim.

He loved Elizabeth. Look how she argued, half lying in her chair, boneless, firing off put-downs in staccato bursts, an automatic rifle of sarcasm. What a trio they were. They ought to form an eating club or something. Three singles—they ought to team up. They could buy a group home, pool their money and go in on a nice place near the college.

Elizabeth stood, started putting on her coat. "Let's get out of here."

He and Tim stood up, too. "Where to?" they asked.

"My place. Get something to eat."

fourteen

They ate dinner in Elizabeth's elegant, oak-paneled dining room. Everything was take-out leftovers, but it was excellent takeout—sashimi salad, red snapper carpaccio, breaded veal chop in anchovy sauce— from nearby restaurants.

"Guess you don't cook much," Tim noted, mouth full of mushroom risotto. He and Elizabeth ate like famished dogs, barely chewing, pushing and pulling Styrofoam containers back and forth. They'd switched to wine and were sharing a 2001 Château Magdelaine Saint-Emilion she'd gone down in her basement to get. It was after nine. Andrew ate sparingly; he'd gone beyond hunger, could only take occasional sips of the expensive wine.

"I can make coffee. The housekeeper taught me."

Tim snorted a fine spray of Bordeaux through his nose. Everything was funny to him.

"You have a housekeeper?" Andrew asked carefully. "For this house?" It was important not to slur or trip over his words, do nothing to reveal that, improbable as it seemed, he was most likely the drunkest of the three. He was hiding it in his usual way, to the extent that he had a usual way, by speaking slowly and, according to Dash, with artificial formality. "Cut him off," she liked to say, "when he starts talking like Shakespeare."

"Mrs. Wilson," Elizabeth confirmed, dabbing anchovy sauce from her chin with a linen napkin. "She lives in, but Tuesday's her night off."

Andrew and Tim exchanged looks. They shouldn't be surprised: Outside, the house looked like a small embassy; inside, a posh men's club, all dark, heavy furniture and stained glass and old family portraits. The chandelier over their heads descended from an oak-coffered ceiling.

"You still eating that?" A rhetorical question; Tim forked a piece of veal from Andrew's plate and shook it onto his. "So, Elizabeth. You're, how shall I say, loaded?"

"I suppose. My uncle left me the house. I used to live here with him."

"But you have a mother." Andrew distinctly remembered that; in fact, she'd recently married someone called Carlos.

"Yeah, I have a mother. I used to have a father, too, but he died. So I got a stepfather, then I got another stepfather. When I was sixteen I ditched all that and moved in with my uncle. Who died, and here I am." She spoke in a flat, uninflected voice, just delivering information. Andrew had a sense that he could ask her anything, and no matter how personal she'd answer in the same way.

Tim had the same thought. "Sixteen. Must've been tough. For your parents, too."

"Mother and stepfather, you mean. Oh yeah, they were busted up." She nailed him with her deadpan eyes. "They especially missed busting me out of jail for dope and shoplifting. They wanted to go through more abortions, too. They just couldn't wait for me to return to the family bosom."

Bit of a conversation stopper. Sober, Andrew would probably have cleared his throat and asked if there was any more polenta. Now he said, "I grew up about three blocks from here. I was nine when my mother died. Six months later my father married a woman named Tommie. We hated each other. When they sent me off to school in Connecticut, no one was sorry. Although I can't say the boarding-school experience was a very happy one. I never lived in my father's house again."

Elizabeth's heavy eyelids slowly lifted to show the fathomless black of her pupils. Her scrutiny felt as intimate as a strip search. She parted her thin lips, but then didn't say anything.

Tim stood up and leaned on the table with the heels of his hands. His weight made the wood creak. "Bathroom?"

"Through there, keep going," she said, still watching Andrew.

There was a long, not unpleasant pause after Tim left. Andrew felt almost comfortable under the piercing gaze now, as if he'd aced some test. "Sounds like we have a couple of things in common," he said, feeling bold.

She nodded, so slowly it was almost imperceptible. She stood, snagged her glass and the half-full bottle. "Come on. I'll show you the house."

It was the sort of house in which a round library didn't seem out of place. A billiard room wouldn't have, either, although there wasn't one of those.

"My uncle was a banker," she said by way of explanation, standing back so Andrew could get the full effect of polished wood, ceiling-high shelves, green-shaded lamps, and, most of all, row after circular row of thick, mainly leather-bound books. A sleek computer on the massive oak library table jarred a bit. "This is my office. I decided to use it, not make it a mausoleum."

Behind the table, artfully draped on the wall beside a group of photographs, hung a long black burka, complete with depressing veiled eye curtain. From her last trip to Afghanistan, she said, just before the fall of the Taliban. "First fall, anyway. My real father was career foreign service. I lived in Turkey till I was five, then Italy, back to Turkey."

Andrew went closer to see the photos. Of Elizabeth as a child with her father, on donkeys in the desert, on camels, in a dusty market, in front of a white mosque. She could've been a little Persian or Lebanese girl herself with her tan skin and shock of black hair. Her father was tall and handsome; she held his hand with a proud, trusting smile. There were no pictures of a mother.

"This is Cyprus, outside Nicosia. I went there on a dig in college. Thought of studying archaeology, decided on history. Much cleaner." She was slumped against the wall, watching him, holding her wineglass low in both hands. "Mummy's idea was for me to be a debutante, then marry another banker. So, of course, I became a scholar."

He nodded, in perfect sympathy.

"But not before making her life as hellish as I could."

The drugs-and-abortions phase, he assumed. "How old were you when you lost your father?"

"Ten. He crashed in a Cessna over the Red Sea. Body never found. So. Tell me about you. No, let's go, I'll show you the rest of the house." She shoved off from the wall.

They came upon Tim in the living room. Shoes off, stretched out on the camelback sofa, snoring. "Your chaperone's fallen down on the job," she murmured as they moved toward a curving staircase. She didn't touch him, but Andrew felt as if she'd taken his hand as he followed her a step behind, or as if an invisible web were drawing him along, elastic but irresistible. Which would make her a spider, him . . .

Upstairs, she didn't waste time on more rooms. "Mine," she announced, flicking recessed lights on in another regal, high-ceilinged chamber. This was a suite, complete with sitting room, enormous bath, and a view through an elegant dormer of the cloudy sky. The bed had a canopy.

"Homey," Andrew said. In truth, the room depressed him. The whole house did. Too big, everything too much, and all of it seeming to him to magnify Elizabeth's aloneness. She was like the child in the desert, but without a father's hand to hold in this oversized museum of a house.

No, that was fancy, and he was drunk. He didn't know anyone tougher than Elizabeth O'Neal. Part of her appeal was her ruthlessness, her no-brakes approach to whatever she wanted. He watched her crouch in front of a music system built into the wall, and in a moment, he recognized the opening of *Death and Transfiguration* coming softly from everywhere, no one source; it simply filled the room.

"Like Strauss?" She sat on the bed and patted the place beside her in a peremptory way that was so typical, so . . . Elizabethan. He smiled, and never considered refusing.

She leaned back on her elbows, a maneuver that pushed her breasts up, twin black-covered hills with a crystal winking between. She smelled of smoke and, faintly, curry. Her hair seemed to absorb the light, give none back; if he touched it, it would be like putting his fingers in a well of black ink. The timpani and strings of the music's quiet opening were hypnotizing him.

"Would you be interested in going with me to hear the National Symphony sometime?" A date. He was asking a woman out on a date.

"Not particularly."

"Ah."

"Would you be interested in staying the night?" Only her top teeth showed when she spoke, the space between the two front ones very dark and distinct in the diffuse light. A target for the tongue.

"Ah, well. Thank you," he said sincerely. "Aren't we both drunk?"

"So we're even." She took his hand and slid it under her sweater. It rested on her warm abdomen, rising and falling with her slow breaths.

"Ha." He had no idea what he was saying or what he might say. "Well, you know. I'm afraid I wouldn't be much good."

"We could just practice." Her sly smile set him at ease slightly, that and the lazy slide of her eyelids. Maybe she could take him or leave him.

"It's probably not a good idea. Us. Professional colleagues."

"I won't tell anyone. If that's what you're worried about. It's been awhile for you." She raised one eyebrow. "Yes?"

"Yes. Em, well. Relatively speaking. It's a subjective—"

"Make up your mind, I've got a nine o'clock class tomorrow."

"How about a rain check?" How about a rain check? Had he said that? She sat up and looked him in the eye. "When?"

"When?" He felt like Dash when he said, "What about spontaneity?" She frowned into space, processing *spontaneity*. "All right. Rain check."

The music swelled, brass blaring, the relentless timpani like an urgent heartbeat. They sat quietly, thighs touching, listening to the end of the section, the quiet gong striking while the pianissimo low C sounded ominously from the depths of the orchestra.

"Not to be rude, but would you mind going home now?"

He stood up, mumbled thanks or good-bye or something. When he got to the door he had to look back. She'd pulled her sweater over her head, was straightening it, folding it on her lap. She wore a black lace brassiere. Her skin was milk white, so pale it didn't look real.

He left after Death, before Transfiguration.

Tim slept most of the way home, slumped against the passenger-side door. Andrew drove his car through green light after green light down Georgia Avenue, monitoring the increase in the pounding of an ache on the right side of his head and calculating his chances of having it all day tomorrow if he didn't take another pill soon. Rain blew in squalls that shook Tim's car, almost made it veer out of its lane. In Takoma Park, Andrew pulled into the lot behind the brick apartment building Tim had moved to after the divorce, found an empty spot in back. "Don't forget where you're parked."

Tim jerked upright. "Jesus Christ. I've *already* got a hangover. What the hell. Can't even drink anymore, fucking old age."

They got out, moving like old men.

"Where's your car? At the college. Oh hell, I gotta drive you—"

"No, I'll walk."

"Walk, no, it's fucking raining. It's a mile in the fucking—"

They argued until Andrew convinced Tim he wanted to walk, felt like a brisk hike in the rain, just the ticket, he'd be completely sober by the time he got to his car. None of that was true, but telling Tim that he—Tim—was in no shape to drive would only prolong the argument, and Andrew suddenly was so tired he could barely speak.

"Interesting evening, huh?"

"See you tomorrow, Tim."

"Right. You and O'Neal, how'd that go? I missed half the night."

"Better go in, it's freezing."

"Okay, I'm going. See you tomorrow, pal."

"See you."

He was soaked, wet down to his T-shirt before he got halfway to the car. And not sober but no longer drunk, nowhere near "euphoric," and unable to recall anything over the course of the long night that could've put him in proximity to such a specious emotion. Alcohol, that was all, and now that it had worn off everything was settling back into the familiar old groove. He felt the potential of a bottomless funk he could fall into headfirst if he didn't keep alert. Trudge, trudge, collar up, back to the wind one minute, head into it the next. The memory of Tim's battered umbrella couldn't even bring a smile.

At least the car started. Sometimes it didn't. Shivering, clammy-skinned, he tried to feel grateful as he peered out the fogged-up window at the empty streets, heat on full blast. Dash called him a pessimist, but he never forgot that things could be worse. If you looked at it like that, he was really an optimist.

Of course there were no parking spaces near the house. He ended up parking too close to a stop sign three blocks away. Probably get a ticket. The rain had stopped, just the bitter wind seeping through his wet clothes to his skin to his bones. He'd never get out of this without a cold at *best*. Flu was more likely considering the state of his resistance.

Oh Christ—Hobbes. Mrs. Melman would've walked and fed him at four o'clock, but he'd have gone on the kitchen floor by now—it was close to eleven. Should've called her, Andrew berated himself as he unlocked the front door and turned on the lights. Cold in here. He kept his coat on and went in the kitchen.

"Hobbes! Hey, boy!" Beside the refrigerator, his head throbbed when he knelt to pull on the bundle of blankets and discarded old bathroom rugs Hobbes called home—gently, so as not to startle him. A leg appeared, a haunch. "Wake up, buddy. Wanna go outside?"

The covers were cool, not warm. That should've warned him. His own hands were so cold, though, he didn't notice. He didn't notice anything until he saw Hobbes's gray muzzle lifted in a last grin, the familiar triangle of yellowed eyetooth jutting between dry lips.

Oh no. Andrew dropped to the floor. Hobbes, oh God. It had to happen, he was so old and rickety, but God. If he'd come home on time, if he'd been here tonight—maybe it wouldn't have happened. He touched one soft, curly haired ear, the knob of bone on Hobbes's crown. He'd always dip his head and sigh when you petted him, his lids sagging over his filmy eyes in contentment. No reaction now, no nothing, just stillness, utter vacancy. Hobbes's shell, that's all this flattened pile of grizzled fur was. Sweet old boy. His father's dog.

He was going to cry. He couldn't believe it. His throat hurt; the backs of his eyes stung like salt on a wound. But when the tears came, he felt relief, and what little shame he had, he let it go. Why not weep for a dog? Or for mistakes and missed chances? For self-pity, for confusion. For this empty house.

He folded the blanket in half and carefully wrapped Hobbes's stiff body in it. The bundle felt unexpectedly heavy when he carried it out to the back porch. He laid it on the glider first, but the wind blew a fine spray of rain through the screen just then. He put the dog on the floor by the wall instead, behind a stack of chair cushions. He'd be dry there. Safe and dry.

Tomorrow he'd bury him.

"What made him die?"

"Old age. He was a very old dog."

"Can I dig, too?"

"I'm about finished." And, foolishly, he'd chosen a gravesite too close to the maple tree—Wolfie would never get a shovel through this thicket of roots and rocks. Andrew was having a hard time himself. At least the ground wasn't frozen. "You can help me cover him up, though. Afterward."

"How he die? What happened to him?" In his hooded sweatshirt, Wolfie crouched beside Hobbes's shrouded body, studying the shape, fascinated. He wanted to see the dog, Andrew knew, as much as he was afraid to look at him.

"Well, I guess his heart stopped."

"Did it hurt?"

"No, no. He was asleep. He just passed away while he was sleeping."

"What it feel like? Did he know? What happen to him after he pass away?"

Andrew dropped the shovel and stepped up from the hole he'd been digging for the last forty minutes. A weak, bleary sun in the corner of the sky barely cast shadows. The perfect gray setting for a funeral. Wolfie, on his way home from school, had seen him from the alley and come into the yard to watch. Andrew looked at him helplessly. "I don't know for sure. Think this is deep enough?"

"Did he go to heaven?"

"Yes. He was a very good dog. Want to help me put him in?"

Wolfie stood up and stepped back, wide-eyed.

"That's okay, I've got it." Andrew knelt and lifted the dog in his arms, surprised again by how heavy old Hobbes was. Dead weight.

"Wait, I'll help!" Wolfie put his hand on the edge of the blanket, grabbed a fold of it, and together they lowered Hobbes into the clay-sided grave.

"I have something," Andrew remembered. From underneath his coat, which he'd thrown on the ground when he got hot, he took out Teddy—Dash called it that, a filthy, vaguely beige piece of fake fur with one ear and no eyes. The comfort blob Hobbes kept with him in his blanket jumble even when he kicked or nosed everything else away: covers, tennis balls, stupid rubber toys Andrew bought at the grocery store. "This was his favorite," he said as he bent down and laid Teddy on the blanket, in what he estimated was the crook between Hobbes's paws and his nose.

Wolfie pressed his hands together and closed his eyes.

Andrew cleared his throat. "Well. Hobbes was thirteen years old. That's . . . ninety-one in human years, a pretty ripe old age by any reckoning. He had a good life. A very good life," he embellished, but he was thinking of his father's state of mind when second wife Tommie took off, leaving behind nothing but an eight-week-old purebred English cocker spaniel with champion lineage and one undescended testicle. Edward had just moved to a condo on P Street, depressed, recently retired from the law firm, and getting first hints of the price he was about to pay for working too hard and smoking a pack of cigarettes a day for fifty years. As the new, unwilling owner of a dog, he must've left a lot to be desired, from Hobbes's standpoint. But they'd grown old together comfortably enough, settling into a lifeless routine of occasional walks and long, silent sits.

"Did he ever get hit by a car?" Wolfie came out of a reverie to ask.

"Not that I know of."

"He like to lay out on the front porch. He sure sleep a lot."

"He never bit anybody," Andrew said.

"I snuck him cookies Dash gave me. He liked me."

"He had a big heart."

"Yeah."

Eulogy over, Andrew let Wolfie drop shovels of dirt into the grave until he got tired. "Got to put his name on top or something," Wolfie said when the job was done. "Like a cross. You got any flowers?"

"How about a nice bush?"

"A *bush*."

"Yes. I could get an azalea and plant it at the head."

"When?"

"In a couple of weeks. Mid-April, I guess."

"No, we got to put something now."

They looked around the wintry backyard.

"That rock," Wolfie said.

It was a big, shapely stone Dash had wanted in her flower border for a decoration. "Too heavy," Andrew said, remembering hauling it there for her.

"We can do it. He got to have a mark."

They managed it by rocking and shoving the stone out of the rut it had sunk into over the years, carrying it between them for a few feet, then kicking and rolling it the rest of the way.

"There."

"Looks good. Like in a graveyard."

"Headstone. Well, that's it," Andrew said before Wolfie could suggest carving Hobbes's name in it. "Let's go in, it's cold. Want some hot chocolate?"

"My aunt died, but I didn't see her. My sister said she all dressed up, like going to a party. But laying down in the box. Coffin."

"People try to make their loved ones look nice."

"My father might die and I wouldn't know. He could be dead *now*." He sat down on the hard ground and crossed his legs.

Andrew sighed, looking up at the streaky sky, following the black silhouette of a shrieking bird. "Aren't you cold?" he asked as he hunkered down beside Wolfie.

"No." He was starting to shiver, though, and blow into his cupped hands. Small, boyish white scars scored the brown skin of his fingers and wrists.

Andrew reached over for his coat and threw it across Wolfie's shoulders. "How long since you last saw your dad?"

"I don't know. He use to come by, then he quit."

"Well, there are worse things than not having a father." That sounded heartless. "What I mean is, no father could be better for you than a bad father. Sometimes."

"My father . . ." Wolfie made *X*s in the dirt with a stick. "He use to let me put my hand in his pocket, like I was stealing his money. He'd laugh. Sometimes he put his hand on top of my head." Wolfie put one hand on his own head. "Keep it there."

"My father used to laugh at me."

"What for? How old were you?"

"If I'd do something he thought was stupid. Say something he didn't agree with."

"He hit you?"

"*No.*" He looked at Wolfie in alarm. "Did your father hit you?"

"No. How old were you?"

"Oh, your age, or older. Younger." All his young life, actually, until Edward and Tommie sent him away to school.

"Like what? What'd you do to make him laugh for?"

He regretted beginning this. Wolfie's puckish face was screwed up with concern, the dark eyes liquid and sad. "Nothing, just silly things. Okay, one thing I remember. It was his birthday, and I wanted to give him something special. You know? Something he would really like."

Wolfie nodded.

"He smoked cigars. He'd smoke one after dinner every night, and if he was at home, one every afternoon at four o'clock. He kept them in his humidor—know what a humidor is?"

"No."

"It's a fancy name for a cigar box. My father's had a hygrometer inside, but it was broken."

"What's a—"

"It's a dial that reads the humidity inside the box. Cigars can mildew if it gets too damp in there, or dry out if it gets too dry."

"You gave him a box?"

"No, I gave him a hygrometer. Because his was broken. Except"—Andrew started to laugh, to take the sting out—"I didn't know anything about humidity, I thought that little meter inside the box told the time! He was so regular—four o'clock and eight o'clock, every day—I figured that was a little *clock* in the humidor."

Wolfie grinned uncertainly.

"So I pried it off with a screwdriver—"

"How old were you?"

"Seven. Then I took the watch I'd just gotten for Christmas, took the band off, and glued the watch face inside the box, where the hygrometer had been. Elmer's glue. And I gave it to my dad for his birthday." He drew his knees up and wrapped his arms around them, smiling broadly over at Wolfie. "Pretty funny, huh? My father thought so."

"He laugh?"

"He roared." Andrew's mother had fluttered her hands—"No, it's nice, Edward, tell Andrew it's a nice present"—but every time Edward looked at the Bulova dial inside his handsome, wood-inlaid humidor, he'd laughed harder. Not indulgent laughter, not charmed or tolerant, no "aww" in it to make Andrew feel silly and fallible but still loved. Just humiliated.

"Hey," he said to Wolfie, who was pushing his lips in and out, looking worried. "No big deal. Thank you for helping me out with Hobbes. How's school? What'd you learn today?"

"I got a girlfriend," Wolfie said doubtfully, as if half his attention were in the new conversation, half still in the old. "Her name's Tina."

"Is she nice?"

"Yeah. Only she don't know she's my girlfriend yet."

"That could be a problem." He rubbed his cold hands together. He'd known—feared, truthfully—this was coming someday: a call to dispense fatherly advice to Wolfie. Now that it was here, he didn't feel as burdened as he'd thought he would. "Well, does Tina like you? Can you tell? Does she look at you in cl—"

"She not in my class. She don't know me, I see her at recess."

"Ah. Well, that makes it a little more difficult. Are you in any clubs together? Perhaps—"

"I threw a football at her yesterday, got her in the back." He reached up and patted himself between the shoulder blades.

"Well, that's . . . the direct approach. Maybe if you spoke to her, said, 'Hi,' or something, 'My name's Wolfie,' and then began a—"

"Nah, I'm just gonna go and get her. Girls like that." He jumped up. "I have to go now." He threw off Andrew's coat. "See you."

"See you." He was accustomed to Wolfie's abrupt departures, as if an urgent previous engagement had suddenly occurred to him. He trotted down the walk and through the gate to the alley, sneakers echoing on the concrete for a second, then silence.

Once, a long time ago, Andrew had just gone and gotten Dash. She'd liked it.

Beyond Mrs. Melman's roof, a crooked quarter moon was rising in the paling sky. The sweat Andrew had worked up digging the grave had long since dried on his skin; he should go in before he caught cold. He'd have to call Mrs. Melman, tell her about Hobbes. Andrew usually walked him this time of the day. It took forever. He'd lose patience, mutter, "Come on, come on, come on," while the dog limped from grass blade to grass blade, deciding where to pee. If he were here now, Andrew would walk him gladly.

Dash didn't leave him at the altar—the first time she left him—but almost. Three days before the wedding she'd planned and insisted on paying for—a tiny ceremony at the National Arboretum followed by lunch at their favorite Thai-Vietnamese restaurant; immediate family and closest friends only—Andrew appeared at her apartment to show off the Mexican wedding shirt he'd just bought at a men's store on F Street. He'd thought at first that that was it, a terrible miscalculation with the shirt, an item of clothing so unlike anything he had ever worn before, he was sure she would love it. But no, it couldn't have been the shirt, because he'd hardly gotten it out of the bag before she burst into hysterical tears, told him she was sorry she couldn't marry him, couldn't, it was impossible, and ran out the door.

Seven hours later Arlene, his mother-in-law-to-be, called. Dash was there, in Greensboro, with her. How did she get there? The train. She was in her room with the door closed and the lights out.

"May I speak to her, please?"

"Honey, you know . . . I think it would be better if you just came on down here."

He'd only met Arlene once, when she'd driven up to check him out after Dash told her they were getting married. From Dash's stories, he'd been expecting someone softer, rounder, a woman who embodied maternalism, and Arlene was hardly that. She was handsome instead of pretty, taller than Dash, with keen, critical brown eyes she'd turned on him with the intensity of searchlights. When she'd decided to like him, he'd felt as if he'd passed some shrewd and difficult test.

And when she said Andrew should come down, he didn't think it was a suggestion.

The house was a tiny, postwar bungalow on a one-block street lined with replicas of itself. He sat in his car and tried to imagine Dash growing up here, playing in the miniature yard, running on the chalky sidewalks—when suddenly the enormity of what he didn't know about her crashed over him in a hot, numbing wave. His fear was physical; it made his heart race, his palms sweat. It was as close to a panic attack as he'd ever had, before or since. He thought of driving off; his fingers even fiddled with the key. In that moment he forgave her for running away—after all, she'd only given in to the same sickening temptation he was feeling. And it wasn't heartless of her, he realized, it was smart—for God's sake, they'd only known each other *five months.*

He'd gotten out of the car stiff-jointed, like a man going to his hanging. Arlene answered the door. She looked at him and laughed (but in the same sweet, charmed way Dash sometimes laughed at him), and kissed him on both cheeks. He took heart from her unworried face. She sat him down in the living room, asked about his trip, gave him a glass of sweet tea. Then she told him a story that only confused him.

"When Dash was in kindergarten, she made friends with a little girl named Karen Svensdotter. That's all she talked about for days, Karen Svensdotter said this, Karen Svensdotter did that, oh, to have freckles like Karen Svensdotter—well, finally the day came when the mother called and invited her to go home with Karen after school one day. A playdate. Dash was just over the *moon,* so excited, she couldn't sleep the night before. So the mother picked the girls up at school, took them home, and at three o'clock Dash called. In tears. 'Come and get me, Mama, I want to come *home!'*"

Arlene had a mannerism so like one of Dash's—crossing her legs and leaning so far forward to speak to her companion, her breasts almost touched her thigh—Andrew was distracted and could hardly follow what she was saying. It seemed like rambling, anyway. Where was Dash? Why were they talking about Karen Svensdotter?

"She stopped crying as soon as she was out of that house. 'Mama,' she told me on the way home, 'Mama, they all had such little ears!' " Arlene leaned back to laugh. "Little ears, every one of them, the mother, Karen, her two brothers—the whole family had *little ears.*"

"Em," Andrew said, empty-headed.

"Well, it just scared her to *death.* She wasn't a fearful child, but something about it just got her. Those little ears. I guess she thought the Svensdotters were monsters or something. And that was the end of the friendship, needless to say. I don't remember what I told the mother when I called her up to apologize. Nothing about little ears, I'm sure."

She laughed again (Chloe's laugh; pure music), and Andrew tried to smile back politely.

"Now, honey. Don't take this personally, because it's not. What happened . . ." She touched his arm with her fingertips. She still wore a wedding ring, he noticed; her hands were the same bony, competent shape as Dash's.

"What happened is, you . . ." She put her hands over her nose and mouth, an abashed little tent. Then she sat up, squared her shoulders, and gave it to him straight. "Honey, it's your hair. It took an age to get it out of her, but that's what it is. Your wedding haircut, it just—now, it looks *fine* to me, a little short but perfectly nice, not one *bit* alarming—"

"My haircut?" He'd gone to his father's barber two days earlier, mentioned he was getting married. It was shorter, yes, but he'd thought— he'd thought—

"She won't talk about it—truthfully, she's hardly done anything except cry since she got home—but she did say—"

"My haircut?"

"She mentioned that—"

"Where is she?"

"In the backyard. You go talk to her." Arlene stood up. "I didn't tell her you were coming. Honey, everything's going to be *just fine.* Believe me, this is something y'all are going to look back on and laugh at." She gave his shoulders an affectionate shake before turning away, her lips pressed together. As if, for her, the laugh had already started.

His haircut? He walked out through the kitchen, rubbing the bare back of his neck, in a fog of confusion. Dash had left him over a haircut? It made so little sense, he couldn't think. Was he marrying a crazy person? Arlene seemed so normal, though, and so unconcerned. What was he missing? Was he really supposed to take comfort from the fact that Dash had done something just this absurd and idiotic when she was five years old? He couldn't possibly throw in his lot with a person like that. Lunacy, insanity—

He saw her at the end of the neat, fenced backyard, sitting on one of the low seats of a rusted swing set with her back to him, staring down at the grassless patch of ground at her feet as she swung herself listlessly back and forth, back and forth. The skirt of her white sundress billowed over her knees with each forward pass. She was barefooted. Both hands gripped the swing's chains, and her head was bent at a sad, sideways angle. She looked forlorn. Impossibly lovely. He tried to hang on to his outrage, at least his bafflement, but they disappeared together the moment she turned around and saw him.

Because who could resist the rising light in her face or her slow, radiant smile, the pure joy in her eyes followed so quickly by a flood of helpless tears? Who could resist her flying white skirt and flashing legs, the reckless collision of her body against his when she threw herself into his arms and kissed him all over his face? She kissed the sparse hair in front of his ears—formerly sideburns—with extra fervor, and she rubbed her nose against the prickly side of his neck and murmured through her tears, "I'm sorry, oh, darling, I'm so sorry, I love you, you don't look anything like him, I love you, let's get married right away." She cried so many tears, soon his face was as wet as hers.

"Like who?"

"Your father. Why do we have to wait? Let's get married today, do you want to? I'm dying to."

So they did. Not that day but the next, with a minister Arlene knew from sewing altar cloths for the Baptist church around the corner. Andrew's father, a lifelong Episcopalian, had little enough use for Dash already and he balked at that, wouldn't come down with Tommie for the ceremony. A week later Dash and Andrew threw a big party for themselves at the Thai-Vietnamese restaurant, and a week after that Andrew's hair had grown out enough so that the whole issue drifted away, seemed almost dreamlike to him in time. He forgot about it.

Until, two months pregnant with Chloe, Dash took the car—they only had one in those days—and escaped to Arlene's again. That time he didn't go get her.

He thought of calling her now. Not of going to get her, just calling her. To tell her about Hobbes.

She'd probably be on her way to the cabin from work, though, and he didn't like to talk to her while she was driving. Then, too, she'd try to cheer him up, and the things she would say—Hobbes was old, he'd had a good life, better to lose him now than when he was in pain and incontinent—Andrew didn't feel like hearing those things now. Even from her.

He should go in and get warm. He'd catch his death out here. Or he could just stay where he was and feel sorry for himself. Remembering his wedding had put him in a strange mood, hopeful and sad at the same time. Bittersweet. Like recalling the warm, inspiring parts of a friend's funeral.

He put his coat over his head and hugged his knees to his chest. He'd stay out here with Hobbes a little longer.

dash

fifteen

"Thank God for children." Greta stabs a forkful of Cobb salad and shakes her head. She's done her hair in braids today, four thick ones swinging around like orange tails, and one more curled up in a circle on her forehead like a hat ornament. "If I had to deal with nothing but mothers, I'd go nuts. I don't see how you do it."

"Well, you said it—the kids. But you have to admit, not all mothers are like that one."

We're decompressing, over a take-out lunch in the office, from a shoot this morning at the home of Mrs. Valerie Weiss-Slater and her new baby, the adorable Sophie. It was Greta's first location shoot, plus she'd never worked with a child as young as Sophie—ten weeks.

"But God, wasn't that lady a piece of *work*? Could you believe she wanted to *pretend* to breast-feed?"

"Oh, I've done mothers like that before," I say over a mouthful of pickle. "They want the full Madonna portrait, but none of that messy stuff that goes with it."

Beads clack in Greta's hair when she shakes her head some more. It's so much fun to teach her. I have to look at everything through her eyes, which makes it all new. "Valerie should've gotten the Academy Award," she grumbles.

There was a lovely soft-gray light coming through Valerie's gauzy bedroom curtain while we were setting up this morning, and she looked wonderfully maternal in a diaphanous white negligee, doing the sleepily ecstatic look with half-closed eyes and beatific smile—she must've been practicing in the mirror—when all at once she pulled a breast out of her nightgown and shoved it in Sophie's startled mouth. "Hurry," she snapped when Sophie, quite naturally, began to suck.

"I wouldn't have done it," Greta declares.

"You wouldn't have done the shot?"

"No. It's bogus."

She's so cute. "Well, what's dressing up a little girl in a Victorian gown and a big floppy hat and sticking her in a pony cart? Portrait photography's a lot about pretend."

"It's not the same."

"No, probably not. You're right. And I do draw the line sometimes—like when the mother wants total nudity, and it feels more like porn than maternity. But, honey, if Valerie wants to pretend she nursed her baby, what do we care?"

"She's a phony. What if she tells the kid she nursed her? And Sophie grows up believing it?"

"Well—then Sophie will always think it's sweet and precious that she and her mother had that bond, and one day she'll nurse her own child."

Greta rolls her eyes in a way that reminds me of Mo. They think I'm Pollyanna.

"We got some great shots, though, didn't we? Especially the baby by herself." We propped Sophie up with the arm of the sofa under her chest in Valerie's immaculate white living room, and the first thing she did was yawn. I'm fast—I got the pug nose, the puffy eyes squeezed tight shut, and oh, the big, toothless, wide-open mouth. Of course Valerie had to put a fuzzy pink blankie under her—no drool allowed on the furniture—but that turned out to be even better, because then I got the unbelievably delicate pastel of Sophie's beautiful skin. I think if you get that right, a baby's skin, the rest almost doesn't matter.

The phone rings. It's still a luxury to have somebody else answer it. "Bateman Photography, this is Greta, how can I help you?" She's so efficient. She jots down notes while she listens. "Oh, I'm sorry, we're going to be closed all next week. But after the eleventh you're welcome to come in. What about Tuesday?"

Whenever we speak, I make a point to tell Andrew how well she's working out. Because it's true, not just because I want to rub his nose in the brilliance of my choice. The new website Greta designed gets more hits in a day than the old one did in two weeks. She never misses a meter reading, she's good on the phone, she's great with kids. Studio work is still a challenge—we haven't yet repeated the Greta-in-charge experiment (which went pretty well, no major catastrophes)—but I think that's to be expected when you're just starting out. The main thing is, she's flashy. People come in and it's not just boring old me anymore; there's this extremely odd-looking young woman, edgy, arty, still a bit unpolished, head in the clouds sometimes. Somebody interesting.

She hangs up the phone. "A lady and her four-year-old. She doesn't have any idea what she wants."

"Is she coming in for a consult?"

"Yeah, end of April. Spring's really filling up," she notes, entering the appointment on the computer.

"I know, but I still need my week. God, one whole, uninterrupted week in Virginia." I thrill at the prospect.

"You look different. You look good, but different." Greta sits back down at the other side of my desk. "I mean, from when I first met you."

"I do? Well, my hair." I got about six inches cut off last week, a complete surprise to my hairdresser, not to mention me. "I'm old, Harold, cut it all off," I told him. "Old people don't get to have long hair." He didn't want to; he threatened to give me a perm and dye it blue. I was scared to death, but I kept insisting, and now—I like it! It's easy, I don't have to do anything, and it makes me look—the magic word—younger.

"Yeah, but no, it's not just the hair." Greta squinches her pale-lashed eyes into slits, studying me.

"I've lost some weight," I say helpfully.

"No . . ."

"Just from walking. Sock and I take these long walks in the woods—"

"No, that's not it. Oh, well." She gives up, starts throwing lunch stuff in the trash.

I wish she could, but I'm not surprised she can't nail it down, the precise change she sees in me. I certainly can't. As soon as I think, *This is how I feel,* I don't feel that way anymore, I've gone off in a different direction. Greta must see a pinwheel when she looks at me, multicolored vanes constantly spinning, spinning—or one of those trick card decks you thumb through fast and see some jokey scene played out in cartoons. Except my deck's not in order, so there's no coherent scene, just jerky, unconnected postures.

It's not all bad, though. It's as if I'm standing on tiptoes all the time. From excitement, from anxiety, both—doesn't matter; either way, I'm not sleepwalking. Boy, am I wide awake.

"You know what, Greta, you can probably take off right now. Nothing here for you to do, and I have to start sorting through proofs if I'm going to get them online for Valerie by tomorrow. Because come hell or high water, I am *out* of here Friday night."

Greta sort of dithers in the doorway.

"I mean, is that okay? You get your bonus today, of course, for helping on the shoot. And full pay next week even though I won't be in the—"

"I know." She's got one arm in the sleeve of her gnarled green sweater, which she always wears with a long fuchsia muffler. "Um," she says.

"What's up?" She can't have a raise yet. Can she? Maybe she can. She deserves it. Yes! She can. I'm excited, anticipating the good news.

"Um." She falls back in the chair, unwinding her muffler. She's a lipstick freak, always choosing the reddest, the brightest, her round mouth like a tropical flower in her milk-pale face. She takes a deep breath. "Joel asked me to marry him. I said yes."

I don't say, "Oh, wow," soon enough. I'm too shocked. "Oh, *wow*. I'm so *surprised*. How about that." I should get up and hug her. "You and Joel. That's amazing."

"It just happened. I haven't told my parents yet, even. We're thinking June."

"*June.*"

She speaks quickly. "Because we both want a small wedding, tiny, just family, and we'll probably do it outside in a park or something. So no big, like, preparations or anything. And afterward I'm going to work at home. Designing commercial websites. Which I've been doing some of already in my spare time, you know—I told you. And I'd help Joel, too, because his goal is for us both to be independent, work for ourselves, not have bosses. He's got plans already for his own consulting firm, he's got great contacts in the industry and also in the government, which is where it's all at in this town. There's this woman at his work that he'd go in with, she's Chinese, so they'd get minority set-asides."

I stop listening to Joel's consulting firm plans. I'm having an out-of-body experience. Greta has turned into a ventriloquist and her dummy is talking to me. "But, Greta," I manage when she pauses. "What about your career? Your photography career," I specify in case she's forgotten. "What about photojournalism? Travel?" I stand up, have to dissipate some energy. "What about perfecting your art?"

She lowers her head, becoming absorbed in braiding three pieces of fringe on the muffler.

"You know I'm glad for you. If this is what you want. But honey, you're so young—"

"Twenty-five?"

"That's young. Do you have to *marry* him?" I try a laugh, to mask the exasperation. "Couldn't you just live together?"

"He has a son, Dash."

"Right, okay, but—is this what *you* want? Be sure, be absolutely sure. Joel, I can see—and I know he loves you, but isn't it possible the, the *practicalities* might also be motivating him here?"

"Like what?"

"Like wanting some help with little—I'm sorry, I forget his name—"

"Justin."

"—Justin, wanting a mother for him, needing help when it's, when there's—"

"Justin already has a mother." She stands up, too. "I have to go."

"Wait, wait. I am *really* not saying what I mean." I follow her out through the studio. Something's hounding me, I can't let this go. I'm not angry, exactly; it's more like desperation.

In the lounge, she whirls around to face me. "You know, Dash—" Her face is pink; she's about to cry. Oh no! Then I will, too. "You're not my mother."

"Of course I'm not, of course not. But we're friends, and I couldn't stand it if you were making a mistake."

"I'm not. Not for *me*."

"I know you feel that way. I know exactly how you feel right n—"

"No, you don't."

"I do, believe me, I do, but in a few years, or a lot of years, in—say, *twenty* years, you're going to feel differently. Or you *might*, you might feel—"

"*I'm not you.*" Her back is to the door; she swings her fist down behind her and *thunks* the door with it hard. "I want to do this. I love Joel and he loves me. This is not me—*sacrificing* myself. I wish I could be like you. Or your friend Mo—no, not her—but you, I don't know anybody I'd rather be like than you, but I'm not." Her voice quivers. Tears squeeze out of her pale eyes and dribble down her cheeks. "I'm not you."

"Oh, honey, don't cry. Never mind about me. I understand what you're saying, but you're twenty-five—"

"Just because that's how old *you* were—"

"No, listen. We don't always take time to think things through. Forget age—anybody. And you have so much talent. You have a real eye, Greta, and that's rare, you have no idea how rare it is."

"I'm not, I'm not rare. I'm not creative! *You* are—I'm not!"

"Nonsense—you have your whole life, you can be anything. If you settle now because *he* wants you to—and because you're in love and it feels good and you want to be with him—"

"What's wrong with that? I don't understand you! You have the best job in the world. You're not stuck—I don't get why you're *warning* me."

She jerks the door open, clatters down the stairs. Outside, it's a shock to see blue sky, sunshine—this morning it was gray and misty. At the bottom of the outdoor steps, she whips around. "I'm not bolting on you, I'm not quitting *tomorrow*."

"That's completely beside the point."

"I'll work till the end of May, that's what I was trying to tell you. But after that, I'm sorry it disappoints you so much"—more tears—"I'm marrying Joel." She gives a jerky wave. "So I'll come in for two days next week, like we said. That is, if you still care to employ me."

I call after her. Pedestrians on the sidewalk gawk at me. Now, of course, I'm crying, too. This is crazy. Greta keeps going, moving as fast as she can in her wobbly strut, hampered by her ridiculous platform boots. I sink against the warm brick wall and watch her go.

If you're going to laugh about something later, start now. That's a good saying, but I'm pretty sure it doesn't apply here. No, this is a bitter, bitter pill. I don't even know why I'm taking Greta's horrible decision so personally. I feel terrible about what just happened. I've been unkind, tactless, and a bully.

But I'm *right*. I see it so clearly. Why can't she?

Mo calls. "I'm so disappointed in Eleanor Roosevelt," she opens.

"Oh?"

"Guess what her one regret was. In her whole, amazing life, the one thing she wished at the end she could change."

"I give up."

"She wished she'd been prettier. Not world peace, 'I wish I'd been prettier.' Eleanor *Roosevelt*."

"Huh. Listen, I just had—"

"I always respected her, but it just shows you what a death grip, Dash, the material world has on even thoughtful people. 'I wish I'd been prettier'—as if there really is an 'I,' for one thing. No wonder she was so unhappy! She was too attached, she lived in the past or the future instead of the present, otherwise she wouldn't have died anxious."

"How's Liam?" I ask to divert her. It's all about mindfulness and the five hindrances and the four noble truths with Mo these days.

"Liam? History."

"Oh, no! Why?" I liked him, the art-gallery guy. He sounded so normal.

"He was too grounded in so-called reality. We had nothing in common. I'm done with men."

"Oh, sure."

"I am, actually. They're just a Band-Aid, we stick them over an uncomfortable truth we don't want to look at."

I'm afraid to ask. "Which is?"

"That we're all ultimately alone. Everything else is illusion. We live in solitary confinement inside our own bodies, which aren't real to begin with. No man can complete me, Dash. I'm on this journey alone."

"Nobody can complete me, either, but what I'd like is a man who's more like a dog."

"A dog?"

"Freud wanted to know what women want? Well, I know: doglike devotion. Uncritical love and devotion from a nondog. Canine love from a human, i.e., a spouse."

That shuts Mo up for a while. I tell her about Greta, our fight, her decision to marry Joel. "I don't even know how it happened. One minute we're having a nice lunch, the next she's running out of the room and we're both crying. I can't stand it that she's just—throwing her life away! All that potential. I'm heartsick."

"Breathe."

"What?"

"Long, slow belly breaths while you label your thoughts. Then you can see them for what they are. See your own ego. The first step toward understanding the nonself."

"Oh, Mo," I wail. "I'm just not on that journey, you know? I have a self, and right now it's very upset."

Thoughtfully, she changes the subject. "How's Andrew?"

"I have no idea. We hardly speak."

"Are you going to split up?"

"Who knows?" Just talking about it makes me feel crazy. "I have fantasies all the time about living without him."

"Good fantasies?"

"Sometimes. Yes, sometimes," I admit, although that feels treasonous. "It's like I've crossed the line between the unthinkable and the thinkable."

"Divorce, you mean?"

I shudder. "It's this horrible temptation, it's like the devil or some drug supplier whispering in my ear. Now that I've thought about it, I've made it real. The possibility."

"Let me lend you a book."

"On what?"

"Self-abnegation."

"Oh. Well—"

"It'll change your life. That would be good, right? You'd like to change your life, wouldn't you?"

"Damn right," I say, but the fact is, I don't know. I don't know anything anymore.

My eyes sting. My neck hurts. I've been staring so long at the computer screen, clicking through pictures of Valerie and the magnificent Sophie, I've fallen into a trance. When the downstairs buzzer goes off, I jump so violently, I kick a notebook off the desk with my stocking foot. It's six o'clock—who in the world wants in at this hour? I press the button and ask.

"Me. May I come up?"

Andrew? He couldn't know about Greta, or I'd think he's come to gloat. I'm dazed, at a disadvantage; I've been drinking stale coffee for hours, I have bad breath. "Come on up," I say, and hit the buzzer.

Why would he come instead of calling? We haven't seen each other since the night in Fogelman's office, and we only speak when we have to, terse business conversations about Chloe's tuition or who's got the safety-deposit box key. So why is he here? I'm embarrassed when my stupid recurring fantasy revives—I thought I'd killed it: that he tells me he's sorry for what he said and none of it was true. What an idiot I am sometimes. I don't even *want* to make up. And still, I can't help listening for a tone in his footsteps on the stairs, the sound of eagerness or hope. Or, best of all, contrition. "In here," I call, and after a moment he appears in the doorway.

"Good God. You've cut your hair."

So much for reconciliation. "Oh, thanks *very* much. It's lovely to see you, too."

"No, I mean to say, it's, em . . ."

"Forget it. Is everything all right with Chloe?"

"Yes, yes. No, it's attractive, in a way, it's quite modern, I'm sure. Quite . . ."

"Never *mind*, Andrew." Why can't he just lie, like normal people? "Did you drop by because you were in the neighborhood?" I say, moving away, putting the desk between us. He doesn't look so great himself, if we're in a contest. Unlike me, he could *use* a haircut. His skin color is off and his eyes are watery. He could actually be ill, but he'd never tell me now. Never again. Thanks, Dr. Fogelman.

He tosses a couple of envelopes on the desk and sits down in Greta's chair, crosses his stork legs. "Have you forgotten what day it is?"

I try to think. It's nobody's birthday, not our anniversary. We met in the fall, not the spring. "I give up," I say, intrigued.

"April fifteenth."

"April fifteenth." It sounds familiar. We first had sex on February 2; I write it on every new calendar (in code) with all the other annual reminders. "I don't know, I give up. Tell me."

He sighs. "Income taxes? Federal, D.C.?"

"Oh! Right." Deflated, I watch him fish the forms out of the envelopes. He finished the taxes ages ago, but he likes to mail them at the very last second to save on interest if we owe anything. I feel stupid again. As if he's given me a heart-shaped box, and inside on a bed of velvet is a pencil sharpener.

"Do you want to go over them?"

"No, but they . . ." No, I won't fall into that. Every year he asks if I want to read the returns, every year I say no but they better be right, I better not end up in jail, ha-ha, and he uses this smooth, oily voice to say don't you trust me? Ha-ha—a humor ritual. But we're not having those moments anymore, or if we do by accident, they feel false, and then we become horribly self-conscious.

How will this work next year? Maybe by then we'll be filing separate returns. I'll have to go to H&R Block.

I hate these thoughts, but they come more and more often. The devil whispering in my ear. How will we split up the dining-room furniture, I wondered the other day. Andrew can have everything but the sideboard, which was my mother's. Which one of us gets to go to Parents' Weekend in the fall? Which one gets the house, or will we sell it and split the proceeds? Andrew must have the same thoughts. But we can't talk about them yet. We're in the lull, the silent, frightened phase, when it's still too painful to speak.

I sign the tax forms in the right places and he folds the pages, puts them in the proper envelopes, seals them up. "So what have you been up to?" I ask, trying for a casual, friendly tone. Normal.

"Nothing. Work. I spend a lot of time at school. I'm rarely home."

"Oh?" I say encouragingly, but that's all he's going to tell me about what he's been up to. It feels strange, being together in a room again. I can smell him. I know what's in his wallet. I know what the texture of his tweed jacket feels like, I know what hole his belt buckle is in. How cold, to know someone so intimately and yet be so estranged. This is the kind of thing that happens to other people.

Business over, Andrew glances around the office vaguely, pleasantly, as if looking for additions or improvements. His eyes light up when they fall on my big leather duffel in the corner. "Ah," he says— and later I'll try to deconstruct his precise tone when he said it. "You're staying over tonight, then leaving tomorrow? For your week of solitude."

"Right. I do, once in a while."

"Do what?"

"Stay over. When things get hectic or I have an early shoot. The couch isn't bad, I've got a pillow—"

"What do you mean? You stay *here*?"

"Yes." We stare at each other. It dawns on me—I am so slow today— he thought I was coming *home*. "Yes, I do, I stay here every great once in a while. Not often. Well, what did you expect?"

"Nothing, that's great. That's just great." He shoves the envelopes in his coat pocket, uses both hands to shoot himself out of the chair. "That's perfect." His anger freezes me; I can only look at him. "Who takes care of your dog?"

"Cottie sometimes, or—Owen. Owen's got her tonight."

"Owen." He says it not just with distaste, but with venom.

"What's wrong with that?" I stand up, too.

"I don't know, you tell me."

"Tell you what? What does that mean?"

"Not a damn thing."

I trot after him through the dim studio. It's like a bad dream—I just did this, except it was Greta who was furious with me. "Hold on a damn minute, Andrew." He halts in the door to the stairs. "You're the one who's better off without me—that's what you said. What happened? Did you finally get *bored* enough?"

"Don't worry about it."

"Oh, believe me, I'm not worried!"

"Good."

"Good!"

He starts down the steps.

"Hey!" I yell. "I'm not mad at you. Are we fighting? I don't even know how you are. How are you?"

"Have a good week, Dash. Find yourself. I'll be at work if you need me."

"Oh no, you will *not* make me feel guilty for—" The outside door slams behind him.

"—for my free week. My free week!" I shout, because the first time my voice echoed so pathetically in the empty stairs. "I can't wait. You won't be there, and I will never once be bored. I have resources!"

sixteen

Friday p.m. — It begins!

Chilly rain started on way home, scotching plan for long walk with Sock to launch vacation. Forced to sit by fire and drink wine after dinner. Too sleepy to write now, but mean to keep journal over entire week, tracking spiritual/mental/physical progress. Forward or back.

Saturday

Indecisive April still can't make up its mind. Am I winter? Am I summer? Snow flurries in a.m., sunny & warm by afternoon. Ate scrambled duck eggs for breakfast—Owen gave them to me—he has duck flock on his farm. Delicious. How clever, growing your own food. He has cows, too, and huge vegetable garden he's already begun planting.

Took Sock for walk in afternoon. Saw, acc. to nature book: wild violets, fiddlehead ferns, crested dwarf iris, wild strawberry, mountain laurel. Also something like gorse or vetch, v. sweet-smelling. Everything is waking up. Budding trees look like clouds of green mist. Saw: a hawk, two sparrows, swallows (?), a goldfinch. A butterfly! Also deer, but they are so commonplace to me now, they're not remarkable.

Fell asleep during meditation again. Mo taught me new way, hand mudra, you hold your left fist in your right palm above your navel and think about nothing. Does wonders for insomnia.

Sunday

Am thinking of going to church. Would be first time in long time. Pretty day, but windy, clouds zooming across crystal-blue sky. "Pneumonia weather," Andrew calls it.

Took my time and made beautiful salad for lunch, work of art, felt guilty eating it. Fell asleep afterward trying to read Ayurveda book Mo lent me. Slept TWO HOURS.

Didn't go to church. Played with Sock—puppy therapy—then held private service by pond, v. reverent place. Saw no wildlife. Was hoping for something, fish, an otter, a fox. Nothing. Except birds, and I couldn't recognize them. Must study more.

Oh, blah-blah-blah. Had thought to start a sort of naturalist's daybook, complete with sketches and simple but profound nature observations. Forgot I can't draw and am not profound. Would so much rather look at and/or photograph nature than write about it. Am consigning this diary to wastebasket. A. is right, I don't stick to my projects. Damn A.

"Hi, Ma."

Talking to my mother is a lot more therapeutic than keeping a journal, anyway. I lean my elbows back on the porch step and fix on the brightest star in tonight's busy sky. "Hi, Mama." She doesn't talk back; I'm aware these are *monologues* I have with my mother every evening, usually during Sock's last outing before bedtime.

"Andrew hates my hair." I pull my sweater up around my ears—not used to having a bare neck. "Not that I give a rat's patootie." That was one of my mother's sayings. "But you should've seen his face, like I'd gotten snake extensions or something. God."

Down the mountain, an owl hoo-*hoo*-ahs. A barred owl; I looked it up. I know some of the stars now, too. "That star, Mama, is Alioth, and it's eighty-one light-years away. Four hundred and twenty trillion miles."

Chloe knows the stars. She taught them to herself, just because she was interested. She was a little girl about ten minutes ago. She could read when she was five. "May I have some sugar?" I'd say, the same thing Mama used to say to me, and she'd run over and kiss me. Her hand in mine was always so tight and trusting. A boy named Dickie Hoyle broke her heart in second grade by abandoning her on a play-date, and when I called her apologetic mother to complain, I burst into tears. (Chloe was stoic, dry-eyed.) My favorite photograph is of her sitting on the Easter Bunny's lap—some mall foolishness—in her silver snow jacket and red galoshes, pressing her fingertips together and frowning up at the bunny with an expression that remains classic Chloe: polite, secretly baffled, endlessly tolerant.

"I knew those were precious times, Mama. I knew they were going by too fast, everybody knows that. Where I went wrong is, I thought that would protect me, the *fact* that I knew. Knew and appreciated, felt grateful and blessed every day. But it didn't slow anything down, not for a minute, and now . . . I don't know, something's going on with time, it's not passing the way it used to, and I *hate* it. Because you know all it comes down to is good-bye."

Mama's star flickers and keeps mum.

"I have to grow up. I have to stop minding the way things are. Accept, go with the flow. Maureen's talking about becoming a Buddhist."

Maybe middle age is when you make a choice. You can continue to be a child and just get older, or you can take the plunge into adulthood and just get older. Neither one saves you from pain, oh no, not by a long shot. But at least with the latter there's less whining.

"I'm going in, my butt's cold. I love you, Mama. Wish you were here. Sock, come on, girl!"

She flattens her butt in the moss to pee one more time, then she comes. She's so good. Maybe I should get lots of dogs, the next best thing to lots of children. No, that would be childish. Or would it? I hope it's not that whatever feels good is infantile, whatever hurts is mature. Oh, surely not, but I'll put it on my list of things to think about this week. I must never tell Andrew I have a list.

The cabin had no closets when we bought it, not even a kitchen pantry till Mr. Bender made us one. What did people used to do with their clothes? I've been hanging mine on hooks around the molding of a high faux wainscoting Andrew and I thought to nail to the bedroom walls a few years ago. They're sort of decorative—at least my light-colored summer clothes are and a few of my hats—but really, a woman should have a closet. So I asked Owen to build one, and he did.

It's small, but that's okay, so is the bedroom. Tomorrow he's coming over to put up the hanger rod and build an overhead shelf, and today I'm painting it. I'm using Lantern Glow, the exact shade of yellow-gold you see in all the house magazines but can never find at the paint store. And there it was in Flohr's Hardware on Monroe Street. It's sunny and perfect, I adore this color, I might paint every room in the cabin Lantern Glow.

Engine noise—gravel churning. Somebody's here. I put my sticky paintbrush down and cross to the window.

Owen? *Today?* I recognize his tan pickup through the trees before he wheels into the clearing and brakes. Sock has a remarkable disinterest in barking—so far; Owen says some dogs come to it late. She skips out to meet him, tail whirling, rear end squirming. She loves Owen.

Christ, I think on my way downstairs, *I'm a mess.* No makeup, my worst clothes, paint on my arms, probably my face. I've still got on my bedroom slippers. "Hey," I call from the porch, shading my eyes. "You're here *today.*"

"Got free early, thought I'd get that shelf in for you."

"Great!"

He always looks so healthy. I feel waiflike when I'm with him, and blonder for some reason. Today he has on several layers of clothes that make him look even bigger. I don't bother asking if he wants any help unloading stuff from his truck; I'd just get in the way.

Owen and I work well together. When he did the kitchen cabinets, there was no awkwardness between us while we stripped and stained and varnished. I don't know why I thought there would be, except that I talk so much more than he does.

"We can work around each other," he says when I tell him I'm in the middle of painting the closet. He's already measured and sawed for the shelf and rod, so now, unless he made a mistake, all he has to do is put them up. Still, this involves hauling a big plastic bucket of tools up the stairs, and then he has to put on his thick leather tool belt that's so heavy it always pulls his pants down a little and makes him look like a gunslinger. He shrinks my bedroom down to dollhouse size when he's in it, but he's not clumsy. He's quite graceful for a man his size.

"Don't you love this color? Isn't it fabulous?"

"Real pretty." He smiles, because that's a joke now, how many times I've asked him that. I like his soft-voiced, Virginia-Piedmont accent. "Real pretty."

"How's Cottie? I haven't talked to her in days."

"Doing good."

"Is she still walking?"

"Every morning."

"She hated that treadmill. Does Shevlin go with her? How old is he, seventy-five? He could use the exercise, too, I bet."

"Walking's for yuppies, he says."

"Ha. Of course. Stay in shape the old-fashioned way, with hard, honest labor."

Owen chuckles, but he'd never jog or walk for exercise, either. What foolishness, he'd think. Like his father-in-law, Owen's a man of action. Men of action don't join health clubs to use their Nautilus machines.

He measures something with his big, retractable measurer. "Danielle was over for the weekend."

I almost drop my brush. Partly because a local appearance by the elusive Danielle is a rare event, like a hummingbird in winter, but even more because this is the first time Owen has ever brought her up without a lot of not-so-subtle prodding from me. I'm intensely curious about her. We've never met; she's here and gone in a flash, like a movie star, and I hear about it afterward from Cottie.

"Really?" I sound very nonchalant.

He hunkers down, half in and half out of the closet, changing bits on his power drill. I stare down at the top of his head, his wide shoulders and strong, bulging thighs. If he doesn't say anything else, I'm going to pour this can of paint on him. "Yeah. She brought Matthew."

"She did? She usually leaves him at home, doesn't she? With her roommate?" Someone named Lisa who's a sales rep, like Danielle, at a cosmetics company.

"Yeah. Usually."

"How old is Matthew now?" Seven.

"Seven." For a while we can't talk over the noise of his drill. "He's in second grade. Real smart."

Matthew is Danielle's son from a very short first marriage. That husband is completely out of the picture, so Matthew is all hers. She and Lisa, who travel a lot in their jobs, have some sort of monetary/ care-sharing arrangement, so somebody is always there to look after him. I get all this from Cottie.

"I don't think you've ever told me how you and Danielle first met." This is so disingenuous, I can't look at him. I have to edge Lantern Glow along the white molding with extra care and concentration.

Another pause.

"I've known her practically all my life."

"Oh. Were you childhood sweethearts?"

"Nope." He puts a screw in his mouth and talks around it, squinting up at a metal bracket on the wall. "We didn't start up till I got out of the army. Then she got married, which set us back a bit."

His arm is in the way, I can't see if he's smiling. "And a baby, too," I say tentatively. "That probably took . . . some adjusting."

"No."

"No?" I prod after another damn pause.

"Matthew's never been a problem. I miss him more than her. What'd you think of that wild turkey meat? Too gamy for you?"

End of confidential revelations.

I finish my painting job before he finishes his carpentry job, so there's nothing to do but go down and clean my stuff in the kitchen sink. After that, I have time to put on some lipstick and fluff up my new short hair. Exchange this sweatshirt for a cardigan I left in the living room. *What's going on?* I ask myself in the bathroom mirror. As if I didn't know.

It's nice that I understand myself, because I certainly don't understand Owen. I'm used to men flirting with me, old men, young, attractive, not. It doesn't mean anything, they just like me, because I like them. I enjoy that little *thing* that happens, mutual awareness, unspoken acknowledgment of interest. Nothing comes of it, you have it and go on, it's just pleasant knowing it's there.

Owen and I, as far as I know we never have that *thing.* He's fond of me, that's obvious in his kindness, all the time he puts in doing things for me—of course, I *pay* him, but not that much, he's certainly not over here all the time for the money—but he never flirts. Occasionally I'll detect an appreciative look when he first sees me, although I might even be imagining that. So what is the problem? Does he find me sexless? Old? Does he dislike my city ways? Does he disapprove of my leaving Andrew?

We almost collide at the top of the stairs, me going up, him coming down with his bucket of tools. "Oops," I say, flustered. He started out with two shirts on and a T-shirt; now he's down to the T-shirt. I can smell him: fresh sweat, sawdust, and muscle. "Um, would you like a cup of coffee?"

"Got anything cold?"

"A Coke?"

"That'd be good."

We squeeze past each other.

"Oh, it looks great! Hey! I have a closet!" And I can't help thinking how completely beyond Andrew this project would be. I know I'm not supposed to mind. People like us, urban professionals who supposedly live in our heads more than our bodies, we've talked ourselves into half believing we're more evolved because we don't know how to do anything. But I don't know a single woman who, all other things being equal, wouldn't rather have a man who can do things.

Although, in fairness, Owen probably couldn't teach a course on the American Revolution.

While he loads up his truck, I set out sodas, cookies, peanuts, pretzels, olives, carrot sticks, hummus, and pita pieces. The cornucopia effect; I learned it from Cottie. When he comes inside, Sock trailing, he asks if he can use the bathroom. I rattle ice cubes while he pees so I can't hear. I don't know why.

"How's the washer-dryer? Any leaks?" He pulls out a chair and sits down at the table, frowning at a napkin in a wooden holder I put at his place.

"Nope, not a one. Owen, would you like a beer instead? I didn't even think to ask."

"This is fine." He takes an enormous swig of Coke, ignoring the lemon wedge I stuck on the glass. Leans back, getting comfortable. Looks around the kitchen. "So. How do you know what you're eating?"

"You asked! Finally—you've been so *discreet*." We look over at the big paper labels for tomatoes, corn, asparagus, beets—anything colorful—I glued behind the sink for a backsplash, and crack up. They brighten the room, no question, but over in the glass-fronted cabinet are the by-products of my cleverness I forgot to plan ahead for: lots of naked, anonymous cans of who knows what. "The other night I had lima beans and corn for dinner with a side of succotash." That's not even true, but it makes Owen laugh harder. "You're crazy," he says, as if it's a compliment.

He tells me about some genuine oak parquet squares he can get for practically nothing if I want them for the living room. "Hm" is my answer; I love the old pine boards. "Maybe in the kitchen, though. Instead of this linoleum." He looks taken aback, unsure. Parquet in a kitchen?

"Forgot to tell you—Miz Bender said be sure to call and tell her what's a good day for you two to get together."

"Oh, good. I'll call her this afternoon." Cottie and I are going out for lunch one day this week. "You always call her 'Mrs. Bender.' She told me you're as close to her as a son."

His blond eyelashes go down and he smiles, showing a crooked eyetooth. "I'm the same. She could be my mother."

"How did you lose your parents?"

"You mean Miz Bender didn't already tell you all about it?"

I show my open palms, look innocent.

"My father got blood poisoning from a tractor accident, and my mother got cancer."

"When you were very young?"

"Not that young. Twelve, Mama died. My father, I was fifteen. Lawyers wanted to sell the farm, but I wouldn't let 'em. Made 'em lease it."

"And the Benders took you in."

"Eventually. After a spell with my uncle and aunt down in Staunton. Pretty bad spell."

Cottie didn't tell me about that. I can see Owen's not going to, either.

"Benders knew me from church, knew my family. Some people talk about charity and doing what's right, helping out your neighbor when he's in need, and other people do it and don't say a word. Benders took me in and never made me feel beholden or like I had to be thanking them all the time. They even—" He pauses a second. "Even lent me some money when I got out of the army, get the farm going again. And that had nothing to do with Danielle, they just wanted to help me get started in my life."

I'm not surprised that Cottie never told me that, either.

"Do you like living by yourself? Or do you get lonely on your farm sometimes?"

He has light, clear eyes, and when he goes quiet or shuts down, he turns them away so I can't see them, as if otherwise I'd always see the truth. Andrew's a bit like that, too. Owen leans over to retie his boot lace and says, "Oh, I'm used to it. I get along fine. Too much to do to get lonesome."

I fall into a reverie I've had before, that Owen and I are married. We live on his farm. I tend the big vegetable garden and dress venison and can things in my spare time while he does the heavy outdoor work, planting the fields, castrating bulls, and what not. I don't have too much spare time, though, because I'm also the local vet. We're very *real* people, salt of the earth, nothing frivolous about us. I take his name. Our lives are simple but meaningful.

Sock puts her paw on his knee, and he pulls her up on his lap. A different kind of reverie comes over me. Sock splays her long adolescent legs over Owen's, and the worn corduroy stretches over his thighs, pulling the seams tight. His thick fingers disappear under the fur around her neck. She yawns in ecstasy, turning her head this way and that for more, shameless as a cat.

Owen's asking me something. I hear "week going?" and take a startled stab at the answer. "Oh, very well so far. I read and walk, I have my projects."

"Like what?"

"Well, black-and-white studies of the pond, that's one. In fact, the one thing I forgot to do is bring down my old enlarger. I used to develop pictures in a little bathroom darkroom—I could do that down here, just for fun. I miss film. Digital's great, I'd never go back, but sometimes I miss the darkroom."

"You should do that, then."

"I think I will."

"You're sure good at a lot of things."

"Me? I thought I was only good at one thing."

He shakes his head. He and Sock are both looking at me through half-closed eyes. "Cottie thinks you're about the smartest woman she knows."

"Oh. Pshaw." I trace a drop of condensation down the side of my glass with my finger. "What do you think?"

"I think it's gotten a lot more interesting around here since you came." He smiles. In a friendly way? A seductive, inviting way? Is his answer a factual observation or an overture? Is he oblivious to what he does, or is he doing it on purpose to make me crazy?

He picks up my camera, hanging by the strap on the chair next to his. His fingers look too big on the black case, fumbling it open, pulling the camera out. I'm a bit unnerved. Be careful, I want to say, don't crush it. He finds the power button and swivels it on. The lens hums out. He looks at me through the viewfinder.

"Don't take my picture."

"Why not?"

"Here, I'll take yours."

But he leans back, won't let me have the camera. He closes one eye and turns the focus ring. "Smile."

"No."

"You have a pretty smile."

"I hate having my picture taken. I know, the irony." I give him a flat-lipped smirk.

"Don't do that. Smile sweet. Then you develop it and let me have the picture."

I don't know what kind of smile I give him, but he takes the photo. I imagine the blacks and grays being born in developer, the whites emerging. It's me, all right. I've got antlers. Headlight glare flashes back from my dazed pupils.

Before he goes, he checks the stove in the living room and tells me I've got creosote, not to light another fire in there till I get it cleaned. Maybe this is all I want from Owen, manly advice, someone to look out for me. That's a comfortable role. He plays it well, and it doesn't confuse me.

I'm in a tricky phase, though. Anything could happen. I have a certain feeling in my skin, as if it's unnaturally thin, ultrasensitive. From past experience, I know this feeling can sometimes precede an impulsive act.

I walk outside with him. It's a bright, breezy, hopeful afternoon, warm in the sun, chilly when a cloud hides it. The sound of the wind is different from only a week ago, softer and more encumbered now that the buds have turned to baby leaves. April's mean streak is over.

Owen is one of those people who take forever to say good-bye. I don't think it means they hate good-byes—*I* hate good-byes, so I expedite them, kiss-hug-disappear. I think they just don't know how to leave. Owen presses the small of his back against the truck while he tells me about a porch swing he'll let me have cheap because he bought it in the fall when nobody wanted a porch swing. About how he'll kill the mice in the cabin walls if I don't have the heart for it (I don't, and I'm not letting him, either, but I say I'll think about it). About how these burrows in the ground here are from voles, not moles, and I should encourage Sock to eat, not just sniff them—why, his dog, Rex, eats so many, he'd be fine if Owen forgot to feed him for a week.

Then: "Do *you* ever get lonesome?"

I drop the stick Sock and I were mock-fighting over. "Who, me?"

"Your husband never comes down anymore. I know there's trouble. Miz Bender didn't say, but . . ."

She probably implied. I'm touched that Cottie hasn't told her own family everything I've told her about Andrew and me. I'm also amazed that Owen is finally saying something to me directly, no gallant circuitry, about my marital situation. I've referred to it plenty of times, but till now he never has.

"Yes, sometimes, sure. I'm lonely. But like you," I say deliberately, "I'm getting used to it." That's an invitation: mine to his. I'm already anticipating his response—*we should keep each other company,* something like that. Because to me, and now, obviously, to Owen, inquiring about whether a person is lonely or not is almost always an invitation.

He opens the door of his truck. "See those jammed-up oak leaves up there?" I follow his pointing finger to high, bare branches, a dark mass of something or other among them. "You got a flying squirrel's nest. Come out some night when the moon's full and watch. It's a sight to see." He gets in the truck and starts it up. "Okay. See you."

That's it? "Thanks—the closet is wonderful—I'll send you a check." Sock barks at the truck, which has begun to reverse; I scoop her up in my arms. "How much do I owe you?"

"I'll catch you on that later." He shifts gears and drives away.

I think that's what he said. Or "I'll get you on that later"? "I'll get with you on that later"? Any way I construct it, and I try several more combinations, I can't make it a double entendre.

seventeen

I've never seen Cottie Bender in a dress before, nor with her long braid pinned up on her head. My glance goes right over her amid the afternoon crowd at the Velvet Cafe until she waves to me from a back booth. I hurry over, wishing I'd dressed up more; the only concession I've made to our lunch date is to put on slacks instead of jeans. I didn't know it was fancy. "Sorry I'm late! Have you been waiting long? Chloe called right as I was leaving—"

"Just got here. Sit." She's finished most of a glass of iced tea, so I know that's a fib.

"Sorry, sorry, but then we got into a *fight,* and so then we had to make up before we could say good-bye. *Sort* of make up."

"You and Chloe?" She has a garnet circle pin on the collar of her long-sleeved shirtwaist dress, and clip-on earrings that almost match it. She leans toward me in sympathy. "You had a fight?"

"You won't believe what she said, Cottie."

"Oh no. What did she say?"

"I'm still in shock."

"What?"

"She's decided to major in drama."

She sits back. "Oh. Really?"

"The theater." I put my hands on my cheeks. "After all these years of knowing exactly what she wants to be, a historian, a scholar like her father, now she wants to *act.*"

"Oh, my. Well," she says with a tolerant chuckle, "if that's what she really wants . . ."

I look at her in disbelief. But she doesn't know Chloe, doesn't understand the complete absurdity of this so-called decision. "How could she be so *impractical?* Chloe's the smartest one in the family! I *thought.*"

Sue, the waitress, appears. I'm too distracted to read the menu, I practically know it by heart now anyway. Today's special is turkey and stuffing with choice of two vegs. I order that and Cottie orders the big salad.

"This is so crazy, and she will not be reasoned with," I go on after Sue leaves. "She got *angry* with me. I'm still upset. We rarely fight. We disagree constantly, but we rarely fight. And the worst is, Andrew doesn't mind. *Andrew.* Or so she tells me—I haven't spoken to him yet. I called him immediately, but he wasn't there. And *then, before* that, Greta tells me she's marrying *Joel.* What is going on?" I stick my fingers in my hair and pull. "I don't get it, I just don't get it."

Cottie looks at me as if I'm a riddle she can't solve.

I flutter my hands. "Never mind, let's not talk about it now, boring family business. How are you? You look wonderful, truly—Owen said you're feeling good, too."

So the conversation changes, but part of me is still back on the phone with Chloe. She mentioned it almost in passing—"Hey, Mom, I'm switching majors"—then she was *surprised* when I wasn't thrilled with the news. "What difference does it make?" she kept saying. "Why do you care so much?" Why do I *care* so much! Because it's impractical, impulsive, unwise, and immature. "Do you know how many people make a living in the theater? One percent!" (I have no idea.) "Since when have you been *practical,*" she said to me, and that set me off. I said the one thing I now regret: "Let's not forget who's paying for your sky-high tuition." At least I didn't add "young lady."

"I don't get you," we ended up telling each other, and hanging up practically in tears—me, anyway. And to hear that Andrew has *no problem* with this—I can't get over that. If it's true, it's just to spite me. Everywhere I look, I am having the rug pulled out from under me. No one's behaving the way they should, and I don't understand why *I* keep looking like the bad guy.

Cottie pours oil and vinegar on her salad from the smudged glass bottles Sue brings. "I should've gotten that," I say, spreading a pool of yellow gravy into my mashed potatoes. "You're such a sensible eater."

"Only recently."

"But haven't you always been slender?"

She nods. "I was sickly as a child, never have been able to put on much weight."

"Rheumatic fever," I remember. Owen told me.

She examines a chunk of iceberg lettuce on the end of her fork. "Never thought I'd make it to old age, to tell you the truth. Since I was nine, every year I've given myself about four more years."

"Oh, Cottie."

"I never thought I'd make it off the operating table after surgery. Never thought I'd get this far in my recovery."

"Cottie *Bender*."

She grins, then looks down. "I've got a little confession to make. Remember when we first met?"

"Of course."

"I had in mind that you were a particular kind of person that I could be friends with, like I couldn't be with anyone else. Not Shevlin, not Owen or Danielle, none of my friends from church." She gives a hooting laugh. "Definitely not them. Somebody I wouldn't have to be so damn cheerful and hopeful with, frankly."

"Oh." I put down my fork.

"Because you came from the city! You had an artistic job, and you're so smart and dress so chic. Your husband's a professor, your car isn't American. Sophisticated, that's it. I thought you might be the perfect person I could be my secret self with."

"But why?" I'm not getting this. I thought she just liked me. "Anyway, what secret self?"

She looks around, as if checking for eavesdroppers. "I am a pessimist. And"—she leans forward for this—"I *might* almost be an agnostic."

"I think I knew that," I say slowly. I feel surprised that I'm not more surprised. "So with me . . ."

"With you, I thought I could be negative. Honest."

"Well, sometimes you have been. I guess."

"I don't know if I have been or not, but the point is, I was wrong. And not that it matters anymore, but it's turned out, you're a bigger optimist than Reverend Ashe—our pastor at church."

"Well, that's what everybody *says*."

"It was foolish of me to make you into a certain type of person before I knew you, that's what I wanted to say. I'm sorry."

"Oh, please. Just so you're not disappointed."

"No, I'm not disappointed." She smiles her sweet smile.

I try to think of something I could confess. "I thought you were going to be much squarer. A country lady."

She loves this; her eyes light up and she colors. "I *am* a country lady."

"Yes, but I didn't know you'd be so worldly."

"Worldly." She rolls the word out, savoring it like a mint. "What in the *world* are you talking about?"

"Well, you told me you used to sneak cigarettes when Shevlin wasn't around."

"Used to," she agrees, patting her chest.

"And . . . you know."

"What?"

"You know." Now I'm the one lowering my voice and checking for listeners. "What you'd say to him," I whisper. "In his coffin."

"Oh!" We cover snorts of laughter with our hands. Cottie once told me, I forget in what possible context, that if Shevlin died first, she would feel compelled to tell him the truth at last. She would whisper in his ear as he lay in his casket, "Honey, I always voted Democrat."

"How did you meet him?" I ask.

"How did you and Andrew meet? You go first."

"Oh, at a party on New Year's Eve."

"And did you like him right away?"

"Right away. As soon as I saw him." I don't tell her I kissed him the second I set eyes on him. She might get the wrong idea about me.

"Why? What set you off?"

"Oh, I don't know. Well, he was cute. And sort of courtly, I thought. Knightly. And I could tell he liked *me*—I always like people who like me."

Cottie laughs.

"He was twenty-eight and I was twenty-four, but it seemed like more. Almost as if he was from a different era. I don't know who I thought I was in those days. I'd get an idea of myself, but then it would change, and . . . But I was happy most of the time, and I think people like that in other people."

"Andrew liked it in you."

"Yes." I could see myself appealing to him that night, I could see him letting go of some of his reserve. "That's seductive, don't you think, watching someone fall for you? Of course, it was happening to me just as fast, so I didn't have time to gloat."

I don't know how to explain to Cottie a feeling I had from the first, almost as soon as I saw him, that—*Here is someone who knows things I'd like to know.* Things about life, that's as specific as I could be. Secrets about how to live, what the best things to want were. Maybe something about rectitude or discretion, a quieter, calmer way to get through my life. Of course, it was all mostly unconscious at the time, and even now it's not exactly crystalline. I thought he had something I wanted, simple as that. Although that night it was mainly to know how the back of his neck would feel, just below the shaggy hairline.

"So anyway, we just hit it off," I conclude. "Now you go—how did you and Shevlin meet?"

"Well." Cottie sits back, blots her lips with a napkin. "I was an old maid, living at home with my father. Who was on disability for a leg he lost from diabetes. My sisters were married and older, it was just me. I had adored my mother—you and I have that in common—but my papa was another story. Deacon in the church, real strict, and very pious. Shevlin didn't even go to church, claimed he didn't believe in God. So wicked, that seemed to me. And attractive."

"Yes."

"I was a good girl, but I had a tongue in my head. He said that's one reason he liked me right off. We met at a dance social at the fire hall— he brought another girl. He looked dark and dangerous, like a tough customer. And quiet, like he was thinking dangerous thoughts. I couldn't take my eyes off him."

I squeeze my arms, give a mock shiver.

"Well, he got away from that girl he had with him and got me on my own and he said, 'I'm calling on you.' "

" 'I'm calling on you.' "

"But the *way* he said it. It was old-fashioned even then, but neither one of us were spring chickens, we were both in our thirties, that whole sixties business had passed us by."

"So then?"

"So then, that's just what he did. Papa *hated* him. Called him the devil, which was all I needed." She smiles. "But no, it wasn't like that, I was too old to fall for a man just because my father disapproved. Though I'm not saying it didn't help."

"And he pursued you," I remember. Cottie had felt like a dandelion in the wind.

"He did. Me, I was sick of singing in the church, being the girl every boy treated like a newborn rabbit. Shevlin was never disrespectful, but he surely did let me know I was no newborn rabbit. One time . . ." She chases a last bit of tomato around the bottom of the oily bowl. "We used to meet in the cemetery on occasion for a date."

"The cemetery?"

"It got so tiresome dealing with Papa every time we wanted to go out, so once in a while we'd meet in the cemetery. Well, this one night I couldn't go at the last minute, Papa wanted me to help him with his bath, so I missed our date. I was sitting in my room feeling blue when who waltzes around the corner and through the door but Shevlin. In my room! It was such a *shock*. At first—but then it just seemed natural as anything. We sat on the bed and visited—which is about all we ever did, strange as it might seem now, even in the cemetery. We were talking and laughing, feeling safe because Papa was downstairs with the radio on, we'd fixed up the dining room like a bedroom so he wouldn't have to use the stairs—"

"How did Shevlin get in?" I interrupt.

"Through the front door and up the steps, that's how. Which is just like him, I know now: He always takes the direct approach. Well— somehow, I guess with his X-ray ears, Papa figured out something was up, because all of a sudden we hear this *thump. Thump. Thump.* The sound his crutch made on the stairs." She puts her hand on her heart. "I have never been so scared in my life. Shevlin—you ought to've seen him. First he tried to get under the bed, but the space was too narrow, plus I kept my suitcase under there. Then the closet, but the door wouldn't close. *Thump. Thump.* I had my sewing machine under the one window. It took the two of us to shove it aside, and Shevlin tore his pants and his underpants on the window crank when he squeezed through."

"My God."

"There was this horrible crash just before Papa came in—I thought sure Shevlin was dead, but he fell on top of the hydrangea. It broke his fall." Her shoulders shake; she dabs a tear of mirth from her eye. "We have laughed about that almost every day since."

"What did your father do?"

"He made us get married. Which is all we were after to begin with."

"Cottie, what a great story." She sighs in agreement. "Andrew would never do something like that."

"No?"

"No." He wouldn't even come down and get me when I was pregnant with Chloe. All he could do was call and *reason* with me. Mama was on his side. I see I'm not quite over being mad at *both* of them for that. "No, it would be too undignified," I tell Cottie. "You can't laugh at Andrew. He's got a lovely sense of humor, but not about himself. I'm the only one who can tease him."

"Well, there."

"Yes, but even I have to be careful."

She drums her fingers on her jaw thoughtfully. "Owen would never do anything like that, either, I don't believe. Sometimes I wish he would. If he'd ever take the bull by the horns, I believe Danielle might go back with him."

I can't think of anything to say to that. I stare back blandly. Yesterday Mo asked me, "Are you going to have an affair with Owen?" "Maureen!" I put all the innocence into my voice that I'm now putting into my face. It didn't put Mo off at all. "Well, are you?" I laughed indulgently. "The chances of that happening are about a hundred to one," I said. "Practically nil." She said, "*Prac*tically," and I changed the subject.

Sue comes over and refills our iced-tea glasses. No thanks, we tell her, no dessert for us today.

"What's funny," Cottie says, stirring sugar substitute into her glass, "is that after Shevlin got baptized again, he took to going to church like it was the Blue Tick Roadhouse, which, believe me, he used to attend regularly."

"He got baptized *again?*"

"My father insisted on it. And this time it took, Shevlin's the Bible clerk at church, and he does so much work on the grounds he might as well be the sexton." She shakes her head for a long time. "I'm not as fond of church as I ought to be. Which I can tell you," she says with a sly smile, "my *sophisticated* friend. I don't say it to Shevlin nor Danielle. Especially not Danielle, who I doubt has set foot in a church since she moved to Richmond. Raising Matthew like a little heathen," she says fondly.

"Andrew goes to church."

"Andrew does?" She's astonished. Another stereotype blown away.

"On holidays. He says he likes the music. He doesn't make a big deal of it—God has his place, no need to get all emotional about him. He's like the president of the United States: You respect the office even when you disagree with his politics."

"Well, I declare." Again she glances around the restaurant, thinning out now that it's after two. "I hope you don't mind if I confide this to you." She leans in. "I get lonesome nowadays. For . . . you know."

I look dumb, in case I'm mistaken.

"Intimate relations," she clarifies in a murmur. "Shevlin is so careful of me since the operation. I keep telling him I'm *fine,* but he doesn't like to take a chance."

"Oh, Cottie." I'm so touched by this, her eagerness, his reticence, the sweetness of it. I think of Andrew, how nice it was with him the last time. I think of what a nice phrase *intimate relations* is. "I miss it, too," I confess. "Not so much the sex"—I whisper that; the Velvet Cafe, at least to me, is not a place in which one says "sex" out loud. Maybe at dinner, but not lunch. "Not the actual sex so much as the closeness."

"Oh, I've got the closeness. What I would like some of now is the actual sex."

We start up again, cackling, sagging against the wall of our booth. Sue brings the check just then and wants to know what's funny. "Whoo," Cottie says, pushing my wallet back at me, taking out hers. "Nothing, honey. Foolish woman talk is all. Just foolish woman talk."

"*Beautiful* afternoon." Cottie puts her head back to catch the sun, slipping her arm through mine. The sidewalk's narrow; pedestrians have to go around us, but we don't care. We're in a good mood, we feel entitled. "What should we do now?" she asks. "Do you have to get back?"

"I've got the whole day."

"Let's go in here."

Treasures and Things, Dolley's antique store. A hundred percent Things, in my experience, but I stop in all the time anyway. Must be because I'm an optimist.

"Are these tacky?" I hold up salt and pepper shakers shaped like cows standing on their hind legs.

"Definitely."

Mr. McDorn, who owns the place, is a nice man, but he's usually too busy talking your ear off to do anything as dull as dust or straighten up or put price tags on things. It's like your dotty old grandmother's attic: no rhyme or reason, not to mention an asthmatic's nightmare.

"I wonder if Shevlin could use this." Cottie fingers a metal contraption, some sort of tool, evidently, since it's in the store's loosely gathered tool section.

"What is it?" I ask.

"I'm not just sure. Something for cows?"

"Maybe Owen could use it, then."

"Or it might be a trap."

"You mean, a trick?"

She gives me an amused look. "No, honey, a trap. For some poor animal."

"Oh." Before my eyes, the metal contraption becomes hideously ugly. I'm glad when Cottie puts it down and moves on.

We wander around, picking up and putting down, admiring, making cracks. Mr. McDorn waylays us in the particularly decrepit used-book section, where I hang back and eventually drift away, letting Cottie tackle him; she's known him longer, she can handle his barrage of words better. He must be lonesome, I always think, and let him go on for as long as he likes. Cottie's perfectly sweet but also brisk; soon we're out and on the street, and I don't even feel guilty for not buying anything.

Cottie has to pick up a prescription at the drugstore. While I wait, I buy hand cream on sale. Part of my arsenal for the nightly lube job: moisturizer, lip balm, body lotion, hand lotion, foot cream. It's a wonder I don't slide out of the bed. It's our hormones drying up, apparently. "Wait'll you're my age," I heard a woman say to her friend on the subway. "Wait till sex is painful." Not "uncomfortable"; she said "painful." Can that be true? If so, talking about it must be the last taboo. Next time sex comes up in conversation, I'll ask Cottie; she'll give me the true story.

The drab, run-down Madison Theater keeps an unpredictable schedule. "Look," Cottie says as we stroll by the streaky ticket booth, "something's playing." True: About a dozen teenagers are loafing in line for tickets to see a romantic comedy I read a snide review of about six weeks ago. Cottie and I look at each other.

"Want to go?"

"If we don't, we'll just have to go home."

"I'll call Shevlin."

The theater smells like butter and wet wool. We take seats on the aisle three-quarters of the way down without asking each other if that's all right. As soon as we're seated and comfortable, the lights go out, as if the projectionist has been waiting for us. "*Excellent* idea," I murmur as the credits roll. We bump shoulders conspiratorially.

How many movies have I seen with my mother? Or Chloe? I like going to movies with them more than anyone else, more than with the closest friend, more than with Andrew. Even the lamest film is bearable if I'm with Chloe—if I was with Mama; in fact, a terrible movie is better than a mediocre one, because then we can make cracks, be sarcastic, make it a competitive sport, our wit against the film's inanity.

This one is fairly inane. The hero's moroseness is supposed to attract the bubbly heroine, but that seems unlikely. All they could possibly see in each other is amazing facial perfection.

My mother took me to see *Annie Hall* when it first came out. Of course we both loved it. I didn't understand all of what *bittersweet* meant until then, and it hit me hard. I was glad to have my mother with me. The film seemed so modern, and she was so old-fashioned. Or no-fashioned; she was just Ma, my often-resisted, occasionally appreciated buffer between childhood and adulthood. We talked about the movie all afternoon, afterward. She understood better than I did why I loved Annie, why she was the first grown-up role model I ever had, not the Bionic Woman or Hayley Mills or whoever. (The second was Vanessa Redgrave in *Julia*.)

I was thinking about that experience, which seemed even more complicated in retrospect, all mixed up with my fear of growing up and a ferocious impatience to get on with it, not to mention figuring out what kind of woman I wanted to be—when I took Chloe to see *Amelie*. It was R-rated, but I had a feeling it would be appropriate for her and it was. What a tender, intoxicating, romantic film. I adored it, the daydream quality, Amelie's exquisite shyness, and her impishness, the wonderful *Frenchness* of it all. Chloe and I got ice cream afterward, our habit, and talked over the movie. She thought it was okay. *Okay?* I was still in a happy haze. "It was a little too much, Mom. Like a Disney movie." She was fourteen; she still had braces on her teeth, she still had freckles. "It was more a fairy tale than a real story. I mean, what was she so *afraid* of?"

It's disappointing when your child doesn't agree with you, especially when you know you're right, but it's also hugely exciting. Discussing that film defined our differences in a way nothing quite had before, and never so easily or naturally. I loved my daughter even more, if that was possible, for who she was, who I could see her becoming. And I like to think she added a little bit of ballast to her already crowded cargo hold of tolerant affection for Mom.

What's this? I'm not paying much attention to this movie, but sometime after the beautiful lovers break up and before they will, I'm certain, get back together, I begin to weep.

Quietly, thank God. Silent tears slipping down, wetting my hands in my lap. The screen is a complete blur. This will stop in a moment, I assure myself, reaching for a tissue in my purse. I mop my eyes surreptitiously, facing away so Cottie won't notice.

But a second later it starts again. This time there's no stopping it, and when Cottie slips her arm through mine, I start to cry in earnest. It's an embarrassing, unexplainable lapse. And strange, because the tears came so much sooner than the emotion that provoked them. Whatever it is. The usual, I suppose. Loss. I feel incomplete. I'm missing.

I glance at Cottie, try to speak, apologize—she's got tears in *her* eyes. Is it sympathy for me, or could she be thinking of her mother, gone but still deeply missed after fifty years? Or of her daughter, who flies in and out of her life at random intervals, uncatchable as a butterfly?

I lean my head on her shoulder. It comforts both of us, I think. On-screen, the morose lover convinces the poignantly brokenhearted but still effervescent heroine that they belong together. Yes, well. Get it while you can, children. Don't look ahead. There's no percentage in knowing what's coming, because you can't prepare for it. And once it happens, there's nothing to do but endure.

"I could've driven you home," I tell Cottie while we wait in front of the theater for Shevlin to pick her up. At five o'clock, the sun is a glowing ball just starting to sink over the mountain. My mountain. A flock of starlings falls like a net over the mansard roof of the bank across the way, rises up, falls back again.

"I know," Cottie says, "but this is fine. He likes to do it."

I imagine he does. It's so sweet. I wouldn't dream of asking Andrew to drive me somewhere or pick me up. Is that another loss? What a mood I'm in. "Well, Cottie, what can I say. I'm sorry for being a noodlehead."

"Now, don't say that."

"I don't even know what was the matter with me."

"Sometimes we just need a good cry."

"Usually not in a public place, though."

"When I was going through the change, I cried through the whole funeral service of a man I never met in my life."

"Oh, I do that all the time."

We sling our arms around each other and watch cars stop and go at the intersection, Dolley's rush hour in full swing.

"Well, I'm not one to go around cheering people up," she says.

"I think you are."

"Bad things are bad things. And they always hit when you least expect them—for some reason, whoever's in charge made that a rule."

Maybe she isn't one to go around cheering people up.

"Life's nothing but saying good-bye, if you care to look at it that way."

"Oh God," I say with a shiver. "I don't."

"Me, either, but sometimes you can't see any alternative."

"So then what do you do?"

"What I do is try to stick myself into it more. If I'm the one who has to let go, then I try to *do* it, not have it *done* to me. It doesn't hurt as much that way, plus you can learn something in the process."

"I guess."

"Not that learning something does you any good next time. You think it will, but it doesn't. Oh, honey, we just have to go through it all."

Shevlin's truck pulls up to the curb. Despite the fine weather, he's got the earflaps down on his old green cap. I'm not sorry to see him; I don't want any more of Cottie's hard wisdom right now.

"Did I make you feel sad?" Worry lines crease her face. "Lord help us, that's the last thing I meant to do."

"You didn't."

"Anyway, I forgot the main thing."

She's become very dear to me, I realize, her long, thick-skinned face, the way it breaks up and shines when she smiles. Her unvarying kindness to me. "What's the main thing?" I ask.

"The main thing . . ." She spreads her arms wide, pulling out the blue wool of her cardigan like benevolent bat wings. "The main thing is we're here right now, alive and kicking. What a shame to waste a minute because it won't last. You can't stop change, so you might as well give it a big hug and get on with it." She salutes me, then hauls herself up into her husband's Ford F-150. The muffler's bad. Roaring off down Madison Street, they sound like reckless teenagers in a hot rod.

Reaching for the car keys in my coat pocket, I pull out something wrapped in paper—and smile, because I know what's inside before I open it. A couple of cows standing on their hind legs.

Five whole hours in the house by herself—a record for Sock, who's wild to see me. A quick survey of the downstairs reveals no damage;

it's either upstairs or my dog has turned into an angel. We put off finding out by taking the flashlight and walking down to the road.

It's too early for crickets, or if it's not, I can't hear them over the tree frogs. Sock is fearful of the dark, sticks with me instead of exploring the woods this far from the house, but I'm not. I only take the flashlight so I won't trip over a rock or a rut. Nothing spooks me; I never have crazy thoughts about bears or snakes or depraved mountain men. I'm a hundred times warier about being out alone at night in D.C. than here.

"Hi, Ma." Instead of a star, I see her in the moon tonight, a kind-faced half-moon wearing a patient smile. "Cottie and I had a nice time today. You don't feel replaced or anything, do you? Because that would be . . . that would be nuts."

Sock and I stop fifty feet from the road—I'm still nervous about her and cars, plus I don't care for us to be picked out by anyone's headlights at night. It's quiet though; not a single car passes as we stand in the shadowy lane, the flashlight off, sniffing the air and listening to night sounds.

"Mama? I wish . . ."

The dog and I start back for the cabin.

"I wish I'd been better. Andrew says no, but I think I could've been a better daughter if I'd had time. If I'd just thought. I'm so sorry about Mr. Dreessen. I wish you were here, so I could tell you. I miss you, Mama, and I can't seem to . . ."

I pick up a stick on the side of the drive, use it for a walking stick until Sock takes it from me. I didn't even know how sick my mother was. When she called to say she couldn't come up for her graduation, Chloe was disappointed but not devastated. They weren't as close as they could've been—that's another one of my regrets. They should've seen each other more often. They should've loved each other as much as I loved them.

The hospital called two days later. Mama had had a heart attack in the night. She'd managed to call 911. I can't bear to think of that, her fear and pain, how alone she must've felt, dialing the ambulance by herself. I should've tried harder to make her move up here. I was half-hearted about that. Self-involved.

She died in the hospital. I was in the air—they told me what time, and I figured out I was eating mini pretzels and drinking orange juice when my mother died. This is the part I can't let go, it's like a burn wound that will not heal. I couldn't have saved her, but I could have held her hand so she wouldn't have been alone when she left. That's all I wish. That we could've been together when it was her time.

Mama had beautiful skin—I have my father's dry, Irish skin. I skip the nightly lube job, though, despite having a new jar of hand cream. Too tired; going to bed early.

How did it happen that Sock sleeps with me? At first I'd find her at the foot of the bed in the morning, then she began to jump up even when I was looking, now she has *her spot* beside my left hip. I like it, though. I like to put my hand on her back—she always faces away from me; some kind of modesty, or perhaps I snore—and feel the soft up and down of her breathing.

The clock dial glows red in the dark: 9:52. Behind my eyelids I see silent pictures, scenes I'm either imagining or remembering from today, lots of people, all strangers, in perfect Technicolor, walking, talking, gesturing, laughing. This happens once in a while, and usually presages a sleepless night.

Sock moans, burrows deeper when I turn on the light. I'm reaching for the hand cream, but at the last second my hand veers to the phone. I punch in Chloe's speed-dial number.

I hope she's not in the library. She's such a good child, she turns her phone off when she's there, lest she disturb other students.

"Hello?"

"I want you to major in drama."

"Mom, hi. I was going to call you."

"Darling, erase everything I said, I don't know what I was thinking. I desperately want you to major in drama, or anything else you feel passionate about. Actually, I sort of do know what I was thinking."

"What?"

"But it doesn't matter now. I got mixed up, that's all, I reversed you and Greta."

"Me and Greta?"

"Do you think she's still awake? Oh, she would be, it's early. I have some names to give her, photographers I know who might want their websites redone."

"Mom."

"Sweetheart, I just want you to know you can do anything you want. Why would you ever listen to my advice anyway, you're a hundred times smarter."

"Well, in this case, I wasn't going to."

"So I noticed. What if I'd said I was going to cut off all funds?" She laughs gaily. "Where are you?"

"Walking back to the dorm."

"Is it a nice night? It's beautiful here."

"Did you talk to Dad?"

"Not lately, why? Oh—he didn't talk me out of anything."

"Okay. I just thought—"

"No, no, I came to this brilliant realization all by myself, your father had nothing to do with it. I gave . . . I think . . . I sort of reversed . . . I gave the right advice to the wrong people. I made Greta myself and— well, I don't know what I did with you. I was trying to be practical for you. Really, really motherly, trying to make up for . . ." Oh God, trying to make up for not being daughterly enough? This was all about *guilt*?

"Practical, Mom. I don't know."

"I know. Not my strong suit."

"And you should know, I might change my mind again. I could decide to major in anthropology."

"Oh, you'd be *fabulous* at that."

"Or archaeology."

"They're not the same?"

"Or French."

"Ooh, *formidable*."

"Hi," she says to someone, then back to me. "So how's your vacation going? Have you bonded completely with the land yet?"

"We are as one. I had lunch with Cottie, she asked all about you." I tell her about the movie we saw.

"Sounds great. Hey, you still miss *me*, though, don't you?"

"My best movie pal? Are you kidding?" She is, but I'm not. If she knew how much I miss her, it would ruin this conversation. "Okay, babe, I'll let you go, I can hear you've arrived." Chatter, doors slamming. "I love you the most."

"Love you, Mom."

"And honey? I just want you to know, even though I didn't see it coming, it makes absolutely no difference to your father *or* to me that you're a thespian."

She hangs up groaning.

Except for a couple of brisk, all-business conversations about how things are going this week at the studio, Greta and I haven't spoken to each other since our fight. She sounds spacey when she answers the phone. "Uh-oh," I say, "did I wake you?"

"No."

"Did I . . . get you from something—"

"I was playing a computer game. What do you want?"

"Um . . . how are you?"

"Fine." I picture her at her computer, zapping aliens or piloting some virtual heroine through a maze. I see her in her nightgown, her carrot hair sticking out like candlewicks. After a pause, she says grudgingly, "How are you?"

"I'm fine, too. Hope I'm not calling too late."

"No, I told you."

This is going to be harder than I thought. Well, nothing to do but plunge in. "Okay, here's the thing. I'm very glad you're marrying Joel."

"Oh, Dash." In two words, she sounds tired and dubious.

"No, anyone can see he's nuts about you. You're *perfect* for each other."

"You don't have to say this."

"But I mean it. I think you'll be great, and twenty-five is *not* too young to know what you want."

"Well, *I* don't think so."

"And . . . I'm proud of you for knowing what you want to do with your life. It's me I feel sorry for, I'm the one who's losing you, but I really admire you for knowing your mind and . . . well, I just wish you happiness, that's what I'm calling to say. And success, and satisfaction, and a long, long life with Joel and little—shit, I can never remember—"

"Justin."

"Justin. You, Joel, and Justin, a ready-made family. It's so right, and . . . I was so wrong."

"Thanks, Dash. It means a lot, you saying that."

"And I apologize for all the other things I said." Might as well make it official. "Just disregard all that, please. I wasn't in my right mind."

"No problem." Her laugh sounds big and relieved. "Totally forgotten. But how come, I mean, where did . . ."

"I was crazy, what can I tell you? Temporary insanity." I can think of no kindhearted way to explain to Greta that, basically, I made her up. It would be insulting to tell the truth: that from the moment we met, I took her for a person she's so far from being (me) that I couldn't see her at all. And then I wanted her to make all the decisions I didn't make twenty years ago. What willful blindness, what monumental ego. I'm ashamed. "Let's have a party." What a *brilliant* idea. "Would you like to?"

"A party?"

"To celebrate your engagement! We could have it at the studio. With men if you want, or it could be more like a shower, all women. But I think men, don't you? Then we can drink more."

"Um . . ."

"All your friends, and Joel's, Mo would come, some clients, some of the neighbors . . ." I start naming people we know in common. "We could do it outside if that's too many people, it'll be warm by then. And . . . I know, a group photo, something fun and creative, not just bodies lined up. A keepsake, something really special for you and Joel. I'll put on my thinking cap."

"Wow, that would be *so cool*."

"I know, and afterward, after you're all hitched and everything, I've got a million photographer pals and they all need new websites, most of them. Whether they know it or not, and I know exactly who to tell them would be *perfect* for the job."

"Dash."

"What?"

"Thank you. Thanks for—"

"For nothing! This is all for me, a hundred percent my pleasure. Truly." Guilt and regret are wonderful motivators. So is hearing Greta laugh like a conspirator—like a friend. Like someone I'd love to get to know.

andrew

eighteen

Andrew dreaded Wednesdays. His only class ended at eleven—it should be his favorite day. But, being the shortest, it was also the day he'd designated at the beginning of term as the one on which he drove out to Olney and visited his father. So he hated it.

He circled the well-tended grounds of Meadow Grove, closing in on the low, handsome brick building, Grove One, that housed his father and eleven other elderly souls in need of assistance with living. Whose white car was that? *Dash's?*

Yes—he recognized the license plate as he idled past, pulling into the last spot in the row. Dash was *here*? She used to come with him once in a while, but visiting Edward was even more oppressive for her than it was for him, so he assumed she'd quit when she moved out of the house. He shouldn't be surprised, though. How like her to come. How kind. He hadn't seen her since the night he brought the tax returns to her office.

He glanced in the rearview mirror to see what he looked like, what she'd make of him—and at the same moment the front door of Grove One flew open and she came striding out.

She looked fit, strong, preoccupied. She had on turquoise jeans and a yellow pullover. Running shoes. She tipped her head back to see the clear sky, and her shoulders rose as she took in a deep breath. He knew exactly how she felt. His reaction after visiting Edward was the same: huge relief; a fresh appreciation of freedom.

He got out of his car.

"Andrew!"

If he had a hope that she'd come today, *his* day, on purpose, her obvious surprise at seeing him dashed it. She gave him an air kiss before they had to move aside for an incoming car. "Can you stay and talk?" he asked, gesturing to an empty bench in a patch of shade near the building.

"No, gotta get back. I just came up to get something—it's still my free week. Greta's handling the office and she says everything's fine, we're making money." She leaned against his car and folded her arms. They could talk here, her posture indicated, just not for long.

He didn't like her bringing up money. It wasn't her style, and he was afraid it was because of what he'd said the last time—something off-hand and thoughtless, possibly sarcastic, about how he'd be *working* while she was down in Virginia finding herself. "It doesn't matter," he said, "we have plenty." She looked at him strangely. Now *he* was saying uncharacteristic things. "What about veterinary school?" he couldn't re-sist asking. "How's that going?"

"I decided against it. There's too much science."

He bit his lip. "Em, I'd imagine there would be."

"So now I'm thinking of the Forest Service. I could be a forest ranger, I'm good at nature."

Her face was turned from him. He ventured an uncertain laugh. She was joking, wasn't she?

"Oh—Edward's mad at me because I made him sit outside."

"Did you? I've given up on that."

"I know, but it's such a beautiful day."

He glanced around. She was right; he hadn't noticed before. A fresh, warm May day, seventy-five-ish, no humidity. Flowers everywhere. "Chloe thinks he's gone down," he said. "I see him so often, I can't tell. How did you find him?"

"Well . . . he did seem weaker . . . more frail," she said carefully. She was softening her report so as not to alarm him, a well-meant but un-necessary kindness. "His mind wasn't quite as sharp. He talked about his mother—I've never heard him do that before. But he's still himself. That's for sure," she said with a quick laugh, as if recalling something he'd just done or said that was more typical, a slight, some put-down, a deliberate hurt. "I guess I would say, all in all," she finished gently, "he seems to be failing."

"Thank you for coming to see him."

"I couldn't stay long."

"But I appreciate it."

"I should've come sooner. I've been remiss."

"It doesn't matter. Sometimes he doesn't remember *I've* been here."

"You're a good son, Andrew. No, you are—you always have been."

He shook his head, shoved his hands in his pockets, looked off in the distance. How nice they were being to each other. It flustered him.

Her new hairstyle made her look athletic. Younger, too—he should tell her that. He'd bungled it the last time, said the wrong thing, as usual. He blamed it on shock. Her hair had been long for so long, that blowsy, droopy style. He missed it, that was all. Missed the way she would shove her hands in it to lift it up, then let it fall.

"Where's Hobbes? Didn't you bring him?" She stood on her toes to see his car.

"Hobbes died."

"Oh, Andrew. Oh *no,* I'm sorry. When?"

"About a month ago."

"A month! Why didn't you *tell* me?"

He shrugged, uncomfortable. "No reason. I suppose I didn't think of it."

"You—" She stared at him.

He held her gaze. They were stepping up to a new level of detachment, but there didn't seem to be anything he could do about it. "Sorry," he said, knowing that was inadequate. It wasn't even true that he hadn't thought of telling her about Hobbes. But he'd known she would be sad for him, sympathetic, warm, and he hadn't wanted any of that. He'd wanted to do without her.

An old man in a motorized chair with a flag on it waved to them as he glided by. "Hi," Dash called to him with her sunny smile. She should be a nurse, not a forest ranger. Activities director, that was it. She'd cheer the place up.

But now she was angry, rigid. She adjusted her shoulder bag and withdrew a step. The sun, backlighting her hair, blinded him. "Chloe has her English exam today," he said to keep her. It worked; for a while they talked about their daughter.

"Are you all right?" Dash said finally. She sounded ever so faintly anxious. Didn't he look all right? No, she was just taking care of the last bit of business before she could leave.

"Yes, fine. Are you?"

"Yes." She took another step back.

Here it was slipping away again, and they were letting it. He was letting it. This was how their phone calls went: long pauses, mutual dissatisfaction. "We should talk," he ventured. "About things, someday."

She made a vague gesture; a safe answer, since she couldn't know any better than he did what *things* meant. Breaking up? Getting back together? She was the one who used to take charge of this kind of business. *Andrew, we need to talk,* she'd say, and they would hash out whatever was bothering her. About him, usually. If anything bothered him about her, he simply put up with it.

He followed her to her car. It had a new inspection sticker on the windshield, he noticed. That was his job, getting the cars inspected. They were both learning all sorts of new things, weren't they? The neighbor who always trapped Dash into collecting for the March of Dimes had trapped him this year.

"Is that your enlarger?" The contraption inside a big cardboard box in the backseat. Alongside yellow boxes marked KODAK and sealed with black tape, more boxes of trays and containers and amber-colored jars. Darkroom equipment.

"Yeah, I went to the house this morning and got all this stuff out of the attic. I'm going to do some developing," she said with satisfaction, buckling her seat belt and slipping the key in the ignition. "I can't wait. I just hope I remember how!"

"I see. So you're down there for the long haul, are you?"

"I don't know, Andrew."

"It's a long commute."

"Yes, it is." She fiddled with the miniature silver camera on her key ring. "I've thought of getting a place, something small. Closer in."

"That makes no sense."

She shot him a fierce look.

"It doesn't. You should live in the house. I . . . I should get a place." Silence.

"Is that what you'd like?"

"Andrew—don't ask me what *I* want when you never say what *you* want." She waited a few seconds. It was his time to say what he wanted, but he couldn't think what it was. The engine turning over sounded like an explosion. He got out of the way.

This is really happening, he thought. This is now, the present moment. It's real.

But it wasn't. That was Dash's car driving away, that was how she held her head, the way she rested her elbow in the open window. Despite everything he knew—and not only about his wife; also about history—at bottom, he wasn't a man who could really believe in change.

His father lay in his expensive recliner with his head back, mouth agape, fast asleep in front of his blaring television set. Dash had brought him flowers, yellow tulips in a mason jar. The spacious room looked like a judge's chambers—Edward's conceit when he'd first moved in: all his diplomas and certificates behind his old desk and high-backed chair, one whole wall of bookshelves and leather-bound legal volumes. Ironic, now that he could barely read a newspaper. He spent his days in the recliner, dozing through sixteen hours of CNN tuned to a deafening pitch.

Andrew muted the TV and Edward roused, blinking, dabbing spittle from the side of his mouth. "Oh," he said without surprise, as if Andrew had just returned from the bathroom. "Grand Central Station."

"How are you, Dad?"

"Eh?"

"How are you feeling?"

"Fine. I feel fine." His standard answer. Andrew could only hope it was true, but Edward had congestive heart failure, chronic bronchitis, the beginnings of emphysema, and chronic obstructive pulmonary disease. He tottered on his thin legs on the rare occasions when he was upright on his own power. He breathed oxygen through a tube in his nose twenty-four hours a day.

Andrew pulled the heavy desk chair over, positioning it beside the recliner so they were both facing the television. It was easier to talk that way, not looking at each other. As if they were sitting in a car.

"Dash came to see you."

If he hadn't heard, Edward frequently said nothing, pretending he had.

"Dash came," Andrew repeated, pointing to the flowers.

Edward grunted. "Nice of her to stop by."

No sarcasm intended, Andrew decided. His father was softening toward Dash in his dotage, possibly realizing all the things he used to loathe about her hadn't taken the family down in disgrace after all. The proof was Chloe.

An aide came in, one of the kind, dark-skinned women with exotic accents who, as far as Andrew could tell, took care of all the old people in the country. "Medicine," she sang in bright, carrying tones. Her nametag said she was Mercedes. She handed Edward a pill in a small paper cup, another cup full of water. "Drink it. Drink. Take your pill!" He smiled up at her, cooperative, obliging. The staff was always telling Andrew what a nice man his father was. The first few times, he was positive they'd confused him with another resident.

After Mercedes left, Andrew fell into a familiar quandary, whether to tell his father about Hobbes. Weeks passed, and he kept waiting for him to ask about his dog, wonder why Andrew hadn't brought him, at least *mention* him. But Edward seemed to have forgotten all about Hobbes. Poor old boy, he deserved better.

Edward startled him by suddenly asking, "So what are you going to do about her?" His eyes, normally filmed over with boredom or weakness or ennui, were sharp and clear, and they were focused on Andrew.

"About . . ."

"Your wife!"

"Em. We haven't decided what will happen."

"Why not? How long has it been?"

He should never have told him they were separated. Why had he? Some idiotic bid for sympathy? "We're working things out, Dad. Don't worry about it."

"I'm not worried." He smiled his thin-lipped, patronizing smile. "I gave you credit for being a little smarter, that's all."

"As smart as you were?"

They glared, side by side, at a story on some Middle East bombing atrocity playing out on the silent TV.

"Just don't take too long," Edward grumped. "They leave."

He couldn't be talking about Tommie, his social-climbing harpy of a second wife; except for the money, he'd been nothing but relieved when she left him. About Ellen, then. Andrew's mother.

All his life Andrew had wondered what their marriage was like. His memories of his mother were vague, more like dreams. She was the one he'd run to from monsters in his nightmares; she'd hold out her arms to him and he would be saved. He didn't know if it was a real memory or a photograph he'd looked at so often it felt like a memory—of her sunny hair that smelled like a Mars bar, coconut and sugar, and of her warm body, always welcoming, embracing.

She'd died of cancer when he was nine, but he could remember nothing of her illness. Only her absences, the last one explained by his father as Mother having gone to heaven. The Batemans weren't church-goers, so the concept was shadowy. Andrew had imagined it as Bethany Beach, where they rented a cottage every summer. "This is heaven," his mother would say as she lay on a towel in the sand, shading her eyes to watch the sun go down.

"Do you need anything, Dad?"

"Like what?"

"Socks, underwear, toothpaste."

"No, thanks. You wouldn't get the right kind anyway."

"Probably not. Any shirts for the cleaners?" They didn't do them right here at Meadow Grove.

"On the floor in the closet."

Andrew yawned. The warm room was making him sleepy. "Chloe says to give you her love." The old man wrinkled his lips for a smile. Andrew told him about her exam schedule, her plans to intern at an experimental theater in D.C. this summer. Edward put his chin on his chest, but kept his eyes open. He rarely left this room anymore, but his clothes were still a matter of pride to him. You'd never find him in a sweat suit or one of those matching velour outfits favored by so many of the other male residents: casual Friday at the law office—not that there had been one at Bateman and Tate—that was as far as Edward would let himself go.

But his eyesight was failing; it was a mercy he couldn't see the dandruff or the shaven white whiskers littering the chest and shoulders of his fine sweaters. Unmatched socks, uncut hair, food stains on his trousers, jagged fingernails—Andrew was used to them by now, but they'd appalled him at first, shocked him on a shivery, deep, personal level. How *horrified* his father would be if he knew. And even though the fact of Edward humiliating himself had a certain quality of closure, even symmetry, Andrew had wanted desperately to save him. But the mildest offer of help met denial or disdain, and finally he'd seen that the only way to "save" his father was to collude with him.

He thought of Wolfie, the story he'd told him about gluing his watch inside Edward's humidor. What if that small, indelible childhood humiliation had been some sort of watershed event for him, or the last among many, after which the entire point of his life was to disappoint his father? Get revenge on him by meeting his low expectations? If so . . .

If so. He couldn't imagine a decent end to that bit of subjunctive thinking. If so—good job? Happy now?

On the television, black people in some African nation held signs, protesting in front of a barbed-wire fence. They looked furious, all of them men, their mouths twisted, spitting anger.

"Dad, did you know Thomas Jefferson owned slaves?"

"Eh?"

"About two hundred. It's not a secret, we've always known it— historians. We just didn't talk about it. Two hundred slaves. And when he died, he didn't free them. Washington freed his, but not Jefferson. A servant or two, that was it. Not even his mistress, or the children he got from her. What do you think of that, Dad?"

Edward's eyes were closed, mouth slack.

"Nowadays we talk about it, of course. As we should. Gloves off. Practically a cottage industry of Founding Father bashers these days, everybody hard at work. They do it with computers and spreadsheets now, models, paradigms, statistics. Jefferson would've approved, actually. He loved anything newfangled. He'd have liked a new light shown on himself, too, because that would bring a balance. He was all for balance. And reason, and temperance, men behaving well. Health in mind and body. Health—he used to soak his feet in cold water every morning, thought it would keep him from catching cold. When his wife died, he went a little crazy for a while. Couldn't rest, couldn't sit still. He'd get migraines."

Andrew leaned forward, holding his head in his hands. He might be getting a migraine himself; he could feel that premonitory ache on the right side of the back of his neck. Why was he talking about Jefferson? His father wasn't even listening.

"He was definitely a racist—he believed blacks were inferior to whites. Truly believed it. But you'd have to, wouldn't you, to make a man your slave? I don't know if he was a hypocrite. He warned against the 'amalgamation' of the races, and he had children with Sally Hemings, his slave.

"How am I expected to defend that? I can't. When I try, I hate the words I have to use, even though they're true—he lived a life of his times, he can't be judged by ours, in every other respect his principles were irreproachable, he was born too soon . . ."

Andrew sat up, still holding his temples. "He was my height. Six-two and a half. Very close to his father, extremely close. He married Martha when he was twenty-nine and she was twenty-four. Dash and I were twenty-nine and twenty-five. I think of these things. He never made a speech. He had weak vocal cords, couldn't talk long without getting hoarse. So he wrote. The Declaration of Independence took him seventeen days.

"If you know a man well enough, you can forgive him for almost anything. Don't you think so? Not that a historian's job is to forgive. But a man's might be."

He sat in silence awhile, staring at a commercial, images of a woman laughing with happiness because her laxative worked.

"I can't decide what I should do. Jefferson was only really happy at home in the country, but he made the sacrifice and returned to public life when he thought he could do some good. Became vice president. What do you think I should do, Dad?"

Edward snorted himself awake. He dabbed moisture from his lips, readjusted his oxygen tube. Regarded Andrew pleasantly. "I wanted to be an actor," he said. "When I was a young man. Tell Chloe that."

"An actor? You did?"

"I played the Stage Manager. College play. Stage Manager, that's the biggest part."

"*Our Town*," Andrew said, astonished. This was news to him. If it was true.

"Loved it. Told my father—your grandfather—*that's* what I'm going to be. An actor." He put his head back, opened his mouth wide in a pantomime of mirth. "Funniest thing he ever heard! That's what he said. Funniest thing he ever heard."

The smile faded to bitterness. Instead of acting, Edward had studied the law and joined Bateman and Tate. He'd wanted his son to make it Bateman, Tate, and Bateman.

He reached for the TV remote and thumbed the volume back on. Andrew's cue that the visit was over.

nineteen

At home, he went for a run, relying on Dash's say-so that it was a beautiful day. But everything had a gray tinge he attributed to depression. He couldn't think of anything to look forward to, nothing he wanted to happen. He had forty journals to read before exams started next week, after which he'd have 130 exams to read. He had never looked on the task as drudgery before, simply another chore like bricklaying or floor waxing. Garbage collection. Why not? What the hell was it good for? Studying history, one could argue—and he was ready to argue it—was another make-work industry, like greeting cards. It kept a certain number of people occupied and off the streets. Deluded people.

"Why don't you just go down there and get her, Dad?" Chloe suggested when he called her. He wanted company, not advice, so he went silent. Alertly, she changed the subject.

His stomach hurt again. He shouldn't have gone running. Not his stomach, more in his diaphragm. He emptied a roll of Tums into a coffee cup and set it by his chair, for convenience, while he read student journals.

Elizabeth was right, he was a voyeur. Not by choice, though; if he wasn't already depressed, reading about how depressed his students were would have pushed him over the edge. Some even had good reasons to be. This boy, Stephen Berger, sat in the back row and never spoke, just stared stonily out of thick black glasses when he wasn't sleeping. On tests he was never more than average because of mediocre writing skills. But in his journal, Stephen became eloquent. His flimsy journal persona was Stephanus Bentham, a student at the University of Virginia. He wrote of classes, classmates, the obligatory current events in his usual spare, flat style, but when he chronicled Stephanus's home life, the words poured out in a flood. His father was an abusive, alcoholic monster, his mother an ineffective wraith. He feared every day for his fourteen-year-old sister who was alone now, no one to protect her.

How could it not be true? And what in the world was Andrew supposed to do about it?

And here was Sasha Maloney, a sweetheart of a girl, blonde, cheerleader perky, good head on her shoulders. She wrote page after page about "Lavinia," a silversmith's daughter who suffered for her "lewd, ungodly thoughts and perversions"—read lesbianism. At the end of the journal, she killed herself by drinking silver polish.

How could he not be affected by such revelations? All the journals, even the ones with better-disguised alter egos, revealed intimate things he felt humbled to know. Helpless to change. Tonight they weighed on him like hands pulling at his coat.

When he wasn't turning a page or scratching a note in a margin, the room was utterly silent. Hobbes had been more company to him than he'd known. Without his scruffy presence the house felt empty and vast, extravagantly too big for one person. Peace and quiet. He'd craved them not that long ago. They felt like a trick he'd fallen for, a swindle. Like—what was it?—the Love Canal, the idyllic community that had turned out to be polluted with toxic wastes.

The phone rang. He knocked a stack of journals off the ottoman in his hurry to answer it.

"Hey, Bateman. Feel like going for a swim?"

"Elizabeth?"

"No one's here but me."

"Where?"

"Sports Center. It's faculty swim night, you'd think someone would be here. But no."

"Wait for me, don't go. Give me thirty minutes."

It took forty minutes, ten to locate his swim trunks. Parking the car, practically sprinting into the campus sports complex—empty; everybody studying for exams—shucking off his clothes in the men's locker room, Andrew kept telling himself she hadn't waited and he didn't care; in fact, he was relieved. Big hassle, eliminated.

Doors from the men's and women's lockers opened on opposite sides of a metal balcony over the deep end of the pool. His first whiff of warm air smelled of strong chlorine. He heard splashing below. She'd waited!

No. When he peered over the rail he could see—somehow, since they were unidentifiable from here—that neither of the two women swimming laps in adjacent lanes was Elizabeth.

"What did you do, walk?"

He leaned over farther, looked sideways. She smiled up at him, stretched out on the first bench of bleachers, using a rolled towel for a pillow. Without his glasses, details blurred; he saw her white skin and black swimsuit, her black hair. Blinding white skin. "I knew you'd look like that," she said, her voice maddeningly uninflected. She curled up from the bench and stood. Wet dark hair cascaded to her shoulders. "I'm going in," she said, impatient, and made a running dive into the water.

He watched her, unsurprised that she swam lithe and fast as an eel, barely making a splash. The women beside her, their hair obediently covered in bathing caps, swam like . . . he couldn't think, but compared to them she was a mermaid. The concrete steps to the pool area felt gritty and warm under his feet. Funny how simple shoelessness could make you feel half naked; take away your watch and glasses—there went the other half. That was how he felt, naked; open and exposed to the wet, steamy air, already starting to melt into it.

He threw his towel on the bleachers, over which the swim team's banner hung: MASON-DIXON OTTERS. He used to swim for his prep school's team. What were they called? He couldn't remember. "I knew you'd look like that." Like what? Hairy legs, pale feet, the blue and green bathing trunks Dash had picked out for him a few summers ago. He walked to the lane next to Elizabeth's and jumped in.

The shock wore off in seconds. He treaded water, waiting for her, but when she reached the wall she ignored him, spinning off the side and reversing like a pro. Of course. He set off at a moderate crawl, smiling to himself. Elizabeth, Elizabeth. Her abruptness and her attitude of weary contempt for almost everything didn't put him off anymore. He liked them. And God, it was good to be in this pool, out in the world, up *against* something. The water felt like a hard, sinewy barrier he had to break through, and he could, his arms and shoulders were strong, his legs were kicking machines churning him forward. He fell into a rhythm he thought his body had forgotten. His mind turned off. Back and forth, back and forth. When he tired, he flipped onto his back and blinked up at the vaulted ceiling high above, and it was like floating in a flooded cathedral. He caught his breath and swam some more.

At a turn he paused, hanging onto the side with one hand. What was different? Besides the fact that he was alone in the pool. The lights—someone had turned off the overhead lights; the whole echoey, cavernous building seemed to be illuminated only by the pool lights. He heard the slap of feet and turned around to see, dimly, Elizabeth descending the steps from the balcony. She smiled her snaky, come-hither-if-you-dare smile as she passed, heading for the shallow end. The siren look jarred intriguingly with a big red beach ball, exercise ball, she carried under one arm. Swim-team equipment. Where had she found it? Maybe she was *on* the team. No, but nothing would surprise him. He pushed off and swam underwater to the other end, coming up only twice for air.

"So how are you?" She threw the ball to him and slipped into the water, agile as a dancer. "Help me with this." She couldn't unhook the heavy lane divider from the side of the pool. He lifted it up and out and let it fall, glad to be useful for once. Part of her allure and part of her tiresomeness was her disdain for help, especially men's. "This one, too," she said, and he lifted out another lane divider. Now they had a place to play.

"I'm fine," he said. "Great, in fact. Lots of journals to read, but I'll be done before exams." He lofted from the water to catch a high pass, pitched the ball back to her with smoke on it. "How are you?"

"I'm pissed."

"About—"

"My merit raise. I told you."

She was furious with Richard Weldon for, among numerous other things, not signing off on her demand for a raise based on a year's superior performance. She'd only been teaching for four years, but she wanted tenure and a promotion to associate by the end of next term, too, a year earlier than usual, and she blamed Richard for thwarting her.

"If I were a white male," she snarled, slamming the ball hard, so a plume of water hit Andrew in the face.

He'd heard it all before. "You'd be tenured and on sabbatical by now." He threw the ball in the air and whacked it at her, volleyball style. Bull's-eye. It hit her on top of the head. "Hey, sorry," he started, but Elizabeth laughed. She laughed. Not for long; soon she was back to bitter bitching about Richard—"I've got an eight o'clock class next term, Bateman. Eight o'clock. If that's not punishment, tell me what is"—but that flash of self-knowing humor doubled his affection for her.

"I might leave." She batted the ball between her fists, short, hard punches on the surface of the water, showing off her biceps. "I could go just about anywhere. Maybe not Ivy League. Although why the hell not. I know Binghamton would piss themselves to get me."

He didn't know if that was true or not. "Why did you come here? Why Mason-Dixon?" She'd arrived two years ago from a bigger, more prestigious school.

"Old time's sake. The old neighborhood and all that." What a sneer she had. Her cynicism used to disturb him, but lately it provoked only a touchy tenderness. He'd always known she was a train wreck, but now he cared about her. And rooted for her, the way he might for the headstrong principal in a disaster movie. "Of course, if *you* were the chair." She lay back in the water. Her hair floated around her face like black seaweed.

"You're a terrific swimmer," he said.

"I know. I'm part fish."

Mermaid. He, too, had always known she would look like that.

"If you were the chair, Bateman."

"I'd miss teaching." She had red polish on her toenails. Shocking intimacy. He couldn't get over it. He stared at them as if they were her breasts, her pubis.

"Oh, balls. All those journals you have to read. You wouldn't miss that."

"They teach me things."

"What things?"

He bent his head back, put his ears under water as warm as a bath. Closed his eyes and listened to the heavy, rushing silence. When he spoke, his voice sounded disembodied, like someone else's. "No life is bland to the one who's living it. The coolest student can be the most troubled. The funniest in the most pain. No one escapes loneliness."

A nautical pinging sounded pleasant in his ears. He could stay like this, limp in the water with his knees bent, toes almost grazing the bottom. But just then he felt something, a hand on his heel. He straightened and looked down. The mermaid was circling him, her back arched, feet thrusting. Above him, blackness; light below, sinuous, aqueous silver blue. Everything alive was below his waist. He sank to his knees.

Her hair curling away, behind the corner of his eye, just brushed his shoulder. He turned the other way, but she'd already reversed. He feigned that he couldn't find her, only accept the slide of her fingers on his neck, behind his knee, along his spine. Until finally a firm grip under his arms, lifting him. They surfaced together.

They stood chest to chest, thigh to thigh, the closest they had ever been. His eyes were level with the part in her streaming hair, the jagged white zigzag seeming too vulnerable to him, childlike. She lifted her face and kissed him without touching him with her hands. She was smiling when their lips parted. With pleasure, not slyness or triumph. He reached for her—she glided away. He caught his breath instead of chasing.

"Not enough time," Elizabeth said, gesturing toward the clock at the far end of the pool. He pretended he could read it from here. "My house is closer than yours."

He ducked under, shot up in the air, shook water from his hair like a dog.

"Right?" She was backing up toward the ladder. She scooted her hands along the water's surface, patted it gently, splashed it. She turned her head sideways, looking at him between spiked lashes. "Right, Bateman?"

Too long a sacrifice can make a stone of the heart. Who said that? Probably Tim after a few pints. "Right," Andrew answered, although he doubted if right had anything to do with it.

Dash would approve—in a way: He was being spontaneous. He was putting his clothes on like a man in a race. The only way to be spontaneous was to move, not think.

Nothing to think about anyway. This would be free and conse-quenceless because, for reasons of her own, Elizabeth, who wasn't in love with him, wanted him. That was a blessing to be counted, not a puzzle to unravel. Most men wouldn't think twice. Most men would think he was unbalanced, weighted down by pathology for so much as hesitating.

Was he hesitating? He had to look at himself in the foggy mirror to comb his hair, had to peer into his own eyes. They looked worried. In the same way he'd wondered all his life when he would die, and how, he had also wondered when, or if, he would have an affair. A sense of inevitability had tracked him, a cloud of dread and avidity that lifted gradually as he got older and began to see that it might not happen, might not be fated.

Fated? Because of his father, a serial philanderer? To hell with that. Whatever happened tonight, he swore by *God* it wouldn't have any-thing to do with Edward.

Elizabeth. Remember how she'd looked, how she'd felt snaking around him underwater, supple, seductive, a pale-limbed Lorelei. Think how it might be with her, how she would look without her clothes. How aggressive she would be. He was surprised she hadn't initiated sex in the swimming pool. An uncharacteristic moment of discretion.

Once, over a weekend when Chloe had stayed at a friend's instead of going down to the cabin with them, he and Dash had swum naked in the pond. He hadn't wanted to. It was freezing—it was last spring, be-fore her mother died, before everything went haywire. "You can't come in with your clothes on," she'd warned him as she'd stripped hers off in the chilly sunshine. "Not one toe, Andrew, don't even think about it. Naked or nothing." Yipping at every step, she pranced into the water while he stood on the bank and laughed, watching her lips turn purple, her skin pebble with gooseflesh, her nipples shrink to buttons. The last thing in the world he'd wanted to do was get in that cold brown water, with or without his clothes. But her teeth started to chatter and she looked so miserable and bossy and tickled with herself. Her hugging arms made pretty round hills of her breasts—he'd wished he had her camera. "Ch-chick-chicken! Come on in, it's warm as toast." What could he do? He'd undressed and waded in, and when he got to her, he'd put his arms around her to try to warm her. She'd stuck her foot behind his knee and tripped him. They'd gone crashing into the frigid water together while she shrieked with laughter.

Outside, Elizabeth was waiting for him, slouched against a light pole with her hands shoved inside the pockets of her trousers. Behind her, the balustraded roof of Mason Hall, the oldest building on campus, looked medieval silhouetted against a hazy pink sky. The night was quiet and sweet-smelling. Elizabeth lifted her head and smiled. "Two cars this time," she said, and pushed off from the pole, heading for hers.

He thought of her museum-house, the high-ceilinged bedroom and the canopied bed with its heavy quilted coverlet. It couldn't be a black room, but that was how he remembered it, black or brown, everything shadowed but modern, a carpet thick as mulch. He pictured the room candlelit, shadows flickering on the canopy overhead. Elizabeth's hard, elastic body astride his. Her hair tickling his face. Her viperish smile.

He called to her and she stopped, turned. "Let's walk."

"Walk?"

"Here." He gestured across the bright, empty parking lot to the concrete footpath that wound up a slope to the main campus. "Around." He spread his arms. "It's a nice night."

She stood motionless, watching him with glittery eyes. She lifted her top lip in an unambiguous snarl.

"Please," he said, and waited for her to whirl around and stomp off, to curse him, both—but she raised her handsome shoulders and let them fall. Then she stalked past him, knees unflexed in that peculiar gliding gait she had, and headed across the parking lot.

The campus usually bustled this time of night with noisy or sleepy students crisscrossing the quads, going home from the library or a party, a friend's dorm. Tonight it was hushed, and every residence hall window was lit up. Nobody was having a party; students at the library weren't leaving yet. Part of Andrew always felt sorry for them, their tension and worry palpable in the air, as if they were hiding out from the plague, and part of him always thought, *Serves you right. If you'd studied all term, you wouldn't be in a cold panic right now, would you?*

Midway up the winding path, between Wilson Hall and the Science and Technology Center, he began, "It's not that I don't find y——"

"Shut. Up."

He coughed into his hand and obeyed for a while. Elizabeth was no ambler; he had to stretch his stride to keep up with her. "Listen. I would very much like to be with you. I think you're—spectacular."

No response but a sneer.

He paused, trying to choose his words. One of his problems was that he didn't understand himself. He'd never made a decision, so there was nothing to defend. How could you explain a reflex?

"Haven't you ever done it before?" She strafed the words out so fast, it took a second to process the question. Cheated on Dash, he assumed she meant.

"No."

"Never? Jesus. Should've known."

He hung his head. For the first time he thought of how much male admiration and envy he could've bagged by going home with her. For doing something macho, too, not scholarly—imagine it. Tim would eat his heart out.

"Why the hell not?" She stopped walking to face him. A nearby lamp lighted one side of her long, narrow face, left the other in shadow. Under the disgust and irritation, she looked genuinely baffled.

Why the hell not. Excellent question. He used to be conscious of his fidelity, like a piano student playing a difficult piece note by note, or an athlete learning a complicated skill muscle by muscle, concentrating on every move. But he was a professional now, he didn't have to look at the music, the goal line; faithfulness was in his bones and muscles, a learned memory.

He shrugged. "Habit" was all he could say.

Elizabeth looked revolted. "God, I need a drink." She began to root around in her huge black handbag, and he was relieved when she pulled out a pack of cigarettes, not a flask. Mason-Dixon was officially smoke free, but it didn't seem like the right time to point it out.

"Let's sit," he suggested. They had stopped in front of one of the uncomfortable wooden benches some wealthy alumnus had gifted the college with a few years back. Too bad he hadn't donated the concrete slabs they had to be bolted to when students began to steal them or shift them around to inappropriate locations.

"I don't want to sit."

"Please. A minute."

She swore, tossed her bag on the bench, plopped down.

He took a seat on the eight or so inches of edge she'd left him. "I'm going through a strange time."

"Right. Who gives a shit. Not me, okay? Nothing about you is interesting to me, Bateman. Got that?"

"Quite. I'm pretty clear on that." She make a sound of disgust and cursed him some more, but under her breath now; he only heard the sibilants distinctly, "asshole" and "shithead."

"I'd like to tell you something. I'd like to be serious, and I want you to listen, even though you're angry with me."

"Make it quick, I've got things to do."

He waited until a couple of fast-walking students passed out of earshot. Elizabeth tapped the sides of her shoes together, legs stretched out, half blocking the path. She looked like a disgruntled bird of prey in profile, chin tucked, lips sour, brows scowling. He liked her very much.

"I don't know what you're doing." Not a graceful beginning, but there was no hope for eloquence here, or tact, or face-saving. "You have the makings of a superb historian. You're young and brilliant, you have passion for your subject, you're ambitious. And you're screwing it up."

"Bullshit. Anyway, you're the one who's screwing up. You're nothing but a coward for not taking Richard's job."

"We're not talking about me."

"*I'm* talking about you. You're afraid Flynn will bury you in his book, so you won't even take a chance."

"You don't understand—"

"Hell I don't! You've got things to say, but you're afraid of coming off sounding reactionary or racist. You pretend you're above all the politics, but the truth is you're in a bind and you're paralyzed."

That hit a nerve. It hit all his nerves. He opened his mouth to argue, but nothing came out.

"Wow. Look how much better you are," Elizabeth observed nastily, "at attacking me than defending yourself."

"I'm not—I'm not attacking you."

"Sounds like it to me."

"No, I'm only saying . . . You must see what it is you do. The ways in which you undercut yourself." She was right: He was on much firmer ground when the subject was *her* professional failings.

"Yeah? How do I undercut myself?"

Very well, he would tell her. "I have no idea what your relationship with Richard is, and under any other circumstances I can think of, I wouldn't care."

"What's the word on the street?"

"You know."

"Don't you want to know if it's true?"

"No." He assumed it was. And not just Richard, either. "But if it is true, does that strike you as professional behavior?"

"Oh, get off it." She leaped up. If she'd been angry before, now she was furious. "You pompous jerk. Clue, Professor—this isn't Williams-burg. What are you, dead? Do you understand the sexual dynamics of this place at *all*?" Two book-laden coeds walked by, but she didn't even lower her voice. "Listen to me: Everybody screws everybody. Nobody gets his shorts up his ass about it but you. It *happens,* we go *on.*"

"Sit."

"Professional behavior," she spat. "Please, don't make me—"

He stood. "I've got things to do, too."

"Okay!" She sat.

"I'm not having a lot of fun myself, you know. In fact, this sucks. The whole situation—it's much harder on me than you. Believe me."

She snorted, but he could see she appreciated that. "Finish the lecture."

"It's not a lecture. I want to say—all right, it sounds like a lecture. But we're friends, aren't we? Potentially? That's what I'd like," he said truthfully. Amazing, after all that had happened between them—not the least of which was her calling him a coward—friendship was a role he could still feel comfortable in. "So please, permit me to say, as a friend, I think it's possible you might—have a problem with authority figures."

"I do have a shrink already."

"I might have the same problem, actually."

"*You.*"

"With my father. It manifests itself in other ways."

"Clearly." She smiled thinly.

"Elizabeth . . . Richard tells me things. No, nothing personal, just that you are . . . a thorn in his side. You say he's holding you back—he is. Because he thinks you're hard to work with, unpredictable, and inconsistent."

She made a rude noise. "Inconsistent. Meaning he can't get it any time he wants it."

"Maybe so. Love, hate. Father figure, married lover. Don't you think it's time to break out of that cycle?"

"What *cycle?*"

He put his hands on his knees. "As manly a man as everyone knows me to be, the thought did cross my mind that part of my irresistible charm for you could be the slim possibility—"

"No, don't go there."

"—that I'll change my mind and decide to take Richard's job."

"That's not true."

"Thank you, but let's say it is, for the sake of argument."

"Jesus," she murmured. "What you must think of me."

"I think a great deal of you. And if I *were* chair, you and I would start with a clean slate. I'd do everything I could for you. I'd expect nothing in return but professionalism. In the context of our cordial friendship."

"Right."

"You wouldn't be my girlfriend or my daughter. I wouldn't be your lover or your father. We would like and respect each other. As we do now, but even more, I hope, because . . . it would be real."

She put an elbow on her thigh, her chin in her hand. Tilted her head at him. Her sideways smile skewed cynically, but for once there was a hopeful light in her eyes. "Well, Professor. If even half of that's true." She stood up, hefting her bag onto her shoulder.

Half, he thought. Pretty good percentage. They began to walk back along the path the way they'd come. The first fireflies were out, sending hopeful signals in the trees and shrubbery, even the grass. The sound of crickets was louder than the traffic; he could imagine he and Elizabeth were strolling somewhere in the country, not a busy suburb northwest of the capital. "What?" he asked. "If even half of that's true."

"It's obvious. Bateman, you have *got* to write that Jefferson chapter and become the new chair."

"Well," he allowed, looking up at the starless mauve sky. "I guess it's something to think about."

dash

twenty

"Marriage starts in the dream of the other," Mo said to me once, before she developed her Zen mind. "If the dream matches for one, it's a wonder. If it matches for both, it's a goddamn miracle." She said, "Marriage only makes sense when there's money and children." And she said, "It's complete insanity to think two people can stay together happily for sixty or seventy years. So why do we get so upset when it fails? Why do we watch each other's marriages flame out and feel so frightened? Can't we learn? Don't we see?"

I know and I don't know why I'm thinking of that as I drive toward the river, toward Owen Roby's house, on this perfect May afternoon. The same way I know and I don't know why I just washed my hair, why I put on the black shorts that make me look skinny from the back. Owen called this morning and invited me to watch ducklings hatch. How wholesome is that? I also have on the silver earrings Greta said make me look like a gypsy.

I never told him, but I drove by Owen's place once before. Out of curiosity. You can't see much from the road; the house sits back a good ways, and a cluster of tall old trees obscures half of it. It's white with a silver tin roof, two stories, and a railed second-floor balcony over the front porch. How nice to have access to the outdoors from your second floor, I thought the first time. I wondered if the balcony led from Owen's bedroom.

I can hear a dog barking before I'm halfway down the dirt drive. Must be Rex, the vole eater; we've never met. So many outbuildings, some painted, some not, the roof shapes all different. This is a working farm; nothing's for show.

Well, no, now I see metal tubs of geraniums on either side of every front porch step. And you could call the American flag a decoration; Owen's got a small one jutting out from the upstairs balcony. Where to park? Behind his truck, I guess, beside a big fuel tank on stilts at the side of the house.

The front entrance is pretty because of the geraniums and a porch swing and some painted wicker furniture, but there's no walkway to it, barely even a path through the grass. I guess he never goes in and out that way, and neither do his visitors. I start for a smaller door on the side, which I surmise leads to the kitchen. There's a sound like *"Whup,"* like an army command, and Rex, who's never stopped barking, instantly shuts up. I follow the command sound to the back of the house, and there's Owen. Kneeling in the bright sun in one of the perfect rows of an enormous vegetable garden, patting soil around a plant.

"Thought that was you," he says as I pick my way through the neat, lush lines of who-knows-what, taking care not to step on anything but dirt. As I go closer, I watch for that pleased, appreciative look I'm used to getting from him but never know what to do with. And there it is. He sits back, resting his palms on his thighs, and smiles while he looks me over head to toe. What does it mean? What? I'm tired of wondering.

"What are you putting in?"

"Okra. Second planting."

Imagine planting okra twice. I squat down beside him, aware that my pink-painted toenails look rather fetching in my strappy sandals. I look him over, too. He has an actual red neck, damp from perspiration above the collar of his T-shirt; below the line, his skin looks as smooth and pale as mine.

"You smell good," he says.

I look into his eyes, startled; I was just thinking the same about him. I smell like herbal shampoo, Owen smells like—earth. And sweat, and tomato plants, and hot cotton. The body part that most attracts me is his thighs. They're so . . .

"Could you use some pansies?"

"Hm?"

His big, dirt-stained hands are delicate as they separate the roots at the bottom of the second-to-last okra plant. "I got too many pansies last year, and every one made it through the winter. You can have all you want, they're around the side." He tilts his head in the direction of Rex.

"Great, I know just where I'll put them. Thank you."

The sun is hot and in my face. I think of sunscreen, skin moisturizer, a straw hat. I bet Owen never thinks of those things. "What is everything?" I ask, gesturing to the garden.

He grunts, finishes planting the last plant, and stands up. My knee cracks embarrasingly when I join him, but then Owen puts both hands on the small of his back and groans briefly while he stretches—that makes me feel better. "Corn, sunflowers, tomatoes, peppers over there. In there, broccoli, another kind of pepper, eggplant, kale, cabbage, collards, beets. There's cucumbers, yellow squash, zucchini, butternut squash. Beans along the fence."

"Wow."

"Over there's carrots, onions, horseradish, garlic. What's left of the spinach. Little bit of lettuce."

"*Owen.*"

He grins at my amazement. "Got a fruit tree orchard in back—apple, peach, plum, pear, and cherry. Asparagus all along that fence." He points toward the driveway. "Pick some when you go, just snap 'em off. Little late in the year, but they're still good."

I shake my head.

"Mushrooms in the basement."

"Really!"

"No. Kidding about that."

I punch him on the arm. No give; all muscle. "What do you do with it all?"

"Eat it, give it away, put it up."

"You mean, can? You can?" I picture him in a kitchen over a steaming pot of mason jars, wearing an apron.

He nods, picking up his trowels and things, leading the way out of the garden. "Got pretty good at it last fall when Miz Bender was outta commission."

"Where are your cows?" I ask while he puts stuff away in one of the leaning sheds the backyard is full of.

"My what?"

"Your cows, all your cows." There's a half-stone barn over there in a muddy field, but no cows that I can see. For that matter, I can't see any ducks, either.

"My cattle? They're down the hill, grazing down in the floodplain. I don't have any cows."

"Why not?"

"Beef cattle."

"Oh, bulls. Well, what's the difference?"

"A cow's a female. Them you milk."

He's smiling, as if he thinks I'm kidding and he's going along with the joke. I should let him keep thinking that, but something compels me to say, "I thought cows were brown and bulls were black and they could be either sex."

"No, you didn't."

"I did."

Now I know what compelled me—the chance to make him laugh. He *roars*. He keeps looking at me to see if it's a joke, and each time he realizes it's not he laughs harder. He has to lean against the side of the shed. When he pulls himself together he stares at me through damp, smiling eyes. I think—I could be wrong—in some strange way I've gone up in his estimation. Whatever I was to him before, I have outdone myself.

"All righty, if you're done," I say, "where are the ducks?"

"This way."

He keeps them by a thin, slow-moving creek about fifty yards in back of the house, almost invisible behind a tangle of willow trees and leaning sycamores. Ducks! I didn't hear them before, they must've been taking siestas in the sun, but when they see us they all start quacking at once. They won't let us go too close—me, rather; Owen knows better than to try—but they stop waddling away or hopping into the creek as soon as I stop moving. Wow, *ducks*. Some are white and some are brown. I try to count, get to about fifteen, and give up. "What are they, what kind?" I'm struck by how far back their legs start, how far apart their eyes are.

"The whites are Pekins. They grow fast, seven pounds by seven weeks if you manage them right. Lot of fat in their meat."

"My God, they're adorable." Their tails stick up in little tufts, and they have bright orange bills and feet. Storybook ducks. "So those must be the Khaki Campbells," I deduce, pointing to a brown one. Owen gave me Khaki eggs once—they were delicious, much better than regular eggs. "It's so *pretty* here," I tell him, although the natural beauty of the spot has been spoiled a bit by all the little utilitarian sheds and pens, the windbreaks and wire runs he's built beside the creek. One of the sheds has a black cable, an electric line, running to it all the way from the house. We head toward it.

"Watch your head," he says, holding the door open for me. I duck in, but there's no need; he's the one who has to bend his head or it'll brush the low ceiling. The warm, close air smells like a nest, earthen and alive. Except for two small windows, the only light is coming from the box on a wooden table and a lamp inside a rubber swimming pool, a kiddie pool on the straw-strewn floor. I can hear soft, impossibly high peeping. Owen pulls a string, and a bare bulb in a corner of the shed comes on.

The box on the table is an incubator. The kiddie pool is a duckling house. Straw and wood chips line the rubber bottom, and a gooseneck lamp—how appropriate—shines down on a huddle of babies, tiny hand-fuls of fluff with perfect beaks and perfect little webbed feet. "Oh" is all I can say. I sink to my knees beside the pool, holding my hands together so I won't reach out and grab anything.

"God, they're . . ."

"Yeah," Owen agrees.

The cuteness is overwhelming; I've gone gooey inside. I'm sorry there's no mother, though. I was imagining a big fat mama hen sitting in a pretty nest on a bunch of eggs, which would conveniently hatch, one by one, as soon as I got here.

"Can I touch them?"

"Well . . ."

"Okay, I won't."

"It's better if you don't handle them too much right now, or they'll imprint on you. Makes for problems later on."

"I can imagine." But still. "How many are there? One, two, three . . . four."

"Four there in the brooder, two more eggs up here, and a wet guy I haven't moved yet. One egg I had to throw out, the duckling was deformed, but that's pretty good, two bad eggs out of eight."

"Two?" I get up to see what's inside the incubator, a plastic box with a transparent lid. "Oh my God. Look at him." A dark, stringy-looking bit of wet down on extremely unsteady legs, cheeping piteously while he stumbles and lurches and flings himself around the small enclosure. "Won't he hurt himself?"

Owen frowns. "Well, now, he just might." There's a small roll of corrugated cardboard on the table, only about three inches high and the same in diameter. Owen opens the incubator lid, drops the little tube of cardboard on top of the duckling, and quickly closes the lid. "That'll settle him down." It does; he can only crash into the sides of the tube now, and it also keeps him upright. "This one's a lot further along since I last looked, but this one . . ."

"Which, where?" He points, and I finally see the main attraction, the reason I came, the big show—an actual duckling actually hatching. No wonder I didn't notice, though, it looks like . . . a lot of wet tea leaves in the bottom of a pearly white cup. With a beak! "Oh my God, oh my God!" And tiny beady eyes that look—I must be imagining this—exhausted. "Can't we help him out? Oh, and *this* one." There's another egg, still intact—no, now I see a hole, the smallest chip in the top, darkness inside.

"That one's probably not gonna make it. Hate to keep opening this, drops the temperature—" Owen lifts the lid again, carefully snatches the unhatched egg and brings it out. "Can you hear?" He holds it between our ears—I stop breathing to listen.

A faint scratching, just once. A weak peep.

My heart's in my throat. I stare at Owen. "Can't you . . ."

"No." He puts the egg back in the incubator, bending down to read the number on a thermometer inside.

"Why?"

"You can't help them. This is a test, right here. That duckling got through the embryo into the air sac, now it's got to get out of the shell, and it's probably not going to."

"What if you crack it open for him?"

"Something's probably wrong with it. My ducks are production bred, meat and laying. I can't afford to help out the weak ones." He smiles. "I know how you feel."

"But, Owen, he's *in* there."

"Look at this guy, though. I didn't think he'd make it, and look."

But I keep hearing that soft scratching sound, exactly like a baby's fingernail. That one little cheep.

The duck in the teacup-shell doesn't seem to have moved. "How long does it take?" I ask. Owen's arm touches mine, that's how close we're standing. I feel the heat of his body. The soft hairs on his arm brushing the soft hairs on mine.

"Three or four days."

I pull back. "Three or four *days*?"

"From the internal pip, yeah, the first breaking of the membrane. Ducks take a real long time."

And no cesarian sections allowed. Maybe my duck will still hatch, though. Owen thought this one wouldn't, and now all of a sudden he's lifting his head and using one stumpy wing like an arm to try to get some leverage on the egg edge, try to sit up. That lasts for an exciting, hard-to-watch minute or two before he sinks back down, palpitating from the exertion.

"I can't stand it," I say, and turn back to the wading pool to look at the babies.

Their makeshift nest is called a brooder, Owen informs me, and the eggs were laid by the brooder hen—"the broody," he calls it, smiling back when I laugh.

It's so funny how we've begun to acknowledge our differences. A stride forward from the time when, out of politeness, we pretended we didn't have any. It's a measure of intimacy, I think, how frank you are with another person about how foreign he can seem. "The broody"— how old-timey, how Farmer Brownish. When I happened to mention my book club not long ago, Owen kept repeating "Book club? Book *club*?" as if he'd never heard the term, and it turned out he hadn't. "You read a book in a *club*?" It just wouldn't compute until I compared it to Bible study, then the lightbulb went on. Now he teases me; he'll pick up the newspaper on my kitchen table and say, "Did you read this with your club? What'd they think of the funnies?"

"How long do they have to stay in this here *brooder*?" I ask him, sitting on the floor by the ducks and crossing my legs. I've got on shorts; straw sticks to my thighs and I pick it off in a prissy, city-girl way. Owen hunkers down beside me, forearms on his knees. I bet he can't even cross his legs—they're too muscle-bound.

"Couple of weeks."

"How do they learn to swim?" Motherless, fatherless, not even allowed to imprint on Owen. They're like aliens set down on a new planet with no instructions.

"They can swim right now. They love it, the second they stick their foot in. You oughta see a duck's first time, that's comical." He sees the question I'm about to ask. "But I keep 'em out of water till they're a lot older, and they don't miss it. Can't miss what you don't know."

"That's mean."

"No, it's not. A young duck can drown if you don't watch it every second, which I don't have time to do."

"A duck can *drown*?"

"Sure. They're like wads of cotton. Put 'em in water, they soak it up and sink. So you have to keep them warm and dry. *Dry*."

"I doubt if Mother Nature keeps them warm and *dry*. What if you supervised them?"

He sighs. It's fun to exasperate him. "If I had nothing else to do but play with ducks—like their mother—I'd fill a paint roller pan with warm water. That's got a low slope, a ramp, see, so they could get out when they wanted a rest. And I'd watch 'em splash around in that all day."

"But you can't because you're a busy man."

"I'm a busy man."

White smile lines fan out from the corners of his light-brown eyes. A slant of sun through the dusty window makes his blond beard hairs glitter. I told Mo I'd never be unfaithful, and she said, "What does desire have to do with principles? Passion isn't in the head, it's in the blood." I was a wild girl twenty years ago—is that all gone? No, it is not.

But it's not just lust. Owen intrigues me. Under his deliberate, easygoing manner there's always a tension, something unsettled about him. He keeps his mouth closed, the jutting lips clamped shut, jaws flexed.

Even when he smiles, his lips look defensive. Truthfully, I'm not sure what I want to do more, mother him or kiss him.

Beep.

It's not a duck; it's the pager he wears on his belt. "Damn," he says, checking the readout. "I've got to return this call."

"Go. I'm fine, I'll just sit here."

"Sure? Might take a few minutes."

"No, go. You're a busy man."

Luckily I have ducks to distract me when he leaves. It's so tempting to touch them. Two could easily sit in the palm of my hand. I would be a bad duck raiser, they'd make me their mama in the first five minutes of their lives. I want to touch one's little bill, find out if it's soft or hard; I love the two tiny nostrils at the top, on either side of the most delicate bend. Their eyes must see two completely different worlds, they're so wide-set.

I must have some ducks.

I get up to check on the hatchlings, but nothing's changed. The heat in here is starting to get to me. I step outside for some air.

The grown-up ducks waddle away from me or jump in the creek, burbling along between its low, grassy banks. Butterflies, buttercups, smell of fresh earth. Through the willow-tree leaves, I can see a mountain in the distance, another one hazy behind it, and a third hardly at all. The muted colors go from jade to amethyst as your eye sweeps the range, and then there's the blue, blue sky.

Farm life. It has its ups and downs, I imagine, like any other life, but the satisfactions must go very deep. Tending the land, growing something from nothing, working the soil with your hands. The simplicity. I must tell Owen that my mother's grandparents were farmers. In Lithuania. They grew beets and potatoes.

Rex is barking again, a monotonous repetition of the same boring, bored pitch. Following the sound, I come upon a small, upright platform made of plywood, the bottom half stained red. It has two red canvas conelike things nailed to it upside down. What could they be? I go closer to find out.

Halfway there I freeze in midstep, front foot poised just off the ground. I must look pretty silly. That's not red canvas. It's bloodstained canvas. I know why the cones are upside down. Owen sticks the ducks in headfirst. The feet probably protrude from the top when they're snugly in there, their wings immobile. Do they quack? Unlikely; they'd be too terrified. They don't know what's coming, but I bet they can smell the blood. He chops their heads off, I suppose, and lets them bleed into the ground. What does he use, an ax, a hatchet? He'd make sure it was razor sharp—he'd want it to be quick.

What I hate most is that there are *two* cones, for efficiency. So one duck always dies and one always knows it's about to.

I'm conscious of my hypocrisy as I shrink away from this killing place, a knot of revulsion cramping my stomach. "What did you think," I mutter, "what did you expect?" Meat and laying, that's what Owen said, but I only thought of eggs. The sunny side of farm life, baby animals, milking contented cows. Owen's cattle, down in the lower forty or wherever they are—they're *beef* cattle. I eat steak. I eat duck.

I watch my feet—my sandals and pink toenails look idiotic to me now on the trampled grass—and take the path back to the house.

Owen's talking on the telephone in the kitchen. Old-fashioned kitchen, everything almond yellow, lots of rooster-themed bric-a-brac, pineapple stenciling around the low ceiling. It's as if his mother stepped out a few minutes ago to set the table in the dining room.

Owen holds up one finger, not to shush me but to say he'll be finished soon. It's a business call, something about kilocalories and the optimum ratio of phosphorus to calcium in gluten meal. He circles the finger in the air, which I take to mean "Make yourself at home, look around, go anywhere." Good: I want to explore.

The house smells old, like a vacuum-cleaner bag that needs changing. In the living room, the floorboards creak at every step under worn sculpted carpet, two shades of green to match the flocked wallpaper. Heavy curtains with elaborate swag valances hang over mottled sheers at the front windows. The television's new, though. It's huge, one of those projection screens that take up half a wall. The couch across from it is plaid, well-worn, with cushions stacked at one end. I picture Owen sprawled sideways, flicking through hundreds of channels beaming in via the satellite dish on the roof. The local paper and the *TV Guide* clutter the coffee table, and plastic wrappers by a dish of hard candy, a can of Pepsi with a glass of melted ice on a coaster. A *coaster.* That gets me.

An old pump organ sits near the unused front door, its dusty top covered with photographs. In their formal wedding picture, Owen and Danielle look equally nervous and uncomfortable. I recognize her from pictures I've seen at Cottie's, but she looks younger in the wedding shot, vulnerable and childlike. Scared to death, actually. Not a good start for a marriage, but then hindsight is everything.

Except for one picture of Owen with the Benders—he in his army uniform, practically bald, Cottie and Shevlin vigorous-looking in their fifties—all the photos are of Danielle, either by herself or with little Matthew. Here she's in Owen's kitchen, lazy-eyed, saluting the photographer with a can of beer; here with Matthew on the back of a horse, his thin arms clutching her waist from behind. Here a formal pose in front of an enormous yellow forsythia, high as it is wide, in her Easter Sunday navy suit and white pumps. She wears her dark hair shoulder-length but short on top, a style I've always disliked. She's pretty. I think of her as a blonde, so there's always an instant of surprise when I see a picture and remember, no, she's brunette.

I never gave Owen the deer-in-headlights photo he took of me that day in my kitchen. It turned out about the way I expected. If I had given it to him, I know one thing: It wouldn't be among these pictures on top of the pump organ. This is a shrine to Danielle.

I don't know if she'd make him happy, but if she were here she'd wake this house up. This wouldn't be a shabby, lonely, one-man room anymore. Owen wouldn't fall asleep on the couch and wake up in the middle of the night with his clothes on, mouth sour, some kickboxing tournament playing on the giant TV screen. I think of her as a blonde, and I thought of him as a strong, sure man with endless resources and a soft-spoken, rock-solid self-confidence. But I believe he's as sad and alone as any of us.

"Stay for supper?"

He's so big and solid, yet he moves so quietly. He stands in the doorway with his fingertips in his pockets, watching me. I feel like a snoop, an unmasker. But it's myself I've unmasked. I make my living with my eyes, and I've been looking at a complicated man through only one or two facets of a prism that has more sides than I can count.

Why do we feel so frightened when other people's marriages fail? That's what Mo asked me. "Can't we learn? Don't we see?"

I know why. Because we want it so badly. We're not blind, we see people screwing up right and left, we know the odds are miserable. We want it anyway. If you were stranded in the desert you'd still want water, even knowing there isn't any. We want love, a lover, because otherwise it's too lonely. To care for someone else, to toss your lot in with theirs, to make their burdens yours, to try to make someone else happy, to have that be part of your job—it keeps your heart from darkening.

"Thank you, Owen. I don't think I will."

twenty-one

*O*nce, when Chloe was four or five years old, I let her come into my darkroom while I was working. This was strictly forbidden, a taboo we had reached a grumpy understanding on after innumerable serious conversations and corrections. I don't remember why I relaxed the rule on that day—a Saturday, Andrew's day to mind her while Mommy did a million other chores that had backed up during the week and sometimes, rarely but sometimes, got to play in her darkroom. Maybe it was the sweetness of Chloe's knock on the bathroom door, the poignancy of her entreaty, the fact that I was in the process of printing pictures of her recent birthday party and she knew it—whatever the reason, I broke the law and let her come in.

"Don't touch anything, honey. In fact, don't move. Put your hands in your pockets and just stand still."

"Stinky," she pronounced the room, wrinkling her nose. She loved the red light. "But I can't *see*," she complained when I got back to work at the enlarger. Good; I wanted it to be boring, so her lust to see what went on behind the tantalizing closed door would go away and leave us both in peace. But then, I also wanted her to understand the *process* as much as she, my ceaselessly curious child, wanted to understand it. I put my left arm around her waist and picked her up.

"Look. See how the light shines through the *negative* onto this paper and makes a . . . ?"

"A . . ."

"A *positive*." It was a photo of Chloe blowing candles out on her cake. Needless to say, she was spellbound. I managed to time an exposure one-handed before I set her down. "Now, watch." The best part, gently swishing an eight-by-ten sheet of blank paper in a tray of developer and watching an image form. Absolute magic. It's what it's all about.

Chloe took it in studiously, matter-of-factly. It wasn't magic to her.

She was a child; everything was magic. All phenomena were at once amazing and just what you'd expect.

I had a system: developer on the toilet seat, stop bath on the toilet top, water in the sink, fixer in a tray on the edge of the bathtub. Very ergonomic; all I had to do was pivot. I was washing my miracle print in the sink when I heard a *whoosh,* followed by a shrill wail. Chloe had pulled the tray off the tub edge and drenched herself in fixer from the chest down.

Andrew's footsteps pounding up the stairs. Me calling, "Wait a sec!" Andrew flinging the door open. I couldn't help it, I was still in darkroom mode, it was a reflex—I yelled, "My papers!" I'd left the box open; Andrew had ruined them. They were expensive.

We had a terrific fight, Chloe screaming through most of it. "The fumes!" he kept saying. "She could've been burned!" No, she couldn't have, but he blamed me so unkindly, so eloquently, and he was completely right—that was the ghastly part. I'd broken the rule out of foolishness and thoughtlessness and vanity, putting our child at risk. We bathed Chloe in the shower together, by which time Andrew's anger had gone silent. (Much more terrible.) I could not bring myself to admit guilt yet, but I had no defense, none, so I went on the attack. He was never here, how dare he go all Father of the Year on me, I did everything, I took care of Chloe and kept the house and held down a job while all he did was stoke his ego by being charming nine hours a week to a bunch of undergraduates. We didn't speak for days.

The past wasn't really that long ago. Who said that? Maybe I did.

This bathroom darkroom is even smaller than that one was, now that Owen's put the washer-dryer in. Although that's come in handy—I use the open doors of the washer and dryer to hold my chemical trays. The enlarger sits on a kitchen stool. Precariously. The acrid smell of stop bath is what's bringing back these old memories, I believe. And giving me a headache, as usual, but I don't mind. "You have the best job in the world," Greta said during our quarrel. It's possible. In any case, this is my lot. I take pictures.

Which is it, you're good at what you love or you love what you're good at? I hang dripping prints with clothespins from a wire in the shower and admire my handiwork. Pond studies, mostly, with slow black-and-white film, the old-fashioned way. The pond at dawn, full day, dusk, by moonlight. Mood pieces. They please me enormously.

So do my pictures of Sock. They're really good. But, of course, as soon as you put a dog—or a child—in a photograph it's not "serious" anymore. (Unless they're starving.) Luckily I don't care about any of that anymore. I could do fine art if I wanted, I've got the skill, the eye. But I like my children. My stinky darkroom. Maybe it was coming back to it, and back to film—coming back around to the beginning—that's redeemed for me what I do for a living. I don't know. But I find I'm anxious to get back to work, and I haven't said that in a while.

If there were another great flood, I could build an ark and repopulate Earth just with the fauna living on, in, or around my pond today. There's a turtle sunning itself on a rock; it's got a dragonfly on its back. All the baby birds fledged and learned how to fly, and now they're doing whatever teenage birds do—hang out, sing a lot. Ride in jalopies.

I've come down here this afternoon without my camera. That's so unusual, it must be significant. Do I think I've photographed everything? What arrogance that would be, and besides, the evidence is abundant and everywhere that I haven't. I don't have the playful submerged mystery of a minnow school, I don't have a frog's inflated throat in close-up, I don't have the shadow of a bird on the water surface, I only have about half the butterfly population and not a single real keeper among those. I could go on and on. Like, buttercups—I can't get that brilliant acidic yellow. When a dragonfly stops short and holds still, tense and poised—I can't get it, he just looks stuck in air. Oh, and I don't have any shots of the mosquito bites on my ankles.

Still, I've come down here without my camera, and I think that means, or is connected in some way to, this sense of . . . not *completion* exactly—I mean, talk about arrogance—a step, I'll say, a movement toward completion. It's possible I might be finished here for the time being. It's only a sense, certainly not a fact, because I haven't come *close* to finishing all the projects I had lined up for my free week— although that wasn't the point, of course, to finish projects. A few things have settled inside me, that's all. I won't make too much of it.

The way it ended with Owen yesterday has something to do with this *finished* feeling. And this achingly beautiful spring, the most perfect unfolding of a season I've ever known—because I've watched it so carefully, lived so close to it, my *eyes wide open*—is nearly over and it doesn't need me anymore. Everything's begun, everything's in progress. The mountain can take care of itself now.

"Hi, Mama," I say, imagining she's that bird up there, coasting so high in the sky it might be in another dimension. The difference is, when I talk to her now, I don't feel so sorry for myself. The pain isn't so harsh and jagged; it's settled into an ache, and sometimes the ache is sweet, almost a comfort. She's gone and not gone, and she will always be with me, and that's the best I can have.

When did this change happen? I feel less frantic. Cottie has something to do with it. And time, prosaic old time. And Chloe . . . something about Chloe. When she tells me what she wants, what she hopes for, my first reaction isn't fear. Or if it is, it's fear for her, not me, and that's a sea change. My baby is growing up, not abandoning me. Poor thing, she couldn't abandon me if she tried. Not that I'm cured. If I could, I would keep three steps ahead of her for the rest of her life, hacking down trouble and heartbreak with my machete, making straight her path. Fortunately, I can't. She can do it herself, and I even get to take some of the credit.

Mo told me that when Mark was a baby, she used to chant over his crib, "Let go, let go, let go." In nature it's simpler; the bird teenagers, the little goslings in the pond, they probably wake up one morning knowing the free ride's over, this is the day they'll have to find their own breakfast, use their own wits to hide from the scary predators. The parents are nothing but relieved. Good riddance, they think, now we can get back to the business of living for ourselves. Much less stressful.

I'm thinking some parent-bird wisdom got through to me this spring. That's how it feels, as if I absorbed it through my skin. Osmosis, filtration, transmigration. Andrew learns with his brain; me, with everything but.

I might be ready to go home. Back. Home, back, whatever. Can't stay here forever. It's been lovely, but—security is when everything is settled and nothing can happen to you. You might say it's the opposite of living. I miss talking! Friends, crowds, the Metro, noise, the Safeway. I look forward to teaching Sock how to walk on a leash. I look forward to being one of those people who follow their dogs down Columbia Road with a plastic bag. We can go to the park on Sundays, she can jump in the creek at Beach Drive. We'll join a dog park and make all new friends.

Mo needs me, that's another reason to leave. I'd like to slash a clear path for her, too, with my machete. She's given up men! She said she was going to, but I didn't believe her. But now it seems to be true, and I blame it on this we're-all-ultimately-alone business she's taking way too far. (Interestingly, she doesn't want *me* to give up men. "When are you going to sleep with him?" she asked me the other day—meaning Owen. I was shocked. Well, I say shocked. Shock was on top of a squirmy hill of reactions I didn't feel the need to examine closely.) Mo, levelheaded Mo, is going off the deep end with her self-abnegation and ego destruction and freedom from desire and all the rest of it. It's fine up to a point, but where does it end? Belly breathing in a cave by yourself? I must save her. Who can I fix her up with? So that's another reason to pull up stakes and go home. Back.

Which leaves Andrew. I sit down in my spot on the dock, my perch, and peel an orange. I've been saving Andrew for last deliberately, because he's the hardest. I thought if I cleared the decks, got rid of everything else but him, I could see more clearly. With Owen out of the picture, that's another distraction gone—if he was ever really in the picture. Now that he's out, I like to think he wasn't. Am I rewriting history? Well, it's my history, I can write it any way I want to. The point is, I miss Andrew. That's nothing new—I've missed him since I left him. But I'm trying not to trust every little emotion that comes along; be more like him, in other words. What I wouldn't give for some clarity. Things have gotten *muddier* since I scooped Sock up and stormed out of the house, and I'm getting tired. I want resolution.

So I'm off—I'm charging up the hill through the thick, buggy grass, not even picking up my orange peels first. And I am smiling and frowning with purpose, because it's good to know what I'm going to do about Andrew right *now,* at least: I'm going to call him up and apologize for never admitting I was wrong to let Chloe in the darkroom.

The past wasn't really that long ago.

I couldn't do it at the time, because it cut too close, would've pained me too much. *Bad mother.* There was for me then, and probably still, nothing worse. I was ashamed. And proud. Pride—I always thought that was Andrew's sin. I forgot it's mine, too, when the stakes are high enough. And where does pride get you? Look at us.

Inside the house, the answering-machine light is blinking. I almost don't play the message back—I'm impatient now, dying to apologize. I love apologies. Most people don't, but to me they're like good medicine, or what confession must be like. Apologizing to Greta was positively therapeutic.

"Dash." Andrew's voice comes over the machine. "Call me when you get a chance. I'm at home."

I'm laughing as I pick up the phone. What a riot if *he* were calling to apologize for something. But that's silly. I rein in my expectations and punch the number.

"Hello?"

I pull the phone away from my ear and look at it. Like in a cartoon. "Elizabeth?"

"Yes?"

Elizabeth O'Neal is in my house?

"This is Dash."

"Hello, Dash. I guess you want Andrew."

Muffled rubbery sounds—her hand on the receiver.

"Hi. Em. Hi."

"What's she doing there?"

"Em—are you leaving?" Now it's his hand on the receiver. I hope it's sweating. More muffled squeaking, then he comes back on. "Em, hi." It's all he can seem to come up with.

"Oh, she didn't have to go on *my* account."

"No, it's all right. She was in a hurry."

"Why? Down a pint, needed a fresh blood feed?"

Shocked silence. I'm shocked myself.

"That's not nice," Andrew says, and he's right; I hang my head. "Elizabeth is a troubled young woman. She doesn't deserve your scorn."

My *scorn?* That's too much. Anyway, *my* scorn? I've been putting up with Elizabeth O'Neal's obnoxious disdain since the day I met her.

"You're right," I say, "she's a very troubled woman, and she's not that young. What the hell was she doing there?"

"She brought a shrub, a sort of tree. For a present. To plant in the yard."

"Huh. Why?"

"I don't know. People give people things. She just did."

"Well, wasn't that nice of her. A *tree*?"

"Yes. A kind of evergreen—"

"Maybe she wants to hang upside down in it at night." Before he can chastise me again, I say, "What did you call me for, Andrew?" That reminds me of why I called him. Funny, all that eagerness to apologize for an ancient mini-sin—gone. Vanished like the undead at daybreak.

"I called . . . hold on two seconds." Pause. When he comes back, he's crunching something.

"What are you eating?"

"Nothing."

"Something."

Impatient exhale. "A Rolaid."

"Do you have indigestion?"

"I think it's . . . never mind."

"What? Go ahead, tell me."

"All right, because I'm sure it won't alarm you. I think it might be my heart."

He's right, I'm not alarmed.

"I made an appointment with Dr. Kim for next week."

"Andrew—you are the only person I know who has a regular cardi- ologist and no heart problem. You have a *strong* heart. This is stress, or worry about your father. Or not eating right." I think he eats ice cream for dinner.

"I'll relay your theories to Dr. Kim," he says huffily. "The reason I called . . ." Another pause while we both try to shift gears, at least return to neutral. "I've been thinking about our situation. I think it's time for us to make some decisions, Dash. I think we should be speaking to each other. More."

A gelled feeling inside me thaws. "Oh, I do, too. Definitely." I thought he was going to say something else, but I've already forgotten what. "We should be talking, I couldn't agree more."

"I don't want us to go back to Fogelman, though."

"No, I don't either. We could just do it on our own."

"Actually, Tim knows someone."

"Oh. Another therapist, you mean?"

"Yes."

I'm silent.

"Not the one he and Meg saw before their divorce. Someone Tim heard about from someone else. It's a woman. I thought you'd approve of that."

I've been leaning against the sink. I listen to the slide of my T-shirt against the cabinet as I bend my knees and slowly lower myself to the floor. "Sure. Yeah. A woman's perspective for a change. Can't hurt." I roll sideways and stretch out. The dog comes over to lick my face. I can see cobwebs between the light fixture and the ceiling. "Is this what we should do?"

"As opposed to what?"

"I don't know." If only we could synchronize our watches. If only Andrew would want me back the same times I want him back.

"No, I really think this is for the best," he says after a long silence. "Don't you?"

"What is?"

"Seeing someone. Get things moving. Get the ball rolling again."

I picture a big white ball, big as a car, rolling and stopping, rolling and stopping.

"In whatever direction it's going to go," he adds.

"Right. Could go either way. Where will I live?" That sounded plaintive. "I mean, the commute from here, if this is an indefinite . . . separation . . ."

"I've been thinking about that, too, and I think you should have the house. Tim says I can move in with him."

An electric tingle coils around my spinal cord. I picture my veins as tiny white Christmas tree lights blinking on and off. "Well, that's . . . that's a . . . Tim's little apartment?"

"There's a sofa bed in the living room. And starting tomorrow he'll be in Boston for a couple of weeks. Visiting his brother."

"Starting tomorrow. Well, then."

"It'll be convenient for me to be near the college library. I can work there."

"On what?"

"Different things."

Different things. If he doesn't want to tell me, I don't want to know. Are we throwing in the towel? In a very civilized way? Of all the conversations we've had since this whole thing started, this is the worst. I think of the phrase "the banality of evil." And "a whimper, not a bang." Underneath some sort of quilt I feel very angry, but I'm too enervated to do anything with it, the quilt is too heavy.

We leave it that he'll call the woman therapist and get a few dates for a first meeting. When we hang up, I stay on the floor with the phone on my chest. It's the middle of the day. The quietest time. I can smell Sock's dog food because the bowl is over there on the floor by the refrigerator. Smells like leather.

I don't want to move back to the house by myself. Let him stay there, he likes it so damn much. *I'll* get an apartment. Near the studio, tiny, an efficiency, because money will be tight for at least three more years. I'll work hard, and once a week, Andrew and I will meet for marriage counseling.

Well, that evokes so little enthusiasm, it must be mature. And Andrew suggested it—that makes it doubly mature. I try to get up, but I can't move. Sun shadows float across the ceiling. A fly bats at the window screen to get out. The day is slipping by. I was going home tomorrow, but now I don't care if I do or not.

Elizabeth O'Neal brought Andrew a tree.

The phone is still on my chest—when it rings, I jump so hard it almost falls on the floor before I can grab it.

"It's Miz Bender."

Owen's voice, but so strange and thin, like a wire, all the tones on one line, I hardly recognize it. Why is he saying it's Cottie?

"Owen, is it you? What's wrong?"

"Her heart. Shevlin said it was going too fast. He did CPR. The ambulance came. They took her."

twenty-two

"They're stabilizing her."

Owen and I take heart from that, but a few vague, semireassuring sentences later the nurse rephrases. She says, "They're *trying* to stabilize her," and that's different. We go back to our scared, stiff-shouldered stances, next to each other but with nothing to say, in the hallway adjacent to the ER waiting area. We tried to sit in there at first, but we had to stand up and move even after Owen turned off the television set—some entertainment news program; listening to it was physically painful.

"Her husband is with her," the nurse adds, but we knew that already. What we can't decide is if it signifies something good or bad.

"I'll go get us some coffee."

Owen shakes his head. "Not for me."

I don't want any, either.

I squeeze back against our section of wall, where we're trying to stay out of the way of aides, office staff, nurses, doctors, patients, relatives, even a policeman bringing in a drunk. Who knew there were so many emergencies in this sleepy county on a sunny afternoon in May? It's good, that means they know what they're doing here, but also bad, because what if the doctors are overwhelmed? I don't know what to wish for. I hate hospitals. Owen asked me to meet him here, to wait with him for news, and I wanted to, but if he knew how profoundly disoriented I am here, he might do without my company.

But this is not my story, it's his. *Not my drama, not my drama,* I tell myself, and take hold of Owen's wrist. "She'll be okay. They'll stabilize her, and she'll be as good as before."

He looks into my eyes, trying to see if it's true. "Yeah. She'll be good." He twists his hand around till we're palm to palm, our fingers locked. "She's gonna be okay. This kind of thing happens, I read about it. It's not that . . ."

I follow his eyes. Shevlin, coming around the corner, stops when he sees us. His foxy face seizes up, like a baby's before it starts to cry. I'm frozen; can't move or speak. It's too much, I can't bear it. He pulls on the bill of his cap, and when his hand comes away he's himself again, just older looking, grayer. He doesn't seem surprised to see me, but I doubt he's paying attention to details right now.

Owen goes to him and takes his arm. "How is she?"

"It happened again. She was fine, and then it started up, same as before. They had to shock her again, and I . . . can't watch that."

"Let's sit." Owen steers him inside the waiting place. People are spaced out, no one wanting to sit next to a stranger; only two empty chairs are left together. I force Owen to take the second one, but then a girl on Shevlin's other side says, "Here, sit, I'm going out to smoke anyways," so I take her seat. Somebody has turned the TV on again. Instinctively, Owen and I lean toward each other, forming a protective half circle around Shevlin.

"What happened?" Owen asks. "Tell us what happened."

"It was at home. She was fine, she was just starting supper, standing in front of the sink washing lettuce. Gonna make another goddamn salad."

Owen doesn't move, but I can tell he's startled. Shevlin never swears.

"I wasn't paying attention. I was gluing a cup handle back on a cup, sitting at the table, not paying any attention. Now I recollect she said something like 'Whoo' or 'Whoa,' some such, but I didn't even look up." He stares down at his rough, open palms, moving his knobby fingers. He has a black nail, the fourth finger on his right hand. "Then she said my name, and I knew. She said it real calm, but her voice wasn't right. She was looking at me, holding her chest. 'Call 911,' she said, and I started to, but she—she called to me again. I rushed up—she'd've fell if I hadn't caught her. She still dropped like a stone, she'd've broke something, I barely got ahold of her head before it could hit the floor. And then . . ." He whispers. "She wasn't breathing. I felt her neck, she wasn't breathing."

He can't stop the tears that overflow his red-rimmed eyes and roll down his cheeks. He turns toward me, away from Owen, while he hitches up his jacket and pulls a blue-checked handkerchief out of his back pocket.

He gives his throat a harsh clearing. "I called 911 and told them, and they said do I know CPR. I learned it here," he says to me while Owen nods, "they did a course back in January, I took it on purpose."

"That's right," Owen says. "You took it for her."

"So I started up, and I kept on till they came." He scrubs his eyes again with the handkerchief. "They shocked her with the machine, and she come to. They said I could ride on the ambulance with her, and she was talking and everything. She said it was like her heart running backwards—but she was good, saying she felt all right and not to worry—but just now it started up again, the racing. I couldn't watch." He covers his face with his hands.

"They'll fix it." I clasp his shoulder and hold on. "That's what they do. She's in good hands, she'll be all right. She will be." He looks up and nods, searching my eyes the way Owen did. This is all I can do for them, say the things they desperately want to believe. "You did everything right, Shevlin. You saved her. If you hadn't been there and done everything exactly right, who knows what would've happened? But you were there, thank God, and now all that's left to do is wait."

"Yeah." He blows his nose. "I didn't call Danielle yet."

Owen is sitting ramrod straight, gripping the sides of his chair, as if by staying strong and stoical he can control this situation. Shevlin may break down, but Owen never will. "I'll call her," he says.

"She's not in Richmond, she's down in Charlotte, North Carolina, at some convention. I don't have the number on me."

"I'll get ahold of her." If it bothers him that his father-in-law knows where Danielle is but he doesn't, Owen doesn't show it. "I'll be right back."

I reach for my purse. "Do you want my cell—"

"I got mine." He walks out into the hall.

I keep my hand on Shevlin's shoulder, bony-feeling and trembling under his corduroy jacket. I rub it softly, and I think it's a comfort to us both. It's a fluke that I'm here; it should be someone he knows better, or one of the church ladies who helped Cottie after her operation. Then again, would he feel better with or be any likelier to confide in one of them than me? He's a much tenderer man than I thought, Cottie's strong-hearted lover. I think of him sneaking into her father's house to see her. I think of him diving out the bedroom window and landing on a hydrangea bush. They've been together for forty years. She wants to have "intimate relations" again, but he wants to be "careful of" her.

I don't want their love affair to end. I want to put my arms around Shevlin, who would be horrified. Why is life so *mean* sometimes? Why are we here if it's just to lose everything?

"I got her." Owen takes his seat, flopping down as if his legs just gave out. He looks worse than before, the skin stretched tighter around his mouth. "She can get a flight out real early tomorrow."

Shevlin nods for a long time. "How'd she sound?"

Owen looks helpless, as if he doesn't understand the question, or its implications go so far, it's too painful to answer. He mutters something, then drops his head and covers the back of it with his hands. What could she have said to him that would make him feel even worse?

Both men seem too desolate to do anything but sit here, not even speaking to each other. I take over as the one who asks the triage nurse, passersby, the occasional white-coated doctor, what's going on. "They're still stabilizing her," they all say. "The husband can go in if he wants."

I go to the cafeteria and bring back drinks and cellophane-wrapped sandwiches nobody touches. I study a poster hanging in the hall that says heart disease kills one out of three women in America. I keep saying positive, optimistic things to Shevlin and Owen, but the longer this wait goes on, the less faith any of us have in the words.

I've fallen into the role I always play in hospitals—trying to be strong for my family. Andrew's a mess, Chloe's a child, there's never been anyone else *but* me. I'm not even any good at it. Less so since my mother died. I don't want to think about that now, but how can I not?

I never even got to see her at the hospital, because by the time I got there they'd taken her away. And at the funeral home, she looked so little like herself that the service healed nothing, it only made me feel more abandoned and unconnected. The wax-faced woman with permed-looking gray hair—who told them to *curl* my mother's beautiful straight hair?—wasn't her at all. And yet, when I knelt beside the coffin, I overflowed with harrowing, intense, passionate love. I kept whispering while I patted her shoulder in her beige suit—I was afraid to touch her skin—"I love you, Mama. I love you, Mama. I love you, Mama." It feels as if I've been crying ever since.

Shevlin should go back in the emergency room. It's hard to watch, whatever they're doing to Cottie, but he should go. He should tell her what he feels right now. While he can say it to her face, his eyes wide open.

A doctor I've never seen comes into the waiting area. Shevlin stands up, then Owen and I. The nametag on his breezy white coat says DR. PITTMAN. He's short, cherry-cheeked, pear-shaped, with intense blue eyes.

"It's good news," he says to Shevlin after perfunctory nods to Owen and me. "She's stable now, and we're moving her out to CCU, where they'll keep monitoring her, give her some medicine to make sure her heart rate stays steady. So she'll be here overnight, and then we'll see how she is tomorrow."

No one says anything.

He looks at us. He's carrying a clipboard. "Okay? Okay, then." He takes a step back.

Shevlin takes one forward. "She's okay?"

"Should be. In her case we know what caused the V-tach, and she's strong, she's in good health otherwise, and I think she's got a good prognosis."

"What happened to her won't happen again?"

"Could happen again. We'll try out different antiarrhythmic meds, try to control it like that, or we might try ablation, although I doubt it, but that's a curative treatment for certain tachychardias. More likely for something long term we'll want to do an EPS test to see if she needs an ICD, implantable cardioverter defibrillator. That emits a shock when it senses a V-tach coming."

"Like a pacemaker?"

I stop listening to the exact sense of Dr. Pittman's words and concentrate on his reassuring voice, the way his intelligent, focused eyes never leave Shevlin's, how his chubby cheeks expand when he pronounces long *e*'s. Cottie's not going to die. An implant, a little machine in her chest is going to save her. I can't speak or I'll burst into tears—I didn't realize until now how hard I was trying to prepare myself for different news—but I join in profuse, extravagant thanking of Dr.

Pittman by patting his arm and shaking his hand. We're as grateful as if he brought Cottie back from the brink of death with his own clean white hands. Who knows, maybe he did! But when he's gone, I tell Shevlin *he* did, and he laughs and cries while he gives me the longest, fiercest hug anyone's ever given me before.

It should be pitch-black out, not just starting to get dark. It should be the next *day,* not a measly six hours since I was playing with pictures of Sock in my darkroom. But time's not real in hospitals, I should know that by now. A soft, clear twilight is falling over these hills I love. I lean over the steering wheel to watch a flock of birds flapping their wings in a lazy, unmistakable, going-home-to-bed frenzy. The sun comes and goes depending on whether I'm at the top or bottom of a hill, and even its setting is gentle and soft, not piercing or dramatic. I should feel completely at peace. I smell fertilizer when I pass the just-turned fields, honeysuckle by the fallow meadows. All's right with the world—so where's my contentment? I can't explain the restlessness I feel until I catch myself grappling for my cell phone in my purse and dialing one-handed.

It's been a long time since I couldn't quite savor an experience fully, couldn't *possess* it, before telling Andrew about it.

And he's not there! This is so wrong.

"Hi. I wanted to tell you something," I say to his voice mail. Now I realize it isn't even about Cottie. No, it is about Cottie, but she's only the starting point. "Call me. Let's talk—I really want to."

In fact I almost start in, fill up his answering machine with words, because I am so tired of not talking to my husband. Cottie's going to be fine, I want to say. There can be happy endings. Life is very dear, but it's so short, it's so short, and pride takes up so much precious *time.* I don't give a damn about Elizabeth O'Neal. Shouldn't I come home? Shouldn't we be doing something? Cottie's going to live!

But he might think I'm hysterical. I must be more systematic and organized, at least get him on the *phone* before I start speaking. If it were the other way around, I'd rather he said these things to me than to my machine.

No, hell no, I'd take them any way I could get them. He could tell Sock for all I care—how in the world did we come to this? Enough is enough. I trail my hand out the window and let the cooling air blow through my fingers. Things seem to be falling away, all the . . . weeds, the nettles, everything that was obscuring the object underneath. It's this house of ours, somewhat decrepit—it needs paint, shingles, new glass in the windows—but it's still sound. What it needs is someone to stand up for it. If Andrew won't, I will. I wanted him to go first, but this is fair—I'm the one who started the breakdown process. First me, then him: We let it go, didn't do the upkeep. Turn your back on an old house, immediately it begins to sag. Rust never sleeps. Constant vigilance, that's what you need. It's not romantic, God knows, but neither is dry rot.

I'll go first, I'll commit to the rehab. It's not too late. It couldn't be. Andrew just needs to see me with my sleeves rolled up, a bandanna around my head, carrying a hammer, one of those long silver level things on my shoulder. Why am I thinking in all these contractor analogies? My God—Fogelman! Oh, Andrew's going to laugh and laugh when I tell him. All this craziness and confusion, all the running around and fretting and dead-ending—when what we should've been doing was moving purposefully together from room to room, remodeling the House of Love.

andrew

twenty-three

"ey, man, you ain't puttin' *that* on the grave."

"No, I'm not."

"'Cause that is *the* ugliest flower I ever saw."

"I'm not putting it on Hobbes's grave, I'm just setting it out in the sun." And just his luck, Wolfie happened to be skipping by in the alley at that very moment. Under other circumstances, Andrew would've been happy to see him.

"Good, 'cause that is one ugly flower."

"It's a tree. A cedar of Lebanon. Very old. It's mentioned in Gilgamesh, which was written thousands and thousands of years ago."

Wolfie came closer, squinting at the squat, drab, short-needled sapling in the elegant porcelain pot. Elizabeth's peace offering. "Wow," he said more appreciatively. "It *look* old, but not *that* old."

"No, the species is that old—this is a . . ." Oh hell, Andrew didn't have the strength to explain it. When he bent over to slide the pot farther into what was left of the sunlight, he felt, in tandem, a stitch in his back and a roll of nausea in his stomach. What the hell was that? Was it one ailment with two separate manifestations, or two discrete afflictions?

Wolfie had his basketball under his arm, as usual. "Wanna play some one-on-one?"

"Not right now. But some other time."

"Yeah, you don't look good. You movin' like a ol' man. What up, you sick?"

"No, no. I'm fine."

"You look whipped. You should get in the bed."

"Thank you, Doctor."

Wolfie thought that was a riot. He followed Andrew to the back porch, bouncing the ball between his legs, showing off. "I could come in," he said, "but I got a date."

"A *date*."

"Yeah, that girl Tina I told you about."

"Tina," Andrew said appreciatively. He put his hand on his midsection and pressed. A pain there came and went. "So the direct approach worked."

"Yeah." Wolfie spun the ball on his fingertips for an expert few seconds. He looked taller, fuller-faced than the last time Andrew had seen him, which was about a week ago. "Sometime we could go out together."

"Who?"

"Me and Tina, you and Dash." He dribbled the ball in a tight circle, darting Andrew a sly glance.

"Em. I don't think that's very likely."

"How come?"

"I just don't." Not today, but sometime soon, he and Wolfie needed to talk.

"How come? You still like her, don't you?"

"I have to go in."

"You do, right? So just go get her. It's easy."

"Thank you, Ann Landers."

Wolfie's face wrinkled in disgust. *"Who?"*

Andrew wanted to put his hand on his head, the way Dash did. Brush his bristly scalp and feel the hard bones in the delicate skull. "A wise old advice giver," he said. "Very famous and rich."

"Yeah? So, see, that make two of us. You ought to listen up." He whirled and ran down the flagstone walk, faked a jump shot against a utility pole. "Later, man!"

"Later! Have a—" He was already too far away to hear. "Nice date," Andrew finished weakly and went in the house.

Upstairs, he got the Pepto-Bismol out of the medicine cabinet and slugged down a dose without measuring. His face in the mirror gave him a queasy start. He looked, if possible, worse than he felt. He stuck out his tongue, pulled one eyelid down, felt the glands under his jaw. Symptoms of heart attack included nausea. Restlessness and apprehension as well. With a so-called silent heart attack, there was no chest pain at all.

"I'm just coming down with something," he assured his reflection.

Stomach flu, a virus. No reason to call Dr. Kim and push up the date for his appointment. If he dropped dead between now and next Thursday, Dash would be sorry. That was something.

The ache in his middle returned when he lay down on the bed. He tried sitting up on pillows, but then his neck hurt. Every position he tried was either painful or uncomfortable. Chloe had one of those back-pillow things with arms; he got up and went in her room.

He could hardly tell she was gone; except for her clothes and her computer, most of her stuff was still here. She took after him: She traveled light and she wasn't sentimental.

He thought of their last conversation, a phone call yesterday in which she'd told him he needed to get back into marriage counseling with Mom. She was quite adamant about it. He'd teased her that one freshman psych course had turned her into an expert. And yet today, with Dash, he'd made the same argument, that time was passing and they weren't doing anything, that they needed to be more assertive, get the ball rolling again. If nothing else, he'd liked the way he sounded, like a man who meant what he said and knew what he was talking about. He couldn't be sure what Dash had made of it, though. She'd sounded . . . disengaged. Uninterested. Weary of something.

It made sense for her to come home and him to move into Tim's place for the summer. He started a mental list of what he would take. He felt monastic, as if his possessions weighed him down. What was the smallest suitcase he could get away with? Simplify. Really, why take more than one change of clothes and some underwear? His laptop and some books, that's all he needed. Why was Dash the one who'd gotten to slough things off and live at the cabin? He felt like camping out, like living in a Quonset hut. Minimize. Peace and quiet hadn't worked very well, but only because they weren't peaceful and quiet *enough.*

He dozed off.

When he awoke, it was pitch-dark and he had no idea where he was. Oh—Chloe's room. He staggered into the bathroom, splashed water on his face, and swigged down another capful of Pepto-Bismol. Wandered downstairs. The phone hadn't rung, but the light was blinking on the answering machine. Someone must've called while he was outside with Wolfie.

Dash's voice. "I wanted to tell you something," he heard against a background of high static—she was driving. She sounded wrought-up, on edge. He played the message again. "Let's talk," it ended. "I really want to."

God.

He put a cup of water in the microwave. Longing and anxiety were an uneasy mix, like the curdled milk he tried to stir into his instant coffee. What now? There had been a time when he loved and was entertained by his wife's emotional eruptions, but nowadays they seemed to come just before she cut him off at the knees. *What now?* He had very little hope, none, that Dash was calling to tell him good news.

He went upstairs and put on his shoes. While he was at it, he combed his hair. He sat on the bed and picked up the phone, but then he put it down. This room was too small or something, the lighting too intimate. Conscious of behaving neurotically, he went downstairs and dialed Dash's number from the bright, high-ceilinged kitchen.

"Hello?" She made it sound like a demand, as if whatever he had to say had better be good.

"Em, have I caught you at a bad time?"

"Andrew!"

"Yes. Em—"

"I can't talk now, I'm sorry, I really—Owen's here, I have to be with him, I have to. Sorry—I'll call you later, okay?"

"Okay," he said blankly. Then, "What?"

She hung up.

He stared at the floor for a while, thinking what he always thought, that the yellowed wax needed stripping and had for several years. He took an absentminded sip from the cup of congealed coffee, and while he was swallowing he played back in his head the sound of "Owen's here, I have to be with him, I have to." The swallow reversed itself in the vicinity of his diaphragm. A substance like beige yogurt spewed from his mouth with disgusting force, hitting the front of the dishwasher with an audible splat. Either the sound or the sight dredged up more nausea; he made it to the sink just in time to vomit again. He put his hands over his eyes and retched until he was empty.

When he could stand up straight, when he could think, he went back to the telephone and punched redial. It rang until Dash's machine came on. He hung up.

I have to be with him. It could mean something else. Although what? *I have to eat dinner with him. I have to hold this board so he can hammer a nail in straight.*

She'd sounded agitated, distracted, definitely unwilling to talk. He looked down to see his car keys in his hand. *"I have to be with him."* Like hell.

Where was his wallet? On the newel post, where he'd left it. Hot night; he wouldn't need a jacket. Good thing Hobbes was dead; otherwise he'd have to take him along, and he got carsick.

I'm carsick, Andrew thought, taking the P Street curve too fast on Rock Creek Parkway. He could throw up again right now, pull over and puke out the window. What stopped him was the novel certainty that that would be psychosomatic behavior. Psychosomatics: the relation of psychic conflict to somatic symptomatology.

On Route 29 he caught sight of the speedometer and jerked his foot off the gas. Besides the pain that came and went in his right chest, he had a persistent ringing in his ears and a bitter taste in his mouth. *Just drive,* he thought, because it was hard to credit any of his senses anymore. Some sort of cognitive disconnect was happening, an episode of distance between his perceptions and reality, making it impossible for him to conclude anything definitely. He wavered between two opposing convictions: that nothing was wrong and that he was having a myocardial infarction.

What would Thomas Jefferson do?

Not about a heart attack. What would Jefferson do if he found out Martha was having an affair? An absurd proposition on its face, they couldn't have been more devoted, but just say. *Think about it to focus your mind,* he told himself. He'd posed that same question to his conscience in various moral quandaries before now, but never in circumstances this dire.

But imagine it. Thomas, sick of revising the legal code, comes home from Williamsburg unexpectedly to find Martha, his lovely, fragile wife, the mother of his darling little girls, in the intimate company of . . . a neighbor. A freeman, but rough and unrefined, uneducated.

Someone Thomas knows only as the man who . . . comes to butcher the hogs every October. With Martha! In the long alcove bed, in the beautiful bedroom Thomas modeled after a temple by Palladio—no, wait. He designed the sleeping alcove in the 1790s, and Martha died in 1782. Never mind that—what would he do?

Nothing precipitous. Tom was a mild, sweet-tempered man, reasonable to a fault. Disciplined. He wouldn't reach for a musket and blow the villain's brains out. Throw him out, though—he might do that. Bodily and with pleasure, and enough violence to assuage some of his fury and confusion. Right, he'd heave him out of the house—then he'd confront the tearful Martha, who would be prostrate, incoherent with remorse. *Why?* That's all he'd want to know. My dearest love, can't you tell me *why?*

Then—he'd forgive her. In time. Because his heart was gentle and humane, and Martha was the love of his life. (She died at thirty-three; he promised on her deathbed he would never remarry, and he was true to his word.) He would find it in himself to forgive her, even though she and the hog slaughterer had committed the greatest betrayal he would ever know. His noble heart would overcome.

Dash—sometimes she couldn't help herself. She was born rash. Think of the time she talked the manager at Clyde's into letting her jump out of a cake for Andrew's fortieth birthday. Think of the time she bought Chloe a pony. Because it was there, grazing near a PONY FOR SALE sign, and Chloe had admired it. Andrew, the bad guy, had to straighten it all out, and thank God Chloe's heart wasn't broken. At eight, she already had her mother's number.

The pain in his side was gripping him tighter the closer he got to the cabin—surprise. When this was over, no doubt it would miraculously disappear. Would he tell Dash? He might be able to forgive her for a once-in-a-lifetime fling, flirtation, dalliance—such *chipper* words for the most devastating blow he could imagine—but it would take all of his magnanimity. There probably wouldn't be any left to tell her she'd been right all along. He was a hypochondriac.

dash

twenty-four

What a magical night. The full moon is enormous, a perfect yellow ball rising behind the black pines. I couldn't stay in. I brought my salad outside and sat in the old wicker rocker, the bowl between my knees and a glass of wine precarious on the armrest. "To you, Cottie," I toasted. I toasted Dr. Pittman, too, and everybody in the ER and the CCU, and when I got toward the bottom of the glass, which went straight to my head, I was in a mood to toast my mother.

"Mama, did you intercede on this deal? Even if you didn't, here's to you, because I know where your heart is. Thank you. For always loving me. I'll always love you." I cried a few tears.

Now I'm sober again, relatively speaking, although I still have the music up loud. This I'll miss. If I go home and Andrew and I reconcile and live happily ever after, I will miss this feeling of absolute freedom from having to be anything for anyone but myself. And it's all right, it's not that nourishing anyway, I can definitely live without it. But I'll miss it. It's not even particularly mature. What is it? A little wine, a yellow moon, music I love, and no one around. Just in this moment, I feel *ecstatic*. Possibilities come to me, brand-new thoughts, as if I am making actual, measurable personal and mental progress. An illusion, no doubt, but I like it. If it's a state that requires solitude to replicate, I can always tell Andrew to go away for a while.

I don't know why I'm feeling so optimistic about us, actually. The other half of ecstasy is agony. Which I am imagining now as drifting farther away from my husband out of inertia or sullenness, until there's nothing to do but construct a life without him. Then I wouldn't like solitude so damn much, would I?

Maybe Mo is on a higher spiritual path than I am, maybe the goal really is to "be no one," and therefore need no one, but I don't think so. Truth is, I want that hard shoulder next to me in the bed at night, that other flawed human being who knows me better than anyone else ever will. For as long as I can have him. I want that even more than doglike devotion. And when I can't have him, because he's had a heart attack or I've lost my marbles or he's walked in front of a bus, *then* I'll take to heart Mo's god-awful truism that we're all, every one of us, alone, and I'll soothe myself with whatever I've got at hand, whatever's left. But before that, I intend to hold my loved ones close, very close. And tell them all the time how dear they are to me. And count myself unbearably lucky.

Yes, but what if it's not up to me? What if, deep down, Andrew doesn't want me back? How unamusingly ironic, just when I am learning how much I want him back. I always wanted him back, but a different Andrew, or a different me. I thought I was dying for *change,* but that was a mirage: What I wanted was to go back to the *pre*change time, the *old* us—a Peter Pan–like wish I hope I've outgrown. I have my fingers crossed.

But I still want passion. I won't live without it. Why should I set that aside along with youth and looks and menstruation and good skin? I don't want to. I don't want to. Cottie never did, and she's my heroine. I take off my wedding ring, read the inscription inside, run my finger over the etched gold, like a message in Braille. I want all of Andrew back, but especially the part of him that once tramped it out in the snow for me.

Well, for Pete's sake. I can't believe someone's coming. What time is it? Headlights shine through the trees before I hear a car's engine. "Sock," I call, so she won't get run over, and so she'll come and protect me if it's a rapist. She ignores me, starts barking and wagging her tail; she recognizes the sound of the engine before I do.

Owen's truck.

Well, hm. This isn't how I saw the evening going. I get up to greet him—then stop. Is it Cottie? Oh God! Something he didn't want to tell me on the phone? He stops the truck too fast; tools slide up and strike something metallic in the bed. He throws the door open and puts one foot on the ground. Something's wrong; it takes him forever to set the other one down. The moon is behind him, I can't see his face. Walking toward me, he stumbles on a rock or a dirt clod in the driveway, and his white teeth flash. He chuckles.

I fold my arms.

He hasn't seen me yet. When he does, he says, "Dash!" as if he forgot where he was going, but now that he's here he's pleasantly surprised. "How are you?"

"Fine. How are you?"

"Great!"

"So I s——"

His arms wrap me up and he lifts me completely off my feet. What can I do but laugh and hug him back? He sets me down, takes hold of me by the shoulders, and kisses me on the mouth.

"Whoa." I sound a little shaky. It started out exuberant, this heady kiss, but it turned into something else so fast, I wasn't prepared and I let it last too long. I put my hands on Owen's stony biceps to put some distance between us. His eyes are dancing. Sexy blond beard stubble has grown in since I saw him a few hours ago. He smells incredibly . . . real. I've been intrigued by those assertive, jutting lips of his since I first saw them. He is such a *rock* of a man.

And now I'm not interested in him at all. Timing, my God, it's everything. If he'd kissed me before, if he'd kissed me *yesterday* in the garden or in the duck house—who knows? My whole life might have changed. I'm so thankful it didn't, I want to kneel down in the driveway and say a prayer.

Luckily I know how to deal with this. For some reason I've had a lot of experience in this particular area. "Why, Owen Roby. *Thanks*," I say with a laugh that's equal parts surprise and matter-of-factness. I know just how much humor to put in the laugh so it's the sound of mutual fun—never ridicule. My, aren't we silly people, and aren't you something, and wasn't that a delightful, *one-time* experience? It's not a strictly feminist response to male aggression, I know, but it's my style, and more important, it works. And life goes on.

Owen—what a nice man. He steps back and grins, looking down at his feet. "Me and Shev, we got a six-pack to celebrate. I went and drank three of 'em. I'm drunk!"

"Three beers, wow." I gesture playfully to the rocking chair on the porch. "Maybe you'd better sit down."

"You wouldn't have anything to drink around here, would you?"

"Coffee?"

"Nah." He glances up at me through his eyelashes, very boyish and winning, hands in his back pockets. "I'm still celebratin'."

I do an exaggerated, put-upon sigh. "Okay, come on in. I can probably dig up a dram of something or other somewhere."

I happen to have three bottles of beer in the refrigerator; I'll give him one, but I don't know if I'll tell him about the other two. What a cheap drunk—I love that in a man. Andrew's the same.

I get a Coke for me, and we go in the living room.

"You *like* this music?" Owen flops down on the couch and takes a long pull from his Corona. "Scuse me," he says after a satisfied belch. I turn off the Pretenders and sit next to him. "Here's to Miz B.," he says, and we toast. "After you left, I went in and saw her. They got her breathing oxygen and hooked up to this and that, but she looks fine. She talked just like herself."

"That's fantastic."

"They're talking about letting her come home in a day or two. I still can't get over it. When she went in for the valve last year, I was scared, sure, but I had a feeling she'd be okay. Maybe because *she* was so sure, and she talked us into it, me and Shev."

"I can see her doing that."

"The night before she had to go in, we were all in this motel restaurant near the hospital having dinner, except Shev and I couldn't eat. And bad as it was, somehow she got us to laughing. Called it the Last Supper, you know, and started telling all these"—he breaks off to laugh—"these terrible jokes about what we're supposed to do when she's gone, what to have at the wake, songs she wants at the funeral, Perry Como and Peggy Lee, she wants 'My Way,' by Frank Sinatra—"

All at once he's not laughing anymore. He squeezes his eyes shut, but the tears flood his face, it's like a dam bursting, and he grits his teeth but a terrible, devastating sob escapes. It's horrible. Shocking.

"Owen, it's all right, she's—no, that's okay, go ahead. Go ahead, it's good." I hold him and he gives in to it. Chloe used to let me comfort her like this. Owen cries so hard, so heartbrokenly, it's as if this is his first time.

"I saw it all going," he says against my neck. His tears are scalding. "I don't want to lose. Everything again. It hurts. I couldn't—"

The phone rings.

He pulls away, hiding his face, rubbing his nose against the arm of his shirt. The only thing that stops me from letting the goddamn phone ring is the certainty that it's Andrew.

I put my fingers in Owen's hair and squeeze his temples. "Two secs," I promise, and make a dash for the kitchen before the machine can come on.

Yes, it's Andrew. Dear Andrew. He sounds especially dithery, but out of my other ear I hear the screen door slam. Owen is *leaving*? "I can't talk now," I say in a rush, "I'm sorry, I really—Owen's here, I have to be with him, I have to"—if he's still here. "Sorry—I'll call you later, okay?"

No, he's still on the front porch. I'm so relieved—it would've been awful if he'd left like that. This feels like a second chance.

I go and stand beside him at the rail. What should I say, I ponder as we watch the moon rise and listen to the frogs singing. "I'm okay," he says, his voice thick and nasal. "If I can just stand here for a minute."

It takes me a couple of seconds to get it: He wants to be by himself. "Oh. Sure." I mumble something about coffee and make a sheepish exit.

I take as long as I can in the kitchen. If he feels humiliated because he broke down in front of me, I don't know what I'll do. It seems best to leave him be, but I wish there was something I could do besides absent myself. I take a pile of laundry out of the washer and put it in the dryer, and I fold the clothes that were in the first dryer load into neat piles and carry them upstairs. I want him to get tired of being alone and come inside without being asked. But time passes and the coffee's getting old, so in the end I pour us two mugs, lots of milk and sugar in Owen's, and take them outside.

He's out in the driveway, throwing a stick for Sock. When he sees me, he comes over and sits beside me on the stoop. He blows steam from the coffee mug I hand him and takes a sip. After a pretty long time he says, "Sorry about that."

"Don't be silly. It's been a hell of a day."

He won't look at me. "I never did that before."

"So what?"

"It was the beer. I don't drink usually."

"Would you forget it? I'm all emotional today, too. It's good for us.

To carry on once in a while. What are we supposed to do, bottle things up forever? We'll explode!"

He laughs a little. But then he doesn't say anything more, and I follow suit. It's a peaceful silence, calm, tension free. I believe, in all the time we've been friends, it's the first time we've ever been completely at ease with each other.

The moon has come out from behind the trees. It's platinum white, not yellow anymore, and so bright you could read a newspaper by it.

"Hey, Owen. Let's go for a walk."

We set off down the drive, Sock ranging ahead. Here in the woods, the crickets finally outchirp the frogs. Lightning bugs flicker like clouds of little match heads firing on and off in the trees. There's a coolness in the air that won't last much longer; in a week or two the nights will be warm and buggy. But for now I rub my bare arms and let the mild chill remind me that nature is separate from and ungovernable by me. Hence the thrill.

At the road, there's no need to hang back in the shadows and watch the infrequent cars hiss by—a man is with me, I'm safe. But the dog, who except for riding in them has hardly any experience with cars, can't resist sniffing around too close to the road, and I have to pick her up. Owen still isn't talking. I'm tired. There's nothing I'd like better than to crawl in bed and doze off reading, Sock at my hip, but I can't let Owen go until he's his old self. That's what he came for, I think, more than to celebrate for Cottie, certainly more than to kiss me.

Eventually we head back to the house, the uncanny moonlight limning every rut and crevice in the lane. I'm pondering my strategy for cheering him up when Owen says, "It's not just Miz Bender. Danielle's leaving."

"Leaving?"

"She told me today when I called her from the hospital. It's her job, they want her to transfer to Atlanta. She'll take Matthew with her, and that'll be it."

At last I can ask him, "Do you still love her?"

And he says, "Yeah," with no hesitation.

We walk along in silence.

"But she . . ." I don't know how to phrase this kindly. "She doesn't . . . ?"

"She says she loves me, too."

"*Oh.* Well, then—"

"But she won't live with me, so how could she?"

"She won't live with you?"

"She says she can't live here. Can't live here. What does that tell you?" He picks up a stone in the road and sidearms it into the woods. The clatter when it lands frightens the dog, who scuttles backward against my legs.

What does it tell me? That Danielle likes the high life in Richmond. Or Mom and Dad cramp her style, especially Dad. Or she hates Dolley. Or she thinks the schools are better in Richmond, or she's afraid of commitment, she's allergic to tobacco fields—who knows, and what difference does it make? Danielle says she loves Owen: That is the salient fact, and news to me.

"Why don't you go with her?"

We're home. He collapses on the porch stoop, leaning back on the old boards with his elbows. He makes a hopeless, amused face.

"Owen, it just seems like you're all jammed up, and one of you needs to remove one obstacle, one log, to get the stream flowing again."

"Go with her and do what?"

"Anything! I've never known such a jack-of-all-trades as you. You could do anything, or keep doing what you're doing now. Don't they have farms in Georgia?"

"But this is home."

"Not to her."

He doesn't hear that. "If she really wanted to be with me, she'd be with me."

"She's probably saying the same thing. 'If he wanted me, he'd come and get me.' Like Shevlin went and got Cottie. He didn't think and mull and sulk, he just *got* her. Did she ever tell you that story about how one night he sneaked—"

"Snuck in her daddy's house to see her. Yeah." He leans over, unlaces the work boots he's had on all day, and toes his feet out of them. It's a tribute to our friendship, I suppose, that he not only doesn't ask if it's okay, he groans with relief while he massages one foot and then the other, as if he were by himself, sitting on the edge of his bathtub. "Yeah," he says, "but then Shev jumped out the window and ran off. He didn't face up to the old man."

"No, but he set a *tone*. He let Cottie know she was *it*."

He rubs his eyes with the heels of his hands, scratches his fingers through his thinning hair. Thick-shouldered and indecisive in his holey socks, he looks like an overgrown boy.

"A woman wants to know that," I tell him. "A *person* wants to know it. It's such a lonely world. If somebody has to have you, you're not alone, you've got a partner, someone to go through it with. Cottie and Shevlin, they're partners. I don't know Danielle, but if she's like either one of her parents, she understands how it is with them and she wants to have that, too. She'll want you to want her, Owen. So much that you act out of character. She's yours if you do that. I really think so."

I feel drunk. This is just the kind of intense personal certainty I feel about someone else's life, and don't mind telling them, when I've had too much to drink.

"What do you mean, act out of character?"

"Oh, I don't know. I know you have to be yourself, of course, who you are is who you are, but . . . Who did she fall in love with? What were you like then? Were you the exact same man you are now?"

"People change," he says, defensive.

"Sure, and sometimes they don't change at all, and those are two good reasons why they split up. But if Danielle used to love something in you and it's gone, or it's hiding . . ."

Sock is a very empathetic dog. She's been sitting on the porch, alert to all the night sounds, oblivious to us, but now she pads over to Owen and looks up into his face with limpid, searching eyes. "No pressure," I start to say, to acknowledge the comical obvious—but I don't really want to lighten the mood. I'm trying to make a point.

"I guess I was . . ." Owen straightens up and puts his hands behind his head. "Looser. Maybe she liked that?" he asks the moon. "Maybe I didn't work as hard. I had, you know. More time."

"For her and Matthew."

"Yeah."

That'll be one hundred dollars. The friendship discount. I have nothing more to say, but I stay with Owen, watching the moon and the lightning bugs and listening to the frogs. I feel as if I'm half gone, as if I have one foot here and the other dangling in space. Here, but not here. My other half is in limbo, and it's driving me quietly nuts. I can't *wait* to put my halves together. I can't *wait,* but I have to. Inside this pure paradise of a night, I feel as if I'm full of amphetamines or steroids, Mexican jumping beans. "Be right back," I say finally, and drift into the house.

I know I can be presumptuous, that I'm not shy about dispensing advice to people who haven't asked for it. It's probably a flaw, although I think the fact that no one ever complains is a point in my favor. Immediate family excluded. And Owen did come over for counsel, whether he knows it or not. So I'll let myself off the hook on that one. Now all that worries me is . . . there's probably a psychiatric name for it. Not transference. When you say things to your client that actually relate to *you,* not necessarily *him.* When you mistake the patient for yourself.

Oh well. La-la-la. I fold the last load of laundry with a light heart, because even if I did give Owen advice that applies to my life, what's to say it doesn't apply equally to his as well? It's not as if either of us is so damn unique.

My, I'm full of moods tonight. As I set my clean, folded clothes at the bottom of the steps, a little cloud falls over me. Wrong: I wasn't giving advice to *myself* via Owen, I was giving advice to Andrew. I want *him* to sneak in the house. He can jump out the window afterward, in fact I'd expect him to, but first I want him to set that *tone.* I want to believe he has to have me. Like the time he came and got me at my mother's house. I never—it hits me for the first time—I never gave him credit for that. I've never been so happy to see anyone in my whole life, scary, horrible haircut and all, and yet I never appreciated what it must've taken for Andrew to do that—come and get me. The pride he had to swallow. I took it for granted. Oh God, I want to make amends.

Now I want Owen to go home. It's late, this party's over. Could I just flick the porch light on and off? I'm tired of talking and listening and being sympathetic. The doctor is out.

Oh, for Pete's sake. Owen has moved from the stoop to the wicker rocker and fallen asleep. Well, that's just great. Now what? If I wake him up, I'll have to talk to him some more. He probably shouldn't drive yet, anyway. I go in and get the flannel blanket from the living room, bring it back, and tuck it gently around his shoulders. He looks pretty cute, I have to say, with his feet crossed in their holey socks, arms folded, bristly chin on his chest.

I move out into the grass, yawning. The dog has gotten into the habit of not peeing unless I'm with her. "Okay, babe. *Business.*"

Successful, she scampers up the steps and waits for me at the door. She likes our nighttime routine as much as I do—a strange man asleep on the porch can't interrupt it. "Snack?" We go in the kitchen. Her snack container is an old tin tea box. She gets one biscuit and one chewy thing, and I've taught her to sit politely until I set them on the floor, not maul me for them. "*Good* girl."

Lights out in the kitchen, the living room. I'll leave the porch light on for Owen. And I guess I'll leave the door open. Night, pal. Get up in about thirty minutes and go home, I advise him telepathically.

God, what *now*? Lights, car lights coming up the driveway. Oh, impossible. It's Shevlin, who else could it be. Well, he'd better not be drunk! This is *really* getting . . .

The car comes out of the tree thicket and turns; through the screen door I see it in profile before it turns again and the headlights momentarily blind me. Not Shevlin. Andrew. Oh! He read my mind!

I punch the screen door open, laughing. I just want to get my arms around him. He climbs out of his car without turning the lights off, *so* unlike him, and he doesn't even close the door. I'm *thrilled.* I wait for him in the yard, hunching my shoulders and clenching my hands, a shivering ball of pent-up welcome. How often do we get to have our heart's desire? At the very moment we want it most?

The dog, still inside, is barking like a maniac. I glance back and see Owen shuffle down the steps in his socks. Big and sleepy looking, the blanket still wrapped around his shoulders.

Oh.

"Hi, Andrew," I call gaily, and start toward him. He looks funny. Grim, not glad. He's pale as an egg, sweat gleaming on his forehead. Why is he walking like that? He's got his hand in his belt, why is he . . . Oh my God.

"Andrew!" No. No, he's empty-handed—what was I thinking?—but his face is so strange. "Andr——"

"I forgive you." I *think* that's what he says before he shoulders past me, glittery eyes on Owen.

"Wait, now. Honey? Hey, no, this isn't at *all* what it—wait!"

Even if sleepy-eyed Owen wanted to defend himself, both of his hands are full of flannel. But he's missed all the signals I am now overloading on. He has no idea what's coming, and all I can do is shriek in a helpless, girlie fashion as Andrew draws his fist back and socks it into Owen's chin. The blow doesn't look that hard, and it's all but silent. Owen's feet never leave the ground, but he falls straight back and lands on his behind in the grass.

"Sonofabitch had it coming."

Owen's all right, sitting up and rubbing his jaw. I don't have to run over and hold him up or anything. You see that so often in the movies. And I'm supposed to glare furiously at Andrew and say, "How *could* you?" but my sentiments are mixed. Especially since Owen is all right.

Andrew sounds out of breath. "You're coming home with me, Dash."

"Okay."

He waves his hand at poor Owen. "I'm better than this guy."

"Well, for me."

"So you're coming?"

"Yes." I feel shy. "I was coming anyway."

I'm not sure he hears that, though. His eyes are rolling back, showing the whites. His knees buckle and he folds rather than falls, like a ladder or a tall scaffolding with lots of hinges and joints. I have time to scream again and reach out two futile hands before he drops, with a sound like bones cracking, in a slack pile at my feet.

the batemans

twenty-five

"But the sonogram wasn't conclusive because his liver is swollen and it was hiding his gallbladder. So then they did a CT scan, and between that and the blood tests they finally figured it out. It took half the night."

"His liver is swollen?" Chloe's voice was anxious.

"Yes, but that's not serious, apparently—it's his gallbladder. He's got a stone the size of a golf ball."

"Oh, my God!"

"And don't you know he already loves saying that. It's going to be the *big analogy* this year." Dash pursed her lips at Andrew in a jokey kiss from the edge of the empty bed next to his. He rolled his yellow eyeballs at her. "He's got a lot of bruises, too, but luckily he didn't break anything when he fell."

"Is he in pain?"

"Not now, they've got him on an IV with painkillers and antibiotics."

"But he was before?"

"Yeah. It was pretty awful." Chloe didn't need to know how awful, the unstoppable vomiting, the nightmare race to the hospital in the backseat of her car, Owen driving. Or the sight of Andrew doubling up in pain in the ER while they did test after test, with interminable waits between them. "He has acute cholecystitis, which means inflammation, caused by this stone. Which, did I mention, is big as a golf ball?"

"Let me talk to her," Andrew said.

"I was reading this pamphlet on gallstones in the waiting room—you know how they have all those leaflets on diseases that got you in the ER in the first place—and I know exactly why he has his stone."

Andrew made a sighing sound and held out his hand for the phone.

"Ice cream. Fatty foods, that's a cause of gallstones, and it's the only profile he fits. He's not a woman, he's not overweight or old, not diabetic, not a Native American. I'm telling you, it was the ice cream."

"May I please speak to my daughter?"

"Dad eats ice cream?"

"Like a child at the beach."

"Dash—"

"Mom—"

"He wants to talk to you. Sorry to call so late. Love you, babe—I'll call tomorrow, right after the surgery."

"Okay, Mom."

"And don't worry—the doctor said it's strictly routine. Here's Dad." She handed Andrew the phone.

He wedged it between his ear and the pillow, because his left arm had a needle in it and he was afraid of pulling it out. "Hey, kiddo. When are you coming home?"

"Daddy! Oh, poor you! How do you feel?"

"A lot better now. A lot better, I feel practically well."

"Was it terrible?"

"No, your mother exaggerates. A little discomfort, all gone now."

"And the operation is really routine?"

"Absolutely, they've done it a thousand times. I'm not at all worried." Nerves fluttered in his stomach at the same time a rush of blood surged to his neck. For years he'd lived in fear and dread of what was going to happen tomorrow. Thirty-two thousand people a year never woke up from surgery. They died unconscious. They went under, they never came up. "So how'd you do on your last exam?"

"It's tomorrow."

"Oh no, that's right. I'm sorry, I wouldn't have had your mother call if I'd remembered."

"It's cool, Dad. I was still studying, I haven't gone to bed yet."

"Well, you better turn in soon, it's after two o'clock. If you don't know it by now, you never will."

"So how come you're down in Virginia with Mom?"

"Em . . ."

"Are you two back together? Pretend you've been kidnapped—just say yes or no."

"Well. Em. I think so."

Across the room, Dash raised her eyebrows like antennae.

"Oh my God! Since when? Daddy, this is so great!"

"It's quite recent. Ongoing, you might say."

"Okay, I'm hanging up."

"No, don't do that. I just called to say . . . to hear your voice and say . . . you know."

"I know."

"That I'm proud of you. How happy you've made me, all your life. I couldn't have invented a better daughter."

"Oh, Daddy."

"So, that's it. I just wanted to tell you, make sure you know. I love you."

"I love you, too."

He looked over at Dash, who had tears in her eyes. She beamed at him as they trickled down her cheeks.

"Good luck tomorrow," Chloe said. "They just do it through a little hole in your belly button, right?"

"Right. Laparoscopy." His testicles retracted. "Nothing to it. Recovery's a breeze."

"And I'll talk to you right afterward."

"You bet."

"I'll be *home* on Saturday."

"Oh, I'll be home by then, too," he said confidently. "We'll pick you up."

"Both of you? You and Mom together?"

"I don't see why not. Currently."

Chloe's laugh was pure joy. "Daddy, this is the *best* news."

"I know."

He handed Dash the phone and shut his eyes for a moment, to think about his good fortune, having his wife back, and his bad, the circumstances under which it was occurring. Diarrhea had never figured in his vision of their reconciliation. Nor jaundice, nor a semiprivate room. Dash wasn't taking him back out of pity, was she? He must ask. He could hear her low, intimate voice, telling Chloe something about bile, something about liver enzymes. When he opened his eyes again, the nurse named Amika was fishing his arm out from under the covers and wrapping a blood pressure cuff around it.

Then she was gone and Dash's face was in his, practically nose to nose. "It's going away. The yellow." She pulled down on one of his eyelids. "Must be the medicine kicking in."

"Do you have to leave?"

"Now? No."

"Tonight. I wish you could stay."

"I already asked them. Unless you get a roommate in the middle of the night, I can sleep in that bed. They were very nice about it."

He closed his eyes again. His blood seemed to pump more freely. Warmer.

"Slip over." She had lowered the bed rail and was sliding under the sheet. He obliged, not minding the muffled stabbing sensation when he moved, a mere ghost of what it had been. "I like drugs," he murmured, trying to settle on his left side to give her more room. Whatever drug was dripping into his vein right now, they should put it in the water.

"It would be a better world," Dash agreed. Oh, he's said that out loud. She lay on her side too, facing him, one arm light across his stomach. "This okay? Does anything hurt?"

"Not now." He studied her face, looking for changes since the last time he was allowed to be this close to it. Tiredness was new. The circles under her eyes were partly smeared mascara, partly fatigue. He stroked his finger over her cheekbone and watched her closed lashes flicker, the corner of her mouth twitch. "How are you holding up?"

She yawned; her breath smelled like coffee. "This is the second time I've been here today. Do you remember?"

"Your friend Cottie. Her heart." Some of the things she'd told him during the long wait in the emergency room hadn't quite sunk in, they'd discovered later. But he remembered Cottie. Her husband had saved her life.

"Owen's taking care of Sock." Dash opened her eyes to say that. Everything she'd told him about Owen he recalled with perfect clarity. And believed, so he ought to feel sorry for hitting him. And yet he didn't.

"You should go to sleep," she said. "Although all you have to do tomorrow is lie there."

"Piece of cake." His skin flushed hot, then cold. He rested his wrist on his forehead and stared at the shadowy line between the wall and the ceiling. "Just in case, though. Some fluke. I'd like you to do something."

She raised up on her elbow. "Are you worried? Andrew! Nothing's going to happen tomorrow."

"Oh, I know. But just in case. I'd like you to tell my father they offered me the chairmanship of the department."

"You never told him?"

"I didn't want to give him the satisfaction."

Silence while he, and he imagined she, contemplated the stupidity of that.

"So just tell him I was going to take it."

"What? You were? *Are?*"

"If I'd lived. No, I know, but tell him. I decided to take the job."

She was quiet. Then: "Not for me, I hope. In fact, I don't even want you to take it." She picked at the sheet, eyes downcast. "It kills me that I've been as mean to you as he was. Edward."

"No."

"I have. I've been a shrew. Telling you what you should do, like it was any of my business."

"Well, it is your business."

"Nagging isn't. Making you feel bad about yourself isn't. You're a teacher, a *wonderful* teacher, and you're so lucky to love what you do. I was stupid and mean. I'm just glad you ignored me. Except you didn't," she remembered, sitting up again. "Don't take the job, Andrew. I'm afraid it would be for the wrong reason."

"Darling." She could be so lovably self-important. "I would take it for myself, not you."

"I wish you'd stop saying 'would.' Stop using the subjunctive."

"I think I could—can—help reshape the department in positive ways."

"Well, of course you can. What about Peter Flynn?"

"I'll write his chapter for him. And then the chips will fall where they may." Elizabeth was right—he'd been paralyzed. But not anymore. Maybe it was the drugs, but the problem had never seemed less important, more manageable. "He can bury me in the next chapter for all I care, but I won't throw Jefferson to the wolves just to satisfy the current party line."

He would acknowledge the great man's flaws—as he hoped he always had—but he would also *contextualize* them, and he wouldn't be shy about reminding the nouveau detractors that, despite his moral shortcomings in a crucial (but *single*) area, Jefferson's legacy to the republic was still precious and unequaled.

"He was a good man," Andrew told Dash, who nodded readily, humoring him. She'd heard it before. "I can forgive him his sins—and of course you're thinking, 'Easy for you to say, you're a white male.'"

"*What* a mind reader."

"The interesting thing is that this is all mixed up with forgiving my father." Now he had her attention. "For not being a very good one—but after fifty years it's probably time to let that go." Dash looked puzzled, but the connection had never seemed clearer to him. "If I can forgive Jefferson for being an imperfect man, I ought to be able to forgive my father for the same failing. Don't you think?"

She smiled a slow, appreciative, faintly wondering smile. Instead of answering, she leaned over and pressed a slow kiss to his lips.

A funny time—or not—for a confession to bubble up from his subconscious. "I went on a date."

She pulled back. "Who with?"

"Elizabeth O'Neal."

"I knew it!"

"Nothing happened."

"A date? A real date? And then she gave you a *plant*."

"A half-assed date."

"Who asked who?"

"She asked me. And nothing happened." Nothing to speak of, certainly. "Elizabeth is a sad, troubled, very intelligent young woman—"

"She's not that young."

"A friend and colleague, nothing more."

"But it was a date, you said 'date.' How did it end? Did you kiss her? Come on, Andrew, tell the truth."

Not at the end, and it was more that she'd kissed him. So he could truthfully say, "No." Technically.

"Why not? The sun was coming up, she had to run?"

"Dash."

"I don't know why I'm not more upset!"

"You shouldn't be."

"Good, because I'm not. I'm profoundly unworried."

"Good."

"Good."

Well, this was a first. To his knowledge, Dash had never been jealous before, not on his account. He hoped he didn't feel gleeful or invigorated; he hoped he was better than that. He couldn't help noticing the symmetry, though, a certain unasked-for equilibrium in effect between them. He hoped Elizabeth and Owen Roby weighed precisely the same, not a gram more on either side, on the scale of attractiveness and significance. Hoped, but was reconciled to never knowing.

Dash played with the snap on the shoulder of Andrew's hospital gown and thought about Elizabeth O'Neal. Now wasn't the time, but someday she would have to ask him what he saw in her. Had seen in her. How he could like her and Dash at the same time—unequally, of course—given that they couldn't be more different. Did he like Elizabeth because of that? In spite of it? It added a new dimension to him, just when she thought she'd seen all his dimensions, that he could feel an attraction to . . . the moon instead of the sun, you could say. Yes, very apt. Dark versus light. Spooky versus sunny. Elizabeth's creepy mystery to her open book.

Amika came in again. Since she'd already made friends with her, Dash didn't worry that she'd throw her out or make her get in her own bed. "Five more minutes," she promised, "then he goes to sleep," while the nurse listened to Andrew's heart and adjusted the plastic bags on his IV stand. "Five minutes," Amika confirmed, with a smile that said she'd seen it all and wasn't impressed, and padded out.

"Did you call Chloe so you could say good-bye?"

"Hm?"

"In case you don't make it tomorrow?"

He looked at her disapprovingly.

"I can make light," she said, "because I've *had* a laparoscopy. Remember that uterine fibroid?" He turned pale, she noticed, every time the subject of his surgery came up. "That was nothing. Truly." She took his hand, stroked the knuckles across her cheek. "Are you glad I'm back?"

"What do you think?"

"Gimme the words."

"I'm glad you're back."

"I'm glad you came down and got me."

"Wolfie told me to. He's very wise in the ways of women."

I'm glad we're three, she thought. It's much better than two, and three times better than one. "We're going to be fine now," she said confidently. "Because it's not true that we have nothing in common. Think of it—we both like life. We like where we live, we like our friends, our jobs."

"You like your job? What about forest ranger?"

"No, I've given up on that, too much science again. But I did finally figure out the perfect job for me."

"What?" he asked, sounding cautious.

"Wine bottle label designer. Wouldn't that be me? I would be so *great* at that."

He blinked rapidly, searching her eyes for a sign she was joking, she was serious—she loved it that he hardly ever knew. She cut the suspense by snickering, and his face cleared.

"No, yes, I do love my work. You were right about that, but I think I had to watch Greta give it up to appreciate how much it suits me. Just because I fell into it accidentally doesn't make it an accident, something random like, I don't know, landscape architect—although I would be *fabulous* at that. But what *luck,* really, that I fell into my life's work."

"Yes."

"You didn't. You defied your father to do what you love. You don't give yourself enough credit for that."

"I missed you."

They pressed their foreheads together.

"I missed you," she whispered back.

"I had enough time to make a sensible new life while you were gone, but I didn't. Things never fell into place. When you're gone, it's like gravity . . . gravity . . ."

"Gravity ceases to exist," she suggested.

"Yes," he said, but so carefully, she knew she'd gone too far. "Was it the same for you?" he asked.

"Yes. Well, no. But women are better at being alone than men. I had a good time in the beginning, but it didn't last—and it was very short, the good time, an illusion, really, smoke and mirrors. Childish imaginings of a life on my own."

"I like your hair like this." He had his hand in it, softly rubbing her scalp.

"You're my rock. Your name should be Peter."

"You said rocks are sedentary."

"Yes, but that's the beauty of rocks. You're my ground, my base. I should never have left you. Although I'm glad I did, because if I hadn't we wouldn't be saying these things right now."

She decided not to tell him she'd known all along that leaving him would only be an interlude. "Known"—no; assumed, then, and on a deep, barely aware plane, that she was playing, that this wasn't real. She was scaring herself on purpose, letting herself be seduced by the perverse lure of disaster. Sometimes the deep, comforting assumption that it was pretend disappeared or hid from her, and those were the panicky times. "That night at Dr. Fogelman's," she said. Horrible; that time it wasn't playing. "I *hated* that night."

"Maybe therapy isn't for us," Andrew said.

"Oh yeah, this is much better. Gallstones."

"Big as a golf ball."

"I wish I could stay right here. Don't want to get up."

Andrew smiled with his eyes closed. "Stay."

She sighed, rose. Their five minutes were up. She leaned over him for a good-night kiss. "Here we are in a hospital in Virginia, but as far as I'm concerned we're home. You're my home." She rubbed her cheek against his whiskery face. "My love."

They kissed again.

Her face looked yellow in the fluorescent light over the bathroom sink. She could be the sick one. She peed; washed up; wished for a toothbrush.

She turned all the lights out except the one in the bathroom, and left the door open only a crack. It was still too bright, and nobody was making much of an effort to be quiet in the hall. Hospitals, gack. Amika had made up the bed next to Andrew's for her; she climbed in and lay quiet, testing the slant she was on. She pressed the button on the side, enjoying the low hum and the slow, mechanical descent until she was flat.

"Are you awake?"

Eventually Andrew made a noncommittal humming sound.

"I was thinking. Something Cottie said. She said—marriage is like an old tree. It starts out a sapling . . . no, it starts out an acorn, a passionate little acorn, and slowly, slowly it grows and sends out its branches and leaves, and every year new buds. All the things you did together, every trial you lived through, they're scored into that old trunk. The tree is the thing, not the acorn or the sapling or even the strong *young* tree. After all is said and done, you want the old tree, no matter how misshapen it's gotten from ice storms and lightning strikes or bugs and what-have-you."

Andrew didn't speak.

"I'm paraphrasing." She yawned. She punched her pillow into shape and turned on her side. "Night." And drifted to sleep.

Andrew dreamed of a tree framed in a window. At first it was the oak tree outside his bedroom window when he was a boy. Then it changed, became an old, gnarled, knobby child's book illustration of a tree. Someone was chopping it down. He couldn't see who, he could only hear the rip of the saw, *zz-zit, zz-zit,* back and forth, cutting through the tender, stubborn trunk. Sadness filled him, and fatalism, that nightmare inability to move or change anything. A voice: "It was Lincoln, you know, who said marriage is neither heaven nor hell, it's purgatory." Dr. Fogelman?

The dream turned a corner, as if he were driving, and at the end of a lane a house appeared. Not the cabin, not the house in D.C. A wooden house, square, with four windows, door, and chimney. Dash had painted it Lantern Glow. She was standing on Fogelman's other side; the doctor had his arms around their shoulders. "You know where that wood came from, don't you?" he said. "You know what this is, don't you?" Neither of them wanted to give him the satisfaction, but they couldn't deny it. It was too obvious. Behind his back, they touched hands. "The House of Love," they singsonged in unison.

The last place Dash expected to see Cottie the next morning was in the corridor on the far side of the nurses' station, the equivalent of about a city block from her room. Striding along at such a vigorous, arm-swinging pace, Dash had to hustle to catch up to her.

"Hey, lady! Where's the fire?"

Cottie wheeled around, already grinning. Over the regulation blue-striped hospital gown, she had on her own red wool bathrobe—Shevlin must've brought it to her. She held out her arms. Dash came into them gingerly, but the older woman gave her such a powerful squeeze, she laughed and lost her fear of hurting her.

"You look fabulous. *Look* at you," she marveled, holding Cottie's elbows. "What a fraud. You're not even sick."

"That's what I said. Let me out of here so I can get something done. I left sixteen tomato plants sitting in a tray in the hot sun on the kitchen counter, and do you think Shevlin's going to remember to shove 'em over to the side? Much less water them?"

"I don't *think* so," Dash said, catching her exuberance, laughing again with her, both so glad at how things had turned out. Cottie did look good, pink-cheeked, practically glowing—nothing like impatience to get out of the hospital to turn your medical condition around.

"How is your husband?" she demanded. She took Dash's arm and they set off at her speed-walker's pace for her room.

"He's in surgery."

"Right now?"

"This minute, so I can't stay long. I just wanted to see you, plus I couldn't sit still in the waiting room or his room." Sometime in the night all of Andrew's anxieties had migrated from him over to her. "I don't know why I'm so nervous, it's not even a complicated operation."

"When does he get to go home?"

"Tomorrow."

"Me, too. Shevlin's scandalized. 'They kick you out in one day no matter what you've got,' he says, but me, I couldn't be happier. The sooner the better."

"I thought they were going to put in a thing, a pacemaker or something."

"Not right away, in a week or so. And even that's outpatient."

"How does it work?"

"It's a gizmo they put in right here, right under the skin, like a pack of cigarettes." She pointed to a place above her left breast. "When my heart goes too fast, like yesterday, I get a shock and it resets it."

"Wow, that's incredible. Isn't it amazing? Cottie—you could live *forever.*"

Her laugh sounded pleased but self-conscious, as if she'd already thought of that.

"Here's me." They turned into a beige-painted replica of Andrew's yellow room. The curtain around the bed on the near side was drawn, but not all the way; tiptoeing past, Dash caught a peripheral glimpse of a tiny, white-haired lady, asleep with her mouth open. "Heart," Cottie mouthed, quietly pulling the extra chair from the old lady's side over to hers so she and Dash could sit next to each other.

"I really can only stay a minute. I told him I'd be there when he wakes up."

"I know, I know." Cottie was all but rubbing her hands together. Her eyes sparkled. She leaned close. "Owen says he *hit* him."

Dash covered her cheeks with her hands. It was so much more exciting now, with Cottie to share it with—and being in the *past*—than it had been when it happened. "I was right there. He socked him in the jaw. Owen *fell.*"

Cottie put her hands on her knees and rocked.

"I know we aren't supposed to enjoy that sort of thing, we women. It's absurd. It's not civilized."

Cottie made a grinding sound in the back of her throat. They leaned toward each other, shoulders shaking.

"I guess I won't be seeing much of you anymore." Cottie pulled a long face.

"Oh, you'll see plenty of me. But, no, not as much," she admitted. "I'll be going home with Andrew."

"I'm so glad."

"I want you to meet him. It seems strange that you never have."

"What's strange to me is that you've never met my daughter."

"Is she coming in today?"

"Shortly. Owen and Shevlin went to pick her up at the airport."

"What do you think will happen?" Dash asked. "With Owen and Danielle?"

"That I do not know. They need a push, that's for sure. Especially him."

A push, Dash thought, or else three beers. "I hope it works out," she said. She had such a fondness for Owen, now that she'd lost all interest in him. She wanted only the best for him, like a best friend's son or a favorite nephew. She looked at the clock and jumped up. "I should go. I'm a jack-in-the-box, I can't be still."

Cottie got up, too. "I want to hug you again," she said, and did.

Dash felt teary, patting the back of her fuzzy red robe. "I don't know what I'd've done without you, Cottie. All these months."

"Me, too."

"We were lucky to find each other."

"I know, I think of that. Good timing."

They hesitated in the doorway. Dash had a question she hadn't known she wanted to ask until it popped out. "Would you get married again if something happened to Shevlin?" Mo wouldn't. The last time they'd talked, she said, "I wouldn't marry God."

Cottie looked tickled. "Well, honey, I can't claim I've never *thought* about it. First I said no, never again—that was when I was young. Then in middle age, I said never say never, and maybe I would. So as not to end up old and alone. Which is funny, since now that I *am* old, I'm back to no."

"So you wouldn't? Why not?"

"Oh, it's too much trouble. It takes a lot of energy I don't have anymore." She leaned back against the wall. "The forgiving and forgetting, all the attention you have to pay. How big your heart has to be." She looked Dash up and down. "Would you?"

"Yes. I love marriage. Although," it occurred to her, "I guess I could just be in the middle-aged yes phase. But I *know* I've got enough energy for it."

"Oh, honey." Cottie took her hands, squeezing them between her big ones. "Your man is so lucky. In for good times."

Dash blushed.

The elevator was down on the first floor, according to the dial; she decided to take the stairs. Naturally the elevator bell pinged as soon as she got to the door to the stairwell. She glanced back just as Owen, Shevlin, and a woman—Danielle—stepped out of the elevator into the hall. They didn't see her. They turned and headed off in the opposite direction, toward Cottie's room.

Why, she's lovely, Dash thought. Clutching her purse in one hand, holding her father's arm in the other. Petite and shiny-haired, taking short, fast, anxious steps. Owen towered over her, protective but not touching. He reminded Dash of Shevlin with Cottie, that same delicate solicitousness.

Go with her, she telegraphed to the back of Owen's head. *Go to Atlanta.* It would be worth it, all the trouble it would cause, the energy it would take. The forgiveness and forgetfulness. The big heart—especially that. All worth it.

She would tell Mo that. Not that she wanted everyone in the world paired up at the end, like a Shakespeare comedy—although she *did*— but Mo needed to be reminded that yes, certainly we are all ultimately alone, but how much kinder to yourself it can be to look that fearful truth in the eye with the one you love. Your mate.

Amika was coming out of Andrew's room as Dash went in. "Oh, hi—I left the referral on the table. And I asked Dr. Brooke, who said it would probably be better to wait a couple weeks to start, till he's a hundred percent and has all his strength back."

"Start what? Who's Dr. Brooke?"

"Oh, the allergist. Your husband wanted to know if he could start the tests right away. For his dog allergy? Dr. Brooke thinks he should wait and get well, then see an allergist in D.C., so he left a name, it's on the paper. Tell Mr. Bateman, will you? He asked me to ask."

"Thanks. I will."

Dash sat on Andrew's bed. Pointless tears started as soon as she picked up the pink referral slip Amika had left on the bedside table. It was the nicest thing he'd ever done. She wanted to tell somebody, she wanted to say it out loud in a weepy voice, "It's the nicest thing he's ever done." All so that she could keep Sock. Oh, Andrew.

If he had made this concession, this lovely, loving gesture for her the night she'd stormed out of the house, would it have changed everything? Or only postponed it? The latter, she thought. She'd have been touched, grateful, moved, but Sock was always just a surrogate, a ringer. A pinch hitter in the ball game of her discontent.

Not that she was counting, but with this piece of paper Andrew had moved out in front. She wasn't used to that. They'd been reunited for less than a day, and already it was two to nothing. She didn't know what she would do for him to even the score, not, of course, that there was a *score,* but she looked forward to thinking of something good. Some sweet, spontaneous kindness, an act of selfless love that would awe and humble him, like an allergist's referral. A gesture of the big heart.

For now, though, he was ahead. By *three* to zip if you counted the next gift, and she did. She got to go downstairs and greet him in Recovery.

Acknowledgments

Many thanks to Jerry Cederblom, professor of philosophy at the University of Nebraska at Omaha, for his insights into the workings and politics of a small college's history department. I'm sure he made it all up, of course; I'm sure the dramas and intrigues at Mason-Dixon College never went on anywhere Jerry ever worked.

Thanks also to Rodney Clark, portrait photographer extraordinaire, who was so generous with his time and so patient with my questions.

Sally Kim's kindness, clear thinking, and brilliant editing chops helped make the writing of this book a pleasure, or as close to it as any of them ever get. Thank you.

Finally, thanks to Amy Berkower at Writers House, for generosity and support, loyalty, patience, tolerance, charity, mercy, and any other cardinal virtues I've forgotten. You're a lifesaver.

mad dash

by Patricia Gaffney

Reader's Group Guide

1. Everyone has heard the old axiom "opposites attract." Do they? And can they last? Dash and Andrew don't have much in common. What attracts them to each other initially? What keeps them together in the long term? How important are shared hobbies and interests to a relationship?

2. Dash's mother passes away just months before Chloe, her only child, leaves home for college. How big a factor do these events play in Dash's decision to leave Andrew? What does it mean to be a member of the "Sandwich Generation"?

3. Both Dash and Andrew claim to be annoyed by the other's foibles. What do you find annoying about Dash? About Andrew? What do you find endearing about each of them? Who would you rather be in a long-term relationship with, gender notwithstanding? Why do the quirks we love at first turn into pet peeves over time?

4. The puppy Dash finds on her front porch becomes the catalyst for leaving Andrew. What does the puppy represent to Dash? What does it represent to Andrew?

5. Andrew tried to break things off with Dash after their first night together—why?

6. Like many people in the throes of a midlife crisis, Dash wants to "find herself." What does this mean? Is it even possible? Does Dash manage to do it during her separation from Andrew?

7. Why is Andrew so reluctant to advance at work? How does his relationship with his father contribute to this? How does Andrew get over this problem?

8. Cottie and Shevlin Bender are happy after years of marriage—why? How are they different from the other couples in *Mad Dash*? What lessons can be learned from their successful marriage?

9. While living in Virginia, Dash begins to spend time with the Benders' son-in-law, a local farmer named Owen. Why is Dash attracted to him? Do you think she has more in common with Owen or with Andrew?

10. Dash's friend Maureen is newly divorced after a long marriage. How is her experience of life after marriage different from Dash's? What do you think of her attitudes about love and marriage?

11. On page 134, Maureen says that only married people can appreciate the allure of loneliness. Why is the thought of being alone attractive to married people? Can you relate to that sentiment? Dash thinks women experience this more than men. What do you think? Is this experience the same regardless of gender?

12. Andrew says that Dash was a good daughter, but Dash harbors a lot of guilt about her mother. Why? Is it warranted? Discuss Dash's actions regarding her mother's thwarted suitor, Mr. Dreessen. What effects do motherhood and her own child's flight from the nest have on Dash's feelings about this? Why does this guilt make it harder for Dash to heal after her mother's death?

13. Her flight to the cabin makes the third time Dash has left Andrew. What happened the other two times? Why did she come back in the past? What's different now? What does this tendency say about her?

14. Dash believes she will get a lot out of having a whole week to herself at the cabin. Do you think she gets what she wants out of her week of solitude? Would you enjoy having a week all to yourself? What would you do with the time?

15. During their separation, both Dash and Andrew come very close to committing adultery but don't go through with it. Why? What does Dash learn from Owen? What does Andrew learn from Elizabeth?

16. Dash and Andrew come close to making up many times before they actually do. What keeps them from getting back together? Why do they reunite when they finally do?

17. Since she's already decided to go home, how important is Andrew's arrival at the cabin? How is Andrew's punch significant to Dash, especially in light of her advice to Owen regarding his estranged wife?

18. Once they've reconciled, Dash admits to herself that she never really planned to stay separated from Andrew. In light of this, do you think the separation was a good thing? For Dash? For Andrew? For them as a couple? What do you think its long-term effects might be?

About the Author

Patricia Gaffney lives in southern Pennsylvania with her husband of twenty-eight years and their two dogs, Finney and Jolene.